A L

A Lost Woman

Ann Brooks

To request permissions, contact the publisher at contact@boundtobrew.com

Library of Congress Cataloging-in-Publication Data has been applied for.

ISBN 978-1-953500-08-3

Edited by Pauline Harris and Danielle Manahan

Printed by Steuben Press in USA

Team Publishing
9457 S University Blvd. 819 Highlands Ranch, CO 80126

Boundtobrew.com

Acknowledgments

I am forever grateful for the opportunity that Ethan and Chris at Bound to Brew have given me by publishing my first novel. Their dedication and passion for authors came through in the way that they supported and encouraged me during this publishing process. I am thankful to the creative support of my editor, Pauline Harris, who helped me in numerous ways to improve my story. I appreciated their collaboration in making this story special.

My writing journey started over ten years ago with the conception of this story. Along the way, I have battled with doubt, exhaustion over parenthood, personal loss, and I lost my direction numerous times. But through it all I have had people who never stopped encouraging me, never let me give up, and shined as a beacon at the end of my tunnel. This never would've happened without you.

To my family, who has endured more than I care to admit during this arduous process of writing and publishing my first novel. My mother, who has supported me every step of the way, read every draft, given me the advice I needed to become a better writer, and never hesitated to watch my children for days on end so I could finish my novel. My husband, the person who knows me the best. He knew when I needed to be left alone in my writing, giving me time I never would've had to devote to my dream. He knew when I needed my hand held through rejection and never stopped encouraging me through all my doubt. So many times, I thought about taking a different path than writing, but each time, he refused to let me give up. Always telling me to live with no regrets. My in-laws, who watch my children in the summer, provided them with experiences and love while I wrote this novel, edited this novel, and read it a million times. Without their support, this story never would have made it past the tenth page.

For my sons, who have grown up around a writer. Which means there were times that they were ignored, numerous memories I faded into the background of, as I was engrossed in writing. I am sorry I missed so many things, but I am grateful that I can now show them that their sacrifice meant that I could accomplish my dream. I hope they will always reach for their own dream and never give up.

Through the encouragement of every single family member, my brothers, my sisters, my parents, my grandparents, my aunts and uncles, my cousins, every one of you that advocated and gave me the confidence I needed to write this story, I am so grateful for the endless support.

To my friends, who took the time to read my first, second... tenth draft. To Ashley, a fellow writer friend who was my first Beta reader and editor. Thank you for taking the time during your incredibly busy life with three kids. To Leanne, who barely knew me at the time but read my story and has cheered me on ever since. To Penelope, my childhood friend, who not only read my story, but helped the true beauty of my words shine even brighter. To Trudy, the person who held my hand as I nervously waited for my first agent meeting, giving me the strength I needed to find confidence within myself to finally put my writing out to the public. To Mindy for always pushing me forward and introducing to my first editor, Emily. To Emily, for taking the time to edit my novel. Our endless conversations and your support made this novel come to life. To Amie, who made sure I was making all the right moves to make this book a success. To Steven, a wonderfully talented photographer for your pictures. To Stephanie, who always made sure I looked good. To every person I told I wrote a book who immediately said they wanted to read it and gave their unconditional support. To all my friends who have cheered me along, assured me never to give up, and affirmed that my story was worth publishing. I thank you all.

To all my friends, family, and strangers who will take the time to read my story. I am forever grateful for your time and support. All I ever wanted was for others to read this story and take away a deeper understanding of how our past drives our futures.

This story is for every child that has suffered abuse and labored to break the cycle of violence in their own adulthood.

For my mother, who never wavered in her love for all of us.

For my husband, for never letting me let go of my dream.

Part One: Hurricane A-Comin'

On October 10, 2018, Hurricane Michael made landfall on the Alabama coast as a Category five hurricane. It caused catastrophic damage, with waters rising fourteen feet above sea level and winds reaching 120 mph, as it smashed against the Alabama shore. The waves reached up to ninety feet high, crashing against homes, as the rushing waters pulled anything and everything away. Winds divided trees from their roots, roofs from their homes, mothers from their children. Everything was lost ... the damage so deep, so irreversible, that most people were never able to return to their homes if they still existed.

Chapter One
Present Day

Within the last six months, my classically flawless life had been shattered into pieces—*sharp and deadly*. My fingers grazed over the faint pale line across my ring finger, the wedding ring long since taken off. The divorce had been finalized three weeks ago, ironically on our wedding anniversary. The memories of our life, like ripples in the water, continued to affect every inch of me, spreading slowly and growing larger by the second. I felt like I'd fallen to the bottom of a lake, drowning slowly, unable to find the strength to swim to the light ... *rock bottom.*

For ten years, my ex-husband, Michael, and I built a life, which included our two-bedroom condo in downtown Atlanta, two Goldendoodles, and a successful law practice. None of which I got in the divorce.

The reason behind my divorce was simple if you examined the facts *(he cheated)*. Yet, it was so much more complicated: two-tiny-blue-lines-on-a-pregnancy-stick complicated. The feeling I had the moment I realized I was pregnant was ... *dread*. The idea of being a mother was *dreadful*. Motherhood was never my plan, for various dark reasons. Unfortunately, as it turned out, fatherhood was the plan for Michael.

Without conversation, he decided that we were having this child. It was as if he had forgotten every reason having children was a bad idea. Every cautionary tale I'd told him about being parents melted away, giving way to a *new beginning* of parenthood. But I already had my *new beginning* in him. He was all I needed, but now I could see that I was not enough.

So many times I tried to talk to him, attempting to tell him how much I didn't want this child. I was devoid of all maternal instincts, having had them beaten out of me my entire childhood. But he wouldn't hear any of that now; all he cared about was the baby. No matter how many times I protested, I felt like having this child was no longer my choice. Deep down, I knew that I would lose him if I decided not to have the child. They had become a package deal.

I thought back to that moment so many times. *What if I never told him? What if it never happened?* There was a part of me that knew we would still be together, if not for the pregnancy. The moment I lost the child, I lost my husband ... *I lost everything.*

Chapter Two
One Year Ago

The pressure rippled through my body, like waves in an ocean. Then a riptide of pain took over, pulling me further and further into the depths. I felt like I was drowning in that moment, paralyzed as my body betrayed me, accepting of its fate to die.

The air was unseasonably brisk, the gray sky hanging low and misty, waiting for the perfect moment to drop flakes of snow, but my body flushed with heat. The pain rising and falling as a ship caught in rough seas, the heat radiated to every nerve, setting my body on fire. *I was dying.*

The sound of sirens was distant to my ears, even though I was in the back of the ambulance, racing to my final resting point. Michael crouched on a tiny sliver of a bench, clasping my hand tightly as his body thrashed wildly from side to side. He was calling out something, his eyes burrowing into my own, but I could not hear him. My own eyes started to blur as the darkness crept in from the corners.

"Stay with me," the EMT mouthed, as he pulled a plastic mask over my mouth, the cords slapping against my hot cheeks, but I could not feel the pain. It was nothing in comparison.

My eyes flickered, white ceiling tiles streaming by, lights flashing on and off as my eyes fought to stay open. "Keep her awake!" someone yelled in the distance. *Where is Michael? I need Michael!* I tried to scream, but my mouth was rendered unless by the mask. Then darkness. It was dark for a long time.

My eyes opened. First the light, then the sound rushing back to me, flooding my senses as I attempted to stabilize my mind. First only the color of white, the pressure of a pulse oximetry on my index finger, making it difficult to lift my hand. Then a slow, rhythmic beeping sound coming from a machine just behind my left ear pierced through my mind. The feeling of the harsh, rough fabric of the hospital gown pulled against my dry skin as I tried to move. *I am in the hospital. I am alive.*

"Norah, Norah!" His voice rang in my ears as they adjusted to the intrusive sound. Then, I could feel his hand within my own, lifting my fingers to his soft lips and kissing my palm.

"Michael ..." The dryness made it difficult to talk, my voice raspy as I tried.

"Yes, honey, it's okay. You are going to be okay." But I could tell by the glazed look hidden behind the redness in his eyes that it was not going to be okay—something was wrong.

"What"—*cough*—"happened?" I strained through the dryness. He reached over me, took a small plastic cup, and filled it with water—avoiding the answer. He touched the rim to my lips, forcing me to take a long sip, the water soothing my throat and chilling my warm body all at the same time.

"Tell me," I pleaded.

He hung his head low, avoiding my gaze. "We lost *her*, Norah, we lost *her*."

"*Her?*"

I watched as his shoulders heaved forward, tears spotting his black slacks. Then I remembered. We were leaving for work. He was in a suit, having to be at court that morning, but I was only in a pair of khaki slacks and a white blouse, office-bound for the day. But the pain started right before we were about to walk out the door, causing my body to cramp and pull into itself. Michael reached for me and caught me just as I started to fall; then fragments of memory—ambulance, operating room ... *the baby.*

His red, watery eyes met my own as he nodded, as tears released from under my lashes. There was nothing else to say in that moment. The feeling of loss was so deep, as if a piece of my heart was dragged away with the tide.

A few hours later, the doctor arrived in the room. Our tears had long since dried, but we still were not able to speak. The unspoken words hung in the air like humidity on a hot summer day, pushing against us and causing our bodies to sweat. We both felt the grief of losing the baby, but the true guilt was mine to bear alone.

"Norah, how are you feeling?" the doctor asked as he flipped open my chart. A stethoscope wrapped around his slender, freshly shaved neck, his white coat pocket filled with different colored pens—blue, black, red. He pulled out the red to take notes.

"Sore. Tired." It was still difficult to speak, the dryness persisting no matter how much water I drank.

"That's to be expected." His fingers turned the pen over, and he quickly scribbled a note into the chart, eyes hidden behind thick glasses, following each movement of his pen.

"Doctor, what happened?"

"Well," he returned his pen and flipped the chart closed, pressing it against his muscular chest, "you had preeclampsia at twenty-two weeks. It's a condition in pregnancy where the cells start to reject the fetus, literally clamping down on the cells in your body. It causes high blood pressure to the point, which you were at, that it caused your body to have a seizure."

"I don't remember a seizure." I glanced at Michael, who dropped his eyes to the floor.

"How long have you been having symptoms?"

"Symptoms?"

"Yes, uh, swelling, more so than normal, dizziness, nausea ... any of those?"

"Yes, I am pregnant." Michael's eyes instantly reddened at the word. "I *was* pregnant," I corrected.

"I'm very sorry, ma' am. The onset of preeclampsia can be sudden in some cases. In your case, it appears that it was sudden and frankly life-threatening. Your husband had no other choice."

Suddenly, I realized the guilt I was bearing being the one who couldn't keep the baby alive in her body, the one who did not want the baby, the one who considered abortion, was not just my own. He shared my guilt, his face contorting as he started to sob into his hands. He pulled his hand from my own, our fingers falling one by one away from each other, as he fell into his own grief.

"How did it—" The words caught in my mouth.

"We had to do a c-section." Realization pained in my abdomen. He motioned for permission, and as I nodded, he reached over to lift my gown, revealing the mass of cotton across my stomach. I had been so numb that I failed to notice it before now. As the doctor pulled the bandage to expose my wound, my eyes grew wide, the pain surging through my body. Tiny black string weaved over and under a pink mesh of skin, pulled tightly together. I had only been twenty-two weeks, barely showing, but that small bump that had started to form was now flat. *She* was gone.

"You are healing nicely. In about six months or so, you should be good to try again."

"Try again?" *Why would anyone do this again?*

"While there is a chance you will develop preeclampsia again, this time we will be able to implement some countermeasures to hopefully get you further along in your pregnancy." It was clear that the doctor had never been pregnant, and, most likely, was not a father himself; otherwise, he would not have said it.

"What are the chances, doctor?" Michael's voice sounded faded and unfamiliar to me as he spoke. I desperately wanted to slap him across the face, stop the conversation that was transpiring, but I was too weak to lift my own hand.

"Typically, there is an eighty percent chance someone will develop preeclampsia in a secondary pregnancy; however, with your wife's age, that percentage is much greater. At thirty-five years old, we consider the woman to be at high risk. At forty, the risk of birth defects greatly increases." Suddenly, the doctor realized he was being too blunt as he stared into Michael's squinted eyes filled with horror. He had been looking at me, taking the void look in my own eyes as a sigh of understanding. But really it was a sigh of ambivalence.

"I am truly very sorry for your loss. I think you should both take time to heal. Just not too much time, if you still want to have a child." He receded from the room, a rip current pulling him quickly and violently before we ever realized the damage of his words.

The room grew dark as the sun disappeared and night blanketed the Earth. Michael was gone. I sent him away to shower and sleep, seeing as I didn't need him here. After the doctor left, Michael cried and apologized so many times for taking our baby away—*for killing her.* I told him not to think about it like that, and to instead think about it in terms of *he saved my life.* His guilt was relentless, making my own guilt feel shameful.

At ten weeks, I had made the choice to get an abortion. Telling Michael of my pregnancy had been a mistake, but I was not going to continue to have a lapse of judgment, which is exactly what having this baby would be. I would make the choice, then figure out how to explain my actions to Michael. Surely, he would forgive me. But as I waited in that office, doubt flooded my mind like oil into the ocean, spreading slowly, dark and thick, into my thoughts. Michael would not forgive me; he would leave me. Just as I was slipping through the exit, I heard the nurse call my name. Her call went unanswered.

For the next ten weeks, I forced myself to accept this pregnancy, to feel a part of this choice, instead of a prisoner. I made two other appointments at the clinic, then canceled them both. Even though Michael was making this choice without my permission, it felt as if my choice could not be made without his permission. Yet, no matter how many times I pursued the conversation, he never seemed to understand my position.

So, when the swelling started, first in my feet, then my hands, I assumed it was stress. When nausea lasted all day, I just thought it was something I was eating, not really caring to pay attention to a diet. Then, at work the week before, I fainted. I told everyone at the office I had just had a sleepless night; no one knew we were pregnant. All of these were symptoms that I ignored—subconsciously or consciously, I'm not really sure.

Fall fell away, giving into a harsh, brutal winter. The frigid air gave me cause to wear thick, covering pajamas and cocoon into heavy blankets. Michael tried for months to get close to me, touch me, hold me, kiss me, but like the leaves in fall need to break free of the tree, I needed time to break free of my guilt and pain.

Then winter, like my depression, settled in so deeply that it refused to leave. Snow covered our balcony, a gray-brown color, showing its age. I mourned the loss of the baby, as the trees mourn their leaves, but unlike the trees, I knew my leaves would never return. Even at twenty-two weeks, I was still unsure of becoming a mother. I doubted myself, rightfully so, and the moment I learned that I had lost the baby, I knew ... I knew I would never—could never—be a mother.

Chapter Three
Present Day

The smell of mahogany crashed against my walls. The walls I put up to prevent anything from making me cry today. There was a time I relished the smell, the feeling of standing in a courtroom, a tight black suit tailored to fit my body perfectly, my long, wavy, dark hair pulled back into a sophisticated bun, glasses perched on the end of my nose as I'd prepare to close my case successfully. But not today.

Today, I looked very different. Really, I tried to appear presentable, but the last three months had slowly siphoned any hope I had for my life right out of me. From the moment he told me of his betrayal, the last piece of my heart that I had so desperately clung to after the miscarriage burned, tiny flakes of ash floating off into nothingness.

Gently pulling a stray frizzy hair from my pale, sunken face, I tried to adjust myself accordingly. That morning I couldn't decide what to wear, so with only minutes till I had to leave, I pulled on a simple white shirt and jeans. I was no lawyer today. Just the client.

As the judge stood before us, I couldn't help but glance over to Michael. The memories of that day came flooding back into my mind, the current world melting away as I slipped into a nightmare.

"Norah, there is someone else."

Out of the corner of my eye, hidden behind my hands as I slumped on my elbows resting on our marble countertops, I could see his hand hover above my shoulder. He wanted to touch me, comfort me, but knew it was wrong. He knew he could never touch me again, not after he'd said those words.

"Just with the way things have been lately, I—" He couldn't finish the sentence. *Coward.* I understood, not being naive about our current situation.

"I want to keep this civil."

"This?" I croaked out behind my shaking fingers.

"The divorce."

I should have looked at him, forced him to tell me the truth, but I was filled with shame. This was my fault. When a bridge collapses in the wind of a hurricane, it is not the hurricane's fault, but the engineer who failed to make the bridge strong enough to endure such force. I was not strong enough.

"Is this what you want?" My words were muffled through my hands.

"Norah, isn't this what *you* want?"

Relief washed over my body, for on some level I did want to run away, escape this pain and start over as I had done so many years ago. But this time, I had something to lose—*Michael.* I did not want to lose him; he was my family, my love, my life. No matter how much pain and loss I'd endured, I would still be nothing without him.

I reached across the cold marble counter for his hand, laying my own palm up and ready to receive his touch. I waited, my body suddenly eager to feel him again, despite what he had told me. I knew this was my fault; the part I had been playing for the last eighteen months contributed to his betrayal.

But he did not take my hand. He stared down at my lined palm then shoved his own deep into his pocket. My own hand fell off to my side, the realization that our relationship was over sinking in, the weight of my choices making it hard to hold myself up.

"I don't want this." My voice was only a whisper through the hurt.

"Sure feels that way."

"I'll try harder, I can be better. I just need time. I told you that."

"How much time? How much harder? It shouldn't be like this, Norah."

I desperately wanted him to pull me into his long, lean arms, enclosing me in an envelope of protection. Suddenly, the revulsion I had to his touch these last months melted away like the snow as it yields to the sun's warmth.

"I want children. Can you give me that?"

Shame, like a tidal wave crashing upon a city, overtook my body. If not for the counter to lean on, I would have fallen to the ground. Not only had he known how to hurt me, but he knew when to hurt me.

"No." A single word, just a whisper, changed the course of my life.

The door closed behind me, closing on my previous life as I shuffled into my low-rent, barren apartment. There was nothing here, symbolic of my life. Tossing my black purse aside, pulling off my tennis shoes, and throwing my broken body onto the couch, I was determined to spend the rest of my life wallowing in self-pity.

My phone buzzed, vibrating the entire couch ... *Who would be calling me?*

I should've tossed the phone across the room. There was nothing left in my life, least of all friends. I should have realized that no one I wanted to talk to would actually be calling. Maybe then, my life would've gotten back on track. Maybe then, my life would've been ... *livable.*

"Is this Miss Crawford?" He had a deep, unrecognizable Southern accent, which was hard to understand over the phone.

"Yes, this is she."

"This is Doctor Bishop." *Ugh—*I should've recognized the voice and hung up, but now it would just seem rude. "I am calling on behalf of your mother."

"Yes." My jaw tightened.

I was in no mood to hear from my mother, a woman I had not spoken to in over five years. I did not want to talk to her doctor, either. I was sure she had him call me to pay for her unnecessary medical bills. After all, that's what she typically wanted from me ... *money.* Well, for the first time, I actually did not have any to give, even if I wanted to. The divorce bills cleaned out half of my savings, while not having a job the last six month was taking care of the rest.

"Well, the thing is ... see, well ... your mother, over the last several months, has been getting into ... Well, it's hard to say."

"What is it, Dr. Bishop?" Annoyance seeped through my words.

"Your mother is *sick.*" It was the way in which he said the word *sick* that struck me. My mother was, in fact, a sick person, but judging by his use of the word, he might actually mean she was medically sick.

Then I heard her—*my mother*—yelling in the background that she was fine and wanted nothing to do with her "insolent daughter." Not the worst thing she'd ever called me.

"I've known that for quite some time, doctor, and, no offense, she clearly wants nothing to do with me, so I don't understand how this is any of my concern."

"Miss Crawford, I regret to inform you that your mother is actually quite ill," he reiterated harshly as if somehow that would make a difference. "I'm afraid over the last several weeks your mother has not been taking care of herself. It is clear that she has not bathed, nor changed her clothes in days."

"Doctor, sorry, but that's normal for her. She's probably just been on a bender."

"No, no, I'm afraid you misunderstood. Your mother is forgetting to do these things. I'm even concerned she's not eating. She is very thin." *Jesus, why me?*

"What do you mean she's forgetting?"

"I believe your mother has Alzheimer's disease." *Damnit.*

"Are you sure? I mean, this is just ... uh, not possible."

Of course, I'd heard of the disease and was aware of what it meant. But my mother ... *never.* The woman who held on to everything her entire life and never let anything go was literally going to forget everything? *No way.*

"Yes, I am quite sure. Now she will need to go to a specialist for an official screening and diagnosis, but in my professional opinion, your mother does have Alzheimer's disease. At this stage, she appears to need around-the-clock care."

" *What?!*" I stumbled off the couch. Suddenly, I was very alert. "You've got to be kidding me."

"Your mother has been exhibiting symptoms of Alzheimer's for the last six months. She needs specialized treatment. Over time, this disease attacks the brain. At this point, your mother cannot function on a basic level and needs constant care."

I felt like screaming. My chest tightened, laboring my breathing. *Panic Attack. Deep breaths,* I told myself, *deep breaths.*

"Are you sure she's not faking it?"

"What? This is not a joke. Your mother clearly is no longer able to care for herself. I worry deeply about her health." The laugh escaped before I could stifle it. My mother had been mentally ill my entire life, and not one person in that town ever cared, let alone *deeply worried* about it.

"This is very important. Your mother needs you," he urged over the phone.

I pulled the phone to my shoulder. I just needed a moment to think, to wrap my mind around what this all actually meant. I had been on autopilot for so long, and now I needed to find a way to turn my brain back on and figure out what to do next.

The implications of my mother having Alzheimer's disease was that I would need to take care of her, which was never going to happen. While I should have felt some visceral obligation to care for my mother, there was nothing in this entire world that would make me return to that place.

"Okay, what are my other options?"

"I'm not sure. You would need to take her to get an official diagnosis. Only then can you pursue alternative care for your mother."

I could still hear my mother screaming in the background, but I couldn't focus on her words. I only heard the words of the doctor, now spreading like wildfire through my mind.

"Your mother will need a caregiver of some sort. Whether that is you, a paid nurse, or possibly a nursing home ... that is for you to decide." *This was not good.*

What happens if I just hang up and pretend this conversation never happened? I knew that was an awful thought to have, but there was a part of me, a big part, that knew she deserved it.

"Doctor Bishop, I am just not in a place where I can care for her."

I refused to admit to myself that I was actually in a place to return home and care for my mother. I no longer had a life in Atlanta. There was nothing left for me here except shattered dreams.

"Are there any other options?" *Please, there has to be something I haven't thought of yet.*

"At this point, I'm not sure. Your mother is a ... a special case." His hesitation held the unsaid words—*a drunk.*

"What are you *not* telling me, doctor?" I wanted him to say it out loud, to admit in front of her that she was still an alcoholic, a fact she had refused to acknowledge my entire life. As if her alcoholism didn't ruin my entire childhood, now it was going to ruin my adulthood as well.

"Well ..." His voice softened. "The truth is, your mother is very difficult."

"I am aware of this fact." He had no idea how truly difficult the woman actually was, especially as a mother.

"In truth, she needs *you* to take her to appointments, file paperwork, get insurance. All these things before she can get the help she needs. She won't do it for herself." I was well aware of that fact. My mother never did anything for herself except drink.

This time I could hear her clear as day, screaming, "I don't need anyone, and I'd rather die than live with her again." I wonder if that could be arranged—*bad thought.*

"I think it is best if you come home, Miss Crawford."

Deep breaths. Deep breaths.

"That is just not possible, Doctor Bishop." *Deep breaths.*

"Please," he begged, his voice soft and sad. "She needs *you.*"

Deep breaths. Deep breaths. I am never going home ...

My resolve was strong at first, as I refused to go to my mother's aid. I owed her nothing. But I couldn't get rid of this feeling deep down in the pit of my stomach: *I was killing my own mother.* If I didn't go, knowing what I knew about her, she would die. *Would I ever be able to let that go?*

One suitcase and two hours later, I was in Summerville. Hometown to the Summerville Tigers and Oscar's famous restaurant, nestled in the middle of Nowhere, Alabama. The town had not changed since the early 20th century. Back in the 1950s, this town was run on family-owned businesses *(the hard-working American dream)*, but those were shattered during the recession of 1981 when cheap became the economical need. All it took was one Walmart, and downtown Summerville became a ghost town.

Slowly, I rolled through the center of "*town,*" if you could still call it that—it was more of an abandoned strip mall. Buildings lined either side of the two-lane, cracked street, the windows cloudy with dust. It appeared as if all the stores were closed, windows dark in the middle of the day. A river of dead dreams. The only business that seemed to survive was a small coffee shop at the end of the row. The red-and-white-striped awning covered the large front window, a sign flashing "open" in bright red.

The car stopped at the single traffic light, the yellow glow flashing into my deep brown eyes, which refused to blink. I was frozen in fear. *Turn around, go home ... go anywhere except left.*

Automatically taking a left, the lifeless town disappeared in my rearview mirror, giving way to wide-open spaces. Rolling the window down, the warm air battered against my chilled skin. Just a mile down the road, on autopilot, I took the next right onto a hidden dirt road. The forest barely parted; a person would miss it if they didn't know where it was located. The fact that the road was still unpaved was very telling of how little anyone cared about who lived out this way. Branches clawed at the car, the road so overgrown that only a single car could drive through. Not that anyone else would be coming back this way.

Just when it felt like the forest would swallow me up, it receded. The trees were now tamed back by landowners, as trailers peppered the horizon. My mother's house *(only bequeathed to her in death)* came into focus. It was one of only two houses located back in these woods. There was a decent amount of space between the trailers, with trees to provide cover from peering eyes, but as I reached the end of the road, there were two homes, closer together, with little in between but yard. It was clear which one was owned by a drunk who couldn't remember shit.

The car violently shook as I plowed over the potholes up to the front porch. *Jesus.* The house looked worse than I felt, which was saying something. Like a boxer that went eight rounds too many. Buck-teeth shingles, bruised paint, stringy weeds clinging to craggy bricks.

The car revved, my body, like the car, idling in the heat. I should back out and pretend I never got that phone call from Dr. Bishop. I doubted she had noticed my return. I could just disappear; she would be none the wiser. The house appeared to be crying as I put the car into reverse. The shutters hung loosely, crooked, as my eyes became downcast. The paint frayed, revealing dark wood, as tears formed, bursting to be released. *Damnit.*

Turning the car off, I pulled my stiff body from the driver's seat. Stepping onto the porch, the boards creaked and flexed beneath my weight, the weeds nipping at my ankles. *I might go down with the house.* I knocked loudly. *Nothing.* Shades were pulled down over the dirt-covered windows, making it appear as if the house were abandoned. She was probably passed out in that small flowered chair in the living room, frozen in time from the moment I left this place twenty-one years ago.

"She ain't home, darlin'." My body instantly chilled in the summer heat at the sound of her voice. *There is no way.* I thought for sure she would've died by now. Standing at the edge of the porch, I stared out over the yard, the tall, untamed weeds giving way to freshly cut grass, making a stark property line. Her front porch was only about twenty feet from our own.

Ms. Louis-Bee Kay stood at the edge of her porch, the panels of her house a crisp blue, freshly painted, two rocking chairs set off to the left side of the bright yellow door, giving her a good vantage point to view my mother's living room windows. The houses were designed the same, twins positioned at a forty-five-degree angle away from each other on the makeshift cul-de-sac.

Her misty, gray-blue gaze traveled the short distance and burrowed into my own, sending a radiating shiver down my spine. If it was possible, Ms. Kay looked exactly the same. Her hair was still gray with flecks of black, cut off at her ears and wildly curly. It made her look crazy. All the sagging wrinkles on her face made it hard to determine her facial features or her age. When younger, I suspected that she was a witch, over one hundred years old; my theory was only made more believable at this moment.

"Do you know where she is?" I called across the yard, attempting to be as polite as possible without letting her see my fear. I had a feeling she lived off others' fear, like in a bad horror movie. This was not too farfetched considering I felt exactly like I *was* in a horror movie.

"She's down there at the police station again." I fought to understand her through her thick Southern accent. It was an accent I once had but labored greatly to suppress.

"Same ol' Mama," I uttered under my breath, a slight accent returning. This was not the first time—and probably not the last—I would be picking up my mother at the police station. Unfortunately, in a small town like this, where everybody knows everybody's business, she never had any real consequences for her actions. It was more of a catch-and-release type of system. If only she had been convicted, just one time, maybe I wouldn't find myself having to deal with her now.

"Thank you," I said politely and waved my hand as I returned to my car. *This is definitely a big mistake.*

There was a part of me that wanted to drive straight back to Atlanta and pretend I had never come, but my car drove on autopilot to the police station. *Some things never change.*

"Well, if it isn't Norah Crawford." I swung around just in time to catch his big bear hug.

"Mark, you're crushing me," I laughed as he tightened his squeeze. It had been a long time—*too long.* I allowed his muscular arms to flex against my own. The smell of his aftershave flooded my mind with memories as the feeling of comfort washed over me.

"I thought I'd never see you around these parts again." He gently lowered me back on to my own two feet, which struggled to find steady footing.

"Me neither," I admitted, shame flushing my cheeks. "It's been too long, Mark. How ya been?" Southern hospitality demanded that I ask, but in this case, I genuinely wanted to know how my best friend from high school—whom I haven't spoken to in twenty years—was doing these days.

"You know me, just getting along," he said with that sideways, dimpled, all-too-handsome smile I could never forget. He gently pushed back his wavy jet-black hair, revealing his still strikingly deep brown eyes, which complemented his olive skin. It went without saying that he was popular in school, but as the girls stared at him, he only had eyes for one.

"But you tell me, *city girl.* How've you been?" He nudged my shoulder, acting like we were those two kids forging an unlikely friendship in high school. Only a true friend could pretend like the last twenty years of silence had never really happened.

"Things have been fine." My *fine* was received with just as much skepticism as one would coming from a sleep-deprived mother holding her poop-covered infant.

"Now you wouldn't be back here if things were going *fine.*" I chuckled as he dragged out the word *fine* in a childish manner, providing air quotes to top off his disbelief.

"Just back for a short visit, really."

His thick black eyebrows raised. "Your Mama's back in lock up again," he divulged as if I didn't already know.

"So I hear."

An awkward silence followed our exchange, as unspoken words hung in the stagnant air. Growing up with the town drunk for a mother meant that I was well acquainted with the police department. Subsequently, I received a bit of a reputation, undeserved mostly. People assumed I was guilty for anything and everything. After all, I was unsupervised, unloved, and unruly ... therefore guilty. As I looked up into Mark's dark eyes, desperate to cover up my shame, I could see his sympathy. Suddenly, I got the feeling that maybe he had been the arresting officer. Not that it really mattered. I was sure my mother deserved to be arrested.

"What was it this time?"

Before he could answer, a large, wobbly figure appeared. Officer Morris *(old acquaintance)* stood in the doorway to a rather large office, waving us over. The station was one large room, desks scattered around, covered with papers, files and very out-of-date desktop computers. A few officers wheeled in chairs—*hard at work, I see*—while others walked with purpose. I was sure no one was looking directly at me, but it sure felt like it.

"Well, howdy, Miss Crawford," he sneered with the tip of his oversized, ostentatious hat. His lips parted, revealing yellowed, crooked teeth that made me cringe. His fat fingers waved me over to the door. As we approached the office, I noticed the words *Chief of Police* etched across the glass of the office door. *Well, shit.*

Officer Robert Morris and I went way back, him having been the arresting officer on numerous occasions with my mother and, unfortunately, me. He was the worst one, always assuming I coerced others into my devious acts—*smoking pot mostly.* He hauled me down to the station every time, mostly just so he could see my mother. It was always awkward watching him try to convince my mother to go out on a date with him, assuring my mother that if she did, whatever I had done wouldn't go on my permanent record. She never went on that date, and I never got a permanent record. My mother always could get men to do whatever she wanted; well, most of the time.

"Hello, Officer."

"Chief," he interjected.

"Morris."

Hiking his pants up by the belt, his beer belly a slight smile under his rising shirt, he moved over, and his short, freckled, outstretched arm ushered me into the office. *Chief* was not a good look on him. As an officer, he had been lean and young, but time had taken its toll.

He stood towering over me, looking down his nose as if I were still that small little girl. I was not short, a good five feet seven inches, so that would put *Chief* Morris at least at six feet tall. The awful smell of coffee and stale cigarettes wafted around him as his oversized body stumbled, then attempted to stabilize, his right knee not carrying his weight appropriately. All he needed was a donut in hand to make this picture classically perfect.

"I assume you are here about your mama?" Vomit caught in my throat as his smug look coupled with the smell of men's cologne and donuts poured over my body like oil.

Mark reluctantly disappeared as Chief Morris followed me through the glass doors and back into the office. His hand hovered over my back, an imaginary string between us that made my toes curl. If he touched me, then I'd be in that cell alongside my mother. "Take a seat."

His office was host to two tattered brown leather armchairs, directly opposite an obtrusive solid oak desk. Obviously, he purchased it himself. There was no way this small town could afford such an ostentatious piece of furniture. He slowly and painfully closed the blinds. There was no reason for this. He was just being dramatic. *Really?* I glared at him as he shuffled behind his desk. There was barely enough room between the desk and wall for him to squeeze that fat belly through.

He took a long sip of his coffee, pulling his stained sleeve across his mouth—*torturing me.* He clearly thought he was someone important. In this small town, maybe he was ... to all ten residents.

"Now, your mama's been causing a lot of trouble around here these days." He leaned back in his chair and looked down at me over his wide, pimpled nose, waiting for me to defend her ... not going to happen.

"Exactly what did my mother do this time?"

"Well, let's see," he began, his chair groaning as he shifted his oversized body back toward the desk. Leaning over a thick manilla file, he read, "Loitering, public drunkenness, indecent exposure, public disturbance, and battery, just to name a few things." An evil smile crossed his greasy face. He enjoyed this. I'm sure it felt like foreplay to him.

"I see." I couldn't help but feel slightly hopeful. If he charged my mother, she would definitely do jail time, solving my problem. I doubt the great Chief Morris knew my true goal. I'm sure he thought I wanted her released, which I most certainly did not.

"Do you plan to charge her with anything?" I held my breath, waiting for the answer I so desperately wanted to hear. *Yes, she's going away for a long time.*

"That all depends, Miss Crawford." *Oh no ...* I could remember hearing those same words across the station as *Officer* Morris leaned in close to my mother and gave her a little eyebrow raise. It was an unspoken gesture, one I didn't understand at that age. Now, he raised the same eyebrow at me. I understood it perfectly this time. Everything came at a cost, and I was not willing to pay this fee, especially not for my mother.

"Your mama is sick. Did you know that?" He actually looked concerned, as he appeared to give up on his advance, putting his eyebrow back into its upright and correct position.

"Yes," I admitted. "Her doctor called me yesterday."

"So, I assume by your presence here that you plan on taking care of her?" He looked down at me as if he were a father ensuring his daughter was going to make the right decision. Except he didn't have all the facts, and he wasn't my father.

"I am only here for a short time to get things in order." No way was I letting anyone guilt me into staying in this hellhole.

"Things in order for what?" he asked crossly, his eyes narrowing, lasers of judgment shooting out from all angles.

"I plan on putting her in a facility so that she can get the care she needs. That is, unless you feel that she needs to spend some time in jail for all her offenses."

Immediately, he popped up in his chair, with his large belly, like a boulder, coming across the table, fat finger pointing up and straight at my face.

"Now, you listen here, little lady—" I tried to interrupt him to remind him that I was no longer a little lady, but he didn't allow it. "Your mama may not be the best mama at times, but that woman took care of you the best way she knew how."

Smirking loudly, I was starting to feel like a teenager again, hands crossed over my chest, anger seeping out of my narrowed eyes. He had no clue how little that woman *"took care"* of me.

"Whether you think so or not, that woman did the best she could for you, and now you just gonna put her away in some kinda home? That ain't right."

"Are you going to charge her and put her in jail as she deserves?" I asked, attempting to get us back on track. The last thing I needed was to dig up the past with Robert Morris, of all people. All he knew was that my mother was an alcoholic, tormented by her troublemaking daughter. *How wrong his version of the story truly was.*

"Well, then I'll make you a deal." He closed up the file and took another long sip of his coffee while I began to squirm. I could tell that, whatever it was, I was not going to like it. "You stay here and take care of your mama, and we'll drop all these charges."

I never considered Chief Morris a smart man by any means. Now I was really beginning to think he was just plain stupid.

"I'm confused about how that helps me?" Honestly, I found the deal counterproductive. It would actually work out better for me if she did end up in jail. Then I could go home ... well, not *home*. That didn't exist anymore. But at least I wouldn't have to feel obligated to stay here and take care of that woman.

"Now, I remember a time I offered the same deal to your mama, and she took it. You'd be right to do the same." I narrowed my eyes on him. Of course, he would bring up the past. I had nothing to do with him letting me slide all those years.

"As I hear it, you've become a lawyer," he stated, not questioned.

"Yes, I am a lawyer," I confirmed, adjusting my t-shirt and wishing I had worn something more professional.

"It's my understanding that you can't be a lawyer if you have a criminal record."

"Oh, come on, I was a child. All that would've been expunged."

"You really figure that fancy college would've taken you if you had been arrested?" He chuckled, revealing deep black cavities in his molars. "Sweetheart, you never would've gotten out of this town without me letting you slide all those years."

"That has absolutely no bearing on my life now." I folded my arms tightly against my chest, refusing to let him get to me.

"Well, by my reckoning, you owe your job to your mama and me," he stated with a satisfied smirk on his face. "Now, if there was only some way you could repay us."

"Like hell I do." This was it, the moment I sunk so low I could no longer breathe. Never in my entire law career did I ever allow a client, colleague, or judge get to me the way I just allowed Chief Morris. It was this place, making me feel as if the last twenty-one years had never happened.

"On top of that, as a lawyer, I am sure you know that a nursing home will not take a person with a criminal record. Not of this magnitude anyways." His smile was smug—not so stupid after all. *He had me.*

"Chief Morris," I sighed, defeated. "You have no idea what you are asking of me."

My leg shook violently as I waited for my mother's release, my fingers wrapped into each other, turning purple from lack of blood flow, sweat starting to bead on my temples, and my anger boiling to an explosive point.

I couldn't take it anymore; this was taking forever. I started to pace quickly back and forth in front of the secretary's desk, which was nicely positioned right where you walked into the station. Holding cells were in the back. My eyes were glued to the large black door that stood between my mother and me. Any moment those doors would open, and I'd have to see her. I couldn't promise I wouldn't kill her on the spot.

Suddenly, there she was—*my mother*—standing only a few feet from me.

"What the hell are you doing here?"

My mother shuffled her way through the police department, the only cage that could possibly keep her from the world, dressed in a filthy pink robe. It had been twenty-one years, but the changes were still subtle. Her hair, slightly gray when I was a child, was now a silver dome, wild stray pieces jetting out from all angles, and her frown falling deeper in the corners made her appear like a codfish. Her age was most pronounced by her foggy eyes and wrinkled face. As she padded closer in her dirt-covered slippers, I could smell her natural body odor mixed with liquor. The smell brought back so many memories.

Chapter Four
Little Girl

Their giggles filled the cool spring air. The three girls fell to the ground following a rousing game of Ring Around the Rosie. A little girl lingered off to the side, swinging back and forth. Her dirt-covered feet dragged ever so slightly through the mud. For a moment, she allowed herself to believe that she could be one of those girls. She pictured them skipping home to a loving mother waiting at the door. With a quick hug and kiss, they would bounce off to the dinner table, which was covered with all sorts of delicious foods. She imagined how it would taste. It caused her dry mouth to water. Her own stomach growled. It had been days since she last ate.

She dreamed she was anyone but herself, if only for a moment, before the reality of her situation came crashing down. She swung her leg out, causing her dress to flutter slightly above her knee. A deep purple-and-blue bruise was revealed. Bruises were the only thing her mother ever gave her. Ever. She was filled with shame as her eyes drifted back toward the girls. They were staring at her, like concrete statues in a graveyard. She thought maybe they would come and ask her to play. Then she saw their looks and noted their actions. They all did the same thing: the outstretched finger-pointing, the grimace, followed by hand-covered whispers. They all said the same thing. They all knew the truth.

She stepped lightly on each board of the porch, cringing as the screen door squeaked open. As she tiptoed into the house, she kept her ears open for any sounds—the drop of the ice in a glass cup, the pull of metal on the recliner as it strained against the weight, the click of a lighter ... all signs that she was drinking. But on this particular day, it was silent.

The kitchen was empty, devoid of anything nutritious, but she was starving. It was a risk, for any moment her mother could wake or return, but she needed something, otherwise she would never be able to sleep tonight. Pulling a small wooden stool up to the counter, she pulled her legs up onto the dirty laminate. She swung the cabinet door open, wobbling slightly as she tightened her grip on the door. The shelves were empty, but she had a secret, hidden on the top shelf.

Reaching up on her tiptoes, her fingers stretching as far as they could, finally, they grazed the plastic box. After a few failed attempts, the box moved just enough so she could pull it down. She had stolen the crackers from the store, wrapping them tightly so the bugs would not get to them and storing them here where her mother would never find them.

Her delicious family dinner was only a bag of stale crackers that was tucked between her knees. The room was dark, the only light from the moon staring at her through the window. She did not know where her mother was, nor did she dare to find out. With each bite, she counted out the days she might be alone. Even though there were more crackers, she only ate five, then tucked them back into the cabinet.

Chapter Five
Present Day

Her feet dragged across the worn wooden-planked floor, a rhythmic scuffling sound vibrating against every wall. The short, round woman behind the desk slowly rolled her chair away in preparation. *The wild animal was being released.* My mother held something tightly against her chest; it appeared to be an old purse. Most likely her possessions that were taken when arrested. I rolled my eyes at the thought of my mother ever having anything worth holding that tightly. It was probably booze.

"Well, why are you here?" Spit oozed from the corner of her mouth, perpetuating the viciousness of her words.

"Someone had to bail you out."

She growled through her teeth as a sly, contemptuous smile crossed my lips. Narrowing my eyes in her direction, a direct challenge to her own opposition, I realized she might actually hate seeing me more than I hated seeing her.

"I don't need you."

"Aw, yes you do." It was wrong, but I took joy from this moment. Mother's anger was palpable; I was bathing in it.

We rode in silence under the gray-cast clouds, my mother still clinging to her belongings. I kept waiting for her to yell at me as she always did, but nothing came. There was just this ominous silence. I figured it was her way of punishing me. It was really a blessing.

Once again, I found myself face to face with my childhood as we sat in the car in front of my mother's house. There was a part of me that had been on autopilot, numb to the choices I was truly making. Or maybe I just didn't understand the true magnitude of my choices. My mother was inches from me, the closest we'd been in all these years, with my old torture chamber looming above me.

I'd eventually have to go inside the house. Living in this car was not an option, of course, but the thought had occurred to me that it might be better than going inside. Pulling my fingers roughly through my tangled hair, holding them tightly at the base of my neck, my head resting on the leather steering wheel, I regretted every decision I'd made in the last six months. I knew the moment I stepped into that house, every memory I'd buried in the last twenty-one years would come rushing toward me like a dam releasing pressure. *This was a very bad idea.*

"What are we doing?" My mother's voice pierced my thoughts. I wanted to kick her out the door and speed off into the sunset, but instead, I gathered my mother from the car and ushered her toward the house. She was oddly compliant. I supported her over the broken porch step and perched her against the doorway. *Keys?*

"Mama, where are the keys?" Nothing. She just stared off into space. The silent treatment was so juvenile. "Okay, let's look in here." I attempted to take the item she was holding, but she pulled back.

"Don't touch my things! Who do you think you are?"

"Your daughter. I am trying to get us inside." There was a loud crack of thunder as dark clouds rolled in across the open field. "Before it rains would be nice."

"It's not going to rain today."

"What? Who cares, Mama? Just give me the damn key to the house." I held my hand out, waiting for her to retrieve it from her purse. I was in no mood to fight with her; I just wanted to get inside. Even though I knew the consequences of going inside, once again, I had made my decision, and now I needed to know what would come next.

As if her brain had suddenly clicked back on, she reached into the top of her dress and pulled out a long chain. At the end was the key. *Why? Nope, not going to ask.*

My shoulder leaned against the door as I attempted to turn the lock.

Open, you stubborn piece of—-

The door swung open unexpectedly, causing me to stumble into the foyer. Immediately, I was overcome by the foul, permeating smell, a cough settling in, attempting to push out the horrible taste. The smell did not seem to faze my mother.

Through the tiny tears in the shades, small thin rays of light danced around the house, specks of dust illuminating each move. I dragged my finger over the antique foyer table *(it came with the house, family heirloom),* making a snail trail in the dust. My finger was black. *This place is filthy.*

Sweat started to bead on my brow as the stale heat set in. It was hotter inside the house than outside. I pulled at my t-shirt as it started to stick to my body, the air so thick that I felt as if I would suffocate. She had let the entire house go to shit ... *utter shit.*

From the foyer, there were snippets of each area of the house. The narrow hallway leading straight back to the master bedroom, flanked by a staircase on the right, the carpet crawling up each step almost as dark as the wood. The opening to my left revealed the living room *(odd name considering no actual living ever took place in that room, mostly just drinking).* I could see a fragment of my mother's flower armchair, a corner of the brick fireplace, and a used drink on the side table. There was something next to the drink, but it took a moment to realize just what my eyes were seeing—*flies.* It was a swarm, covering something, only a sliver of white porcelain visible.

Reflexively, I made my way to the object, only realizing it was a plate of rotten food. I should pick up the plate and drink, but flies would disperse, as bats leaving a cave, and I would be surrounded.

Leaving the plate, I walked back across the foyer, my feet dragging over the extremely dirty, old five-by-seven oriental rug that covered a large, dark stain, and I pushed the swinging door into the kitchen.

The fire clawed for oxygen, and the smell of this house engulfed me as I walked into the kitchen. I could feel the vomit catching in my throat as the palpable smell of rotting food invaded my mouth. Every inch of the kitchen was covered with flies and roaches crawling over dirty, food-crusted plates, inside glasses reaching for that last drop of liquor, making homes in open bags of chips and rice. It was revolting and inconceivable that anyone could let this happen. *How had she been living in such filth?* I couldn't hold the rising vomit at bay any longer—I ran to the bathroom.

Returning from the awkwardly placed bathroom under the stairs, barely tall enough to fit a person, I pulled a dingy, yellow-stained lace napkin from a drawer in a distressed hutch in the dining room, which was too close to the kitchen. The swinging door, currently closed at this moment, loomed in front of me. I knew what would happen when I opened that door. The smell would take over once again, the bugs would feel as if they were crawling all over my body, and I would most likely need to vomit again. I pulled the napkin over my mouth and nose, securing it tightly behind my neck.

I just needed to get the basics done: throw the spoiled food away, get all the dishes cleaned, and spray a ridiculous amount of bleach everywhere. *I can do this .... Deep breaths—wait, no!*

Swinging the door open, holding my breath, which didn't help, I saw my mother standing in the center of all the filth. Her body a statue in a polluted park, her eyes frozen, she gazed unblinkingly at an unknown spot on the wall. As I moved into the kitchen, she didn't move. Slowly, I made my way around her body, careful not to disturb the resting lion. Then, placing a gentle guiding hand on either shoulder, I ushered her to the flower chair as if she were sleepwalking.

Before touching anything, I pulled a container of bleach from under the kitchen sink, dark rust-brown trails stripping the front of its solid porcelain front. Holding the spray bottle like a gun, I quickly drenched each pile of bugs before attempting to move the dish, glass, or a bag of food from the counter, jumping back so that nothing found refuge on my sweaty body.

"Are you going to make dinner?" *Damnit.* My movements had awoken the beast.

"No." I could not conceive cooking, nor would I have an appetite for at least a week—not after cleaning this kitchen. When I initially saw my mother after being away for so long, she did appear thinner. I had always assumed that she would drink more rather than eat more. However, *this?* I never imagined it would get this bad.

"Well, what the hell am I supposed to do then?"

"Whatever you have been doing for the last twenty-one years." I threw the dirty kitchen rag down on the counter, exhausted from cleaning and ill from vomiting more than I cared to admit. *Deep breaths.* Bracing myself on the counter, I took three large, deep breaths. *Stay calm. Don't let her get to you.*

"Fine." Suddenly, she was standing in the kitchen doorway. I was shocked she actually moved. That was new. Her bone fingers curled around her thin waist. Her hollow eyes were narrowing in on me, giving her a demented, skeleton-like appeal.

She pushed around me and into the kitchen. I watched as she proceeded to open and shut all the cabinet doors multiple times, accomplishing absolutely nothing. Completely annoyed by her stomping about and the fact that she still hadn't managed to locate a plate, I couldn't stand it anymore. *She is just doing this to drive me crazy.*

"I'll do it," I snapped at her, pushing her aside. "Just go back into the living room." I pointed her in the right direction as she continued to scowl. At least she followed my order.

"I'd like a drink too," she added as she disappeared. For a moment, I could've sworn I saw an evil smile cross over her cracked lips. *She played me.*

Of course, there was vodka in the house. There was always vodka in this house. It was just unlucky that no one in my family ever invested in the stuff. We could've made a fortune or saved a fortune, depending on how you care to look at the situation. The only thing my mother actually ever taught me was how to make a good, stiff drink. Her actions were altruistic, as she wanted me to make her drinks. I pulled the one clean glass from the cabinet and threw in a few ice cubes. No surprise she had at least put some ice trays in the freezer. I poured the clear liquor to the top of the glass. As I took it to her, I couldn't help but feel like that little girl again.

I never should've offered to cook dinner. Leaning on the fridge door, all I could see was an old moldy block of cheese, V8 juice—most likely for Bloody Marys—and a very random container of ranch dressing. Cooking was not going to be easy. I abandoned the fridge and started to rifle through the pantry. Not much of a difference in the way of edible food. Finally, I found an only-slightly-expired can of tomato soup. Surprisingly, I also found some fairly fresh bread. Just a few moldy parts, but it was still good ... *maybe.*

I scraped the mold off of the cheese block and bread to pull together a grilled cheese sandwich. Heating up the soup in the microwave, I managed a pretty decent grilled cheese and tomato soup dinner. Cooking was never my specialty, let alone when I had nothing to cook with that wasn't spoiled or covered in bugs. My husband was the one who mostly cooked; I was the one who ordered out.

"What happened to this place?"

My mom was hunched over, annoyingly slurping her soup. I could tell she hadn't eaten in quite some time. That should have upset me, but it didn't. I knew what it felt like to be hungry.

Even if I were hungry now, I couldn't eat. I was still nauseous over the state of my childhood home. I had convinced her to eat out on the porch in order to escape the awful kitchen smells. Even in the late-summer heat, I opened all the windows and porch doors. It was going to take weeks to air out those smells. I made a mental note to get air fresheners.

Outside, it was a typical Southern night; the air was warm and muggy, crickets serenading us from the woods. We were in the final heatwave of the summer. Mosquitos were desperately trying to get through the screen and to our coursing veins. Screened in porches were a must in the South. I was thankful my mother had not torn holes in this one. I'd hate to have to replace it ... *again.*

"What are you talking about?" Her response time was so delayed that I almost forgot I had asked her a question.

"There was spoiled food everywhere, Mama, coupled with dirty dishes and a smell ... well, I can't tell what the smell is really, but it's awful. What have you been doing?"

"How dare you judge me? You left this place. You left me! Why did you return?"

"Because *your* doctor called and told me you are sick."

"Why do you all of a sudden care?"

"I really don't, actually. But maybe you should."

"Should what?"

"Start caring about something, like yourself and the state of this place."

"Oh, what do you care? This isn't your home."

The moment she said it, I realized that I had been fooling myself. This was *not* my home. I'd known that my entire life. I never wanted this place to be my home ... *so why did I come back? Why did I care?*

"This place is fine. I'm fine." Her thin lips held a tight frown. Things were clearly not fine, but I didn't have the energy to deal with it now. I realized, by the age of ten, that I would always be more mature than my mother. She was always just a large drunk, *lost* child.

"Never mind," I mumbled. My mother was choosing to ignore what was happening. She abruptly stood, leaving the porch and most likely going back to her drink, which I had strategically left inside. I sighed as I realized she'd left her dirty dishes behind. This might be why the house was such a wreck.

I should get up and clean up ... *again* ... but Alabama had a way of slowing things down. As the moon settled into the sky and the fireflies flashed in the distance, I decided to settle in as well. Going back inside would only lead to having to deal with my mother, and even though I had just arrived this morning, I was ready for a break.

My body jolted back to life as my hand slipped off the side of the chair and my head came crashing forward. I was covered in sticky summer sweat. The air was heavy around me, and the night was dark. I must've fallen asleep on the porch. The stress of the day had finally gotten to me. I pulled my legs from the rocker, like slowly pulling off a stale band aid. My watch glowed; it was three in the morning.

I made my way back into the dark house. I took a quick look into the living room to find that my mother was no longer in her flowered armchair. She was probably in bed at this hour. I was thankful I didn't have to deal with her again. I could not handle dragging her drunken, limp body to bed. Not sure I had the strength for it anymore. Pulling my sweaty, aching body onto the couch in the living room, I allowed myself to fall back into my dreams.

"Why are you here?" Her voice pierced through my hazy mind. It took me a moment to remember just how awful my life had become in the last twenty-four hours. As my mother's poisonous face came into view, so did the dire situation of my life.

"Get up." She yanked the blanket from my body and kicked my leg to get me to move. I wasn't really sure what I did to offend her, but I decided not to even ask. No reason to open that expired can of worms.

"I'm here because, apparently, you can no longer take care of yourself." Her contempt for my situation was undeniable; just as much as she didn't want me here, I definitely didn't want to be here.

"I don't need you here."

"Oh, really?" If the last twelve hours had shown me anything, it was that, unfortunately, Dr. Bishop was correct. My mother was not able to take care of herself ... at all. The house was falling apart; it was filthy. And worst of all, she had gotten arrested, which I had painfully learned was counterproductive to my cause.

"Have you seen the house lately?" I stormed into the kitchen after her, turning her attention to our surroundings. I had barely made a dent. Despite my best cleaning efforts, it was still in disarray, and that awful smell was still emanating from the house.

31

"Oh," she said, waving it away with her hand. "So what if I haven't had time to clean lately? What business is that of yours?"

"Mama, the doctor called me, remember?" Even though she had been there at the time, she was still struggling to understand it was, in fact, the only reason I was here. "He told me about the Alzheimer's."

"Oh, that ol' doctor is a quack," she snapped. "He doesn't know nothin'." But I could see in her glassy eyes she understood more than she was willing to admit. There was no denying the state of affairs of this place; she *had* to see it. No matter how much she resisted, she needed me here, which burned her up inside.

"I can't tell you how much I wish I could believe that, but clearly something is wrong." Sullen, she crossed her arms low over her waist and refused to make eye contact, as if admitting it out loud would somehow make this more real. Unfortunately, it was reality.

"The house is a mess; it looks like you haven't eaten or bathed in days. Oh, and of course, there is the fact you got arrested. For a laundry list of offenses, might I add."

"Why, all of a sudden, do you care so much?" Her fierce stare was disarming. I hadn't seen that look in twenty-one years. I knew what it meant. Her frizzy hair appeared to be slithering around her face as she glared at me with those hollow gray eyes. *Crazy eyes.*

I knew things would be difficult coming back to a mother with a mental condition. I knew it would be hard to come back home after all these years. But, for a moment, I thought maybe, just maybe, all these years apart had softened her, made her forget—or at least let go of—how much she hated me. That was wishful thinking, just like wishing on all those stars.

"You know what ..." I didn't have the energy for it; life had beaten me down too much at this point. "I have no idea why I care all of a sudden. In fact, I don't care." She was not the only one who could hold on to her hatred. "The only reason I am here is to help you get your affairs in order so that I can put you in a home." There, I had said it out loud. It was done. *Now she knows.*

"Over my dead body!" The anger, which was so familiar to me, flashed across her face. There were always two speeds with my mother—hatred or anger. Hatred was the look I had grown accustomed to seeing. Anger was my warning sign, like a tornado alarm ringing through my brain. I knew what she intended to do now, the only thing she knew how to do.

"Oh, please, that would make this even better." I stepped toward her, waiting, baiting her to give in to her anger. But she just stood there, glaring.

"You were always an ungrateful bitch." Her words were slow and deep, sliding like a dull knife through my gut. With that, I'd had enough. I stormed out into the morning sunrise, leaving my mother to fend for herself. I could hear her screaming something after me, but I didn't listen. No doubt an endless list of horrible name-calling. Nothing I hadn't heard before. I had perfected the skill of tuning her out as a child; *like riding a bike.*

My heart raced as I made my way through the backyard, the grass so high it brushed against my bare knees. I knew this was a bad decision. This was not healthy for me. I paced around the yard, just at the tree line. Back and forth, back and forth. I could almost see the old path I used to take to the lake. *Deep breaths—calm down.* I rubbed my chest, feeling the pressure building. Thunder rumbled through the sky; storms were coming. *I need to go back home.*

There was something in that word, *home,* that stopped me in my tracks and knocked the breath out of me. *Panic attack.* My hands fell to my knees as I attempted to catch my breath. Just a few short months ago, I had an actual home and a life with a man who, much to my dismay, I still loved. That was honestly the only place I ever felt like calling home. Now, all that was gone, lost forever. If I could no longer call *that* home, what *could* I call home? Honestly, there was no place that I could call *home.* Suddenly, I realized that I was in the same place I was as a child ... *lost and alone.*

I ran, fast and hard, taking the old, overgrown path through the woods. It was second nature to my feet, having taken this path countless times over my childhood. My breath began to steady as my mind cleared. The trees broke after a mile; the lake glistened in the sun. This place always had a way of taking all the painful thoughts away.

My screams rippled across the glassy lake, fading off in the distance as it always did. When I was a child, I thought I would die in this place. I thought that the ground would open up and swallow me whole. Many times I came to this lake to escape, to be alone ... to be *free.* The idea that I was right back in that place was sobering.

For years, I would tell myself of the life I would have outside of this place. It was the only thing that got me through each day.

Only now, I'd had that life and lost it. My eyes opened up, pouring out like a thick gray cloud. It was a familiar scene, crying at the lake. There was nothing to my life anymore, nothing to hope for anymore. A feeling that took me back to my deepest nightmares as a child.

Chapter Six
Little Girl

The little girl traced her hand over the wallpaper. The small delicate pink flowers moved at her touch, or so she imagined. Each wilting flower transformed into a ballerina, dancing slowly across the wall, in a show just for her. She waited patiently for just the right sound of his snores falling into a rhythmic pattern—*he was asleep.*

With each step, her feet as light as a feather, she avoided each loose board. She did not want to wake him. Silently, leaning over the banister, she could see him sleeping in the large brown leather armchair. His fat arms fell over the sides, legs stretched out, making him look like a starfish ... a dead one most likely. Suddenly, his body gave a jolt and a deep snore. She ducked back down behind the banister. He slightly shifted in his chair yet remained asleep. Her heart started beating again.

She could smell the scotch as she tiptoed by him toward the front door. As she gently pulled on the knob, her anxiety grew. Any moment he could wake, preventing her escape. She had spent all day in that room, and she just wanted a few seconds outside. There was a lake not too far away. If she cut through the woods, she could get there quickly. Maybe she would even have time for a swim if she ran. All she wanted was escape ...

Just as she was about to be free, a shadow cast over her small body. Her long, delicate fingers pressed against the door, closing it just as she was about to squeeze out. The little girl's eyes started to burn as her mother blew out a large cloud of gray cigarette smoke. Through the haze of smoke, she could see the evil grin crossing her mother's red lips.

"Where do you think you are going?" Her eyes narrowed, a silent challenge the little girl knew all too well. If she told her mother she wanted to go for a swim, her mother would slice her skin so that it would burn too badly to get into the water. If she told her mother she wanted to go climb a tree, she would cut it down. Nothing she could say was safe, so she said nothing at all.

"You are not allowed to leave." She inhaled the smoke, letting its poison leak from her nose as she added, "None of us are."

Chapter Seven
Present Day

My mother was nowhere to be found. Darkness surrounded the house like a thick blanket. I had spent the entire day at the lake, not realizing it until the sun sank behind the still and glassy water. Today, my mind was lost. As the memories threatened to flood my mind, I logically attempted to place them back in Pandora's box. I could not handle a tortuous trip down memory lane.

I assumed she had retired to her room but did not care enough to confirm. With a deep sigh of submission, I gathered my bags from the rental car and retreated to my old room. *This is it for me.* Kicking the door open with my foot, the stale smell of the room engulfed me, causing a violent cough. It was obvious that the door had not been opened for a long time, possibly the last time I opened it.

There would've been no reason for my mother to go into the room; if not for making her drinks, she probably never would've noticed I had actually left. That really seemed to be the only reason she was upset to see me go off to college ... *no one to make her drinks.* However, as I flicked the light with my elbow, I realized she had been in my room.

The day I packed my hard red suitcase, I knew I would never come back to this room, yet there was so much I still did not take with me. The only thing I cared about was getting out. Standing in the doorway, it suddenly hit me that maybe I should've taken more, like my Cinderella jewelry box that now lay broken on the floor, the little dancer pulled off. Or my CD player, which was crushed against the wall. But most of all, I should've taken the pictures. I had an old cork board, various pictures pinned all over it, but she had ripped them all down, pieces of everyone's faces scattered across the dingy green shag carpet.

Tears burned the corner of my eyes; she had destroyed my room, the only place I had ever had to myself. Reaching down, I picked up the corner of a picture. It was Caroline's face. My eye released a single tear at the sight of her, the porcelain, doll-like skin, with vibrant deep-blue eyes and a sweep of blonde hair pulled back around her ear. I had forgotten about her as well. The shame welled in my chest, the dam threatening to break.

As I picked up the various pieces of the pictures, I realized that my own face had been torn away from every picture. *She literally ripped me out of my own life.* My mother must've destroyed my room right after I left. It appeared as if she shut the door and never opened it again, evident by a thick layer of dust over everything.

Slowly, I began to pick up all the pieces of my shattered childhood, throwing the Cinderella box into the trash, along with the pictures, and then the CD player. None of it could be fixed. She had turned it all into trash, as she did with everything in her life.

After cleaning the kitchen, I could barely lift my arms to run the vacuum cleaner over the shag rug. There was no way I would be able to sleep in this room with all the dust and dirt. *Yet another thing to clean.* Pulling the purple sheets from my bed, dust engulfed me again. I had to laugh slightly over my obvious obsession with the color purple when I was thirteen. At least that part had not changed. The bedsheets, comforter, and even the draperies were all a deep shade of purple.

Of course, none of the shades quite matched, but I didn't care when I was thirteen. For my birthday that year, Caroline and Mark had each given me a purple present, clearly from different places. I didn't care that it didn't match. All I cared about was the fact that I had received birthday gifts at all, the first time in my life. My mother gave me nothing, which, by that time in my life, was expected. I never thought I'd have friends who actually celebrated my birthday and gave me gifts.

It took some scavenging, but I finally found a fitted sheet in the hall closet. It was tucked deep behind some old boxes of shoes. Pulling my sore body into the bed and an old blanket over my legs, I had hopes that there would be a familiar sense of comfort. But there was nothing. I'd hoped I'd have the feeling I used to get every time I got into bed with my ex-husband. It was the feeling of melting into my place in the world. For some reason, I thought that maybe my old childhood bed would give me a feeling of belonging. But no. I felt nothing.

I'm not sure why I thought this place would feel like home. There was nothing of mine really left in this room. She had destroyed everything that held any memory for me. Despite the fact that I had a horrible childhood because of her, I actually did have some fond memories in this room and of my friends. Yet now they were all gone, crushed by my mother.

Chapter Eight
Little Girl

The little girl swung to and fro on the swing as her naked feet dragged in the dirt. It was a hot summer day, but she did not mind the heat. In fact, she preferred it. The warm sun encircled her bare skin, clasping around her shoulders as she thought a hug would feel. The act of swinging, doing something so classically normal, made her feel less lonely. She desperately wanted a friend to play with, but that was not an option. She could never have a friend. What if they noticed the bruises? Or worse ... what if they found out? She could never take that risk. Her mother would never allow anyone to know the truth. She was alone in her suffering ... *forever.*

"Hello."

The little girl turned to find another little girl staring back at her as if they were both looking into a mirror.

She was older, but not by much. She had a deep Southern accent and a raspy voice that did not fit her small girlish frame. Her brilliant brown curls bounced upon her shoulders as she walked and illuminated her bright blue-gray eyes. She was beautiful.

"Well, are you going to say it back?" she demanded.

"Hello," she whispered. She looked back up to the house to make sure no one was watching. All the shades were drawn closed; she breathed a sigh of relief.

"I just moved in next door." She pointed back over her shoulder at the identical house across the street. "Thought I'd come over to say hello, meet the neighbors." She stared at the little girl, waiting, but the little girl said nothing. "Just thought that maybe we could be best friends?"

"Friends?" The word was so foreign to the little girl.

"Yeah, two people who spend time together, talk ... you know, friends." The little girl smiled, envious of the girl's ability to speak so forcefully as if nothing could ever hurt her in this world. For a brief moment, the little girl considered having a friend like this girl. Maybe she could protect her, keep her safe. She definitely seemed strong enough to protect her. Nothing like how the little girl felt about herself.

"Okay." Her voice was only a whisper, fearful that her mother would somehow find out and ruin it.

"Well then, I guess I've made my first friend in this town."

"Me too." They smiled at each other, not knowing that their friendship was doomed from the start.

The little girl heard the door slam. He was home. Terror rose inside every inch of her body. Coming home at this time of day could only mean one thing—*he was drunk.* The screaming started, at first a low growl but then rising to a full roar as his voice echoed through the small house, vibrating every panel on the wall. Without knowing what else to do, she quickly escaped out the window and down the tree.

As she disappeared into the woods, she could hear her mother's screams. The fighting never stopped; her mother's only reprieve came when he was gone or passed out from drinking. But then it would be her turn. She ran all the way to the lake. Pulling off her white lace dress, she dove deep down into the dark waters. She stayed at the bottom for as long as her lungs would hold before she braved the top of the water for air. It was silent ... dark.

In that moment, the little girl decided she would never return to the house. She would rather live here. She could build a house in the forest, bathe in the lake, and eat bugs. That life would be better than returning home ... anything was better than going home.

She allowed her body to float on the top of the water, still and content with her choice to live here. Suddenly, she realized she was not alone. Opening her eyes, she saw her only friend standing on the broken dock, her dark hair wildly blowing all around her face.

"What are you doing?" She smirked at the little girl as if she were running naked through the fields.

"Swimming." The little girl flipped her body so she could look up at the girl, treading water just a few feet from the dock. Her friend stood, hands on hips, staring down at her. The little girl wasn't quite sure what she was going to do.

"Can I join?"

"Suuurrre," the little girl answered tentatively, not really certain of how to react to her newfound friend. The little girl could not even believe that she had a friend.

The girl dove into the lake. They swam alongside each other for several minutes, the girl never asking about the bruises, never asking about why she was here, just swimming. As the sun started to disappear below the trees, the girl turned to her and asked, "Are you hungry? You can come over for dinner."

"I plan to eat bugs."

"What?" The girl looked confused, but then laughed as if the girl was joking. "Okay, yeah, you are coming for dinner. My parents won't mind."

With that, the little girl followed her new friend back to her home. Through the forest, past the fields, she found herself standing at the doorstep of her neighbors' house. Just a short quarter of a mile away from her mother, who was, no doubt, lying in wait. She wasn't sure how long her mother would wait or if she had already started the search, but either way, for some unknown reason, she felt safe here. She felt her new friend would protect her, feed her, and take care of her. Surely, they would not make her go home.

She ate every last bite on her plate, taking in the meal as if she were never going to eat again. The girl and her parents watched, concerned for the little girl. Her bruises were deep, bones showed underneath her dirty, ripped clothes, and by the way she ate ... it was clear to them that she was being abused.

It did not take long for her mother to arrive at the door.

"Please, have you seen my little girl? Please, she ran away, and I can't find her." Her mother was convincing as a concerned parent. She even managed to muster up some tears.

"Yes, she is here." The door opened to reveal the little girl at the dinner table.

The little girl trembled in her seat, praying to God to please make her invisible. No answer.

"Time to go home, sweetheart." Her mother smiled, but she knew better. It was not relief her mother felt over finding her; it was vindication. Now she could have her revenge.

There were endless screams from her room that night. No one ever called the police. No one ever came to save her ... she couldn't help but wonder what happened to her new friend.

Chapter Nine
Present Day

A flicker of light invaded the darkness, and the pain began to come into focus. My body ached, and my mind was fuzzy. *Where am I?* It took a long moment before I realized where I was and why. Moaning, I pulled the blanket up and over my face, unwilling to accept my horrible fate. Before rising from my bed, I briefly considered a bargain with God. However, I wasn't sure exactly what to bargain for. I had lost everything, and it seemed a little too much to ask for it all back, especially considering I was also wishing for my mother's death. He might be a little conflicted about that one.

Pulling my sore body from the bed, I could smell the summer sweat seeping from my pores. I needed a bath ... a nice long, hot, relaxing bath. Making my way into my old childhood bathroom, just down the hall from my bedroom, I realized the shower had most likely not been cleaned since I left. As I pulled back the shower curtain, I discovered black mold on both the tile and grout. I sighed, exasperated—yet another thing to clean.

But I desperately needed a bath. Surveying the tub, I decided that it was clean enough; that was how badly I needed this bath. The water ran brown for a few minutes, then clean water started to fill the tub. Slipping into the warm water, I sunk my entire body as deep as it would go, leaving only my face above the water. *If only I could drown myself ... bad idea.*

With each minute I stayed submerged, the clear water turned dirty, murky, just like my life. Every minute I stayed in this horrible place, my life was steadily becoming darker. My eyes drifted over the previously white tiles. On each wall of the tile, mold threatened clean white surfaces, just as I was allowing the darkness to come at me from all angles, slowly taking over my clear mind. Suddenly, I realized this tub was filthy, and I could no longer stand another second in it.

It was hard to look at my disheveled appearance in the dusty bathroom mirror. I couldn't help but feel the effects of last night's revelation—*I have nothing.* Nothing felt right to me in my own life, a feeling that I did not wish to become accustomed to. I wished I could say I was just at a crossroads, that things would start to come together, but that was not the case.

Currently, I had only one option, which seemed like the worst thing to do. But unfortunately, there was no other. In court, I always had three or four ways I could take a case in order to win. Being flexible and adaptable gave me my edge. An edge I lost the day Michael asked for the divorce. I hadn't seen that one coming, nor could I figure out how to get out of it. I had become stuck, *lost*.

Coming here was only temporary, or so I told myself when I rented a car. *Just go, get things in order, then get out as fast as you can.* Now, I couldn't figure out what I was going to do next. Now that I was away from Atlanta and realizing all I had lost, I couldn't fathom the thought of returning. Not in this state of mind. *So was I really going to stay here?* There was literally nowhere else to go.

On top of that, just the complex idea of starting over right now seemed impossible. All I wanted—no, all I *needed*—was time to think about how I was going to deal with my mother. In my career, possibly my previous career, my process was to take one piece of evidence at a time. Get through everything one step at a time. Make a plan, multiple plans, see all the possibilities, and prepare for them all. That took time and focus, *so I guess this is it ...*

Step one: Deal with my mother. If only I could think of multiple ways to handle that situation.

The house was silent. I was grateful that she did not appear to be awake. This gave me a moment of peace to have a cup of coffee before I had to figure out my situation. My mind was still struggling with the idea of actually staying in this house; however, I was running out of any other options pretty quickly.

Of course, there was no coffee to be found in that rancid kitchen. There was no way I was making it through this day without coffee. Rubbing my temples, I wondered how difficult it would be to make coffee out of tomato juice. Suddenly, I remembered the small coffee shop in town and prayed that it was still open. Grabbing the keys to my rental car, still unreturned, I decided it was best to leave my mother out of this excursion. I didn't even bother looking in the mirror or putting real clothes on. My mind was totally focused on getting that first cup of coffee.

I was in luck; apparently, coffee can survive a recession. I breathed a sigh of relief. The shop was desolate; thank you, God. The fewer people I could encounter while back here, the better.

The lone elderly man stood at the far end of the long bar, wiping down the seemingly clean white laminate counter. Even though the place was severely outdated, it was immaculately clean. Each retro chrome-red barstool was shining in the morning light, which was drifting low through the large front window. The word *COFFEE* stretched across the top of the window, only slightly obstructing the sun. *Don't they have blinds?*

"Just a cup of regular coffee, dark." He nodded, leaving the cloth and making his way over to the cash register, comically slow in my opinion, which caused my caffeine headache to deepen. I tapped my finger on the counter, my agitation growing.

"Well, if it isn't little Norah Crawford." The wrinkles on the clerk's face tightened as he raised his falling eyelids and spread his thin lips into what I thought was a smile. His voice was slower than his movements, if that were possible.

Oh, great. This is awkward, not even a slight recognition. His eyes glowed behind his thick glasses, which made me feel bad that I didn't remember him. This was the curse of a small town—everyone knew everyone, even if they hadn't been back for over twenty years. For a beat, I did question how he recognized me. Surely, I had changed since I left. I made a mental note to give myself a good, hard look in the mirror when I got home. Maybe I could change something, anything, to make myself more unrecognizable.

"Good morning." I attempted to feign recognition. "How ya been?"

"Well, I've been just fine," he said slowly, revealing his three yellowed teeth. *Guess a dentist didn't survive the recession.* It was going to take all day for him to tell me one thing about himself, but at least he couldn't ask about me.

"It's nice of you to ask." I waited for him to continue ... we stared at each other awkwardly. I assumed he was going to continue, but he said nothing. He appeared to completely and suddenly lose track of what he was going to say.

"So, how about that coffee?" I finally probed.

"Oh, yes, yes, let me get that for you." He appeared flustered as he attempted to get the coffee. I gently tapped my fingers on the hollow counter. The smell of coffee filled the small shop; it was intoxicatingly good. *At least I still have coffee.*

"Well, I'll be damned if it isn't Norah Crawford."

Damn, I hate this town. Every time I turned around, I knew someone. Or more accurately, someone knew me. I turned around, fully expecting to have no idea who was behind me; however, this time, I did. And this person stopped me mid thought.

"Brett Hennings." Disbelief flooded my voice as I stared up at the one person I never would've expected to see still in this town. Automatically, as if we had just seen each other the other day, he leaned over and pulled me into a large hug. His body flexed against my own, the thickness of his *"grown man"* muscles tightening around my fragile body. Very different from the Brett I remembered from high school.

Brett wasn't much in the way of looks and poise back in the day, but he sure knew everything. Always the classic geek of our grade, he was often overlooked by most girls. But being assigned his lab partner in tenth grade had felt like winning the lottery. From that moment on, he single-handedly helped me graduate with a good enough GPA to go to college. Suddenly, guilt hit me like a wave as I realized Brett was yet another person who had been there for me despite who I was, yet the moment I left, I'd forgotten him as well.

"It has been too long, Norah." He pulled back from the hug, which, in turn, caused me to slightly stumble. Deeply embarrassed by my lingering touch, I pretended to brush my frizzy hair away from my face to hide my blushing cheeks. Through the tight, tangled strands, I could see the pity welling in his eyes. He could clearly see what I was feeling. There was just something about hugging him that almost made me cry and never want to let go; I made a mental note to keep my distance. The last thing I needed was to break down on him after all this time. *Nothing has changed with Norah, still a basket case.*

Thankfully, at that moment, right before I broke, the man returned with my coffee, simultaneously handing Brett a small cup of dark coffee as well. I politely accepted the coffee, and we both moved together, automatically sitting together at a table near the front of the shop, just underneath the large *E*.

"So what in the world are you still doing in this town?" Brett, of all people, had the most potential and opportunity to do whatever he wanted with his life. Coupled with having money, I was assured he'd become something great in life.

"Now, this town ain't that bad. If I remember correctly, we had some pretty good times here." His insinuation came with a surprisingly warm and handsome smile. I didn't remember his smile being that charming. Again, my cheeks flushed—*traitors.*

"For real, why are you still here?" I deflected, attempting to keep the topic to him.

"My daddy got sick last year. Mama needed me to come back to help run the farm." Instantly, I felt connected to him, our reasons for coming back almost aligned. Of course, he actually wanted to come home to take care of his loving parents, whereas I was coerced into dealing with mine.

"How is he doing?" The moment I asked I could already see the answer all over his face as his eyes wrinkled up at the corners, and his smile became tightly forced.

"He died three months ago."

"I'm so sorry, Brett."

There was no part of me that could understand how devastating it must have been for him to lose his father. Even after all these years away, I could still see his father's bubbly, soft face. He had been a devoted, loving parent, as was his mother. I had a deep feeling of guilt. For the last twenty-four hours, I had been wishing that my mother would just die, whereas I was quite sure Brett had wished the entire time that his father would just *live.*

Brett's daddy had been a dairy farmer, but more notably, the mayor during Brett's more formative years in high school. I often looked up to his dad, thinking that if mine were still around, he would've been like Brett's daddy. Of course, that was just wishful thinking; no one like Brett's dad would've ever married my hot mess of a mother.

"It's a great loss to the town." It was the only thing I could think of to say, having no idea what it felt like to lose a parent you loved. I had never known my biological father, never liked any of my mother's suitors, and clearly, I detested my mother, so the only person I could say I actually loved was my husband. I think I might have liked my grandparents if I had ever met them, but that was another thing my mother denied me as a child. My mother did not exactly have a good relationship with them, or anyone for that matter.

"Thank you for that." He gently placed his hand on mine. There was something about it that made me slightly uncomfortable, but I felt it would be rude to move away. "So what have you been up to?" With that, his hand was gone as quickly as it had appeared. The moment it was gone. I realized I wanted it back.

"I became a lawyer," I announced too quickly. I needed to change the subject, and it was the only thing I had left to be proud of at this point.

"I heard that. I also heard that you got married." His thin right eyebrow was raised in suspicion.

"Divorced." I was slightly embarrassed to admit my failure at marriage, but in the grand scheme of things, at the moment, it wasn't the worst part of my life. Actually, if I was being honest, I didn't mind telling Brett that I was currently single, which surprised me, because I had never felt that way about Brett—*ever.*

Brett, *"the childhood tutor,"* was a skinny, tall geek with thick coke-bottle glasses that always slid down his nose when he was reading, and arms that were too long for his body. He could've run track or possibly even thrown a football, but Brett always told me his father preferred his head in the books than out in the heat. His father had always valued education above everything else, which is why Brett never played any sports or worked on the farm.

Brett, *"the grown man,"* had a muscular body, most likely from the strenuous work on the farm, and contacts. His face was filled with a thick copper beard, which made his jawline more pronounced. His long stringy red hair was now cut short just above his deep crystal-blue eyes, which were now visible and striking. There was also a different presence about him now ... *confidence.*

"Sorry to hear that." His response snapped me from my staring. I hoped he didn't notice, but judging by the look on his face, he did.

"It's for the best, I guess." I shrugged it off, attempting to pass it off so he wouldn't ask more questions. I still couldn't talk about it, especially not with him. "What about you? Any special lady in your life?"

"Oh, me?" He seemed oddly surprised that I'd asked. "No, no special lady for me." He was lying. There was a slight twitch to his left eye, his tell even when he was just a teenager telling me I was not as dumb as I felt most of the time in our free tutoring sessions.

"Why not?"

46

"Just never found the right woman, I guess." He shrugged. It seems as if I wasn't the only one who didn't want to talk about their past, which I had to respect. "So, what brings you back here?"

"Oh, just in town for a visit really." Now it was his turn to recognize my lie, which he did. There was a shared, silent look to assure me that he was well aware of my situation for returning. For a moment, I had thought maybe the entire town didn't know about my mother's illness. I was wrong.

"A visit?" His eyebrows raised in disbelief. "You ran out of this town as fast as you could twenty-one years ago, so I hardly think you are now back, after all this time, for *just* a visit."

"You're right. You caught me. I just had to get back for this amazing cup of coffee." He laughed. "They just don't make it like this in the big city." I joined in the laughter, surprised that I could still make a good joke and thankful that he laughed at it.

"I know what you mean." He understood that I did not want to talk about it and dropped it. I think a part of him related to my feelings. After all, he returned to bury his father. I'm sure he didn't want to talk about that with every person he ran into on a daily basis.

"Well, I should get going," he announced after the laughter died down, a tight smile showing his regret for having to go so quickly. "It was good getting to see you." He slid out from behind the booth.

"Same to you." As the words escaped, I realized I believed each one. As deep as my disgust was for this town, it never extended to the people I left behind, which I was now only realizing upon my return.

He stopped at the door, pausing with doorknob in hand, before saying, "If you end up staying for a while, maybe we can see each other again." Before I could respond, he was gone.

I watched through the window as he made his way across the road. His body began to blur as my own came into view through the window. My reflection was shocking. I groaned and folded over into my hands. He probably only said it to be nice. Hell, he was probably worried about my health, judging by my appearance. I really needed to get it together.

"Can I get you another cup of coffee?" the elderly man called from across the counter, pulling me from my self-loathing. He was probably concerned about my health as well. *Great, that'll be a nice little rumor around town by the end of the day.*

47

"Yes, to go, please," I added, holding my empty cup up into the air. I was definitely going to need an extra cup today.

Back at home, I found my mother piddling around in the kitchen. Initially, she appeared to be cleaning, but I quickly realized she was just picking one thing up to put it in another place with no rhyme or reason to any of it. *This explains a lot about the state of the house.*

"Mama, what are you doing?" I pulled my aching body up onto an old barstool that was tucked away under the peninsula. It was covered with random kitchen utensils and used paper towels. *Gross.*

"I'm trying to find the damn coffee," she snapped, slamming a coffee cup down on the counter. I smirked at the thought of her looking for coffee that she was never going to find. I briefly wondered how long she would look for it if I never told her there was none.

"There is no coffee." I took a long sip of my own coffee. *This would be better.*

"Well, there was coffee here yesterday. I assume you are drinking the last of it?" Her eyes narrowed in on the coffee cup in my hands. I gave a slight laugh at the absurdity of it all. Of course I did not take the last of her coffee, because, clearly, I had a paper cup from the shop down the road. *Idiot.*

"You just think this is so funny. Well, this is my house, so why don't you just get the hell out!" Her screams echoed through the empty house. *Deep breaths. This was only the beginning.*

"Mama, I am clearly not drinking your coffee. As for the state of my living arrangements, it is only temporary, but for now, you better get used to me being around."

"Fine." She stomped off back to her room, *just like a child.* Of course, this worked out in my favor, because now I could deep clean the house in peace, which is exactly what I planned to do the rest of the day.

I lost myself in the mundane, repetitive actions of cleaning. I pulled all the dishes down from the cupboard and stacked them up on the counter because, in my opinion, they all needed cleaning. After watching my mother this morning, they could all very well be dirty, and some of them actually had food on them. *What had she been doing?*

She had no dishwasher, so I washed and dried each dish, cup, bowl, and piece of silverware by hand and carefully placed them back in more logical places. It was almost soothing to lose myself in these actions. I focused solely on the cleaning, my mind forgetting all the pain. I was lost. It felt good to be lost in something so simple.

By lunch, my mother emerged from her room, scuffling down the hallway in those filthy slippers with a single big toe peeking out the top, and peered around into the kitchen, her witchy fingers curling around the door frame as if she were afraid to enter.

"Ugh, you're still here." She was clearly still exasperated by my presence. Dropping her fingers and fearful facade, she moved reluctantly as if I were forcing her to enter. "Did you at least clean up after yourself?" My mouth dropped. *Deep breaths. Let it go.*

"Would you like some lunch?" The last thing I wanted was to fight with my mother right now. The thought of staying here was overwhelming enough, and in my calm brought on by the mundane actions of the day, I realized that I could not handle constantly fighting with my mother as well.

"Well, yes. Best to make yourself useful." Rolling my eyes, I did my best to ignore her scowl.

Unfortunately, there still wasn't much in the way of food in this house, so I attempted chicken ranch sandwiches. I had found a few cans of chicken in the hall closet that morning (*not really sure why they were in the hall closet*). As I mixed in the expired—but not *too* expired, fingers crossed—ranch, my mother shuffled around the dining room. It was almost like a game, trying to figure out what she was doing. She was randomly picking things up, moving chairs ... but she never did seem to find what she was looking for.

"It's ready," I called, throwing the sandwich down onto her plate and starting to make my own. Slowly, as if she were a cat attempting to catch her prey, she moved in for the sandwich. She gave me an odd, almost fearful, look as she took the plate and disappeared into the living room. Shrugging, I made my way to the back screened-in porch to eat my lunch. I still couldn't stomach eating inside.

The fake green grass carpet scratched against my bare feet as I took a seat in the rocking chair. I never understood why anyone would ever put down carpet in a sunroom. Or purchase wicker furniture in bulk. Of course, apparently, in the 90s that was a popular thing to do down here in the South.

It was not a large porch, but she had managed to fit two armed wicker rocking chairs, mostly torn apart by age, the cushions long gone. There was a small broken table in between the chairs. There was a wicker loveseat positioned at the far end, but it was missing a few boards in the seat and, of course, the cushion as well. *Lots of sitting area for just one person.*

From the porch, I could see across the barren, overgrown backyard all the way to the tree line. The grass was high and needed a cut. I doubted she still owned a lawnmower. *Probably sold it to buy booze.* Growing up, I had taken care of the yard ... and the house ... and my mother. I shouldn't be so surprised that it had all fallen to hell since I'd left.

"Where is my damn vodka?" She stood at the doorway into the house, her thin fingers sprawled out across the screened door, casting a shadow of a daddy long leg spider. She even looked like a spider crawling out of a hole as she moved out onto the porch. "Where is it?" Her eyes tightened, wrinkles spiraling out from her dark irises, as her lips curled up to show her rotting teeth, almost resembling that of an animal in attack mode.

"I don't know, Mama." She just stood there, waiting for me to come to find it. I sighed, in no mood to fight her. I got up and retreated inside to help her.

My eyes grew wide as I took in all that she had done in the short amount of time that I was outside. All the dishes were out, drawers opened. Everything I had accomplished this morning, ruined. I could feel the rage building inside me ... *deep breaths.*

"Well?" She pushed by me into the kitchen.

"What, Mama?" I had been so focused on the destruction, I failed to listen to what she was actually saying.

"V-O-D-K-A!" she screamed, throwing a glass against the wall. *Oh great, another thing to clean up.* Throwing my hands up in exasperation, I disappeared back into the laundry room to get a broom. I really didn't need to deal with either of us getting glass in our feet.

"Oh, stop that!" She attempted to pull the broom from my hand as I entered the kitchen.

"Get back!" I pushed her hard, just wanting to make sure she didn't step in the glass. But my rage got the best of me, and my push was a little harder than I'd anticipated. Of course, the fact she weighed nothing might have had something to do with how far she fell.

"Oh gosh, Mama, are you okay?" Instinctively, I let go of the broom and rushed to my mother's crumpled body on the floor. I reached down to help her, but she slapped my hand away. It sounded harsher than it really was, as the broom slapped the ground at the same moment.

"Get out." Her words slithered out through her clenched teeth. There was that old familiar look—*hatred.*

I dropped my offering hand. "Get up by yourself then." I was flabbergasted that she could still hold such deep hatred for me after all these years, especially since I had now come back to help her dying ass. I had every right to hate my mother, but I never did know what right she had to hate me with such passion and dedication.

I returned to the shattered glass that was all over the floor and finished cleaning up *her* mess. After some struggle, she was finally able to pick herself up off the ground, limping away like a beaten dog down the long, dark hallway by the staircase to her bedroom. There was a part of me that knew I should go check on her, make sure she didn't break any bones in the fall, but the silence of the house was too alluring. After returning all the dishes to their rightful places, I moved into the living room where I spent the rest of the evening. At some point, I collapsed into my bed. No dinner, no mother.

Part Two: Strong Winds

The winds swirl as the warm ocean waters feed the storm, helping it grow stronger as it approaches. The trees begin to yield, bending almost to their breaking points as the wind precedes the hurricane. Even in the heat of summer, the air turns cool against your skin, a chilly warning of what is about to come.

With each passing moment, a storm swells, and you must prepare. To stay is to risk your life, so now is the time to board your windows, pack your bags, and leave. But no matter how great the danger, people still stay. Unwilling to move, to give in to the fear, they find a place to protect themselves from the elements. Pulling all their possessions close to them, praying for the storm to die down or turn the other way, they batten down the hatches. They think they can survive.

But what they don't realize is that out there in the distance, the storm grows more powerful than imagined, its course steady and absolute. The thick gray clouds start to churn, whirling around a gaping center as the storm starts to take form.

A hurricane is coming.
I should've evacuated.

Chapter Ten
Present Day

The morning came too early, the sun bleeding through the sheer curtains. The sunlight shone purple across the room, its bright light tainted, just as my life was contaminated by my mother. There was a familiarity to this place, my mother, but I was different this time. Every part of me was screaming to run, but my body refused to comply, just lying there in bed. I wanted to melt into the mattress, disappear.

Finally, my body twitched—first my fingers, then my entire arm, lifting me from the bed. My toes dug into the shag carpet, attempting to find some firm ground to support the weight of my decision. No matter how many times I tried to tell myself to leave, deep down, I knew I was not going to. I was trapped.

So I decided it was time to stock the kitchen, especially since I woke up to another morning without coffee. My entire childhood had been spent walking the two miles to the local grocery store, Piggly Wiggly, at least twice a week. We could never afford much, no more than two bags' worth of stuff each trip. Looking down at my hands, my mind playing a cruel game, I could still see the deep purple and red marks across my fingers where I'd held the bags, praying they wouldn't break.

This time I would take the car. I made sure to brush my hair, gloss my dry lips, and put on decent clothes. Pulling back my normally frizzy, curly, dark hair into a tight ponytail through the hole of a baseball cap, I prayed that this would make me less recognizable. Leaving my mother behind, still in her bedroom, I decided to go as quickly as possible. Hopefully, she'd remain in her room the entire time, and I wouldn't have another ridiculous mess to clean up. I could've made the extended trip to the Walmart in the next town, but I drove on autopilot to the Piggly Wiggly.

The cart squeaked, cutting through the silence of the empty grocery store, as I hurried through, grabbing all the necessities. It didn't take long, especially considering the Piggly Wiggly was not well stocked. Aisles with barren shelves reminded me of the rare time a hurricane was about to hit, everyone in town clearing out the shelves in doomsday prep. I was thankful to find coffee, but there was no vodka. I'd have to go to the liquor store for that one. I briefly thought about not getting her the vodka, for she definitely didn't need it, but then I considered having to deal with a sober mother. The liquor store would be my next stop.

"Find everything, dear?" The cashier slowly scanned each item, examining it beforehand, as if each was a precious ruby. Her bubbly, fat face had two large blue eyes and one overly toothy grin. She was way too happy to be a cashier at Piggly Wiggly in the middle of Nowhere, Alabama.

"Yep." I kept my head down, refusing to make eye contact, hoping she wouldn't recognize me. Of course, I had no idea who she was, but with my luck, she would know me. "Actually, where is the nearest liquor store?"

"Oh, well, it's ten o'clock in the morning. But who am I to judge?" With that, I met her eye to eye. *Yes, who are you? No one.* "Just next to the gas station up the road."

"Thank you." She smiled again. I did not return the gesture.

The liquor store was quick—vodka, a few beers, and a pack of cigarettes. *Anything to speed up the process.* I returned home, but not before stopping at the coffee shop—for two coffees this time. No sighting of Brett, which was disappointing. I would've liked for him to see me in actual clothes, with makeup on, just to assure him I was not a hot mess.

Back at the house, I struggled through the door with the few bags of groceries, a piercing sound vibrating through the house.

"Mama, the phone!" It rang and rang, but there was no movement from my mother. *Damnit.* I dropped all the bags, exasperated, and answered the phone.

"Yes?"

"Ah, Miss Crawford, good to hear you have arrived." Doctor Bishop. *Double damn.*

"Hello, Doctor Bishop, can I help you?" Twisting, I attempted to unravel the plastic bags from the long, curled cord attached to the phone on the wall.

"Well." He coughed into the phone. "I'd like to meet with you and your mother today."

"Why?" She was just at the doctor last week. *How often does she see him?*

"Well, now that you are here, we have some paperwork to complete. It'd be best to complete this as soon as possible in order to move forward with your mother's treatment."

"Treatment?" That was the last thing I wanted.

"Yes, there are a few options."

"You made it seem like there weren't many options on the phone."

"If you could please just come in. Two o'clock."

"If I must."

I had plans today. Well, I had plans to clean the rest of the house. I guess that could just wait till later. After all, I had all the time in the world to get this house in order. There was nothing else to do. I was actually more annoyed by the fact that I would have to deal with my mother today. I was hoping to leave her alone in the bedroom again. The last thing I wanted was another confrontation.

"You must," he confirmed. "I look forward to seeing you both this afternoon."

The phone slid back into the base on the side of the kitchen wall. The long, coiled cord hung to the floor. As a teenager, I could remember pulling the cord as tight as possible to reach the patio so that I could talk without the other person hearing my mother screaming. The phone was just another thing to bring back painful memories.

I took my time putting away all the groceries—in logical, convenient places, of course. The bread in the basket by the pantry, which is where I put the peanut butter and chips. Milk, eggs, cheese, and other perishable items were slipped into the wide-open fridge. Organizing and cleaning were the only things I felt like I could control, so I made sure to do them right. Unfortunately, when all that was finished, there was nothing else to do but get my mother up and ready for her appointment.

My mother had always loathed doctors, mostly because they would tell her she needed to go to rehab. So it was hard to believe that she would be willing to go, but I got the impression that Dr. Bishop was not going to give up. So I made my way down the narrow hallway, past the stairs, to the back of the house, and gently knocked on her door. *Nothing.* How I wished I could just walk away.

After three knocks, I wedged the door open. I could feel a heavy weight blocking the door, though not heavy enough to be my mother. Leaning my shoulder into the wooden frame, I slowly shoved the door open wide enough to slip into the room.

Across the room the drapes were pulled closed, preventing any light from entering. *No wonder she slept so much.* The ground, barely visible, appeared to be a distant mountain range, clothes piled up in every corner and behind the door. I vaguely remember that there was a baby-blue shag carpet; each room of the house had a different color. Not sure what the thinking was on that one. Yet, it was no longer visible.

Attempting to cross the room to her bed was like going through a swamp full of snakes. At any moment, I could be sucked down or killed in a single bite. My heart rate accelerated as if there might actually be something lurking underneath the piles. It was not totally out of the question. The bed wasn't any better. I had to pull back layers and layers of blankets and clothes to get to her body ... *Still alive. Damn.*

"Mama." I shook her shoulders lightly; I didn't want to break her right before her doctor's appointment. "Mama!" Louder this time. "MAMA!" Pushier this time. I placed my hand underneath her nose, still breathing. "M-A-M-A!" Louder and harder.

"Stop!" she barked back, pulling at the layers of blankets, attempting to re-cocoon herself. *Oh, no you don't.* I pulled back hard on the blankets.

"We have to get ready to go. Come on, Mama. Stop fighting me!" We proceeded to engage in a heated battle of tug-o-war over the blankets.

Finally, I let go, exhausted by the childish fight. Realizing that it was going to take more than just pulling off the covers to get my mother ready for her doctor's appointment, I decided to change my approach.

"Okay, I guess I'll just finish off the drink myself." I waited for the beast to smell my trap. Slowly, she started to move, the covers shifting like the waves of the ocean. Cresting the top of the wave, my mother's head appeared. "I got more vodka at the store."

"Well, all right then." Her harsh, dry voice was foreign after her long winter nap.

"Come on, Mama, it's time to go," I yelled through the closed bedroom door, as I had been doing for the last fifteen minutes. She had insisted on getting ready alone, which I preferred to having to deal with her, but now we were about to be late, and possibly drunk.

"I'm ready," she stated proudly, suddenly standing in the doorway, her nose in the air. "Let's go."

"All righty," I agreed, ushering her toward the front door.

It took some time, but I finally convinced her to let me drive *my* rental car. Then came the fight over the directions. She did not agree with the GPS.

"I know the way! I don't see why you wouldn't let me drive."

"This is my car, Mama. Only I can drive it, and it has GPS, so I know the way as well."

"That is sending us the wrong way." She pointed angrily at the screen on the dashboard. "What the hell is it anyway?"

"I told you, Mama, it's GPS. You just put in where you need to go, and it shows you on a map." She gasped in disbelief. My mother never had any form of technology, which was not so out of the realm of disbelief twenty years ago, but now it was just outrageous. Everyone had a cellphone and Wi-Fi, except my mother. I bet if she learned you could order alcohol online, things would be different.

"Well, that is just ridiculous. I know where I am going."

"Good for you." I decided to stop arguing and listening to her altogether. She rambled on the entire way there, leaving me with a massive headache when we finally arrived.

The good doctor's office was located in a medical building, just to the right of the local community hospital, which wasn't much, but good if you got your foot caught in a tractor. It was in the opposite direction of my mother's house from the town center, past an old, rotten park that looked as if it had been abandoned fifty years ago. Just about five minutes up the road, or so my mother said, but it was really fifteen minutes.

An elderly woman greeted us as I dragged my mother through the door. Her face sagging with deep wrinkles and hair a solid silvery white, she perched behind the sliding glass window. The sharp chill in the air was a stark contrast to the summer heat outside, causing my body to shiver. As if the smell in my mother's house wasn't nauseating enough, the doctor's office was filled with the smell of medical cream and overused, pungent perfume. The vomit caught in my throat as I pulled my hand over my nose to stop the invasion.

"Hello, Miss Lillie." The woman stood up, slapping her swollen, pudgy hand against the glass and sliding it open. "Welcome. Glad you could make it today."

"Just checking in." I refused to smile, hoping that she would see that I was in no mood to talk. She slid the clipboard through the window.

"Just sign in here." Her eyes traveled over to my mother, who was currently looking around the office as if she had no idea where she was, despite the fact that she was just here the other day and *on her own*. It was hard to imagine that she had been able to get to her appointment without assistance. I couldn't imagine her actually driving all this way, not without killing someone.

"You must be Miss Lillie's daughter."

"Yes, I am." My stomach turned at the thought that being my mother's daughter was my defining characteristic. Quickly, I signed my mother in and retreated into the corner of the waiting room.

Thankfully it was only a few minutes before the lady called from behind the window, "Miss Lillie, the doctor will see you now." She pointed to the door and nodded for me to go ahead. "Room 311."

"Mama, let's go." She broke her gaze, the fog lifting from her mind as she settled in on what was happening. For a moment, I thought she was going to walk out the front door instead of through the office door.

"Mama, this way." With that, she followed me through the door and into the examination room.

Seamlessly, my mother positioned herself on the typical patient lounge chair that was placed in a more upright position than what you normally find in a doctor's examination room. It would be more comfortable if she would sit back. But, in true Lillie fashion, she refused to conform. I noticed a small round stool was pushed into the far corner behind the door, most likely for the doctor, so I sat in the single armchair just to the side of the patient's lounge chair.

A nurse appeared in the doorway. Her eyes shifted between us before she nervously entered the room. Without a word to either of us, she pulled out a blood pressure cuff and attempted to put it on my mother, who, without looking at the nurse, kept moving her arm so she kept missing it. The nurse did not seem surprised, nor did she react to my mother's childish actions.

After a bit of a struggle, she left without even a single word. There was a part of me that figured this was intentional. It was like they had this unspoken agreement to not speak to each other. My mother typically did not get along well with women. Men, on the other hand, were a whole different story.

We waited in silence.

"Miss Lillie, how are we feeling today?" Doctor Bishop asked, entering the room with that typical grin on his face that all men had when they looked at my mother. I instinctively rolled my eyes. *What was it with her?*

Doctor Bishop was much older than my mother, which was slightly surprising. I thought for sure my mother would've gone to a younger doctor for various and obvious reasons. His white hair and wrinkled face gave his age away. I guessed late sixties ... *Maybe the receptionist is his wife?* He was larger, obese even, and shorter than me without the heels. I noticed the outline of a wedding ring on his finger and wondered if he chose not to wear it while he was working or if he was no longer married. *Maybe it's an affair with the receptionist?*

"I'm fine as always, Doctor Bishop," she mused. My mother was definitely turning on her charm for the good doctor. She should have been an actress. "I honestly don't see why I keep having to come back here." She batted her eyes in innocence. My mother knew exactly why we were here and what she was doing.

"Well, Miss Lillie, as we discussed before," he shot me an all-knowing look, "I believe you have Alzheimer's disease."

"And as I told you before, Doctor Bishop, I do not," she sneered, her thin lips forming a tight line. She narrowed her eyes at Doctor Bishop, but her voice was light and friendly. Leave it to my mother to be sweetly aggressive to someone.

At this point, Doctor Bishop turned his attention to me, which only infuriated my mother. "Six months ago, your mother was in an accident of sorts."

"Accident?"

"Yes, we tried to call you. She was in the hospital for three days."

"Six months ago was not a good time for me." The good doctor didn't appear to believe my excuse, and I had no intention of explaining it to him.

"During that time, the doctor on call documented she was having memory issues and called me. Since then, your mother's health has been declining significantly. She has lost too much weight. I suspect she has forgotten to eat most days." That made sense considering she had no food in the house.

"Oh, good grief, this is absurd," she barked. "Like I would forget to eat." She huffed and pointed her nose in the air at both of us. She pretended not to listen to us anymore, but I knew better.

"On occasion, she has come into the office, and it is clear that she has not had a bath in days, and she is physically aggressive toward the nurse." That explained the nurse's cold demeanor. "On more than one occasion, she has been picked up by the police. They often report she is confused, violent, disheveled." Generally speaking, this was not uncommon for her, but the good doctor seemed very concerned.

He stared at my mother, who continued to refuse to admit she was listening. After some time, he gave up on gaining her attention and continued. "Your mother needs to be watched and cared for in order to ensure she does not hurt herself or get into any further trouble. This is why I called you to come here, Miss Norah."

"You initially talked about a facility that would care for her ... a home?" In all the chaos of returning back to this place, I had not found the time to research any nursing homes, as I had originally planned.

"Oh, yes, well, there are places available for people with Alzheimer's, but as I said on the phone, I don't think your mother is a good fit for those places."

"Why?"

He hesitated, looking to my mother to see if she was paying attention. She seemed lost in an up-close and personal picture of a cow's face that hung on the wall by the door.

"They are all dry facilities."

"You mean no drinking?"

"Yes, and for your mother, that could be very difficult."

"I'm not going to rehab." She was now acutely focused on the good doctor. "I told you I don't have a problem, and I ain't sick." Turning toward me, she snapped, "I'd like to go now." She hopped from the chair and proceeded to leave.

"Wait, it's not rehab, Mama. It's a place that will take care of you."

"I can do it myself."

"No, you can't," I yelled as my mother lunged for the door. Doctor Bishop slowly pushed his chair out of the way as if he knew what was about to happen—*a train wreck.*

"We are leaving. Now!" she screamed, pulling the door back, her escape imminent. I lunged to stop her. Just then, the nurse barreled into the room, needle in hand. It happened so fast I barely saw the needle going into my mother's arm, her face aflame with anger, as she sunk back into the chair, her eyes slowly closing.

"Not the first time," the doctor assured me, no doubt in response to seeing the sheer shock on my face over what had just happened. *What did just happen?* "It's just a mild sedative; she will be fine in about thirty minutes, ready to go again." I did not appreciate the joke.

"As I was saying, your mother is not the best candidate for a nursing home."

"She can't be the only ornery, old woman in the world."

"No, and ornery they can handle. Drunk, violent, denial ... all these things they cannot handle. Not typically, anyway."

"Is there any place that would take her?" I could see my plan going up in flames right before my eyes. There had to be something to stop it from burning me alive.

"The first step is referring her to a neurologist for an official diagnosis of Alzheimer's disease."

"Wait, I thought you said she has Alzheimer's?"

"In my professional opinion, she is suffering from Alzheimer's, but in order to be considered for a medical nursing home, your mother will need a diagnosis from a neurologist." There was a heavy weight pressing down on my chest again as I realized we did not have the money to go to a specialist. I didn't even have the money to pay Dr. Bishop, which I was sure would come up when we checked out.

"Is there anyone you prefer?"

"What?" The hopelessness of my situation was sinking in, fogging my mind. I felt like I had been given a sedative.

"A neurologist you prefer?"

"I don't know, Doctor." My chest was burning as the anxiety started to rise. "I don't even know if my mother has insurance, and if so, then does she even qualify for these services? I just arrived two days ago. I haven't spoken to my mother in over five years, haven't seen her in twenty-one, so no ... I don't have a neurologist I prefer. I'd prefer not to do anything."

I swear the good doctor wheeled back slightly, as if the door was about to swing open revealing the nurse, needle in hand. But instead, he gave me time to calm down before he spoke.

"I know this is a lot to take in. Your mother is not the same woman you knew twenty-one years ago. I know that is hard, but you are all she has now. She needs you."

If he only knew how much I needed my mother all those years. She never came.

"I just want to put my mother in a nursing home and leave."

"Go see the neurologist. Take the steps. I'm sure they will be able to work something out." Rolling my eyes, I could feel the tears burning the corners. "I'll refer you to Dr. Hanto in Alexander City, just a few miles on the other side of the lake. He's an old friend. I'll make a call."

Chapter Eleven
Mother

Her dress floated through the bright night sky like an open-winged bird gliding just above the ground. As she drifted closer to the porch light, the woman in the window could tell it was not a dress but an oversized, sheer robe untied, blowing behind her thin, tall body. She only wore a gown as she quickly crossed the distance between the two houses and up to her front door.

"Please," she called from behind the door, her long nails lightly tapping on the door frame. "Please, have you seen my daughter?" Her voice was filled with despair, so against her better judgement, the woman opened the door.

"It's okay, she's here," the woman assured her, swinging the door open to reveal her daughter sitting at the dining table. It took every bone in the woman's body not to snap at that moment, but she held back.

"Oh, thank god." She wiped the cold tears from her cheek. At least this time her tears would serve another purpose. "Sweetheart, it's time to go home now."

The little girl didn't move, her fear palpable. Making sure the woman could not see her, she glared at her daughter, silently threatening her existence from across the room. The woman snapped her fingers together, and the little girl jumped from her seat. Slowly, she closed the gap between them. The woman could tell the little girl hesitated, waiting for something. She frowned as she realized the little girl was waiting for these people to say something ... *save her*. What she would have to learn is that no one was going to save her.

The moment the door closed behind them, the woman grabbed the little girl by her short, curly, dark hair. Pulling her violently up the stairs, wanting her daughter to feel the pain she had just endured herself, she threw her into the bedroom.

"No one will ever save you," she screamed.

Just before she slammed the door shut, she caught her daughter's eyes filled with tears and pain. For a moment, she almost felt a need to comfort her, but then it passed just as fleetingly.

In the kitchen, the woman poured the liquor over the melting ice. She took a long, relieving sip, allowing the warm liquid to flow into every part of her body. With each sip, her bruises faded, and her memories, which she so desperately wanted to forget, started to become foggy ... then she heard his footsteps. He was home.

The blood was still fresh on her lower lip, something the new neighbor saw, no doubt. In the past, she would've given the standard excuse of running into a door or falling, but she didn't have the energy for that anymore. After all, their homes were so close they were bound to hear the screams. If he didn't care, neither did she.

He lumbered past the kitchen door, and her breath caught in her lungs as she waited to see if he would continue his assault. The air escaped as she listened to him stumble down the hallway toward the bedroom. She had hoped that after today, he would stay out all night drinking or doing anything else but coming home. She cringed at the idea of having to sleep next to that man. But if she stayed on the couch, it would only make things worse. He would expect her to be next to him in the morning. He always liked doing it in the morning. Her stomach turned, causing her to vomit into the kitchen sink.

Then she heard his call, a siren from the bedroom beckoning her to him against her will. Putting the cigarette out on her bare forearm, letting the truth of the pain consume every brain cell, she made her way back to the bedroom.

Chapter Twelve
Present Day

"I want to go to Oscar's." My mother stood by the front door, her tattered brown leather purse thrown over her concave shoulder. It had taken great effort on the part of myself and the large male nurse at the good doctor's office, but I had managed to get my sedated mother home without her waking up. I left her on the couch, hoping it would last the rest of the night.

"How about we just eat something at home, like spaghetti?"

The raw hamburger meat was sitting in the pan on the stove, my hand on the knob. We could go out, save the meal for tomorrow, but I did not want to go into any public forum with my mother. That was a recipe for disaster.

"I want to go to Oscar's." She stood like a defiant child at the door, fingers curled around the thin leather strap of her purse, her sunken eyes narrowed in my direction. Rolling my eyes, I ignored her, hoping she would forget by the time I finished making dinner.

No such luck. As the meat sizzled in the pan, my mother continued with her demands. She was an unmoving statue, repeating the same annoying demand over and over again until I finally caved. Wrapping and sliding the cooked hamburger meat into the fridge for another day, I grabbed my purse as well. The one time I needed her to forget something, her memory was rock solid. There was no use continuing to fight her on the subject; I didn't have the energy after today. *Maybe no one would even be there.* It was still pretty early in the evening.

As I lumbered by her stoic body, my legs and arms still heavy from having to drag her into the house just a couple of hours ago, I could swear I saw a smile curl her lips. Her satisfaction turned my stomach. When I was her little girl, I strived to satisfy my mother, but now it made me cringe. Just the thought of giving her the power to control my actions was nauseating. I wanted to turn around, leave her waiting on the porch. But my feet kept moving on autopilot to the car.

As we pulled into the gravel parking lot, the largest part of the lake glistening in the distant lowering sun, I counted the cars. The fact that we had our pick of parking places right by the front door was a good sign. Normally, the parking lot was packed, cars spilling over into the neighboring businesses.

Oscar's was a historic landmark in town, created only by the fact that, for as long as I can remember, it was the only actual restaurant around. Of course, there were small pop-up places to eat, but Oscar's was the only one that kept its doors open year-round and never had to close no matter how deep the recession roots spread. There was a classically small-town restaurant feel to Oscar's, from the local pictures on the walls and small intimate booths overlooking the only claim to fame in this town—Lake Martin—to the fresh catch of the day always being bass (the only fish you could catch in the lake). It even turned into a semi-bar atmosphere at night, housing a few stools under the small bar at the entrance. My mother was no stranger here. She often found herself wandering in, the smell of alcohol and men drawing her like a shark to the smell of blood.

My nostrils flared at the smell of oak mixed with fried fish, bringing back a wash of memories. Never in my entire childhood did I come to eat with my mother at Oscar's. It was one of the few places in this town that held fond memories. As I scanned the restaurant, my memories came back to life ... people laughing, large colorful gumballs dropping, spiraling down the clear, circular tube before landing in my small hand.

"How many?" The hostess's voice pulled me from my thoughts as I realized the restaurant was nothing like I remembered it to be. It was empty.

"Just two." Since they were clearly not having a rush, I added, "In the back, near an exit please." Best to have a plan for a quick exit, just in case.

After much debate and some harsh words from my mother, the poor waitress was able to appease her by having the chef make a special order of fried pickles and grouper sandwich. The woman was exhausting in everything she did. In turn, I kept my order simple—a fried shrimp basket. I could see the relief on the waitress's face.

Of course, by my mother's standards, the food took too long to arrive, causing her to complain twice before the waitress returned with our food. The poor girl couldn't get anything right. I would like to say my mother's attitude was because of her mental health issues, but she had always been this way. No one could ever do anything right in her book. I remember one time when she threatened to go back into the kitchen and do it herself; that was the last time we went to that place.

I finished my meal in record time in an effort to make it out of the restaurant before the dinner rush started. I wanted to avoid all people at any cost, especially with my mother in tow. I finished paying the bill and dragging my mother out the door when we ran into the one person I did not want to—nor think I would—see in this town. *Caroline.* It was as if my memories of having dinner with her had conjured her out of thin air.

"Oh my god, you have gotta be kiddin' me." I half expected her to throw her arms around me in excitement, but she restrained. Something held her back—*probably the fact that I more or less abandoned her twenty-one years ago.*

Her saucer-sized blue eyes were bigger than ever, most likely over the shock of seeing me after all these years. I couldn't imagine what she thought of me. Shame flushed my cold cheeks. She brushed her blonde hair, the same length as I remember, to her shoulders, as her eyes took in every bit of my appearance.

"I thought I would never see you around these parts again," she scoffed, folding her thin, muscular arms over her petite chest. Her frame had not changed either; always an athlete, it was clear she still kept her body in shape, unlike myself. Suddenly, I realized how it was so easy for the man in the coffee shop to recognize me that day. Caroline looked almost exactly how I remembered her all those years ago.

"Just back for a few days." The lie resonated between us. Caroline's eyes narrowed in my mother's direction, who seemed lost in the pictures lining the walls of the waiting area.

"You look great." Her eyes flickered back in my direction. The air fogged around us so densely with all the things unsaid that I could barely see her face anymore.

As the fog encircled my mind, my anxiety raised as I realized how much I truly missed my best friend all these years. I needed to apologize, tell her everything, but just then, Mark walked through the door with two girls in tow. *No way.* The fog immediately dissipated.

"Mark, look who it is." It was clear by the look on his face and Caroline's genuine surprise that he had failed to tell her I was back in town. Not a secret I would assume Caroline would appreciate.

"I ... uh ... I," I stumbled over the words, as I stared into Caroline's deep-blue eyes molded with Mark's olive skin and wavy black hair on the girl standing at Mark's shoulder. The other girl, shorter and younger, immediately went to her mother, wrapping her long, lanky arms around Caroline's waist. The younger was more of an enigma, with curly golden locks and speckled green-brown eyes. I couldn't seem to place any of her features as Mark or Caroline.

"I know!" she squealed, shaking her head in disbelief, her blonde hair wisping around her porcelain face. My disbelief was not that she ended up with Mark. He had always loved Caroline since they were little kids; I figured it was only a matter of time before he wore her down. I never thought they would actually settle down and have children together though. Especially considering Caroline's big city dreams. Again, shame and regret flushed my cheeks as I realized I no longer knew either one of my best friends. As my life had continued, my journey unknown to them, so had theirs as well.

"After you left that summer, it just sorta happened," she offered, answering my unasked question. She looked up at Mark, waiting for him to provide further explanation, but he didn't. "So, tell me all about you—I just can't believe you are here!"

"As I said, I'm just in town for a few days to catch up with my mother."

She wasn't buying it. We both looked at my mother, who was clearly in her own world over in the corner of the entryway. Distaste flooded Caroline's face, her disapproval of my mother well earned over my entire childhood.

There were times in my most desperate moments that I would find myself at Caroline's bedroom window—the bruises only mounts of sore flesh yet to discolor, tears as small rivers through the dirt on my face as I would climb through and into her room. In the dark, she wouldn't talk as she pulled back the covers to allow me into her life. It was a rare form of comfort. The next morning, I would pretend the abuse didn't bother me and insist on returning home no matter how many times Caroline begged me to stay. I knew I could never stay with her, mostly because my mother would've hunted me down like a dog. After all, she needed someone to make her drinks.

"Look, I understand if you don't want to tell me the truth," she asserted, "but the truth of the matter is, you're not here to see that crazy ol' woman. I'll call you later tonight, and we'll talk," she declared, and with that, she gave me a quick hug, and they were off to their seats.

As we drove back to the house, the lump in my stomach churned my guilt, stirring the shame till it was so thick I felt as if I couldn't breathe. My memory of our first meeting settled into my mind as a lingering nightmare I couldn't shake. There was no reality in which my mother would allow me to have a friend. She couldn't risk someone seeing behind the curtain. Of course, what she never realized was that our house never had any curtains.

It took Caroline two days of calling before she appeared at the front door. Avoiding her calls was necessary, as I was resolved to not face the truth of my betrayal. There was never a moment in our friendship in which she did not defend me to the others, always welcomed me into her home, held my hand while I cried, or pulled me from the quicksand that was my life.

While she never suffered physical abuse from her mother, the absence of her own father connected us, an immediate, unbreakable bond. Caroline had a fierce strength, built over years of watching her mother labor at arduous odd jobs to afford a basic life. It was just the two of them, but often it was just Caroline growing up too quickly. After everything she did, the friendship she gave me, I just left. Wanting to distance myself as much as possible from my life in this town, I left everything behind, including the only true friend I ever had in this world.

Of course, I should have expected her to show up on my doorstep. Once Caroline decided on something, she made sure it was going to happen. Her conviction was at times exhausting, but it was who Caroline was to her core. Without her conviction, I might have never escaped from this town alive. It was Caroline who raced down the dirt road that humid summer afternoon, the sun dancing off her yellow hair, the sweat glowing on her alabaster skin as she waved something small in the air, screaming for me to *get my ass outside that rancid house.*

I could barely read the acceptance letter in my shaking hands. Caroline danced around me, of course having already read the letter, beaming with fervent emotion. Her words echoed in my ears: "You got in, you got in!"

It was more disbelief than anything that I actually had the option to leave after all these years of dreaming of my escape. I

69

finally held the ticket out of this hellhole in my hands, and it was all because of Caroline. School had always been a struggle, not because I wasn't smart, which I only learned in college, but more so due to a lack of understanding how deeply my homelife crippled my ability to learn. Once I was rid of this place and my mother, I discovered that my life could be calm, giving me the ability to focus on my studies and find a level of stability I never had growing up. Without Caroline's conviction, I never would've found a life.

The fact that I refused to reach back for her, pull her into my new life, was shameful. Of course, I always assumed she moved on with her life as well. There was nothing that could've stopped Caroline from achieving her goals. Unless ... unless something happened after I left her behind. The fact I didn't know caused bile to catch in my throat, threatening to force its way out at any moment.

"I know you are home, Miss Norah, and you better open this door." Caroline pounded loudly on the front door. I pressed my back against the foyer wall, willing myself to melt away. I was not going to let her in. I hoped that, eventually, she would just go away, assuming we were not home.

"Dear Lord, will you please open this damn door?" She knocked again. "I'm not leaving," she threatened. *Double damn.*

"Hello." Plastering a large Southern fake smile across my face, I immediately saw she was not falling for my ruse.

"What the hell, Norah?" She slid her body through the small gap, forcing my feet back and the door wide open. "I've been calling for days, and now you don't answer the door?" She started to walk up and down the foyer, peering through each doorway, an odd sense of determination on her face.

"What are you looking for?"

"Where is she?"

"Who?"

"That good-for-nothin' mother of yours, that's who!" Her voice echoed throughout the entire house, ensuring my mother heard every word.

"Caroline, what is going on?" There were so many reasons Caroline should not be here; yet here she was hunting my mother down like she was a rat in the house.

"What did she do to you this time?" Anger consumed Caroline's normally soft features. Her pouty lips pulled into a tight frown, deepening the lines on her face as her eyes narrowed and flashed with anger. Her anger should have been directed toward me, but she was still infuriated with my mother. *Some things never change.*

"She didn't do anything," I affirmed. "I'm just back for a short visit."

"When pigs fly!" she bellowed. Suddenly she turned to me, her eyes filling with glassy tears as she braced her hands around my frail shoulders. "You got out of here. Why did you come back?"

Every moment we'd ever had came flooding back in that second, a tidal wave of emotions pulling me under, and I couldn't breathe. Tears burned the corners of my eyes; my lip tightened in defiance of my emotions. *I will not cry.* After all this time, the years we lost, she was still every piece of the person I remembered. She was still every piece of me. No matter what happened between us, she wanted me to survive, even if that meant without her by my side. *I owed her the truth.*

"My mother is sick."

"I knew it." She slammed her hand down on the counter. "That witch!"

"She didn't do it on purpose." The comic relief allowed me a moment to recompose myself, pushing the tears back quickly with each finger. "No, it's really not that bad. She is pretty forgetful now."

"You don't forget mean."

"It's fine. I'm not here against my will. It was my decision to return." Technically, it was, but it was under false pretenses.

"Like hell it was! I'm sure your mother called you and guilt-tripped you into coming here to take care of her. You don't owe that woman anything." That was very true, but, unfortunately, it did not change my current situation. Caroline had no idea how shattered my life had become, the loss that I felt every second I was awake. For once, being back home was a needed distraction.

"No, no, it wasn't like that."

"Really? Please, we both know that woman would do anything to get you back here to take care of her dying ass."

"It's just that ... well ... I just ... honestly?" I grimaced at the thought of having to tell her the truth.

"What, Norah? Tell me."

"I have nowhere else to go." The words threw themselves out of my mouth. The truth hitting the wall, exploding in all directions, then oozing down slowly as the depressing thought congealed at the floor. After everything she did to help me find a life, admitting I had lost everything was shameful, as if all her hard work had failed us both.

"What do you mean?"

The look on Caroline's face was a flashback to another time; the first time she saw the bruises on my body. My emotions were as mixed then as they were now: shame that she knew, that my secret was out, that she would look at me differently ... but relief that someone finally knew, and that I was possibly not alone in this anymore.

"My life was—or actually, it did—fall completely apart in Atlanta." I was exposed in that moment of truth, feeling as if Caroline could see every flaw as she always did. Desperately, I wanted her to see the differences I had gained over these years. The drive I had harnessed in college, my own convictions when I went to law school, and most of all the true happiness I had found with Michael. Even if I had lost it all, it had all been there and all because of her. I didn't want her to think it had all been for nothing.

"You are in luck." She pulled a large bottle of red wine from her shoulder bag. "I brought reinforcements."

Our laughter filled the kitchen, echoing down to every part of my body, as Caroline filled the blank air around us with stories of Mark's puppy dog eyes always gazing at her in high school. Her polite, awkward storytelling was replaced with real conversation as she poured us each a glass of wine to the rim. After we each took a long sip, I could see the time for explaining had settled in around us.

"I don't even know where to start." My fingers danced over the various dents and scratches in the round oak table; each held their own memory, as did every part of this horrible place. My mind swirled like the wine in the glass with every moment of my old life, unsure of how to even put it all into words so that she would truly understand.

"How about the beginning?" If only it were all that simple.

"Well, I got married; I guess that's as good as any place to start." She held her emotions in, a rare thing for Caroline, as she waited for what she knew was coming next. "Then, I got a divorce."

"Okay, so the in-between, please."

"So, I guess it all fell apart when I got pregnant." There was an instant fall to Caroline's perky face, as the weight of my words fell upon her shoulders.

"I'm so sorry. I know that must've been hard for you." Empathy flooded her eyes, as she stared at me with understanding, the understanding I had hoped to receive from Michael. After all this time, Caroline understood my reservations more than my own husband, who I thought knew me the best.

"The hardest thing was that he didn't understand. He wanted the child."

She didn't make me say the words, but we both knew how having a child made me feel. Caroline learned in the third grade that my mother wasn't just a drunk—*that, I could've dealt with*—but what she did to me, no child should endure. Caroline knew that, witnessed it on more than one occasion. It was not lost on her that having a child would be difficult, impossible, for me to handle.

"He knew everything." The raw pain of his actions burned in the form of tears. "I told him everything. I thought he understood, but he didn't. He didn't even give me a choice."

Caroline glanced down at my flat, baby-less stomach.

"I lost the baby."

She raised an eyebrow.

"At twenty-five weeks, I got preeclampsia. If I didn't terminate the pregnancy, I could've died." She reached over and placed her hand on top of my own, but I didn't see pity in her eyes. I saw empathy. "What made it even worse was he actually made the decision to terminate the pregnancy."

"How did you feel about that?"

"Uh ... guilty, ashamed over my relief. But it was the fact that he just assumed we'd try again that ruined us. He just wouldn't listen to me ..." My voice trailed as I took a long, soothing sip of wine, the deepness of the alcohol burning the back of my throat.

"He stopped listening to me, so I stopped listening to him. We just fell apart."

It seemed so simple when I put it that way, but there was no way to truly convey the loss and pain I was still feeling. Taking another long sip of wine, finishing my first full glass, I allowed it to flow to every inch of my body. It had been a long time since I drank; my mind began to blur.

"That's not even the worst of it." She cocked a curious head to the side. "He cheated."

"I had no idea ... I should've bought two bottles of wine," she joked, trying to lighten the mood. I allowed her to think that it worked by giving a short laugh. I owed her that for listening to all of my problems. In truth, drudging it all back up made me realize my life was worse than I was willing to admit.

"So your ex-husband, Michael, just sounds like such a jerk." I'm sure there were some other choice words she would like to say about him, but motherhood seemed to have dulled her colorful language.

With the facts she had, she would be right to call him more than a jerk. I did not paint him in the most favorable light, but deep down I knew he really wasn't a jerk. He was just a man who realized he wanted something else in life besides me. *Could I really fault him for that?*

"You know, when we met, I refused to talk to him. I was so focused on law school, I refused him over and over again." I laughed at the thought of it all. "He kept at it though, asking over and over again, until I finally agreed. You know I never wanted to get married, but when he asked, foolishly, I said yes. He was my whole life, literally. I painfully realize that now more than ever." I emptied the second glass. Caroline immediately poured me another, to the rim, finishing off the bottle.

"Can I ask you something?" I nodded approval, wondering why she felt she needed to ask in the first place. "What did it feel like when he told you he wanted a divorce?" Immediately, she was embarrassed by the question, waving her hands and quickly adding, "You don't have to tell me; it was in poor taste to ask."

"No, it's okay. Honestly ... it took me back to the first time my mother hit me." Caroline's eyes immediately started to turn red, water pooling in the corner of her eyes.

"When the person you trust the most in life with your wellbeing betrays you ... well ... it turns your world upside down. You can never look at them the same way."

"Would you take him back?" She was on the verge of tears and her seat.

"Yes." *No hesitation.*

"Wow, you didn't even have to think about it?"

"Caroline, I've had months to think about it. I think about it constantly. No matter what he did, there is still a part of me that loves him, that misses our life together. At this point, I would give anything to get that life back, especially in comparison to this one."

My words hung in the air, a thick, chilly fog that seemed to shake both of us to the bone for different reasons. They were words I had only admitted in my dreams, refused to accept in reality. The thought that I would forgive him of it all, run back into his outstretched arms, was honestly pathetic. But it wasn't just Michael I wanted back so desperately, it was my life.

"So tell me about you," I pressed to change the subject, knowing the silence was about to consume us both in sorrow. Caroline adjusted herself, pushing back her tears and sitting up a little taller.

"Oh, nothing really to tell." Her flippant response was animated further by a dramatic flip of her hair over her shoulder.

"Oh no! I told you all about my dirty little life. Now you have to tell me all about your perfect, happy one."

"Oh, that is so sweet of you for thinking my life is perfect and happy." She paused, and for the first time, I saw a familiar sadness in her eyes. "I guess my good Southern attempt at masking the truth with a smile is working," she quipped, taking a long sip of her first glass of wine. "I love Mark; we have perfect children, but our life is hardly perfect. Being a mother is hard," she confessed. "It is exhausting."

"I wouldn't know." I could see the realization on her face; it had failed to occur to her that she had the one thing I would never have and was complaining about it.

"Oh, I am so sorry." I waved it off; after all, it was my choice. *My choice.* "It's just that ... well, you know ... I just saw my life going differently," she admitted.

"How did that happen by the way?" She knew exactly what I was asking about: *Mark.* I wanted to know how she ended up marrying Mark, having children, and staying in Summerville. After ignoring him for all those years, when she knew he was in love with her all throughout high school, it was hard to wrap my mind around the fact that she stayed here for him.

"Well, after you left early that summer, it was just the two of us ... I found myself lonely, needy." She shrugged her shoulders, a noticeable shame crossing her face. "It just sorta happened."

"What happened?"

"I got pregnant with Katherine." She paused for my reaction, which was my mouth dropping open in shock.

"She's away at college now. Can you believe I have a kid in college?" Well, that explained some of it, but still they could've moved somewhere else in all this time. "I found out I was pregnant two weeks before I was supposed to leave for college. Of course, Mark did the honorable thing and dropped out, too. He took a job clerking for the police department, which eventually led to him joining the force a few years later." She drained the last of her wine and forced a smile.

"So you never went to Savannah?"

She shook her head, holding that last sip of wine in her mouth, refusing to let it go down as her dreams had all those years ago. Caroline had always had an eye for designing. Her dreams were set high to become an interior designer at the Savannah School of the Arts.

"Well," I shrugged, "it seems to have all worked out for the best. Your daughters are beautiful, and Mark seems like he is doing really great." Judging by the look on her face, she was not on the same page of thinking.

"It has," she lied. We both knew it. We both sat in silence. I wanted to say something to help her open up, but that was selfish. Even though she was here, that did not instantly make us best friends again. When trust is broken, it takes time to rebuild; I of all people should understand that.

"I should be going," she said abruptly. "It was really good catching up."

She helped clean up the glasses and trashed the empty wine bottle. As I walked her to the door, she hesitated, taking my hand into her own. Gently, she squeezed it; I knew what she was going to say ... *This place would kill me.* "I want you to call me if you need anything. You promise?"

"I promise."

Shutting the door, I promised myself that I would not call her for anything. The last thing she needed was to be burdened by my life, again. The first time Caroline witnessed the abuse, she begged me to let her help. She had a plan, one that would save me from my mother. But I couldn't let her do it, not then and not now. I learned at a young age that no one was ever going to save me from my mother. It was hard to explain, for there was a part of me that felt responsible for my mother. Trust me, after many years of therapy, I still couldn't seem to get past it. I tossed Caroline's number into the trash right before I passed out.

Chapter Thirteen
Mother

Smoke filled the space around her, the slow, swirling circles mesmerizing in the morning sunlight. The woman shifted slightly on the stool so the dusty ray of sunlight was at her back, blocking any light from her face. There was no light in her life, only the endless surrounding darkness. As she released another cloud of smoke, her eyes squinted against the burn. She felt a fresh bruise forming under her left eye. Instinctively, she raised her long thin fingertips to the cut, flinching at the pain.

She thought of her daughter, lying safely in her bed, and wanted to immediately go upstairs to remind her she was never safe. Neither one of them would ever be safe with him in the house; she learned that the first night she walked over the threshold. Just as her toes touched the wooden floors, so did his hand against her back.

She remembered falling hard against the floor, terror filling every inch of her body. She clawed at the stairs, attempting to lift her shocked body, but he kicked her hard in the side. Large hot tears escaped, cascading down her flushed cheeks.

"Stop, stop," she cried, holding up a shaky hand. "Please."

"Stop?" He dropped down to her, a confused, violent look in his deep-black eyes. "You did not stop dancing with that boy at our wedding, so why would I stop now?"

"What are you talking about?" Fear overtook her entire body as she realized he was referring to one of her classmates she had befriended as a child. "We are just friends." She had only danced with him once ... *just once.*

He pulled her up by her curled, styled hair, the pain searing down her spine as he raised his hand. Before she could block his large, hairy forearm, his hand slapped her hard against her cheek. She could feel the warm blood as it started to fade down her face.

"You are mine." His words slithered over her wet, prickled skin, the alcohol invading her senses. *He was drunk.* "Don't you ever forget it." He released her hair, causing her head to fall quickly, painfully, back onto the floor.

He left her there ... on their wedding night.

She pushed the end of the cigarette into the glass ashtray, the last swirls of smoke dissipating into the distance, just like her memories. For years she prayed to be saved from her husband's drunken rages and abuse, but no one ever came. Now, she prayed to forget, another unanswered prayer.

The woman could not help but feel she was cursed to live this life. Unsure of what evil sin she had committed, there was conviction in her belief that there was no God, no person, no amount of drugs or alcohol to save her from this hell.

Gently, she silently pushed the door open to her daughter's bedroom. The little girl lay utterly still, no doubt dreaming of a better life, as she so often did when she was little. Of course, her life only got worse, as would her daughter's. There was nothing she could do to stop him, nor was there any part of her that would. The little girl needed to understand. She needed to know the truth of life, so when the day came that her husband kicked her in the back ... she would see it coming.

Chapter Fourteen
Present Day

A painful ringing vibrated through my dazed mind as I attempted to wake up. Sleep eluded me throughout the night, my tangled sheets visual evidence. Talking about my ex-husband brought all those buried feelings to the surface, which did not help with my nightmares.

"What are you doing?" I shuffled into the kitchen, wishing I had on dark glasses to block the blinding sun from feeding my hangover.

"Why are you here?" she barked, slamming the frying pan on the stovetop. The sound reverberated through my ears as my head spiked with pain. *Ooowww! Too much alcohol.*

"I'm staying here for a while. I'm your daughter, Norah," I affirmed, assuming that she was having one of those momentary memory lapses the good doctor had mentioned.

"I know who the hell you are," she sneered. "I want to know why the hell you are in my house." I needed coffee to deal with this. Pulling out the previously prepared pot of coffee, I poured a large black cup. It was nice to have coffee and a clean kitchen, which I suddenly realized my mother had ruined again. My head prickled with annoyance.

"Remember, I'm here because the doctor called." She still didn't understand. "You. Are. Sick." Her eyes narrowed in on my face. Clearly, she did not like being told she was sick, or it might have been that I was speaking to her like a child.

"I'm not sick, you little brat." She threw the pan across the counter. It slowly slid to a stop just before almost knocking over my cup of coffee. "Don't you roll those snooty eyes at me. You have no idea what you are talking about. I want you out!"

"I'm not leaving, Mama." *I have nowhere else to go.*

"Like hell you aren't; get out!" She pointed her long, boney finger toward the dining room. I looked back over my shoulder and pointed as I raised a questioning eyebrow. She quickly changed the position of her finger, but not her opinion.

"No, I'm not leaving. You can't make me." My stomach turned over; I needed food. I took the pan she had thrown across the counter and started to prepare some eggs, which only made things worse.

"What are you doing?"

"Cooking breakfast." She attempted to look over my shoulder, but I gave her a stiff body block.

"I told you to get out!" As a ninja anticipates its opponents' silent moves, I turned just in time to grab her raised hand. "I'm not a little girl anymore, Mama. You can't hit me!"

She tried to pull her hand from my grasp, shock resonating from her face, but I wasn't letting go. Suddenly, I felt a sense of empowerment. As I stared into my mother's defiant, fearful eyes, I realized I was not going to let go of her hand. If I let go, I would be that little girl again.

"Let me go," she demanded, pulling back hard against my grasp. But she was weak, fragile, and easy to hold.

"I'll let go when you calm down."

Her mouth dropped in disbelief, unsure of how to handle my defiance. For a moment, I thought we'd stand here till she died. My mother was never one to let go of anything, let alone her perceived power over me. Finally, her eyes narrowed, and her arm relaxed. In response, I let go.

A part of me knew she would try to hit me; it was all she knew how to do. So it did not take me by surprise, but I did realize something about myself in that moment. I was not going to let her do that to me—*not again*. If I had to live here, take care of her, and relive all those awful memories in this house, I sure as hell was not going to let history repeat itself.

"I am going to be staying here, Mama, at least as long as you are," I scoffed. I proceeded to make breakfast, cracking each egg with ease and watching it spread across the pan. With each crack, I pictured my mother's head.

"Your life must be pretty bad for you to come here." An evilness glassed over her eyes as her cracked lips tightened into a thin line. *What kind of mother relishes her daughter's failures?*

"That husband of yours no longer wanted you anymore." An odd sound started to rumble in her chest. "So you have to come running back to mommy." Laughter seeped out from behind her gritty teeth. I knew my mother was cruel, evil, but there was something about the way she laughed at my pain that gave it a new level of hatred.

"No, see, *your* life is the one that is so bad." I slammed the spatula down on the counter in front of her to gain attention and release my growing frustration over this torturous conversation. Her laughter paused, silent hatred filling the air between us. "Just look around you, Mama. No one else is here. You have no one. Your life is so bad that I'm the only one to take care of your deranged, dying body ... and you hate me. I had a great life, wonderful, but you just can't believe that, can you? Your life is so horrible, you can't even imagine the fact that I actually could have a decent life."

"My life is horrible because of you." The words trickled slowly from behind her tight lips, like lava from a volcano about to blow. Her words cut deeper than if she had yelled or hit. She always had a way of doing that, making me feel as if *I* were the reason she was an awful person.

"You're a drunk." *Two can play at this game.* "You have nothing in life, so don't you dare blame me."

Pushing back from the counter, leaving the eggs half cooked, I added, "And don't you dare judge me; you're the last person who can do that."

Escaping from hell, slamming the front door behind me, I realized I forgot to grab the car keys. For a moment, I thought about going back in; the keys were just inside on the wall, but it was too risky. The hatred was tightening in my chest, my breathing increasing in rate ... I had to leave, now. So I picked a direction and started walking, determined to get as far away from her as I possibly could.

It did not take long for the late summer heat to engulf my skin in a thick, humid sweat. Curls started to frizz at the base of my neck, and sweat, pooling then slowly reaching its tipping point, started to roll down my spine. None of it mattered to me, as my anger consumed every feeling, every emotion, every thought.

Suddenly, without realizing my steps, I had walked the two-mile stretch of broken, hot asphalt to a shipping container thrown on the side of the road. A single cracked sign read *Outhouse* at the foot of the gravel path. I should've paid attention, realized the familiarity of my path a mile ago, and turned around. But here I was.

The place hadn't aged a day since I last saw it. Leave it to my mother to locate the one bar within walking distance from our house. Days would pass, the food dissipating, when she would finally return, alcohol thick on her skin, clothes filthy with dried vomit and sweat as she'd bellow for me to make her a drink. She never asked if I was okay after all that time alone, nor did she ever explain where she would go. But I knew she was at the bar; I could smell the cigarettes in her hair.

There was a time or two I had walked the two miles to this place to find her when I was younger. Pulling her arm, I was barely able to move her drunken body from the stool as the bartender laughed. They all laughed. Not one person helped me as a little girl. I stopped trying at age ten, realizing I was better off alone than with her.

My thoughts betrayed my other senses as a truck pulled into the gravel parking lot. In the distance, a horn honked as a hazed figure emerged from the cab. His hand waved, pulling me from my memory. Shame flooded my entire body as I realized whose truck it was.

"Norah," he called, slowly trotting over in my direction. "Are you okay?"

Mortified. That was the best word to describe my current situation. Utter mortification. "Brett, yes, I—uh, I'm fine." Stuttering didn't help.

"Do you need a ride somewhere?" he offered, glancing down at my dirt-covered toes. My very worn Birkenstock shoes had done little to protect my feet from the dusty, dirt roads. The bottom of my jeans was bathed with a thick layer of dried mud. It was clear I was not out on an intentional walk.

"Oh, god. I ... well ... I got locked out of my house." As the lie unfolded from my mouth, I saw every flaw in it, as did Brett.

"Norah, do you need anything?" His concern was paralyzing as I acknowledged just how awful this all looked to an outsider. Bare feet; frizzed, sweat-soaked hair; braless boobs poking through my tank top. I was sure I looked like someone who went two days too many at Woodstock.

"So it's just that I got into it with my mother back at the house and needed to take a walk. That's all." I attempted to reassure him that I was, in fact, not going completely batshit crazy. "I was just going to take a short walk down the road, but then I got lost in thought." Somehow, Brett was nodding in understanding at my ridiculous story, compassion filling his eyes.

"It's hard taking care of an ill parent. I, more than anyone, get that." He placed an empathic hand over his own heart, as if he were feeling it break all over again. "How about I buy you a drink?" He motioned back toward the bar. A drink was the last thing I needed right now. "A coffee," he added quickly, as I realized the bar was closed and he was motioning back to his truck.

"No, no, thank you. I really should be getting back to the house." There was definitely a part of me that wanted to—of course at a more reasonable hour and in actual clothes—pull up on a barstool, our legs gently grazing each other as we moved closer, and feel a connection with Brett, but every minute I was close to him I felt raw, exposed. My body pulled me toward it, but my mind tugged back against the rope, winning the game.

"Maybe another time then." His tight side smile confessed his disappointment. I was sure my fidgety body was revealing my own. "Sure you don't need a ride?" he offered one more time, a flicker of hope hidden behind his crystal-blue eyes.

"No, I prefer the walk." This particular walk of shame was not unfamiliar, unfortunately.

As the distance between us grew, I could feel the pull on the rope to turn around, accept the drink, accept the ride, but my mind would not relinquish its hold. The words echoed in my mind, reverberating the raw pain that I still felt over Michael. A part of me thought I could lean on Brett, or maybe Caroline, but deep down I knew why I was unable to accept the ride or call Caroline. *I deserve this pain.*

I shivered as I stared up at the ominous house, a fearful chill spreading across my body. The sweat that poured down my body in the middle of the day now felt like ice in the cool night breeze. As I approached the house, I noticed someone watching me from a distance. A figure rocked back and forth, the shadow of night masking her face, but I could clearly see the outline of her shotgun. *Ms. Kay.* I swear nothing had changed in this damn town.

"Midnight stroll?" Ms. Kay rocked forward in her chair, leaning over the shotgun slung across her lap. Her porch angled toward my mother's house, forcing her to lean out so I could acknowledge her presence as I reached the porch steps.

"Not sure why you care."

There was never a moment in my childhood in which Ms. Kay ever showed any interest in what was happening, so why now? She'd have to be an idiot to not realize what my mother did to me just a few feet from her front door. Of course, there was a slight chance she didn't know ... *slight*. But that would've been difficult, in my opinion.

"How's that mama of yours doin'?"

"Why do you care?"

Suddenly, I felt a deep need to unleash my anger on someone. Ms. Kay seemed like a good target. Turning on my heels, I stomped through the darkening sky and her precious grass, just waiting for her to say something, right up to her porch.

"Your mama's been roaming around here for months now. Something wrong with her?"

Again, why do you care? Why was she *now* showing an interest in my mother and my current situation? It was infuriating. Slamming my foot down on each wooden step, I made my way right up and into her face. She tightened her grip on her shotgun, but she still didn't move from that godforsaken rocking chair. *I'm not afraid of you anymore.*

"I'm sorry. Is my mother's current situation a problem for you? Is it an inconvenience to have her 'roaming' around? Are you offering to help? Or just being a concerned citizen?" Her crystal-gray gaze did not even flinch as I rattled off endless facetious questions to make my point.

"Just a concerned citizen, I guess."

"Oh, that is real rich coming from you."

"What the hell is that supposed to mean?"

"The only thing you ever cared about was keeping your grass alive, never mind the innocent child being beaten right next door to you!" Her eyes flickered with fear, just long enough to confirm my suspicions. *She knew.* She knew the whole time. "Stay out of our damn business."

My heart was racing as I slammed the door, leaning back against the solid wood in an attempt to ground my mind. The confrontation with Ms. Kay ripped open a long healing scar. The rawness of it was burning on my chest. For so long, I covered the scars, hid from the pain, but being back in this place was splitting them wide open. Caroline had been right; *this place was going to kill me.*

Having had no intentions of walking around in the humidity all day, I had not been wearing the proper clothing. As I lifted my arms, the smell was overwhelming. I needed a bath ... no, a shower this time. I still had yet to properly clean the bathroom.

The warm water cascaded over my aching muscles as I tightly squeezed my eyes closed. I imagined I was back in our Atlanta condo, the large white-tiled, clean shower raining down over my body. Gently, I rubbed my soapy hands over my skin, down my chest—my eyes grew wide with disbelief as I looked down at my protruding stomach. I knew it was impossible, yet I could feel my hands on my skin ... on the baby.

As quickly as the hallucination started, it disappeared, my hands falling onto my flat belly. Shaking the image from my mind, I turned off the water and jumped out of the shower, unable to risk another episode.

My heart was still racing as I made my way back into the bedroom, one towel wrapped around my body, the other drying my already frizzy hair. My mind was so disoriented that I jumped at the sight of a person standing in my room. It took a moment for me to realize it was my mother, standing perfectly still at the foot of my bed.

"Damn, Mama, you scared me." She placed a defiant hand on her hip and glared at me as if she were waiting for an apology. I scoffed; she was never going to get that, not from me, not ever. "What are you doing in here?"

"Well, are you going to make dinner?" I got the feeling that was not why she was in here, but she failed to remember the true reason. Asking about dinner seemed like an afterthought, not the main idea.

"Have you just been waiting for me to make you dinner?" This morning she literally kicked me out of the house, and now she was asking me to make her dinner? I couldn't help but roll my eyes.

"You said you plan to live here now. So you need to earn your keep." Uncontrollable laughter escaped my lungs. As if I needed to earn my keep; as if I weren't already doing everything around the house.

"Mama, I do live here now; I will make the meals, but don't get this twisted. I am in charge, not you."

"Like hell you are," she started, but I shot her an evil look. She stopped short.

"Make a choice, Mama. Option one: I live here. I am in charge. This means I will take care of the house, the food, and make sure you don't get arrested." She glared, clearly pissed about the last jab. "Or option two: I leave, you get arrested or sent to a home, then die alone." I could tell that neither option was agreeable; she was failing to see any other options. *Join the club.*

Of course, there was another option my mother failed to see; I was not going to enlighten her. She could tell me to leave, go away. Maybe she wouldn't get arrested, maybe she could find someone else to take care of her or a home that would accept her. But then she would be alone; deep down, I saw that she really did understand that she was sick. Through all her denial and protest, at this moment, I knew she was clearly aware of her situation. She needed me, as much as she hated to admit it. Silence was her answer.

"That's what I thought. Now leave so I can get dressed, then I will come down and make us dinner." She nodded in reluctant agreement and started to leave, but just before she was gone, I added, "And, Mama, don't ever come into my room again." Just for good measure.

Chapter Fifteen
Little Girl

The little girl stared at her cracked reflection in the broken mirror. Pulling at her dingy lace dress, she attempted to hide the bruise on her arm, the four small perfectly round finger marks from her mother's grasp. The little girl had few things to choose from, this dress being the only suitable thing for her first day of school. She knew her mother would never let her out of the house with bruises showing, unwilling to risk another visit from social services. It was just last week a woman showed up at the door, asking about the little girl attending the local school. The little girl thought the woman was an angel.

She had nothing to take to school, no food in a tin pail lunchbox, no books on a string, not even an apple for the teacher. All things she assumed she would need, but really, she was naive to the entire system.

Dragging her feet in the dirt, empty handed, she made her way to the school. With each step, she could feel the pain in her left knee, a harsh reminder of the previous evening. There was a part of her that thought she would've left her alone last night, considering it was her first day of school ... but no. She had no restraint.

The walk to school was far, but she didn't mind, thankful for any moments away from that horrible place. Her mind wandered to all the friends she might make, the things she would learn ... maybe even someone would see the bruises, save her. She quickly brushed the thoughts from her traveling mind. The only way she would be able to gain these small moments of normality at school would be to keep her mother's secret—*at all costs.*

She winced as her body slid into the hard wooden chair, the long belt-shaped marks across her back preventing her from sitting back into the chair comfortably. Her bruised knee that had slammed on each stair as she dragged her to her room was now swollen, black and blue. She had her story ready for the teacher.

"You should be more careful." Her mother stood in the kitchen doorway, a ghostly circle of cigarette smoke like a halo around her head. The little girl was confused. "Falling down the stairs." Her mother's lips curled up. "You could've broken something; good thing you only got a bruised knee." Her eyebrows raised, daring the little girl to challenge the story. Realization set in.

"Yes, I tripped down the stairs." All she wanted was to go to school, say anything to make it out of the house. She could feel the tears burning to explode, but she fought against them, knowing her mother would detain her at the slightest sign of weakness in her ability to tell the story.

"That's a good girl. Now run along to school."

Just as the little girl was about to pull the door closed behind her, escape on the horizon, her mother added, "I expect you home immediately after school, and if that woman ever comes back here ..." She paused. "You'll never leave this house again."

A bell rang in the distance, the door opened to a flood of kids, all like herself, pouring into the classroom. The voices and laughter filled the silent air as they all took seats. She watched, invisible, from the back of the classroom, a fly on the wall. It was mesmerizing. Their happiness was intoxicating. Her eyes grew wide with excitement. Any one of these kids could be her friend. She was just as they were, in the same class, the same age; she even had a smile on her face ... but it was short lived.

There was a part of her that wanted to join in the conversations, the laughter, but then the cloud lifted, and she realized that she was alone in the back of the room. No one had taken any of the seats around her, nor did they look at her. She was invisible. Even the teacher, as she lumbered into the room, failed to notice the little girl. The teacher, a rather large and aged woman, stood at the front of the class most of the day, calling out questions but never looking in her direction.

The day dragged on. The little girl was invisible. Everyone looked right through her. So she sat silently at her desk, never raising her hand and never calling attention to herself. She convinced herself that it was better this way. It would be easier to keep her secret if no one ever even noticed her presence.

Toward the end of the day, the teacher paused by her desk, looking down over her horn-rimmed glasses at the little girl. In time, the little girl would come to recognize that look as one of pity. She could feel her body start to shake as the teacher continued to stare, waiting for the question she dreaded the most ... but the teacher never asked. The teacher continued her walk down the aisles of desks. In a way, it was almost worse than if the teacher had asked the question. Now, the little girl truly felt invisible, and worse ... alone.

Another bell rang and everyone disappeared, including the teacher, leaving her alone in the classroom. She was never given any books or directions but assumed the day was over. Even though she knew she needed to go straight home, she decided to walk through the fields and by the lake. It would only add a few extra minutes. Anything to delay returning to her prison of abuse and neglect. She prayed daily to be taken away from this place, but nothing. No one ever came. No one ever said anything. No one ever saw her.

As she walked down the dirt road, past the row of houses, she saw the girl rocking on the porch. She had not seen her since that night her mother came to the house. That was weeks ago, but at this moment the little girl felt as if it had happened yesterday. Pausing, she looked up to the girl, waiting for her to come to talk to her, ask her about her day at school, as if somehow now they could be friends again. But the girl stood up and disappeared into the house. The little girl's heart sank because she knew why the girl would not talk to her, why she had stopped coming outside to play. It wasn't the first time she had lost a friend.

Even though the little girl was only eight years old, she knew that people looked at her differently. She ran up the stairs, slamming her bedroom door, throwing herself on the bed. She cried. *How could they see?* She tried so hard to cover up the abuse, but still they all knew. Pulling her sore body up from the bed, she stood in front of her mirror, trying to see what they all saw.

Cracks ran through the glass like rivers on a map, cutting through parts of her body and distorting the image. She saw it: the broken parts of her body, the cracks that tattooed her skin. *How could they look at her?* If they did, they would see. In that moment, she vowed to never look at herself in the mirror again. Her last hope of ever gaining any parts of a normal life was shattered. She would always be broken, always be alone. All she would ever have was her mother.

Chapter Sixteen
Present Day

I stood in the foyer, looking at myself in the hall mirror. The cracked mirror had been there since I was a child. It was covered with a thick layer of dust that, no matter how much I scrubbed, I could not get off, but it was still just as unforgiving as any other mirror in this horrible house. Through the cracks and dust, my sunken, dark eyes gave me the appearance of a basset hound dog, in my opinion. Coupled with my undyed, mousy, frizzy brown hair uncomplemented by my pale skin and thinning frame, I didn't even recognize myself, nor did I want to. This was a disaster. There was no way I was going.

Losing Caroline's number meant nothing to her, as she endlessly called the house to *"check on me,"* as she often explained when I actually answered the phone out of pure, unnerving annoyance. I figured that if I answered every fifth call, that would prevent her from materializing at my door again. I kept telling myself I had too much on my shoulders already, that Caroline would only complicate things more, so, in turn, I'd just have to keep her at bay for a little while longer until I had everything worked out with my mother. Of course, the dark truth was that if she saw me, really looked at my face, she would see what I already knew was happening. *I was dying.*

As always, this place was slowly pulling me into the quicksand; little by little I was losing pieces of myself. Soon I would just disappear into the earth, gone forever. I planned to take my mother down with me.

"Please, you just have to come," she begged over the phone.

"Caroline, I can't leave my mother. She'll do something completely crazy; I just know it."

"Dear God, Norah, just leave her locked in her room. Literally a month ago, she was alone. I'm sure she'll be fine." Biting my lower lip, I searched for another excuse but was lost for one. "You need to get out of that house."

"I just can't."

"Bullshit." Her words hissed through the phone, a surprising harshness in her tone. "It's fucking Christmas." Her foul mouth brought back memories of her unyielding defense of my character to the other girls in the school yard. Caroline was relentless.

"Fine, I'll come." As the words whispered from my mouth, I knew I wouldn't go. There was no way I could face her, not like this. Even after all this time, she would see the truth in my protruding bones, hunched shoulders, and clouded eyes. Then she would definitely be over at my house every day.

As I placed the phone back onto the base, it resonated within my mind that I had not even realized it was almost Christmas. The muggy, humid late-fall air had failed to cool quickly this year, leaving my body with a feeling of fall instead of winter. Just weeks ago, I had sat outside feeling the lingering sweat of summer, and suddenly it was Christmas. My mind failed to make sense of it all.

Walking back into the living room to find my mother passed out drunk in that nasty flowered chair, a vision of a Christmas long ago came to life in my mind. That year, there had been an actual tree with lights and everything in the far corner of this living room, a fire ablaze in the fireplace, flames flickering light throughout the room. That night, I waited for Santa Claus to come. I remembered overhearing the kids talking about it at school, that a man would bring them presents in the night. I was such a naive, stupid little girl.

Christmas morning came, and a feeling of hope rushed through me as my feet rushed down the stairs. I had never felt like that before as I slid around the corner, ready for the surprise and joy of Christmas morning ... but it never came.

The scene before me was from a horror film, as if Jack the Ripper had mutilated my perfect Christmas morning. I found my mother passed out on the floor, her drink spilled. The tree lights were out on account of the fact that the drink had short-circuited the electrical. The stockings were burning in the fireplace, having been thrown there or pulled down by my mother—either scenario was just as likely.

At first, I refused to believe it, but once the reality of the situation sunk in, I was enraged. Days before, I had pleaded with my mother to not drink anymore. He had left us; she no longer needed to drink to survive. But she couldn't. Not even for a day.

Wiping the tears from my hot cheeks, I refused to let the memory bring back all that pain. I'd had enough of that already. Walking over to the fireplace, I could still see the burn marks on the electrical socket. Suddenly, I realized just what I needed was

Christmas. In a split second, I got it into my head that it would bring me back to life, or at least delay my death another few weeks.

There was a nice chill to the air, just enough to wear a sweater. As the heat had pulled me closer to my death in this house, I felt as if this fresh burst of winter air was going to pull me out of the quicksand. Mother not in tow, as she refused to go, and I didn't feel like a fight, I slid into the rental car. Of course, I had stopped making the payments when I arrived, so I wasn't quite sure how much longer I would even have the car to claim.

Pulling the cap down over my recognizable hair, and glasses over my betraying eyes, I made my way down the rows of trees, brushing my cold fingers on the pines and wondering what on Earth I was thinking. I wasn't quite sure how any of this was going to make everything in my life suddenly better, but still my feet kept moving down the rows, the soft morning dirt thickening to the bottom of my rainboots (all I had).

Stopping at the end of the row, I admired a rather small pine tree, with its thick pine needles and sturdy trunk. It reminded me of a short, fat Santa Claus. This was it. This was my Christmas tree. It was only fitting that it was nothing close to perfect. Much like myself these days.

"I'll take this one," I announced to the man standing a few feet away. He was wearing a thick black vest with a large tree on the back, so I assumed he worked at the place.

"Norah?" Instantly, I could feel my heart skip a beat. Brett, standing just a few feet away, was staring at me. *Oh, great!*

"Brett, uh, good to see you again. You work here?" Instantly, I made a mental check of how I appeared. After our last mortifying encounter, I desperately needed this one to go differently. Otherwise, he would probably call the police and try to admit me to a mental institution. In my favor, I had covered my tangled, unwashed hair, the glasses provided good cover for my dead eyes, and the sweater hid my thinning frame. Therefore, I decided it wasn't completely awful this time.

"No, I do not, but I can help you if you need it?" His mouth cocked to the side, a slight smile crossing his lips as I lost myself in his eyes, but only for a moment. Then I realized how ridiculous I must look to him after all these years and was bothered by the fact I seemed to care so much.

"Oh, uh, it's okay." I attempted to blow off the fact that I had mistaken him for a worker. He really should wear a different vest. "I'm sure there's another strapping young man that can help me." Instantly I flushed, realizing what I was saying only after the words vomited out of my mouth.

Thankfully, he laughed it off. "It's really no bother." He quickly looked around, no doubt grasping for someone who worked at the tree farm, before conceding. He reached around me and pulled the tree up with one hand. *Childhood Brett* never would've been able to do that, but clearly *Grown Man Brett* was just as strong as he appeared. Walking back through the trees, shoulder to shoulder, I was too embarrassed by my last comment to even think about making small talk. We walked in silence.

"Is this your car?" he asked, pointing to the black Nissan Altima.

"Yes, uh, it's actually a rental. Well, it was a rental; now it's probably considered stolen." *Stop talking now!* "But, yes, you can tie it to the top there." What was wrong with me? Why was I acting this way around him? The only reason I could think of—because, of course, it was not that I had any remote feelings for him—was that I desperately wanted to prove to him that I was not a hot mess. It was not working.

"So you are getting ready for Christmas?"

"Yep, there's a first time for everything."

"What? You've never had a Christmas tree?"

"Oh ... uh ..." *I needed to think up a lie and think it up quick* ... but nothing seemed to come to mind. Brett knew my mother was abusive, mostly verbal and at least once physical. But he never really knew the true depth of the abuse. No one did, not even Caroline. If no one was going to say something when she hit me, they definitely weren't going to do anything about her not putting up a Christmas tree and singing carols all night by the fireside.

"Never really had a Christmas, actually." My cheeks burned with embarrassment, which he couldn't help but notice.

"Are you going to Caroline's Christmas party?" Graciously, he changed the subject, sort of.

"No, I have to watch my mother."

"Oh, yeah." He seemed disappointed but quickly recovered. "How's that going, by the way?"

"Not good." Concern flooded his face, and I realized I did not need him taking on my issues. "I mean, it's what you would expect, taking care of a dying parent." *Oh crap! What is wrong with me today?*

"Yeah, I understand that."

"Oh, I'm so sorry, Brett." Once again, I had given more information to support the opinion that I was, in fact, a hot mess. I was really bombing at this, whatever *this* was.

"Have a good Christmas." He waved goodbye and disappeared into the rows of pine trees.

After paying for the tree with the last bit of cash that I had, I drove home, tree and all. Surprisingly, it did not blow off. Brett had done a good job tying it down. *Should I send him a thank you note?* Oh, God, it had only been a few weeks and already my Southern accent returned, along with my Southern hospitality. *No, I was not sending a thank you note. That was ridiculous.*

However, I did consider calling him after multiple failed attempts to get the tree off the car. It was heavier than it looked. I finally managed to get the tree to the porch steps before my arms gave out. *Why was I even bothering?* I had no lights for the tree, nor did I have gifts to go under it. I decided to end this Christmas fantasy. I tipped my beer to the stars as I lit the tree with a lighter ... *watching Christmas burn.*

Chapter Seventeen
Little Girl

The little girl could smell the scent of cinnamon in the air as it filled every corner of the house. She peered into the kitchen, watching her mother carefully placing each piece of dough on the cookie sheet. The little girl swore the ice in her mother's drink clinked to the tune of "Jingle Bells." Suddenly her mother stopped, her yellowed eyes glaring across the room at the little girl.

She froze, unsure of what her mother would do. "Do you want a cookie?" she beckoned. The girl knew it was a trap, but the smell was so intoxicating. She emerged from behind the protective wall.

As she approached, her mother displayed a Grinch-like smile, showing her stained teeth. Reaching her small frail hand toward her mother, her mouth started to water over the taste of the cookie to come. She almost had it in her hand ...

Smack!

Suddenly the girl's mouth was no longer watering. Instead, it was her eyes that filled with water. Her hand was bright red, the pain searing up her arm.

"Bad little girls don't deserve cookies," her mother sneered. The wooden spoon used to scoop the dough was still in her hand. She waved it back and forth, daring the girl to reach for another cookie. It was as if her mother wanted her to reach for another just so she could hit her again.

The little girl looked up into her mother's eyes, realizing that she took joy in torturing her. She never knew what she did to deserve such hatred from her own mother.

Chapter Eighteen
Present Day

The moment I walked through the doorway, I regretted my decision. If I could think of everyone I did not want to see, they were all in this room. This very tiny room, at that. *So why would I come here now?* There was a part of me that wanted to fight against the pulling quicksand, even though I knew very well that the more I struggled, the quicker it would pull me down. But I couldn't help it. Plus, Caroline had greatly downplayed the amount of people who would attend her "small gathering."

"Oh my gosh, you made it!" Caroline squealed as she pushed her way through the crowd. This only made things worse because now everyone noticed my entrance. I forced a smile as she pulled me into a tight hug. "I really am so happy you came," she whispered in my ear. One more squeeze, and then she let go, holding me back at arm's length to check me out. "You look amazing!" she exclaimed as I removed my coat.

"Amazingly overdressed." I observed the crowd. Most people were in jeans and a nice top, nothing as fancy as my little red dress, regrettably picked in the hopes that Brett would be here to see that I was not a hot mess, and even think I was hot. Of course, as I thought about it now, it all seemed naive. There was no part of me that needed to be attracted to or hopeful of something with Brett. I'd only take him down with me.

"No, you are perfect." *Horrible choice of words.*

She took my jacket as she moved me into the crowd, weaving me in and out as people stared. That's if they made eye contact with me at all. I could see the recognition in most people's eyes, however, there were a few who appeared confused. I'm not sure if the confusion came from seeing me here or just seeing me at all. Either way, I knew everyone. It was mortifying.

We made our way to the kitchen without one introduction. Caroline really was a good friend. She knew I would need alcohol before I reunited with the entire town of people who seemed to have always looked down on me and shunned me for my mother's behavior. They all thought I'd amount to nothing. Which, at this moment, was pretty much true. That reality did not help the situation. My want for a Christmas, which I deeply regretted at this moment, had overshadowed this fact. I should've stayed home and forgotten all about Christmas.

"Here." Caroline handed me a beer. "So how are you feeling?" It was an honest question, as she could see I was overwhelmed, coupled with the fact that my life was generally in shambles.

"Regretful."

"No, no, no," she protested. "Please, don't feel that way. Everyone is going to be so excited to see you, and no one needs to know the truth." Her add on was puzzling. What truth was she referring to? The marriage, job, child *(my entire life as I knew it)*, or that I was really at rock bottom taking care of my crazy mother because I had no other options in life.

"For all they know, you are just home to help out your mother," she offered. *Oh, that truth. Got it.* It was kind of her to think the whole town didn't know the whole story by now. After all, I had been home for a month. If I remembered correctly, it only took about two weeks for any gossip to spread through this town. I would have to assume that everyone in this room knew the whole truth and nothing but the truth, so please help me, God.

"I'm going to need a stiffer drink," I admitted, chugging down the last half of the beer. She quickly mixed me another drink of vodka and coke.

"Just remember we don't care what all these people think, remember?" It was our motto growing up. *How could I forget?* It was my first real smile in weeks.

"Stand strong; we are better than the hand that was dealt us." I added the end of it, letting out a deep breath. Even after all this time, Caroline and I could just seamlessly fall back into our friendship. If only I could let her in, things might be different. But the cost was too great.

"Oh my word, if it is not Norah Crawford." *Ugh,* I could never forget that voice. It had haunted my dreams my entire childhood. I rolled my eyes at Caroline, who was already plastering on that large fake smile, a true "Southern greeting," as the woman approached us.

"Hello." My words were forced as I tried not to lean into the awkward and massive hug she gave.

"You look amazing," she exclaimed, her big blue eyes so wide you could drive a Mack truck through them. "Doesn't she look amazing?" she asked Caroline. Caroline politely nodded in response, knowing how annoyed I was by all the fake fuss. "With all that you have been through, it is just a miracle." There's the dig I was waiting for; my large fake smile tightened. I took a long, necessary gulp of my very strong drink. *Thank you, Caroline.*

Courtney May Weston. As if her name could not be any more Southern, she was the quintessential Southern Belle. From her big blonde hair to her oversized pearl earrings, to her deep Southern drawl, she was as *Southern* as a Georgia peach.

"Good to see you too, Courtney." I could say the words, but I couldn't fake the face. Caroline gave me a *look-happy* face, as if it was that easy.

"Home for the holidays?" I knew opening it up to talk about her would buy me some time, and hopefully I would devise an escape plan before I had to talk about myself. Courtney always did love to talk about herself, seeing as she felt she was an important person. In fact, her father was an important person in this town, bringing in much needed money throughout the years, but she was just a mean girl.

"Well, yes, yes I am." She seemed flattered by the fact that someone had asked about her. Maybe it was just in the way she said it, or maybe she just wanted another opportunity to flash a large diamond ring in my face. For whatever reason, she placed her ringed hand gently on her heart and left it there just a little bit too long. I wanted to rip it off her finger, just so she would know that I saw it.

"I live in Montgomery now, in order to be closer to the business." She wanted me to ask, but I really did not want to.

"Oh, Mark needs me." Caroline waved off to Mark in the distance, who was attempting to put together some music. *Sorry,* she mouthed as she retreated back into the crowd. *Great.*

We awkwardly stood there for some time before Courtney finally resolved to just telling me, as if I had asked the polite question. "I am an interior designer. I have just a little ol' store." She waved it off as if it was not a big deal to her, but I could tell it was. Another awkward pause as she waited for me to continue the conversation. I took a long sip of my drink instead.

"My husband's job is very demanding. Oh, he's a doctor," she added, unprovoked. "So, if we want to have kids, I will have to give up the store soon. I do love it so, though, but being a mother will be so much more important." I wanted to vomit on her. Clearly, she knew I could not have children; *cat's out of the bag.* I could no longer take it. *I was done.*

I turned to rudely walk away but was instantly halted by a tall, dark figure.

"Well, fancy seeing you here." He smiled down at me, knowing full well I was attempting an escape. "If you don't mind, Courtney, I have something to show Norah."

He was saving me. I noticed Courtney's wide eyes as Brett pulled me away from her and gently ushered me through the dining room, where most people were too busy eating to notice. We ended up on the back porch.

My hot breath clouded the brisk black night sky. I rubbed my hands up my arms to create some heat, knowing that being out here was better than being back in that house. No way was I going back into the lion's den for my jacket.

"Here." He gestured politely as he removed his coat. My body curled into the warm leather, my senses taking in the familiar smell. Suddenly, Michael's face flashed across my mind, a suppressed memory of us in Los Angeles at Christmas, his leather coat around my shoulders as we walked down Hollywood boulevard as tourists. Michael took me away every year for a vacation at Christmas time, knowing how much I loathed the holiday. Now here I was immersing myself into it. Tears pricked at the corners of my eyes.

"Thank you for the coat and for saving me." I hoped Brett hadn't seen the tears in my eyes. I quickly turned toward the lake in the distance. Caroline and Mark had managed to purchase a modest house on the lower side of the lake. There was no water at their dock in the wintertime, which kept the property cost down, but in the glow of the full moon light, I could still see it flickering in the distance.

"Seemed kind of brutal there." He smiled an all-too-charming smile as he looked back into the room filled with people. As he turned, the light illuminating from the house cast a shadow on his bearded chin, flecks of red dancing in the light while others hid in the darkness. It seemed oddly metaphoric for the person he seemed to be to me now.

"It really is."

"I remember when I first came back," he mused. "Everything was so different, yet the same all at one time. I was different ..." He hesitated, as if there was more to say, but then stopped. The shadow refused to come into the light. There was a moment when I almost asked him to explain, but then I recoiled. Knowing how much I didn't want to explain myself, I had to respect that he didn't either.

"Well, coming back to my sick, deranged mother has just been peachy," I jeered.

"Yeah right, I don't believe that for a second." He gently nudged my shoulder, a friendly gesture that immediately brought back memories of studying in the hidden alcoves of the library, lost to the rest of the world. I suddenly wished we were there together now. I'd give anything to just disappear.

"It's honestly horrible. One of the most awful things I've ever had to do." Brett assumed I was referring to caring for my mother, nodding in understanding. But really, the awful part was all that I had lost.

"Yeah, coming home for those reasons never seems to work out in your favor."

"It seems that all we ever wanted was to get out of this place. Yet here we are." The sobering thought left us in an awkward silence, each of us staring off into the distance, imagining what our life would've been like if we had not had to come back home to take care of a parent. I'm sure he had a life worth living before coming back to all this, but I didn't. As I looked back in the distant future, I saw nothing. I couldn't even imagine where I might be if I had not come back. The blackness was consuming.

"I really did actually kind of miss this place though," he confessed, breaking the awkward silence.

"You don't get this view in the city," I added, wanting to move past my feelings of emptiness.

"Before my father passed, we would just sit on the back porch admiring the farm. As if we were in a museum taking in a masterpiece. It was quite calming."

"I know what you mean. The city is busy. It's nice to slow down out here." I took a deep breath, taking in the cool, clean air. It truly did feel different down here.

"Do you think you will go back after all this?" *What did I have to go back to? What did I have to stay for?*

"I actually think I will stay." The answer clearly surprised him and me. He nodded in approval, with that all-too-familiar side smile. It was a lie. I still didn't know what I was going to do, but for some reason I wanted him to think that I was going to stay.

"Well, in that case, maybe we will see more of each other." It was more of a statement, but there was a hint of a question, or maybe it was hope. Either way, I felt the same. For the first time in a very long time, I wanted that hope back, even if it was just in friendship.

"I would very much like that," I admitted to both of us.

"Oh my gosh, there you are," I heard Caroline call from the doorway. "It is too cold out here!" she exclaimed, rubbing her arms as she joined us on the porch. "At least light the fire." She made quick work of lighting the logs in the already prepared fire pit. The fire did feel nice as we all stood around warming our hands.

"It's been a long time," Caroline said, finally breaking our silence.

"Way too long," Brett added, eyes directly on mine. I awkwardly looked away, but I felt it. That feeling you got around someone that meant something to you. *Was it just friendship or something more?* My brain was only in a place to consider friendship; anything else would just be too confusing right now.

"It's good to have you back, Norah." Brett's smile was tender like his words. I couldn't help but notice that Caroline caught the look between us.

"Brett, I could really use another drink. Would you mind telling my husband to bring me another?" Caroline did not really need another drink; she just wanted us to be alone, most likely to probe about *the look*. I got that, but I regretted her sending him away. Of course, he politely obliged.

"I am really glad you came, Norah. I think you should start getting out more." She winked and motioned back toward Brett, who was disappearing through the sliding glass door.

"That's quite difficult in my situation." Not to mention, mentally, I was not ready to put myself out there again. In fact, I was not sure I ever really could put myself back out there again. Nothing was worth that kind of pain, even Brett's smile. Friendship I could do, but romance? No thank you—never again.

"I know it all seems impossible right now, but it did when we were kids too. We just have to fight." Her words were encouraging as ever; that was what she was good at. Caroline could encourage, or light a fire under my ass, depending on the way you thought about it.

Just then, Mark emerged with another drink in hand for Caroline. "It's good to see you again, Norah." He cheered his glass against my own.

"Thank you. Really, I mean it; thank you both for all of this. I don't deserve your friendship."

"Of course, honey, what are friends for?" Caroline said as she wrapped an arm around me, taking a jab at our Southern upbringing by calling me *honey*, something that made me smile and roll my eyes at the same time.

As the evening came to an end, I remained to help Caroline clean up all the dishes. "The party was a success," I offered as I dried dishes while she washed. I could hear Mark in the background still gathering up all the drinks.

"Yes, it was." Her answer was not what I expected. I thought she'd be prouder of it, but she seemed upset.

"I think everyone had a really great time," I offered, attempting to make her feel better, but it didn't work. "Is everything okay?" I finally asked when she did not respond.

"It's just that I noticed the way Brett was staring at you all night," she admitted. Her disapproval was confusing considering her earlier comment of "getting out there." She stopped washing and turned to me. This was serious. "He's been through a lot. You have been through a lot."

"I know this."

"No, you don't," she interrupted. She let out a deep sigh in frustration. I could tell she was unhappy about something between Brett and I, but honestly, there was nothing.

"Just don't start anything you can't finish, okay?" She wanted me to promise something; what it was, I was not completely sure of at the moment. Yet it was the way in which she asked me, as if it was really important to her, so I nodded in agreement.

"Regular coffee, please." Against my better judgement, I took my coffee and sat at the bar, staring out onto the street, just waiting ... waiting for him. The following moments were filled with me getting up then sitting back down again over and over again. I was indecisive on what I was going to do. Of course, I knew what I should do, yet I sat there, waiting.

Christmas had come and gone, but just as the holiday season lingered, so did the feeling he gave me that night at Caroline's party. As things with my mother continued to decline, I found myself needing something to hold on to as the winds grew stronger. Finally making the decision to come back to the coffee shop for a chance encounter with Brett had been my stronghold.

But I wasn't really sure what I could give him; after losing myself in the divorce, not being able to have children, I was left empty, shattered. My heart was in pieces, and I wasn't even sure I could find one piece to give him, which didn't seem fair. Deep down, I knew I was being selfish. I needed this hope to help me survive my mother and stay away from the storm, like those people who leave at the last minute, knowing they will get stuck in traffic ... *What's the point?* How was this really going to go? *Not well.*

Eventually he would find out I could not have children, and he would be disappointed. He would feel the same way my ex-husband had and leave me. Or maybe he would be okay with it? Who was I kidding? A man like Brett would never be okay with something like that; I was assured he was the kind of guy that wanted at least five children. This would never end well, and end it would, so why even get started?

This is crazy, I determined after sitting for over an hour at the coffee shop, lost in my constant inner battle over what to do. I threw down a dollar, grabbed my coffee, and proceeded to the door.

"See you tomorrow?" called the elderly owner.

"Not likely," I disclosed. I pulled my glasses down as the sun reached my eyes. If I had not been squinting at the bright sun, I might've noticed him, but instead I did not, and we ran right into each other.

Instantly, I felt the warm coffee on my chest. *Great, this is just what I needed.* I was just about to chastise the person for not looking, when I realized it was him. It was Brett.

"I am so sorry, Norah." He attempted to help me clean off, but it just resulted in him rubbing my boobs. "Oh, I am truly sorry now," he stuttered, removing his hands, realizing what he was doing.

"It's okay, really. It was not even hot anymore." I mustered all my strength to appear unfazed, when, in fact, I was burning alive.

"Let me get you another one," he offered. This was the moment I had been waiting for. However, I had just decided that I was not going to pursue this. I could never give him what he truly deserved, which was exactly what Caroline was talking about that night.

"No, I really need to get back to my mother."

"Oh, okay, well, maybe we can set up something?" As I stared into his mesmerizing eyes, a deep, searing pain of guilt radiated through my body. There was something about looking up at Brett that brought back all the pain of Michael. Clearly, I was not ready, nor was I sure I wanted to, move on from Michael. It had all been exciting to pretend for a moment my life was not a complete wreck, that the quicksand had not grabbed hold of me, but that was not reality. In reality, I was marked for death. No point in taking Brett down with me.

"I'm sorry, I really have to go." Walking away, I could feel his gaze following me. The pull to turn around was strong, but I forced my body forward. There was nothing good that could come of turning around. Forward was my only option.

My mother's moments of lucidity seemed to fade fast over the next two weeks. I had realized upon my arrival that she was frequently forgetting things, but now I was aware of how often she seemed confused or lost. Now, she was no longer just forgetting things, or generally what she was doing, but she was forgetting basic abilities. Her functionality was steadily declining, making my job of taking care of her increasingly difficult. The cleaning of the house was endless, replacing all the items my mother continued to annoyingly shuffle around—the food and empty drink cups she would leave out, the laundry, the cooking. On top of all that, I was starting to realize I was going to have to treat her like a small child. Tell her to get dressed, bathe, eat—except this mother-child was very obstinate. I had to keep up with all of this while helping her maintain a steady buzz.

I pushed open the door with my foot, the drinks clinking in my hands. *Might as well join her.* The screen door swung shut loudly, just in time for me to watch my mother wander off in the fields. *Damn!*

"Mama," I yelled after her, quickly putting the glasses down on the small table between the rocking chairs.

"Mama, I have your drink," I called after her like a puppy. *Come get a treat.* She kept walking toward the woods. *Oh, great!*

Running out into the fields, I caught up to her just before she disappeared into the woods. "Mama," I yelled, grabbing her by the shoulders. "What are you doing?"

"Oh, hello. Who are you?" Her eyes were glazed over, no reaction at all on her face. She honestly didn't know who I was. *Is that the disease? Or did God finally answer my prayers?*

"Oh, you have such pretty eyes. I feel like I know you." *What is happening?*

"Mama, it's me." Still nothing. "I'm your daughter, Norah." Her face slowly changed, contorting into a deep frown, showing her true contempt. For a moment there, I thought she actually forgot she hated me .... That was wishful thinking.

"It's okay, Mama. I have your drink ready."

"Well, it's about damn time." She shoved me, probably as hard as she could, but I barely felt it, as she made her way back to the porch.

Rocking gently, I stared at my mother over the rim of my glass, the coolness brushing against my lips, wondering just what was happening. Caroline had joked that "you can't forget mean," but for a brief moment, I had actually seen a different person out there in the fields. Her big doe-brown eyes gazed up at me as if I were a complete stranger, not the daughter who filled her with hatred. Of course, now she had that look back on her face, the one of pure disgust, as she so often had unless she was passed out drunk or flirting.

"Drink," she barked. She wouldn't even look at me, just held the glass out for me to take and do my duty. I had been doing my duty since I got here, and frankly, I was getting pretty tired of dealing with her being so rude all the time.

"Go get it yourself." My own glass still had a few sips, so I would at least finish my own first.

"You ungrateful little ..." There was so much more to what she was going to say, but I stopped her dead in her tracks.

"Listen, Mama, just shut up. No one is listening to you." Wrong thing to say.

"You get out right now! I mean it!"

She threw her glass down, maneuvering her body toward my own, clasping her cold fingers around my forearm in an attempt to get me to leave by force. Her lack of strength was comical.

"What are you laughing at?"

"You! I'm laughing at you, Mama."

"Just get out of my house." With that, she released me and stormed back inside.

Once I was sure she was not coming back out, I allowed the tears to escape, gliding down my chilled skin. They burned against my cheeks as the tea burned my throat. Each moment, each day, I could feel myself slowly fading away as my mind became lost in relentless thoughts of my impending, dreadful future.

I had refused to allow myself to think of Brett these last days, knowing that the raw pain of my still-open wounds was probably never going to heal. This, coupled with my mother's growing aggressive annoyance, solidified the fact that my life had become complete shit. There was no denying the storm that was headed my way. Nor was there any way to get out of its path.

Part Three: Landfall

The low, dark clouds swell as they unroll on the horizon like a thick gray blanket. The winds are gone as the storm pulls all the energy, generating an unimaginable force. Time has run out. There is nowhere to go now, no place that the hurricane cannot reach. The stillness in the air creates a false sense of calm, a frozen moment of hope, just before the storm unleashes its destruction.

Suddenly, you are surrounded. The winds surge, challenging the Earth's hold on the ground, pulling everything till it breaks free, lost to the storm. A thick sheet of rain conceals the world, blinding you to what is happening. The silence breaks—howling sounds of wind, giants stomping the Earth as trees fall, glass shattering, and a thunder that stops your heart. Your body braces for impact, knowing it cannot take the force; it will not survive ... but your body, unlike your mind, often refuses to give up even against insurmountable odds.

Shelter is your only option at this point. The sun disappears, and darkness takes over. The moment a hurricane makes landfall, all is lost.

Chapter Nineteen
Present Day

"Norah." The sound of his voice made my breathing stop, stirring up feelings that caused my heart to swell with love yet ache with grief. The blood drained from my body, a feeling of being weightless, as I realized who was on the other line. *We were connected*, even if it was only a phone call.

"Norah, please," he said again. "Talk to me."

Every logical molecule in my brain told me to hang up the phone, my hand quivering as I gripped the cold plastic. With the other, I wrapped a tight tourniquet around my finger with the long curling cord that connected to the base. The kitchen was eerily silent at that moment, time freezing, as I stood there, unable to speak.

"Norah, it's Michael. Please just let me know you are okay." There was an urgency to his voice, a need I refused to allow myself to believe was there. He had thrown me away, abandoned me when I needed him most, so it was hard to believe that he still cared about my wellbeing. *Why is he really calling?* The question gnawed at my mind, forcing me to finally yield and respond.

"I'm fine." My voice was steady, even-toned, but my entire body betrayed my true feelings, shaking violently as I waited for his response.

So many emotions threatened to explode. *Pain*—hearing his voice brought back memories of losing the child, my marriage, and my life. *Anger*—that he changed the rules, that he cheated and ruined us. *Sadness*—that we were only connected by a phone call and not physically together. *Fear*—that he was going to find out what my life was really like these days. Then there was a very small part of me that felt the *excitement*—he'd called. *Maybe he changed his mind?*

"Norah," he breathed relief into the phone as that bit of excitement grew. "Why are you there?"

The fear took first place in my emotional lineup, unsure of how to even articulate what had happened in the last six months. I could not fathom that there was even a place in my current world to acknowledge the life I once had with my ex-husband. Just the agony his voice brought back was unbearable. *Can I really be honest with him?* The truth weighed heavy as I considered what to reveal.

"My mother is sick." That was the simplest form of the truth.

"Why are you there?" he asked again. *Sadness.* Suddenly, I needed to feel his touch, to have his arms wrap around me, as they always did, naturally taming the storm that raged just under the surface. My throat tightened, silent tears cascading down my burning, flushed cheeks.

"Why do you think, Michael?" The lump in my throat burst as I said his name.

There was a deep gush of wind through the phone, a long, drawn-out sigh that seemed to be filled with everything we could never say to each other.

"Why are you doing this to yourself?" he asked, his words attempting to navigate through the sea of emotions.

"I had no other choice." I could also see him standing before me, his face drawn into a deep frown, lines barely visible through an overgrown stubble of despair as he pulled his fingers through his thick, dark hair in mental exhaustion. Even though it had been months since I'd seen him, suddenly my mind could conjure his every feature and mannerism.

"I am so sorry for that, Norah."

Anger. Closing the dam, the tears halted immediately. I vigorously wiped the reminiscence from my cheeks. He'd said *sorry* many times; the words had lost their true meaning. Just hearing them now brought back his insincerity, betrayal ... My excitement died. He would never want me back, never regret his decision, because he never thought he was in the wrong.

"What do you want?"

"I just wanted to make sure you are okay."

"I'm okay."

"Somehow, I don't believe you."

"Luckily, it's not your concern anymore." Pulling the phone from my ear, I was just about to slam it down on the base, but his voice called to me, as flies are drawn to a fly trap, the light too alluring to ignore. "What do you want from me?"

"Why didn't you call me?" Now there's an idea. *Why didn't I call him?* I mentally started making a list of all the reasons I would not have called my cheating ex-husband. "You know I will always be there for you."

"No, Michael. You will not always be there for me."

"Oh, come on, Norah, you know that I still care for you. I just needed—" He stopped short, knowing the words would rip through my heart.

"I can't do this." My energy was draining, the feeling of losing our child crashing against my body. His words battered against me, beckoning me to yield.

"Tell me what you need." His tone was soft, as if he would actually give me whatever I needed. I needed him. *Is he willing to give me that?*

You. That was what I wanted to say as the tears pushed against the dam. My chest tightened as I forced myself not to cry, as a bee refuses to sting, knowing it will kill them, no matter how deep the threat.

"Nothing from you." Silently, I gasped out into the chilled air, my hot breath releasing what my voice held inside. My pride was too deep to let him know the true despair of my life. I would not allow him to realize that he had been the only true possession of worth.

"Norah, please—is it money?"

While money was an issue, one not to be ignored much longer, I could not bring myself to reveal my need, not to him. When we were together, there had been this deep interdependence between us, but it shifted the moment he told me about his affair. It was the realization that he did not need me, only I needed him. This conversation was a painful reminder.

"Why did you call?"

"I needed to talk to you." He paused, the unsaid words trapped in the space between us, delicately waiting to be said as I desperately grasped for them, eager to know. It felt as though he was about to say exactly what I needed him to say: *come home.*

"I just wanted you to hear this from me. Claire is pregnant."

Direct hit.

His words landed like a hurricane, ripping every piece of me apart, flooding my lungs, pulling my legs out from underneath my body, causing it to collapse onto the floor. I reached for the solid ground, grasping for anything that could hold me down, keep me from being pulled into the darkness of the storm, but there was nothing.

The sound invaded the house, the dull tone of the fallen phone, but there was no one there to hear its cry. *I was gone ...*

After that call from Michael, I pulled down the one bottle of wine I had purchased last time at the liquor store *(just in case Caroline stopped by again)* and poured a full glass, not a wine glass. For the first time in my entire life, I wanted to drink to forget.

Within thirty minutes, my hot cheek was pressed against the cold, hard countertop, staring into the glass as I watched the final drop slowly roll down the bottle. The entire wine bottle just did not seem enough on this particular night. *Time to switch to vodka.*

Reaching above the fridge, I found the half-empty handle of vodka and a pack of cigarettes, which I had purchased for my mother. The image of Michael with that woman and their child haunted me, even after an entire bottle of wine. The alcohol was like pouring gasoline on the fire. With each sip, my mind grew darker. My thoughts went from seeing Michael's happy family to wishing something horrible would happen to them. Of course, I had no luck with these types of thoughts, especially since my mother remained alive.

The phone's distant hum penetrated the emptiness, forcing my eyes to flicker, as a sharp pain vibrated through my mind. I knew it was daytime, a small sliver of light coming under the door. With nothing to hold on to, the storm pulled me apart. I was now more lost and beaten than ever, my body refusing to move as my mind attempted to convince it to pull up off the cold tiled bathroom floor. My arms were too weak, my face falling back onto the tile. There was no use in trying.

I could smell the liquor oozing out of my skin, feel the dehydration pulsing through my head. I was hungover, having drunk away all memories except the ones I wanted to forget the most.

Finally, my mind could not take the numbing tone of the phone. My body, mustering all its strength, pulled my sore limbs from the floor. Grabbing the door handle, my head started to spin as I attempted to walk. This was a horrible moment; I had never been this hungover in my life. In the light of day, the drinking had only made things worse.

Once I replaced the phone onto its base, it started to ring nonstop. No amount of lifting and slamming it back down deterred him from calling, so on the second day, I violently pulled the phone from the wall and threw it out onto the yard. Immediately, my purse started to buzz. My cellphone glowed as I dug through pens, candy, and manilla folders. *Thirty messages.* I couldn't bear to listen to them. To hear his voice over and over again apologizing, I was sure, as he always did. He was perpetually sorry, which honestly took the value out of all of them. Even through my drunken haze of a hangover, I knew I would never talk to Michael again. There had been a small part of me that thought we could reconcile, a hope snuffed out by one phone call.

Pulling the vodka down from the top of the fridge, I poured the poisonous clear liquid over three blocks of ice. Vodka straight up, my new drink of choice. The call from Michael had opened the flood gates, the vodka now rushing over me every minute in an effort to release the pressure from the broken dam that was Michael.

"What is that noise?" my mother's voice barked annoyingly, like a dog, nonstop in the background of my life now. She began to search the area, attempting to locate the humming sound. My cellphone vibrated and danced on top of the counter, threatening to take out my drink at any moment. A part of me knew I needed to turn it off, stow it away somewhere in hiding, but I couldn't quite let go of seeing his name flash across the screen over and over again. The phone went black; the sound stopped.

"It's nothing. See, it stopped now." My mother seemed to accept this answer and returned to her chair, drink in hand.

The phone lit up again, pulsating against the laminate countertop, his name scrolling across the top. *Don't answer it ... don't answer it.* So instead of answering, I decided it might be better to listen to the messages. *Mistake.*

"Norah, please call me back. I am so very sorry ..." He let out a deep, exasperated sigh into the phone. "I thought—no, that's the wrong word. I hoped you would understand. You knew I wanted this. Is it crazy to think you would be happy for me?" Another pause, as if the voicemail would answer back. "You are right; that was wrong of me. It is too much to ask." Even over voicemail, I could see him anxiously pacing the living room as he always did in uncomfortable situations.

"Will you please call me back? Tell me what I can do to help you. I will do anything. I still care about you ..." There was more, but I slammed my finger down on the red end button. Gripping the phone as tightly as I could, I wanted to crush it, destroy everything about Michael.

The phone glowed again. *Why does he keep calling?* How many times would he say sorry ... again! How many times would he try to justify his actions ... again! I couldn't take it anymore; the phone had to go.

Pulling a large wooden meat tenderizer from the kitchen drawer, I slammed it down on the phone. Immediately, the light went out. The phone was black, the screen shattered. That was not enough, though, not in that moment. I raised the tenderizer over and over again, bringing it down as hard as I could each time.

"What is going on here?" My mother stood in the kitchen doorway, her drink a crystalized extension of her arm.

"Nothing, Mama. Just please go away." My heart was racing, tears streaming down my face. I couldn't deal with her right now.

"I need another drink."

"Oh, really? That's hilarious." My anger fueled an evil laugh. "You always need a drink. It's a wonder you are even still alive. Tell me something. How did you actually survive without me?"

"You ungrateful, little ..."

"Wow, that's a new one! Never heard that before. How can you forget to bathe but not all the horrible things you think of me?"

"Well, that part is easy." Her eyes narrowed, lips curling downward, pulling her entire face into a hateful stare aimed directly at me.

"What did I ever do to you, Mama?"

I desperately wanted her answer, but she knew that. Throughout my entire childhood with this woman, I asked, begged for the reason, but she never gave me one. Even now, she turned and walked away, leaving a fresh, gaping hole in my heart.

Chapter Twenty
Little Girl

The little girl covered her ears, clasping them so tightly that they burned, but she couldn't bear to remove them. Muffled screams radiated through the small two-story house. Like thunder cracking in a storm, she heard him beating her mother. Over and over again, the thunder pounded through the night. Her mother's voice pleaded with him and screamed out for someone to save her. The little girl wanted to run to her mother, save her, but she feared him.

She could not understand it, but the little girl knew deep down that her mother loved her, even though she hurt her sometimes. She knew her mother had fits of anger, the little girl often upsetting her, but it was not her mother's fault. Her mother was trapped, that much she knew. She never left this place, always drinking and crying when he was gone, which was most of the time. There was a part of the little girl that knew her mother would never truly harm her, but *he* would. Even as a little girl, she knew he was evil.

Suddenly, her mother's screams stopped. Large footsteps lumbered across the wooden floorboards, the door swinging open then slamming shut as he left, or so she thought. Silently, she crept down the stairs, avoiding the creaky boards, moving like a cat on the prowl. Without stepping down off the last step, she leaned over and gently tapped the swinging door into the kitchen. A flash of horror, her mother's broken, bloody, motionless body sprawled out across the tile floor.

She waited, listened, but it was silent. Slowly, her toes grazed the floor, then her entire foot. The boards groaned under her weight, causing her to pause, wait ... listen. Then, when she was sure it was safe, she made her way quietly into the kitchen. Leaning down, she gently touched her mother's hair, her face already swelling, her dark, olive skin fading into a deep purple. She wanted so desperately to save her but was unsure how she could ever help. All she could do was lie with her. She curled her tiny cold body next to her mother on the tiled floor.

"Please, save us ..." the little girl whispered out into nothingness. She wasn't sure who she was asking to save her ... anyone would do.

"What are you doing?" Her mother jerked and pulled away from the little girl, pushing her off her body, forcing herself to get up off the floor. "Go back to bed, now!"

The little girl didn't know what she did wrong as she ran back to her room, tears sliding down her face. She was just trying to save her; she just wanted to be loved by her mother. As she ran back to her room, she could hear her mother crying in the kitchen. Then his steps returned, the crackling swing of the screen door as he ripped it open, then the slow, rhythmic beats as it calmed back into place. *He was back.* The little girl trembled in fear; her heart suddenly feeling as if it could push itself out of her body.

"No, please, I'm sorry," she heard her mother begging. Without thinking, suddenly she found herself running down the stairs into the kitchen to see the man's arm raised as her mother cowered behind him. She had to stop him; that was all she could think about in that moment. *Save my mother.* The little girl reached out, attempting to grab his large muscular arm, but failed.

She pulled at his tattered shirt and screamed, "No! Stop! Don't hurt her."

The man slammed her mother's head down hard on the counter, and she fell to the floor, limp. The little girl's eyes grew wide with horror, for her mother must be dead. Slowly, he raised from the floor, the force of his throw pushing him to his knees. The little girl could not stop shaking, her body fearing what he would do next. Her heart tightened, muscles tensed, as he moved toward her. Her mind froze, but her body reacted as her feet took over, running up the stairs, escaping back up into her closet. A familiar hiding spot. Nestling deep in between her dresses, she tried to become as small as possible as she whispered a silent prayer to disappear.

His weight flexed the boards beneath her feet, his shadow passing underneath the crack in her door, threatening to find her at any moment. Squeezing her eyes shut, she prayed harder, pulling her knees as close to her body as physically possible. She held her breath.

"Come out, come out wherever you are ..." he hissed. Suddenly, the doors to her closet swung open, revealing her huddled, shaking body in the corner. Her face was caked with tears as he glared down at her, the shadow of his large gut pressing upon her small fragile body. Suddenly, he reached down and pulled her hard by her hair.

"No," she screamed, thrashing her legs against the man, her own hands attempting to remove him from her hair. She screamed over and over again, but he never let her go, dragging her over to the bed, her feet off the floor. She could feel each hair on her head starting to pull from its root; any moment they would release, and she would fall to the floor.

Then, just as her feet reached the floor, scrapping for stability, he slapped her hard across the face. The pain reverberated through her entire head, the corners of her eyes going black. Throwing her onto the bed, he crawled on top of her, pinning her down by her arms so she couldn't fight back. The weight of his massive body was crushing, pushing her deeper and deeper down into the bed. She was just a little girl.

"Don't you ever try that again, or next time it will be you." He spat the words into her face, the tobacco juice oozing from his open mouth and down his prickly chin. His smell of cigarettes, alcohol, and sweat engulfed her, forcing bile to rise in her stomach, but she forced it down with all her might, knowing that if she dared to vomit, he would surely kill her on the spot. Her body was still twitching, attempting escape no matter how much her mind was screaming at it to stop. She had no idea what he would do next, the fear a tidal wave burning in her lungs, preventing her from breathing.

He leaned closer, inches from her face as his forehead released a small drop of sweat, which dropped against her porcelain skin, splashing in all directions. But he did not stop there. He pushed himself over more, his bare, hairy gut now against her own clammy skin. His face glided inches above her as he pushed his nose into her hair, taking a long, aroused sniff. She could feel a pulse against her bare legs as everything started to go black, her body now motionless as she realized what he wanted most. Terrified tears burned in her eyes, which refused to close.

Then, suddenly, he released her. A single breath caught in her lungs as the waters receded, the realization settling in that he was not going to rape her as she feared. The burn against her swollen cheek started to ignite a fire through her skin, as the events of what just happened started to take hold in her mind.

That was the first time.

But that's the thing about doing something once, especially for an addict. Once the door is opened, it can never be closed.

Chapter Twenty-One
Present Day

Where is the damn coffee ... Each cabinet, once filled with food from my initial grocery excursion, was now empty. Since the call from Michael, everything had gone downhill all too quickly, including my appearance. Drinking had become a daily pastime, along with screaming at my mother. Always in response to her initial outburst of course. No matter how much I did not want to show my swollen, clammy face in town, I had to go grocery shopping. I also needed coffee ... and vodka.

The liquor store was the obvious first choice at nine o'clock in the morning on Tuesday. Pulling the cap over my unwashed, identifiable hair, and placing some dark glasses on my sunken eyes, I attempted to disguise myself as much as physically possible. It didn't work.

Pushing on the glass door repeatedly, unwilling to accept that the liquor store was closed at this totally acceptable time to be buying alcohol in the morning, I failed to notice him walking down the street.

"Norah?" My head hit the glass door, a deep groan escaping from my lungs as I realized the situation I had found myself in. Brett—*again.* He was the last person I wanted to see after being hit by a Mack truck named Michael.

"Are you okay?"

"Yep." If I could have one superpower, it would be invisibility right now, but no such luck. "Just out for some light grocery shopping."

"At the liquor store?"

"You've met my mother, right?" I turned, glaring up at him as the sun radiated around his silhouette, making him appear godly. Those feelings I had initially had been buried, alive at first but now, after all this time, dead. Drinking to forget had burned any last soft edges I might have possessed towards Brett. The match lit by Michael. I couldn't look at him without seeing and feeling the painful stab of my opened wounds

"Yes, I believe I have." His smile was disarming, which I loathed.

"They should open up in about an hour. Do you want to go get a coffee while you wait?" *Yes ... no.*

"I should probably head on to the grocery store. My mother can really get into a mess if left alone too long."

He nodded in agreement. "Just one cup?"

I was not going to have coffee with Brett. I was going to go to the grocery store, ignore everything about my life, go home, and continue to drink away any real sense of understanding over my dire life situation. But for some reason, I followed Brett across the street to the coffee shop. Maybe I was trying to resurrect the dead, because that always ends well.

"Two black cups," he ordered as we took a small table in the back. Reluctantly, I removed my glasses, but not the cap. "How are things going with your mother?"

"Fine." Glad to see he'd decided to just jump right into it. The moment I took the seat, saw the look on his face when I removed the glasses, I knew this was a bad decision.

"Yeah, I don't believe you."

"That bad?" It had been some time since I looked at myself in the mirror, unable to face what I was becoming, so I wasn't really sure how bad it had actually gotten in the last three weeks.

"It's understandable. Taking care of a parent can be difficult."

"You have no idea." Immediately, I saw my mistake all over his face. My mind was blurry, hungover, and I'd failed to realize the true impact of my words. "I'm so sorry, I didn't mean ..." I wasn't sure what I didn't mean, or meant, only that I wish I hadn't said it.

"I'm probably the one person who does understand. My father may not be your mother, but they are both our parents. They are both people we love."

"That is where you are wrong."

"You may think you don't love your mother, but deep down you do."

"No, I do not." His blue eyes flared in disbelief. "You have no idea what she did to me," I added defensively. No one could ever comprehend the true depth of my mother's hatred and abuse.

"I can't even begin to imagine what that horrible woman put you through." Suddenly, I wanted to wrap my arms around Brett and cry endlessly into his shoulder. His words bridged a long, dredged canyon across my heart. "But I find it hard to believe that you would be here, doing all this for her, if you didn't—somewhere,

119

deep down—have feelings of compassion for her." The feeling was gone. Lost now, as I realized his words were filled with as much *sorry* as Michael's had been all those times. No one could ever understand; that was my punishment.

"I should go. I have a lot to get done."

"Norah, I didn't mean to upset you. I just ..." His lips curled into a pity-filled smile as his eyes glazed over with sorrow. "It's just that ..." He pulled his hands up onto the table as if wanting me to hold them. A part of me needed to grasp on to something steady, ride out this storm in the shelter of Brett's arms, but just as I felt myself leaning toward him, he pulled them away. "I just think you need help."

Help. My logical mind understood completely that I did, in fact, need help. I needed help getting my life back together and disposing of my mother into a long-term living care facility. But that was not the help to which he was referring. No, he meant mental help. Or maybe rehab help. Either way, he wasn't really offering the type of help I needed, and I definitely didn't want it.

"I'm fine."

"Norah," he whispered as I started to walk away, anger and shame blending together to create a toxic black paint over my life. "If you ever need anything ..."

His words faded into the distance as I raced from the store, regrettably tripping over every chair pushed out into the aisle. It was an empty offer, one given out of pity and guilt. I realized that the one person who had made me feel again, if only for a moment over coffee, was now never going to look at me the same way. If there was any piece left of my heart, it was now gone.

Chapter Twenty-Two
Mother

The woman stared at the little girl, her bouncing curls swaying in the slight breeze of the fall wind, emitting playful sounds as she cuddled the small broken doll in her hands. She was so happy with that doll, which she'd found in a box in the closet. It had been her doll, her only friend as a child. The left side of the doll's glass face had chipped, now missing an entire piece, including some of the blue eye. She was damaged, but the little girl didn't care.

Instinctively, the woman touched the side of her face, the deep-purple bruise in the same place as the doll's. She couldn't help but feel like the glass doll—broken, fragile, trapped. Last night, she thought she could leave, escape the man's abuse, if only for an evening. She did not have grand hopes of being able to leave forever, survive with her daughter on her own. That would be impossible. There was nowhere to go. No money. No hope. She just wanted one night.

She had been supplying him with drinks all evening, attempting to get him to pass out earlier than normal. But as the sun bled across the sky, she could see it in his eyes. He was on to her, lying in wait for the opportunity.

"Where do you think you are going?" His words were slurred, but she understood.

"Nowhere." She pulled a glass down from the cabinet and started to fill it with vodka. This would convince him she planned to stay in tonight. "Where would I go?"

"Ha! Exactly. Where would you go? They don't accept your kind in this town. There is nowhere you can go."

His words were a weight on her shoulders, always pulling her back to this place, keeping her imprisoned in this hell. She had failed to think about the fact that surely someone would tell him they saw her out. She stood out like a sore thumb in this prominently backwoods, rural white town with her dark skin and frizzy hair.

"You are lucky I made a decent woman out of you."

Marrying him was supposed to legitimize her, but she never knew why he had agreed to the marriage. She knew now.

"No one would even care if ..." He licked his swollen lips, a dark film draping over his eyes. In that moment, she realized he intended to kill her. Without thinking, she attempted to run, but he caught her mid stride. It was stupid; she never should've tried.

Suddenly, she felt a soft hand on her shoulder, her daughter's voice echoed through her mind. For a brief moment, she thought it was an angel, that death had finally taken her from this horrible life, but then she realized. Quickly pushing back from her daughter, fear consuming her every move, she screamed at the little girl. If he found her here, he would hurt her, and she couldn't stop him.

She would never forget the look her daughter gave her that night, the fear and pain that filled her small doe eyes. It was the one thing she had passed along to her daughter. Otherwise, she got her father's light skin and curly black hair. Seeing that look reflected in her daughter felt like staring into a mirror, one she wanted to shatter into a million pieces. She never wanted to be this person, but life was cruel. Her daughter needed to know ... then she heard the heavy, drunken steps on the porch.

Just before the world went black, she saw her little girl, a flash of a shadow behind the man. Maybe they would meet again in heaven, because he would surely kill them both tonight.

Chapter Twenty-Three
Present Day

It had become Groundhog Day in this place, the same thing, same day, over and over again. Sometimes, I said things just to make it different, even bait my mother to do something. Leaving the house was no longer an option, because I couldn't bear to run into Brett again, or anyone for that matter. Surely they would notice. Notice my fragile body, the alcohol on my breath at the crack of dawn, or worst of all, the blackness in my eyes. My own reflection had become unrecognizable, ghost-like, a shallow husk of what I once was.

This particular day I spent being thoroughly amused by my mother's ramblings and inability to find the yellow-orange tabby that died more than twenty-five years ago, but I failed to mention that to her. It was just too funny watching her toss old, dusty pillows into the air, slowly, painfully crouching down to look under the couch, chair, and table as she called, "Pumpkin!" It was like watching a game show where you know the person is too stupid to win. Without television, this was the next best thing. Eventually, she gave up and barked for dinner.

Food was dwindling these days, especially since my credit card had been declined last week at the grocery store. Never thought I'd be fifty dollars in at the Piggly Wiggly and unable to pay up—a *new low*. It would be another week before my mother's welfare check came in the mail, so I had to work with a few cans of soup, half a bag of coffee, three rotten bananas, flour, six eggs, and the last sip of milk. I pulled one can of soup from the cabinet; we would have to split it tonight.

"This soup is cold. How could you serve me cold soup, you stupid ..." I stopped listening, as she would continue to go on calling me every terrible thing she could think of. While I had tempered the physical abuse this time, that did not stop the verbal assaults. The ability to ignore my mother was like riding a bike; you never really forget how to do it. Being drunk was helpful as well.

"Are you listening to me?" *No, of course not. Who would listen to you?*

"Yes, Mama. Would you like me to heat it up?"

"Mama? I'm not your mother. You really are stupid. How did you get so stupid?" *Stop listening. Just ignore her. Nothing she says is worth hearing.*

The steam of the soup dissipated, turning lukewarm in the time it took me to convince my mother to sit down and eat. I could have taken a few minutes to reheat, but then I risked her getting up and starting the process all over again.

"Well, are you going to heat this shit up?" Her face bent into a scowl, eyes narrowing in on me, like a challenger inciting a battle.

I refused to give her the satisfaction, so I spooned the cold soup into my mouth. Our eyes locked in defiance. This was my life now.

The last of the coffee steamed over the top of my mug as I cooled it with slow, shallow breaths. Sitting at the desk built into the kitchen, I was going through the mail, pulling out the welfare check before my mother could get her hands on it, and putting together a budget so we could survive till the next one. I heard my mother coming down the hall, her left foot dragging slower than her right these days, then pushing the swinging door into the kitchen. I didn't initially look up, not wanting to engage, but from the corner of my eye, I got a glimpse.

"Mama, go put some clothes on." Immediately, I diverted my eyes, pulling my hand to cover my peripheral vision. That was not what I wanted to see.

She just stood there as if everything was completely normal, clearly not registering the cool breeze against her bare skin.

"What are you talking about?"

Keeping my eyes covered, I slowly inched toward the stove, pulling the kitchen towel from the handle, then dangling it out, enticing the bull. She did not take the bait, so I shuffled my feet, on guard for her to charge at any moment, and attempted to use the small green cloth to cover her breast and well ... the other part. Not to be mentioned or seen—*ever*!

"Stop that," she demanded, pushing the cloth away. *No, look away!*

"No, you need to put clothes on." She stared at me blankly as I labored to keep my eyes high. "Clothes." I gestured toward my own clothes, hopeful the memory of clothing would come back to her.

"Oh, shit." Finally, the light bulb. "Well, what the hell? I don't have any clean clothes. What do you expect me to do?" And she was back, guns blazing.

"I promise I will wash today, but please, for the love of God, go put something, anything, on." She turned, proud as ever, and marched her naked ass back to the bedroom. *Really?* Only my mother would be unruffled by this encounter.

My mother was tucked into her flower, smelled-worse-than-I-cared-to-admit armchair, drink in hand, as I made my way back to her bedroom. I decided to go in stealth style, unnoticed by my mother for fear she would prevent me from gathering up her clothes. I was not about to let another naked incident happen. From now on, I would ensure she had clean clothes *daily.*

The first time I walked into her room, the clothes a carpet on the floor, I knew I would have to take charge of the laundry duties. However, since Michael's call, I had failed at almost everything. The cleaned house was now dirty again, along with all her clothes apparently. This was a wakeup call to get back on top of things. That, and the third night of cold soup.

The always-closed door finally being opened released a sour, decaying smell, revealing the truth behind what was really happening with my mother. Reluctantly, I started to make my way through the room, picking up clothes covered with stains and cigarette holes, underwear soured in urine. Gagging the entire time, I filled the laundry basket, conceding that it would take numerous loads to get through this mess. This was going to take days.

In my drunken haze, I had failed to notice the lingering stench in the house, one that I had assumed was due to it continually being dirty no matter how much I cleaned, but after being in my mother's room, I realized she was the culprit. The alcohol had numbed my olfactory senses, along with many others, but the moment I stepped into her bedroom, there was no more denying it.

She was not bathing. At first, I thought it was passive-aggressive behavior; however, after watching her closely, I noticed she often would walk into the bathroom and just stand there, unsure of what to do. She would emerge from the bathroom, change her clothes, and go about her day as if she had taken a bath.

It was another full day before I conceded to the fact that I would have to be the one to bathe my own mother. Sure, mothers did this for their children every day, but no one should ever have to see their mother naked, let alone bathe her. I had illusions that I could do it with my eyes closed, or that once I got her started, she would remember and bellow at me to leave. Or best yet, that she would be so averse to having me give her a bath she would finally just do it herself.

The first time was difficult, to say the least.

"Mama, would you like some help?" She was just standing there, her sheer white cotton nightgown hanging loose on her shoulders, staring at the bathtub. "Mama?" I questioned again, this time louder so she would hear.

"I can do it myself," she snapped back, but made no movement to undress.

"Clearly, you cannot," I sneered. "You haven't bathed in days. You smell horrible."

"Get out!" she screamed, attempting to push me away, but she was too weak. "Get out!"

I left.

A few minutes later, I returned. She was still standing there. Taking a chance, I began running the bath water.

"Can I help you?" She did not answer, so I gently reached for the sleeve of her nightgown. She flinched. I held back, waiting to see if she would do it herself, but she did not, so I tried again. This time, she allowed me to slowly undress her, much to my dismay. Slowly, I reached down to her ankles, the deep-blue veins like a roadmap across her legs, and lifted the nightgown till I got to her chest. She did not raise her arms, so with one hand still on the clothing, I gently raised her right arm with the other. She did the left on her own, and I pulled it over her head. Thankfully, we did not speak.

Ushering her by her shoulders, I led her to the edge of the tub. On her own, she stepped into the warm bath and slowly lowered herself into the soapy water. I was thankful that the water was murky and covered most of her body. She leaned her head back, resting it on an old, suction-cupped pad on the tub. She fit perfectly, her toes just touching the faucet.

"Mama." I touched her arm, and she moved into a sitting position, her knees pulled to her chest as if she had allowed someone to bathe her before.

I moved the washcloth over her pale, fragile body. At that moment, I didn't see my mother, but a very damaged woman. Her collarbone was oddly visible, shoulders bony from lack of eating, and hair knotted underneath her neck, making it very difficult to run my fingers through with shampoo. *This broken, dying woman is my mother.*

Tears started to fall down my cheeks. Not tears for my mother, but more for myself. I felt as if I were looking into my own future, but with no one to care for me. Suddenly, I realized just how quickly she was deteriorating. How neglected she appeared. *Was that really going to be me?*

Silently, I cried as I washed this shell of a woman who was once my abuser ... *my mother.* By the hunch of her shoulders and the dazed expression on her face, I should have noticed the decline, but it was steady, not like I thought it would be. I thought one day she would just forget, be gone. But now I realized that it was more like a dandelion in the wind, tiny pieces falling off little by little, taken away, never to return.

I was losing my mother ... *I was losing myself.*

We were becoming one in the same.

My mother was losing her memories, her ability to function, and I couldn't help but feel the same way. My memories were there, blazing through every day no matter how many vodka drinks I made, but my ability to function was impaired by drinking. Instead of forgetful, I had become neglectful. The small mundane tasks that had occupied my mind, distracting me from my pain and depression, had been replaced with alcohol-induced comas. Even though I realized what I was doing, I couldn't stop.

Chapter Twenty-Four
Little Girl

The little girl stared at her mother, the deep lines around her mouth as the corners of her lips sagged toward the ground, the flecks of silver in her dark hair that shimmered in the cascading sunlight through the dusty windows of the living room, and the slow rise and fall of her protruding collarbone as she breathed deeply, lost in sleep.

Her mother's delicate, long fingers curled around the short clear glass filled with a brown liquid that smelled like smoke. It was all the little girl saw her mother drinking since that night the man smashed her head into the floor. Even now, the little girl could not get the image to leave her nightmares.

Suddenly, her mother's fingers slipped, and the glass fell from her hand, landing on the carpet, the brown liquid immediately staining the gray fibers. The little girl knew her mother would be angry, so she rushed to the kitchen for a towel to clean the mess. She was in such a rush she didn't notice the man standing in the porch doorway.

Just as she turned, having pulled the towel from the stove handle, his large shadow caught her eye. Her body froze, fear consuming every nerve. Gradually, he opened the screen porch door, the hinges squealing like a pig.

"Where is your mama, little girl?" He pulled at his pants, adjusting his belt as he lumbered into the room. His body was the width of the galley-shaped kitchen. Her only escape was deeper into the house, but she knew he could catch her, find her.

"In there," she whispered, pointing a shaky, betraying finger toward the living room. From where he was standing, he could see her mother's limp arm hanging over the chair.

"Drunk again." The little girl could see the anger and disgust wash over his swollen face. He had been out all night, drinking himself, no doubt, but her mother was never allowed to be drunk. He wanted her to feel everything, suffer everything, just like he wanted the little girl to as well.

His large body stumbled forward. The girl feared he would grab her, but he pushed by her as if she were invisible. A deep sigh of relief escaped from her lungs as she realized she had been spared.

Through the shadows she could put together the pieces of the scene. The man grabbing her mother's arm, pulling her from the chair. Her mother's body hung, swaying as he slapped her across the face. Then her mother's body on the floor, the man turning away. Suddenly, she realized that she was next.

Run! Run away!

Her mind screamed at her to escape, but her body betrayed her every command. There was no doubt that he would catch her, find her, beat her, no matter what she did to evade him. In the moment right before he reached her, she thought about her mother. How could she leave her alone with him; how could she forget her? Her mother had been the only person she had, and now she was gone as well. *Lost in a drunken coma.*

Chapter Twenty-Five
Present Day

A shriek pulsated through the house, shaking the walls and causing my body to jolt and collapse to the floor. Quickly, without thinking, just knowing that something was terribly wrong, I rushed down the stairs two at a time. Surely, she had done something horrible to herself to be screaming in such a manner.

Sliding on socks around the banister, knocking my shoulder into the wall, which actually prevented me from falling down altogether, I barreled down the hallway toward her bedroom door. She let out another shriek as I pushed through the door, halting to examine the room. *What is going on?*

Trapped under the bedcovers, my mother was like the waves at the center of the hurricane, thrashing about wildly in all directions, no reason in their movements, just pure chaos.

"No, stop, stop!" Her words were muffled by the sheets as her fingers clawed at the edges. She was desperately trying to get to something.

She was having a nightmare. I sighed in relief. At least she didn't stab herself; I really didn't want to go to the ER in the middle of the night.

I leaned against the wall, sliding down slowly and pulling my knees to my chest. I would just have to wait it out, make sure she didn't actually hurt herself.

Her fears were starting to calm to just a muffled moan as she attempted to escape her demons. My head folded over into my hands. My eyes heavy, I drifted off to sleep, lulled by her soft moaning. *Some things never change.*

Suddenly, I jolted awake, my arm giving way, dropping to the floor, causing my head to slide forward and crash against my knee. A single ray of light cut through the dark room, across the floor, and up my leg. It was morning. My entire body ached, sore from sleeping against the wall, making it difficult to pull myself up. I stretched my arms, then moved to the curtains. *Time to get up, Mother.* Pulling the curtains back revealed the sun high in the sky; it was at least noon.

Turning around, fully expecting to see my mother, panic set in, as her bed was empty. *How did she get out without me noticing?*

Quickly, I made my way through the house, but she was nowhere. *Damnit, where could she be?*

As I frantically attempted to find her, I suddenly realized what was missing. My mind saw it, but I couldn't fully comprehend it ... the car. *Double damn.* Pulling my jacket off the hook to cover my skimpy pajamas, I raced into the driveway, attempting to discern which direction she'd headed. This was not good. This was, in fact, the worst-case scenario.

If only I had a phone, I could call someone, but no ... even if I could call Caroline, I could not risk her seeing what I had become. I was sure she would stage an intervention. W*hat would I say?* Then, I noticed Ms. Kay's truck sitting in the gravel drive. Crossing the yard, my bare feet trampling down her perfect blades of grass, then climbing the porch steps, I slammed my hand down over and over again on the wooden frame of the screen door till she appeared.

"What the hell?" she asked, shotgun in hand. This might have been the worst decision ever; I could've run to anyone else ... anyone!

"Oh, uh, my mama, she is missing and so is our car. If I could just borrow your car? I need to find her."

"Keys are under the visor," she offered, lowering her shotgun.

"Thank you." I raced out to her old dark-green pickup truck. Struggling with the door, the pullback making me stumble on my unsteady feet, I slid onto the torn, hot leather. It smelled like smoke and cheese, turning my stomach. The keys fell right into my hands, and only after a solid three attempts to get the truck to turn over, it finally came to life. *Thank God.*

Kicking up dirt, which clouded the rearview mirror, the truck raced down the road. I barely slowed enough to make the hard left turn, as the panic rose in my chest. She could be anywhere *with my car*! My mind raced with all the ways this could go terribly, terribly wrong. Aside from all the things that could happen, worse, she was out in public. I needed to find her and put her back into her cage, where wild, deranged animals belonged.

Finally, the town started to come into view, Bubba's Ice Cream Shop like a beacon in the distance guiding me in the right direction. Time seemed to slow as I passed the old ice cream shop, now clearly abandoned. It had once been the place to hang out after school. Of course, I only did that once in my life. The memory flashed across my mind, so real that I actually stopped in the store parking lot, expecting to find my mother.

We were standing outside Bubba's Ice Cream shop, Caroline, Mark and I, eating our ice cream, the summer air thick with humidity. The ice cream shop was a few streets over from the main street in town, the first thing I came to on my walk from the house. On this particular day, Caroline and Mark had been waiting for me. They were new friends; I did not want them to know where I lived or who I lived with.

Most of the kids from our class were there, and for a moment, I actually felt like I belonged in this place. No one had mentioned my bruises; I hid them well. I made friends at school, and my mother had managed to stay off the radar, so maybe this place would actually work out for me. Maybe in this place, I could be different.

Suddenly, out of nowhere, a car came flying across the parking lot and crashed right into the fire hydrant. Water exploded into the air like a geyser releasing pressure. All the kids rushed to feel the cool water against their hot, sticky skin. For a moment, it was like a scene from a movie, children playing in the water on a hot summer day—innocent, comforting.

"Come on!" Caroline urged, pulling against my hand, but I was frozen. I saw what the other children had failed to notice, but soon they would see the person in the car, moving slowly, stumbling from the driver's side.

She was clearly drunk, blood running down her face, feet scratching against the pavement as she attempted to get out of the car. There was a force pulling her back into the car, frustrating her as she called out curse words and yanked against her nightgown. The lace along the top of the gown, yellowed from stains, was bleeding into red as the blood faded down her face, a curtain making its final close.

No one helped her; they were too busy dancing in the streets, celebrating, as if we were all at a water park, but I knew better. I saw the woman, *my mother.* Horror filled my mind as I realized that my perfect moment was gone. Soon they would all see her, know she was my mother, and then they would know the truth.

Suddenly, the nightgown gave way, ripping from its hold, her entire body falling onto the pavement. Our eyes met, both filled with horror and rage.

"Norah, you stupid little ..."

Her words were unidentifiable to most, but I knew what she was saying, what she was calling me. *Why here? Why now?*

They all noticed now. The kids froze, watching, the water still playfully spraying in the streets. They watched as the woman screaming foul language stumbled to her feet, only her wildly fierce eyes humanlike under all the blood. For a moment, I thought about running. If I got away, disappeared, no one would realize she was my mother. She would only be the crazy lady that they would call *Carrie* after that movie where they spilled blood all over the outcast—but she would not be my mother. She could be anything but my mother.

"There you are." She pointed a long wobbly finger directly at me and started toward me ... *too late.* Caroline and Mark stepped back, their eyes glued to the terrifying woman as she floundered, like a fish out of water, toward the three of us. Her eyes remained locked on to my own, the anger so deep. *She was going to kill me.*

Suddenly I saw it, across the street, peeking behind the trees. The dirt-streaked black Altima. Seeing the car pulled me from my waking nightmare. Of course, this is where I would find the car, chastising myself for not looking here first. It was clear by her horrendous parking job she was not aware of how to drive anymore. At least she didn't run it into a fire hydrant. I would need to make sure to hide the keys from now on

From this direction, it was hidden behind a row of trees. Nothing like this could be visible to the Bible beaters in this town, so it was tucked away in the woods, only discernible by a small, broken sign that read *Outhouse.* The name was fitting considering it smelled like an outhouse—booze, piss, and cigarettes. The memory of seeing Brett in this very parking lot only a few short months ago haunted each step as I nervously looked around for his tuck.

In the short time it took me to walk from the car to the bar, I was sweating. It was noon, the winter sun never giving way to the Southern heat, but I did not dare take off my jacket to reveal my tattered, flowered pajamas.

"Howdy, Norah, how ya' been?" The bartender was a familiar siren.

I stood in the doorway, illuminating the dark, smoky room. Of course, as always, I knew the bartender, who also happened to be the owner. I was surprised he was still alive, let alone still working behind the bar. We knew each other well, considering my mother was here every day of my childhood. Oscar's was *the* restaurant in town, turned bar at night for the occasional drinker on a Friday, but the Outhouse was for the drunks.

The door swung close behind me, snuffing out the only light from the sun. Inside the few pale, yellowed light bulbs casted an eerie glow over the space. The lack of windows, which I'm sure was on purpose—otherwise, the customers might realize it was daytime—added to the ominous feel. Across the sea of puke-stained velvet pool table tops I could see the hunch of my mother's bony shoulders.

"Why the hell didn't you call me?" I sneered at the bartender.

Her body lay over the sticky wooden bar as her legs hung limp between the silver poles of the barstool. She was passed out, still in her nightgown, the lace at the bottom covered in dirt, ripped, her bare feet black on the bottom. *This is just great.*

"Your number's been disconnected." *Oh crap, I forgot about that.*

"Well, next time, maybe don't give her so much," I spit out.

That was really all I could think to say. After all, there would be no reasoning with my mother; this was basically her second home. I was surprised it took her this long to get here. She probably forgot.

"Oh, uh, here are her keys. I did make her turn them over before I agreed to the fourth drink."

He seemed so proud, as if he had done some great service. I scoffed, attempting to pull my mother up by her underarms. She moaned. Her fragile body was suddenly as heavy as a brick. Finally, I realized that there was no lifting her by myself.

"Drink?" he offered. I glared at him. How could I possibly need a drink in this moment?

"Okay, yeah."

He poured tequila into a small glass. I shot it down quickly. He poured another. This one I took in slowly, just taking small sips as I waited for my mother to regain consciousness.

Despite my recent actions, drinking was not something I did; it was a new thing I was trying out. I never wanted to be like my mother, and studies show that alcoholism can be inherited. So I hadn't been willing to take the risk, nor did I ever have anything I wanted to forget this badly. Maybe a glass of wine on a special occasion, but never did I once go to a bar and get drunk, not even in college ... until now.

"There you have it!" I slurred, throwing my wobbly hands up into the air. "My life is shit, complete and utter shit ..." A hiccup, a laugh. "Get it? Utter shit." The bartender was unamused. "You know what, though, this drinking thing ..." I paused, pointing down into the empty glass. He filled it up. "This actually does make it all better."

Suddenly, the bar door opened, and a large figure stood in the doorway.

"Did you call the cops? What the hell, Marv?"

"Yes, you need to go home, you and your mama both. We're about to open for real, and I can't have the two of you here. Not good for business."

"What? Not good for business! Are you kidding me? We *are* business to you ..."

"Okay, okay, before this gets real ugly, let's get you home." Mark wrapped an arm around my waist, supporting almost all of my body weight as I fell off the stool. Of all the people, of all the cops ... it had to be Mark.

"Thanks for the call, Marvin." He tipped his hat. *What a smug bastard.*

"Oh yeah, thanks, *Marrrv.*" Childish, but warranted in this situation, or at least that was how I felt in my state.

Mark drove us home, my mother passed out in the back seat, my drunk ass in the front. At least he didn't put me back there with her; that was generous. Really, all of this was decent of him, which I would have realized, had I been sober enough to think clearly.

"I'm sorry, Mark."

"I know, sweetheart."

"Oh god, don't call me that," I moaned. "I'm not that person anymore, clearly."

"You are Norah Crawford. Is that not correct?"

"Oh, shut up."

My head was starting to pound, feeling as if it was going to burst open and kill me on the spot. The last thing I needed was a lecture, or for Mark, of all people, to see me like this. I was never going to hear the end of this from Caroline. She would definitely come over after he told her I'd been drunk in a bar with my mother. She was, for sure, never going to believe "I'm fine" again.

"Just take me home, pretend this never happened. That is what a real friend would do."

"Not really sure about that, but I will do it."

Shit! I shot up in bed. The last memory I had was at the bar, drowning my sorrows and anger in a very potent bottle of tequila. *How did I get here?* My bed reeked of smoke and liquor, making me vomit. Rushing to the bathroom, I made it just in time to launch whatever food I had in my stomach into the toilet. *This was not good.* Slowly, I fell onto the cold bathroom floor; it felt good against my hot, sweaty skin. I just needed a minute.

That minute turned into an entire morning. The sun was just starting to disappear when I finally gained the energy to emerge from my room. Making my way down the stairs, I suddenly remembered my mother. *Damnit!*

"Mama!" I called throughout the house, frantically starting to search every room. "Mama!" The last thing I needed was to lose her *again.*

Too quickly, I pulled my body around the corner and into the kitchen. "Oh shit!" There she was, standing in the kitchen ... *cooking!*

"What are you doing?" I asked, puzzled.

She was wearing an apron—I vaguely remembered it, with alligators all over it—as she appeared to be cooking eggs in a pan.

"Making some damn dinner; I waited forever, but you never came."

She held a drink in one hand and the handle of the frying pan in the other. *She could cook and make her own drink!* Might as well join her, enjoy this fleeting moment.

My mother floated around the kitchen, moving gracefully, knowing where everything was, as she finished cooking scrambled eggs. Not a difficult thing to cook, but for her, it might as well have been crème brûlée. She had never cooked anything in her life, at least not any part of my life. I figured at some point she knew how to make her own drink, considering I was gone for over twenty years and she wasn't anywhere close to sober.

The eggs were not the worst, just bland. It was as if I was watching an old movie, my mother in an apron, cooking, then serving me a plate; it was all weirdly very 1950s. I couldn't figure out if she was accepting me into her home or if she was completely losing her mind.

My head was still pounding, the coffee and eggs providing no relief from my horrible hangover. If only the pounding would stop ... suddenly, I realized it wasn't my headache. There was an actual pounding. *The door.*

"Hey, Norah." Mark stood in the doorway, full uniform, which took me off guard.

"Hey, is everything okay?"

"Yeah, uh, I'm sorry to be the one to tell you this, but we had to tow your car last night." Oh, I forgot about that. "Well, turns out you haven't been making the payments. So, the rental agency repossessed it." He shuffled, nervous to tell me what I already knew.

"It's okay, Mark, I knew it was only a matter of time." He laughed nervously.

"They also wanted me to deliver this." He grimaced as he handed me the letter. Without opening it, I could tell it was a bill. One I wouldn't be able to pay.

"It's okay, Mark, it's not your fault. I've done all this to myself."

"Now, that's not fair."

I held up a hand, unable to receive his sympathy and excuses right now. "It's okay. I'm fine."

"You don't look fine."

"Just stop, Mark. Please, just let it go ... please." He nodded, but I could tell he didn't want to. There was no way he wasn't going to tell Caroline.

I guess that's why I opened the door without checking the next morning. I just assumed it was Caroline following up, since I was clearly not fine. But it wasn't Caroline. The moment I opened the door, I instantly regretted not looking out the window first.

"What are you doing here?" For a moment, I thought it was a dream ... or more accurately, a nightmare.

"I tried to call a million times; I thought you were dead."

"We don't have a phone anymore."

Michael nodded in understanding, his eyebrows raising in disbelief, or it might have been discontent.

"It's just that you, here, in this place; it's not good for you." He lifted a strong, firm arm, causing my breath to catch as he moved closer to my body, my mind thinking he was about to pull me closer. But then he reached out, perching it against the door frame as he leaned his head down into his arm. He genuinely appeared tortured.

Every part of me wanted to slam the door, but my hand refused to comply, clutching the handle. It was his scent of lavender and Old Spice aftershave, reaching out from his body and pulling me into him. My body leaned into his smell, his normally styled hair disheveled, jetting off into all different directions, his suit undone at the top, three buttons revealing the tip of his chest hair. I could see my fingers tracing through the hairs along his chest, feeling the way we use to touch—*stop it! Get a hold of yourself!*

"It's not your concern anymore, Michael."

"It is my concern, Norah. I never stopped caring for you as a friend." The idea of it made me laugh. After everything I lost by his hand, there was no way, not even for a second, I believed that he still cared for me. Yet he was here ... *Why?*

"Why are you here?" I reiterated, standing firm in my position. The liquor was still fresh in my mouth, and no doubt on my breath. *Great, no way he didn't smell it.*

"Norah, I swear I am just here to make sure you are okay. This is driving me crazy, thinking of you in this horrible place." He leaned farther into the doorway, running his exasperated fingers through his thick hair, a deep sigh escaping his open lips. I wanted to kiss him—*No!*

"Just stop! I can't take it anymore. Stop pretending like you care, and go back to your perfect, fulfilling life."

I couldn't help but feel that all of this was fake, especially considering that back home, his life was perfect now, absolutely perfect now that Claire was pregnant. He had betrayed us, given up on everything we had together for the possibility of this child. Now he had it all, while he left me with nothing. That was not a man who cared. And for him to be at my door, feigning concern, was my tipping point.

"I do care for you, Norah."

"No, no you don't. If you cared for me, you would've accepted the fact that I didn't want to go through losing another child. You would've accepted my choice—no, wait, *our* choice—to not have children, but instead, you betrayed me in the deepest way possible." Without realizing it, I felt the hot wet tears begin to pour down my cheeks. *Damnit.* I didn't want him to see me like this. I didn't want to cry. *Deep breaths.*

"I never meant to ..." He released his distancing arm from the door frame and attempted to step closer, as if touching me would somehow make things better. I held up a firm hand, stepping back into the house.

"Come back here, and I will shoot you." The door slammed. *Closure.*

He stood on the porch for a good five minutes, pacing back and forth just as the old tabby cat did before he died. When he finally conceded that I was not coming back out, he left. I never wanted to see him again. My breakdown was mortifying, reason number one, but more importantly, it was the feeling I got seeing him face-to-face. There was still a connection to him. I thought it would have dissipated with time, but it was still just as strong, just like the drink I poured the minute I walked back into the kitchen.

Chapter Twenty-Six
One Year Ago

It all happened so quickly once the decision was made. The moment I realized that I could never give Michael the child he longed for so deeply, it was over. Being lawyers, we both stood alone at our respective podiums, a gorge of emotions and memories between us. I could feel him, only feet away for the first time in two months, and desperately wanted to reach across the distance to him.

At that moment, I wanted to tell him I could have another child. I would do anything to keep him in my life. But the words would not come out, nor had they come out in the last two months in any of our conversations. I had let it go too far. I knew that now, but even though I could reach him through the physical space that stood between us, I could never reach across our emotional distance.

There was nothing to really argue over at this point. It was just a procedure, involving a judge to officially sign the paperwork. I wondered if the judge would notice the small snowflake-shaped wet marks on the pages. Tears I couldn't stop as I signed each page the week before. With each initial, I signed away a different part of my life. *My home*—I couldn't afford to buy him out, so he bought me out. *My dog*—my new apartment wouldn't allow pets. *My job*—we had opened a small law office in downtown Atlanta, one that was really Michael's dream, so I let him buy me out of that as well. I was walking out of this room with nothing, but it didn't matter to me at the time. All I wanted was Michael, and apparently you couldn't get your ex-husband in the divorce agreement.

"Norah, I just wanted to say ..." He paused, running his fingers through his hair, an old nervous habit I had grown to hate in these past few months. We stood outside the courthouse, officially divorced, officially over.

"Don't say it." His eyes locked on mine in shock. Our pain threatened to encircle our bodies, pull us back together, but I resisted. We had tried that path before, and this was where it led. There were some pains that could pull people closer to each other, then there were some, as we had suffered, that created an impenetrable barrier.

"Please, I just need you to know ..."

"No, I don't need to know. I don't want to know. I want you to leave me alone."

"Norah," he sighed, reaching out his hand, attempting to scale the wall between us.

"It's over, Michael. Goodbye."

Before I started to cry, I forced myself to walk away from the only person I had ever truly loved in my life. As I took one last look back over my shoulder, I saw his body disappearing into the crowded streets. He was gone.

Chapter Twenty-Seven
Present Day

Full circle, I was sitting at a bar, drinking. I might as well have been my mother at that moment. The bartender even called me *Ms. Crawford* as he handed me the beer. I gave him an unwelcomed, trying-to-be-flirty-but-not wink, which he didn't return. *Really?* Maybe I was slightly disheveled, sitting slouched over the bar, still wearing my clothes from yesterday, my face puffy and red from crying uncontrollably for the last hour at the bar ... but surely, I could still get this hillbilly bartender to return a flirtatious wink? *Nope.* In that moment, I realized that there was no rock bottom, just a sea of hopelessness. Pretty sure I could drink the whole sea at this point.

"What the hell are you doing?" Caroline appeared in the doorway, as the Ghost of Christmas Present shining an unwelcome light on my current situation. She embodied everything I couldn't have but Michael had wanted from me. Her mom look, complete with jeans pulled high on her waist in an attempt to camouflage her baby belly that she assured me never goes away no matter how many crunches you do. Her messy bun released small, wistful strays of hair that flared around her face with anger as she stared me down.

"Oh, come on, did you call her?" My wobbly finger pointed at the bartender, his face fuzzy from all the alcohol. Surely I had not had that much to drink? I attempted to count them but lost track at five.

"Of course he called me." Caroline could not look more out of place as she hiked the thick leather strap of her oversized bag—not purse, because it was definitely too large to be called that—on her shoulder and proceeded to walk through the smoke and filth of the bar.

"Thank you, Daniel, for calling me." Even though his face was fuzzy, I could swear he gave her a flirtatious wink as she slid money across the bar. So apparently it's just me.

"What's the big deal?" I deserved to be able to get drunk if I felt the situation warranted a drink, or two, or five ...

Either way, after all I'd been through in the last few weeks, then Michael showing up at my doorstep, this drink, these *drinks*, were validated.

"What is going on with you?" Caroline stared down at me, waiting for the explanation, a stiff level of unwanted judgement in her look.

"Don't do that. Don't judge me," I snapped, attempting to stabilize my voice and appear sober. It wasn't working.

"Oh, honey, I will judge you. I will judge the fact that you are making a fool of yourself, getting drunk in a bar ... really? That is what you think will help?"

It was a blistering attack, the truth of her words pressing down on my chest. I couldn't hold it in anymore. The tears were not over her words, just the realization that she was right. It was not going to help. Of all people, I knew that drinking was not going to help anything. Yet I continually drowned my feelings in the bottle. The drinking was making all of this worse, but in the moment, it was the only thing that took the all-consuming pain away.

Immediately, she wrapped her arms around me, and the feeling was overwhelming, a thick blanket to keep the hyperthermia at bay. I needed it more than she could ever understand. After seeing Michael, I could feel my body's need to touch another person, to feel the comfort of another, but I had no one. My mother was definitely never going to give me a hug.

"I feel so alone," I choked out. She pulled me closer, tighter.

"I'm here, I'm always going to be here."

"Even after I abandoned you?"

She pulled back and smiled down at me. "Water under the bridge." I wrapped my arms around her, hugging her tightly. "But honey, you have got to get your shit together. I know things are hard right now, but no more so than when you were a little girl. You got through it then, and you can get through this now."

I hated the impression that everyone seemed to think I was so strong as a child. It wasn't strength that got me through it, but determination, with a heavy dose of fear. Clearly, I absolutely crumbled under the pressures of life, just like my mother. I was a drunk, no denying it.

"It just hurts all the time."

I could barely look my friend in the eye, the shame was too deep, the pain too great. She could never understand how dark my life was at this point, this bar being a good representation. This was way worse than my childhood; at least back then I didn't feel like I had any control over what was happening, but now ... I was an adult, and it was all my fault.

"It will get better, I promise."

"You can't promise that. You don't know."

"Oh, my dear friend, you have no idea what I can promise."

I rolled my eyes at her continued persistence to push her will on others, just like when we were children. Except this time, I didn't believe her. There was nothing she could do that would change my life. I was stuck, slowly sinking in the quicksand ... made mostly of vodka.

"This is all my doing, and there is no way, *no way,* to get around that." Reaching for my drink, I was resolved to continue drowning my sorrows.

"Nope, no, no, no—not another drink. That will not help at all." She pushed my empty glass just out of reach as she signaled to Daniel not to pour me another drink. "Let's go. I'm taking you home."

Pulling me from the stool, Caroline allowed me to literally lean on her as I stumbled out to her car. Immediately my eyes seared with pain as the noonday sun flooded my senses. *Oh god, it's the middle of the day. That's just great.* I barely reached the van, the automatic door sliding open, as if reaching a hand out to pull me back to hell. I didn't remember the ride home.

"Okay, here we go." Caroline lifted my legs into the bed. Pulling my feet across her knee, she undid the laces and pulled my boots off one and then the other.

"Did Mark tell you?" I had expected a visit from Caroline after Mark picked me up the other day, but nothing. It was unbelievable that he actually might not have told her about the incident. That was not his style.

"Yes." She refused to look me in the eye, focusing on pulling the covers tight around my legs, as if that was going to keep me in bed.

"Why didn't you say something?"

"Look." She let out a deep sigh, perching on the edge of the bed and pulling her lips tightly together as if she wasn't quite sure if she wanted to say what she was thinking. "I understand the need to drink in order to forget something, or maybe you are just trying to wash away your guilt. Either way, going down this road will never work out in the end. Don't be your mother. You're better than that."

I desperately wanted to respond, but my mind was filled with a dark haze. I couldn't find the words, or more so the conviction to defend myself. My body was heavy, so heavy that I couldn't lift even my finger as I tried to get out of bed to follow Caroline as she left. It didn't take long for a haze of alcohol to blanket my eyelids.

My head ached as the sun cascaded through the room, each ray penetrating and burning my nerves. So much pain. Now I remembered the real reason why I didn't drink like that—the hangover. Twice in one week was too much. Thankfully, I awoke in my own bed. A thank-you call was well overdue to Caroline, but first I needed coffee.

Dragging my sore body towards the kitchen, I could hear my mother already banging around. I already knew what she was doing: attempting to locate something and unable to find it. *Maybe she was cooking again?* Most likely she had already encountered the item but just wasn't aware that it was, in fact, the spoon for which she was looking. I stood outside the entryway, seriously debating going into the room. I could go to the coffee shop, slip out the back door, but then I risked seeing Brett. Or I could just go into the kitchen, make coffee, and completely ignore her ... This plan was less likely to happen the way I was hoping in my mind, but the thought of seeing Brett was worse. His harsh judgement of my coping skills was not something I'd ever like to encounter again.

Immediately, I regretted entering the room. "Where are the damn coffee cups?" she snapped the moment she saw me. Her voice vibrated through my skull. *Ouch.*

"I'll make your coffee; just go to the porch." I shooed her out of the kitchen so that I could make our coffee in peace.

As I slid into the patio chair, the warmth of the coffee cup burning my hands, I stared out over the emptiness. In the distance, the trees lined the property, a wall imprisoning me in this place. As a child, I had found an escape path through those woods and to the lake, a place where I could find calm in my chaotic life. This place was breaking me down, just as it did when I was a child, except this time I was allowing it, just like Caroline deduced. Even though I could feel it happening, I couldn't stop it. Drinking at the bar, twice for that matter, was a bad choice. I was well aware of that this morning. However, as my mind wandered, all I wanted was a drink to keep my memories locked away. If I could just forget ...

"What is wrong with you?"

"Nothing, Mother." I just wanted her to be silent. That was all I needed today, just silence.

"How much longer are you staying here?"

"'Till you die."

My mother scoffed at my ill-timed response. "And who will be with you when I die?" There was a cold satisfaction in her eyes. "You always think you are so much better than me, but really you are just the same." This was a fact I was well aware of at the moment but would never admit to her. "You thought getting out of this town, away from me, would change you." She let out a sinister laugh filled with joy over my despair.

My chest tightened, my mother's poisonous words rushing through my veins, threatening to kill me the moment the venom got to my heart. I had to suck out the poison, pull back the venom, and spit it back into her face. It was the only way I could survive this attack.

"I didn't think it, *Mother*; I knew. I knew the moment I could escape that I would get as far away from you as physically possible. Why do you think I never came back? Never called? I wanted to forget you and this entire life, and you know something? I did. I did forget you. I did forget all you did to me as a child. I had a happy life, a good life, one that was ripped away from me. So yes, I am back now, trying my hardest to find my way back to some semblance of a livable life. But you, you don't even have a shot in hell. You're done. You are dying ... and it can't happen soon enough."

The steam from the coffee rose off the fake green grass carpet on the porch, melting the small plastic sticks. I had thrown the coffee cup down, the pieces now scattered all over the ground. I wanted to hurt my mother with more than just my words. I needed her to feel my pain, but I stopped myself. After throwing the cup down, I retreated back into the house. A dark feeling settled in as I realized she would cut her feet if she attempted to walk back inside. It would be dark before I cleaned the mess and allowed my mother back into the house. Even though I knew it was wrong, I felt vindicated, justified. It was not the only time I justified my actions, nor would it be the last.

Part Four: Weathering the Storm

As the hurricane beats against the earth, the storm engulfing everything in deep darkness, there is nothing else to do but hide. Find a place with four solid walls, no windows, a sturdy roof, and batten down the hatches, because it's going to be a long night weathering the storm.

It is a terrible feeling—the unknown. At any moment, you could be pulled from your shelter by the force of the wind. As the water starts to rise, you climb higher and higher, not knowing if it will stop before the ceiling forces your head under. In the darkness, your actions become about survival.

In survival mode, your mind loses its sense of rational thinking, only considering what you need to do to survive the current moment. There is no long-term thinking, no thoughts of what consequences you may suffer from your actions. You are only focused on survival in the moment. Making choices just to keep you alive.

There is a part of you that recognizes that you will do anything to survive, thinking that when you emerge from the hurricane alive, your actions, or sins, will be absolved. But for every action, there is always an equal and opposite reaction ...

Chapter Twenty-Eight
Present Day

There is never a progressive change in the seasons down in Alabama. The change is always sudden, without warning. One day could be filled with hot, humid air but then the next morning there is a cool dew on the grass and frost on the windshield. Fall always seems to arrive too late and winter stays too long down in the South, in my opinion. I missed the changing of the leaves, their colors becoming a vibrant orange and red as they died. Their death was beautiful, full of color, much different from the one I was witnessing now.

My mother was dying painfully slowly, a winter lasting well past its time. The first couple of weeks with my mother, I thought the season was changing, her mind fading off. But then a random cool breeze in the night faded into another humid, hot morning, bringing back her memory clear as day. I preferred the mother who looked for the nonexistent cat or muddled around the house mumbling nonsense to herself, but unfortunately, I more frequently received the ill-tempered, poisonous snake that slithered around the house waiting to strike. Even if she couldn't remember where to find her liquor and cigarettes or take a bath, she still managed to be the same ol' mean bitch I knew her to be. Winter had settled in, and it didn't seem to be going away.

"If you don't hold still ..." I threatened.

My mother's naked shoulders were hunched over, her knees pulled tightly to her chest, the cold, murky water swirling around her calves. No matter how much I did not want to do it, it had to be done. I needed for her to release her knees, stretch her legs, and allow me to wash every part of her. Bathing my mother had become a daily routine, one I loathed.

"It's cold," she barked.

"Then wash yourself!" I yelled, throwing the soapy, dingy-white washcloth on her face. The cloth hung for a moment, then started to slowly slide off her sagging face, the wrinkles seeming to merge together.

I pushed back from the tub, overestimating the strength of my anger, as my back hit hard against the door. I pulled my hands tightly under my armpits to stop the violent shaking as I attempted to control the anger. I wanted to hurt my mother. I could feel the tears burning to escape, the shame of my thoughts confirming my deepest fears and my anger boiling over. I could no longer stop them as they poured down my inflamed cheeks, marking my gray leggings to the point where they appeared to be polka-dots. My life had become impossible to deal with in the last few weeks—*four months total.* No amount of alcohol could numb the disgust I now held for my life. I could feel myself changing, slipping away into the darkness, and I didn't stop myself. I allowed the depression to set in.

"I'd like to get out now," she whispered.

I looked up to see my mother, but all I saw was a scared little girl. There was a part of me that was so angry with her every second, but then there were moments, such as this, when it was clear she wasn't the woman I hated. She wasn't anything.

"Fine," I conceded, rising from my position on the floor, reaching out to help her.

I remember how embarrassed I was the first time I gave her a bath. Seeing my mother naked was not something I wanted burned into my memory, but there it was. The bath had not been the worst of the chores I would now have to do for my mother. Aside from the still-constant cleaning, now I had to clean her soured clothes, bathe her daily, and just recently, I had to wipe her ass.

I gently placed the towel around her frail shoulders and ushered her toward the bedroom. She sat down on the edge of the bed and waited while I retrieved her clothes. Mostly, she preferred nightgowns and slippers, but today we had an appointment. So I found a clean dress, yellow with bright red and purple flowers designed all the way down to her ankles. She stared off into space, in a trance, as I proceeded to dress her. The light cotton fabric easily fell over her body, a curtain covering the show I never wanted to see. Pulling a pair of loose sandals from the closet, I slipped them onto her sallow, cracked feet. I realized I should lotion her feet and cut her toenails and fingernails, but there was no time for that now.

After I found Michael on my mother's front porch, I decided it was time to plug the phone back in. That, coupled with Caroline demanding the same or she'd physically check on me daily. There was a part of me that wanted the phone to start ringing again the moment I pushed the cord into the wall jack, but there was only silence. Caroline wasn't even calling. So, when the phone rang a few days ago, I eagerly picked it up, desperate to talk to anyone other than my mother.

"Is this Miss Crawford?" The voice was unfamiliar, but Southern, so it had to be local. There was a risk it was a bill collector, which would not turn out well for us, but again, I was desperate for conversation.

"Yes."

"Oh, good. I must say I've been trying to get a hold of you for some time now."

"The phone's been disconnected. I'm sorry, who is this again?" For a moment, I thought maybe I blacked out and missed the introduction, but I didn't.

"Oh, yes, this is Ruby from Dr. Hanto's office."

"Who?"

"Oh, uh, the neurologist you were referred to." Suddenly, I realized that Ruby thought I was my mother. Turns out the good Doctor Bishop had completed the referral to the neurologist as he said he would, relinquishing all further responsibility for my mother's fate. I'm sure the nurse was ecstatic.

"Yes, yes, of course. Sorry, I was never given the name." At least I don't remember it. "It's my mother who has been referred; this is her daughter, Norah."

"Well, just wonderful. It is an arduous time. Having family to help is critical to patient care."

"You don't know my mother."

"Well, uh ..." she stuttered, clearly flustered by my dark comment. "We look forward to meeting her. I am calling to schedule an appointment."

"When?"

"We have a few openings this week. What time works best for you?" *Literally any time of day; we do nothing.* Though, when I thought about it, I'd preferred an afternoon to have ample time to get my mother together and on board with travel. She did not go anywhere, especially considering she no longer had a car to steal. Alas, neither one of us needed to be caught out in public.

"Afternoon is best."

"We have three on Thursday."

"Uh, yeah, okay. Where is the office located?"

"We are in Alexander City."

The realization that my mother and I had no way to get to the doctor's office over forty-five minutes away in the next town only came with the morning light. As I stood at the kitchen window, my lips slowly blowing the steam off the top of my coffee mug, I gazed out past the chipped, broken boards of the porch, over the dew-covered weeds, and directly at Ms. Kay's old pick-up truck.

The smell of boiled peanuts seeped from her doorway, the broken, pulled screen the only thing between me and her shotgun.

"Mornin', Ms. Kay, I was wondering if we ... uh, if we could borrow your truck." Judging by the look on her face, I would need to explain. "My mama has an appointment today and, well, they repossessed the car after that little incident of her stealing it and driving it to the bar a few weeks ago."

Ms. Kay peered around me. My mother was standing on the bottom step, her eyes narrowed in on Ms. Kay, the anger palpable between them. For a second there, I almost inquired what was going on between them but then realized we didn't have the time, nor did I have the conviction to care.

"Uh, you know she's not well," I offered in an attempt to explain why my mother apparently was so disgusted with our neighbor she didn't even know. Never once in all my childhood did I ever see them speak or even look at each other. We were not those kinds of neighbors.

"I know I said some things a few weeks ago ..." She still didn't appear convinced. Borrowing Ms. Kay's truck was our only option. I needed this to work. "I apologize for my rudeness; I was very angry, as I always am in this place." She nodded in agreement, and I wanted to punch her in the face. I was not sorry for the way I spoke to her; she deserved it. Nor did I think it was this place that was the cause of my words; it was her. She was a horrible, old woman who could've done something all those years ago. If not for the fact that I needed her truck ...

"Okay." She glanced down at my mother again, who still was unreasonably pissed off at Ms. Kay. "Only because that woman clearly needs the help."

"No shit."

"Keys are under the visor."

I waved an ambivalent "thank you" as I retreated back down the stairs, regretting every moment I had to be nice to that horrible woman.

"Let's go," I called to my mother as I pulled myself up into the pick-up truck.

The inside smelled of minty cigarettes. The combination made my stomach turn and saliva pool in my mouth at the same time. It would be a miracle if I made it to Dr. Hanto's office without vomiting all over the car. Instantly, I began to manually roll down the dust-streaked window. There was dirt all over the passenger-side seat, and it immediately clung to my mother's clothes as she got into the truck.

"Oh, god, what is that smell?" She frowned and rolled down her window, which was pretty amazing considering she couldn't remember to wipe her own ass. "Why the hell are we asking that ol' bitch for help anyway? There is no point to this."

"Mama, this appointment is important."

"Bullshit."

"Let's put it this way. If you want more money for booze, we have to go to this appointment so your Medicare check increases by $100 a month." Plus, there was still a small sliver of hope that there was a nursing home out there that would deal with my mother. Of course, I wasn't sure what I would do if I didn't need to take care of my mother anymore. *This is why I'm depressed.*

"Okay, let's go."

"That's what I thought."

I knew the enticement of money for liquor would make my mother compliant. However, in this particular incident, it was the truth. Having gone through all her bills and records, while using what was still left of my lawyering skills, I realized that having her officially diagnosed would increase her Medicare check in order to cover medical expenses. We needed the money, especially since everything I owned had been poured away over the last two months.

"Welcome, Miss Crawford. We are so happy you could make it today." The voice was familiar—*Ruby*, who was not at all as I expected. She had a discernible Southern accent that did not match her amber complexion and colorful head scarf covering her hair. Her deep-brown eyes scanned my own appearance as she slipped a clipboard through the plastic. I realized she probably thought me the patient, with my dried-out hair, which I had not even tried to quell, jetting out wildly around my sunken, thinning face. A disturbing combination of a skeleton and medusa. The look was topped off perfectly by my dirty yoga pants and oversized t-shirt.

For the first time, I deduced that I looked worse off than my mother.

"Can you fill these out, please?" *Can.* She definitely thought I was the patient.

"Yes, I can," I assured. "It's my mother that has Alzheimer's." She nervously shifted her eyes, looking away in embarrassment.

"Yes, of course," she assured me, but I could see the lie all over her face.

Turning around, I saw my mother already sitting in front of the television, wide-eyed and watching, as if she had no idea they ever existed. Which would not be extremely farfetched, as we never had one in the house. The waiting room was small, only a few chairs positioned directly across from each other. Taking the seat across from my mother, I prayed the television would hold her attention the entire time while I completed the mounds of paperwork on the clipboard.

The questions were simple at first: Who referred you and why? Address and healthcare information. Patient history (*yes drinking—daily; yes tobacco—daily; other medicines—unsure, didn't find any in the house, so no*). Family history ... I wasn't sure what to mark at this point. We had no family history. I left it all blank. The last part was a review of systems, which I found to be an interesting use of the term. After I read through all the possible "do you have ..." questions, I finally just checked yes to all.

A few minutes later, a short, blond-haired, overly muscular male nurse appeared at the doorway and called my mother's name. His dark-navy scrubs hung tightly to his broad chest, accentuating his thick, sculpted muscles, as he gave us each a warm smile. We followed him through the doorway, down the long, bleak hallway and into room number three.

"Miss Crawford, I am going to take some vitals. Is that okay?" He pulled the blood pressure cuff over next to my mother, who took her expected seat in the center of the room. There were a few seconds of intense anticipation as we both waited to see if my mother would comply with his request. When she extended her arm, we both let out a silent sigh of relief. He nodded and started his work, appearing thankful he didn't have to wrestle her onto it. I got the feeling he might be used to that sort of thing here—a good reason to have such large muscles.

"I'm going to need to draw some blood," he announced, pulling out a large needle from a sterile plastic bag. "This will pinch slightly, but I promise it will be over quickly." He waited again for my mother's approval, which she gave. So far, this was going way better than I expected.

My mother flinched slightly at the needle prick, but he was good, getting the blood to flow into the small attached container on the first try. As he finished putting a cotton ball over the small drop of blood and pressing down, he glanced in my direction and gave a slight nod.

"All done here now. The doctor will be in shortly."

My leg shook uncontrollably as we waited in silence. I knew at any moment my mother's mind would turn back on, aware of her situation; then, like a caged animal about to be fixed, she'd attempt to escape.

"Good afternoon."

Dr. Hanto entered the room, his name stitched into his white lab coat, covering a well-tailored pin-striped suit, which matched perfectly to his dark, slicked-back hair. If I didn't know him to be a doctor, I would think he worked on Wall Street. He had the same polished, arrogant swagger to him.

"How are things going?" he asked, his accent the only non-Southern one I had heard since arriving here. Taking his respected seat on a stool, slightly turning back and forth, I was annoyed how unaware he was of my current struggles, so I decided to enlighten him.

"Honestly, it's horrible. Worse than I ever could've imagined."

"Well, it's my understanding from Dr. Bishop that your mother could possibly have Alzheimer's disease. Caring for one's mother with Alzheimer's disease can be difficult, as if the roles are reversed, making you feel like you are caring for a child." He was implying that it was to be expected, a return of services in a way, but what I was doing for her was not, should not, be *expected.*

"I had to bathe my mother. Just take a moment to let that sink in."

He stared, unaffected by the horrible vision that should have been dancing through his mind right now.

"Naked. I saw my mother naked."

"I understand." He pulled up the clipboard I had filled out, flipping through the pages, taking a moment to read, then flipped them back and continued, "I see here you reported her functioning level as quite low at this point. Is there anything she is able to still do for herself?"

"Drink," I jeered. His eyebrow raised in concern. "My mother's an alcoholic. Dr. Bishop didn't mention that one?"

"No, it was not in her file." He scribbled it down on the clipboard. "Anything else?"

"I mean, no, nothing comes to mind. I pretty much do everything for her at this point, even wipe her ass." Again, he appeared unphased.

"Well, we are going to complete some tests. Then, we can move forward with a treatment plan."

"Wait, it was my understanding that there is no treatment."

"Correct, there is no treatment, but there are things we can do to increase the care and comfort of her life." I wanted to tell him there was no reason for all that, that I had little care for my mother's wellbeing, but I knew he would take it the wrong way.

"First, we will do a physical examination, then a mental examination." Sliding on his stool, too close for safety in my opinion, toward my mother, he suddenly appeared compassionate. His deep-brown eyes widened, and his brow tightened in concern as his hands moved gently over my mother's neck and wrists.

"Your mother is quite thin. Is she eating?"

"Not often. I try, but eating is ... well, difficult." Especially considering most of my dwindling funds went to alcohol these days.

"We will probably need to start her on some vitamins. Would liquid or pill form be easier for you?"

"Liquid." *I can stir it into her daily drink.*

"Exercise would be helpful as well." I nodded in agreement, not wanting him to know just how little I was worried about my mother's health.

Once the physical examination was completed, he proceeded to ask my mother a series of seemingly useless questions. My mother answered most of them incorrectly, which was unfathomable considering they were questions such as, What is your address? What were the names of your parents? How many children do you have? *None, by the way, gee thanks.* The oddest of all was the picture test. Endless objects, all common, but she only

155

answered half correctly. Apparently, she didn't know what a dish was anymore. Well, that one actually made a little bit of sense.

"We are finished with the testing. I will meet with you both in my office. The nurse will come get you," he announced, seamlessly disappearing from the room and leaving behind pure silence.

Sitting there, confused by my mother's own confusion, I couldn't form the words to ask her if she had been truthful on the tests or if she was faking to get sympathy, or maybe keep me around to take care of her. It was hard to discern just what was my mother's sinister plot to kill me or a mental health disorder. Her abilities and deficiencies were perplexing, there being little rhyme or reason to what she could remember and what seemed lost in her mind. Which made me lean more toward her faking it than anything else. I wondered if the doctor would be able to tell that sort of thing. Maybe he could release me from this servitude. *Wishful thinking ...*

"Well, Miss Crawford, I can confirm that your mother is suffering from Alzheimer's," Dr. Hanto confirmed as I slouched deeper into the oversized leather armchair in his barren office, thankful my mother was left in the waiting room under the watchful eye of Miss Ruby. "Judging by my evaluation, she is in stage five." I'm sure he misread my face, taking my sunken, painful look as remorse for my mother's diagnosis, but it was the fact he extinguished my hope that she was faking it.

"How many stages are there?"

"Seven clinical stages of Alzheimer's. Stage five involves moderate to severe cognitive decline, including difficulty with daily tasks ... eating, bathing, cleaning. She forgets prominent pieces of information, like the fact she has a daughter." His compassionate look in my direction indicated that I should feel better about her not mentioning me, but deep down I knew that was no memory lapse. That had been on purpose.

"So what happens next?"

"Well, stage six is severe cognitive decline. She will forget most things, and you will need to do everything for her, which may involve feeding her, especially if she continues to lose weight." *Maybe she could just starve to death—bad thought!* "Stage seven is the final stage, which will be total memory loss, including speech." *That would be a gift from God. If I make it that long.*

The tightening pain in my chest started to swell, causing my breathing to quicken as the realization that all of this was real and far from over started to build in my mind. Pulling my shaking fingers through my tangled hair, my leg bouncing like I was giving a child a pony ride, my anxiety boiled over as it sunk in that what I was dealing with was only the tip of the iceberg.

"Dr. Hanto, I'm not sure I can do this."

"But yet here you are *doing it.*"

"I want out."

"I understand your frustrations. We do have a caregivers support group that I can connect you with?" Before I could object, he scribbled the address down on a piece of paper. "They meet once a week here in Alexander City." I stared at him in disbelief.

"No, this is not what I need. I can't leave her to attend some support group."

"Have you thought about some help?" *Yes, now he is talking my language.* "It is rather costly, but you could hire a nurse to tend to her twice a week. I think that would be good for now." My heart sank.

"I don't have any money. No job. No life. Nothing." I wanted the ground to give way, allowing me to sink into the earth, disappear forever.

"I could refer you to a doctor to prescribe you an antidepressant."

"What?"

"Sometimes, in situations like this, the caregiver can suffer from depression. It is a very difficult time."

"More than you know." I let out a deep sigh, knowing that I could not take the medicine. After terminating the pregnancy, I took antidepressants, a fact I never told Michael. Of course, my brain worked differently, according to my doctor, and the antidepressant only made it worse—suicidal worse. So that would not be an option.

"Probably not the best idea." I pulled my hair tight, feeling the pain deepen on my scalp as I attempted to calm my anxiety. "Can I ask you a question?"

"Go on then." He closed the file as he pushed back slightly from his desk, taking a more relaxed position as he settled into answering most likely what he thought to be endless naive questions. Of course, there was only one question that mattered to me most at this point.

"How much longer do you think my mother has?"

"Well, let's see ..." He flippantly grazed through her file, the anticipation causing me to practically shake right out of the chair. "Dr. Bishop noted that she first came to him last winter, so close to eleven months ago. He reported the symptoms began the summer before, but knowing that she is an alcoholic, it was hard to really pinpoint a specific moment in time."

"Oh, that's good to know," I jeered. "So for almost a year now." I had stopped taking the good doctor's calls five years ago.

"It seems, though, these last few months, the disease has progressed more quickly." His eyes squinted in concern as he reviewed the information. His forehead crinkled, a sudden realization coming to the forefront of his mind.

"Yes, your mother's long-time abuse of alcohol has ... how do you say, given fuel to the fire." *Figures.* "Your mother seems to have lived a hard life." It was more of a muse than a question, so I didn't answer. He could never understand our lives, as I was sure he couldn't touch our level of despair with a ten-foot pole. While Dr. Hanto had chosen an admirable profession, helping those at what one would consider the worst points of their lives, it was clear that he came from privilege. His arrogant air, his relaxed stature in his fancy suit, and something about the wave of his manicured hand as he spoke, all signaled that he had never suffered true hardship in his life.

"Unfortunately, with your mother's condition, it is best to continue to allow her to drink. Which, in turn, limits her ability to go to a nursing home." *As if he read my mind.*

"Really?"

"Surprisingly, the Alzheimer's will probably take her before cirrhosis. But these nursing homes are ill-equipped to deal with severe physical health issues, as they are focused on the mental health of the patient." I really figured they would have been one in the same in places such as that.

"Well, that's great news." The sarcasm in my tone was not missed.

"I'm sorry, but there is no scientific way to determine how long each stage will last; it's different for every person. At this point, it's best to just keep her life as normal as possible. Comfortable. If that means letting her have a drink ... well." He shrugged, condoning the fact that my mother was an alcoholic. "Honestly, if she is difficult now, alcohol withdrawal will only make it worse."

"Any chance it might actually speed it up?"

At first, he looked confused but then flipped through those damn papers again before saying, "Looking at her medical history here, probably not." Shocked by his lack of judgement, I was slightly impressed that he considered the question without chastising me for wishing an earlier death on my mother. Especially since he had no hint of what our relationships truly was to either of us.

"Is there anything that could make any of this better?" It was not lost on me that Dr. Hanto might be the only person that could give me information to lessen the blow of my life right now.

"Unfortunately, not really. Caring for a loved one that is ill will always be challenging. It's hard to watch those who once loved and supported us deteriorate before our eyes. The role reversal is a difficult one, but people are often more than capable of doing so."

Desperately, I wanted to scream that there was no role reversal here, as this woman never loved me, never cared for me, never supported me, so why should I ever be doing all this for her? I should leave ... leave her to die in her own shit.

"Thank you, doctor. I understand."

It was all I could say in that moment, knowing he could never understand the true depth of my mother's hatred and my contempt. This was our silent burden to bear.

"Ma'am," Ruby called from behind the glass window as I attempted to make a quick and unnoticed exit. "Ma'am, there is a co-pay with your mother's Medicare, and we need to schedule the next appointment."

"Co-pay?" I knew I should've ignored the woman. We did not need to waste our booze money on an outrageous co-pay. My plan had been to allow all her medical bills to go into the ground, along with her dead body.

"Yes, it's twenty dollars." The woman's naive eyes stared up at me from her desk, waiting for something ... but even twenty dollars was a stretch right now. I needed that cash for when we stopped by the liquor store on the way home.

"Can you bill her? I'd prefer to pay all her medical bills from a particular account and well, I'm so sorry, but I seem to have forgotten my checkbook."

The woman glanced reflexively at the large bold sign taped onto the window which read, *All co-pays due at the time of service.*

"I'll make sure to bring it next time. When is that appointment again?" I forced a large fake Southern smile across my face, one that apparently did the trick.

"Uh, let's see. How about in six weeks ... uh, that puts us right at about April 19th at three in the afternoon. Is that okay?"

"Yes, that's fine."

The sound of the house key hitting the small blue clay bowl on the entryway table rang through my ears, vibrations making waves in the clouds of dust specks that danced in the rays of light peeking through the dirty windows. There was a haunting feeling to this house, made only more believable by the dark, damp hallways and empty, silent rooms.

"Move it." Her crisp words cut through the waves, pulling me from my trance as she pushed by me into the living room. "Get me a drink." I think I'd prefer a ghost to my mother.

I wasn't sure what I expected to gain from our appointment with Dr. Hanto, but whatever it was, I didn't get it. I could tell by the feeling in the pit of my stomach that things were only going to get worse. In my mind, at that moment, I could not consider how it could possibly get worse. The thought only deepened my depression and need to drink.

Chapter Twenty-Nine
Mother

"Drink!" His voice bellowed from the living room. "Now!" The smell of liquor on his breath and sour sweat on his dirty white t-shirt brought an intense, reflexive fear that caused her body to sweat. Cigarette smoke billowed up from his mouth, morphing into devil horns above his head. Day after day, he just sat there in that chair, drinking and smoking. The only time he rose was to beat and rape her. Pulling the bag of frozen peas from her eye, she painfully limped to the fridge to get ice.

One, two, three drops of ice in the glass cup. "Hurry up," he barked. The ice continued to clink as she attempted to pour the smooth brown scotch over top, drops falling to the counter. Quickly, she wiped them away. If he noticed, he would surely beat her for wasting his liquor. The smell of the drink made her gag, thoughts of him forcing his mouth onto her own, the liquor and smoke invading her tongue. Suddenly, the glass dropped to the floor, shattering, her hand shaking from the memory.

"What the hell?" She could hear him moving, the spring in the chair flexing as he started to raise. *No, no,* she thought. *If he gets up, he will hurt me again.*

"Sorry, *sweetheart.*" The words caught in her throat like acid rising up. "My hand just slipped. I'll clean it up and get you a drink; no need to get up."

"Well, hurry the fuck up." The spring flexed as he lowered his fat, disgusting body back into the chair. Silent tears fell down her burning cheeks as she realized she'd just narrowly avoided another beating. Grasping her hand over her mouth so he would not hear her cries, she slid to the ground in hopelessness.

She could never escape him, be free of him; he made sure of that. Deep down, she knew that even if she walked into the center of town, bruised and bleeding, no one would believe her. More likely, no one would care. After that first night home with him--the kick still caused her to limp weeks later—she had started to develop an escape plan. Running all the scenarios in her mind, thinking of everything, she planned it over and over again in her mind. But every time, he caught her; every time, she failed. She was trapped.

"'Bout time." He licked his yellowed teeth as he took the glass from her hand. A flash of his body on top of her caused her to stumble backward. "What's wrong with you?" He glared in her direction.

"Nothing." The fear overtook her body, betraying her in her moment of need. With every ounce of strength, she held back the tears threatening to erupt, but he saw the smoke. He knew she was on the verge ... just the way he liked her.

He took a long sip, draining the glass, and she knew. A sinister film draped over his eyes as his lips curled up on either side. She knew what was coming.

The first time, she ran, tried to fight him, but it only made it worse. Now, her body froze before him, waiting for what was to come. She couldn't stop it. Closing her eyes, she willed her mind to go to another place, any place. Desperately, she tried to escape, but the smells ... smoke, liquor, sweat ... she couldn't push them away. They invaded every sense of her, just as he did.

Reaching the toilet just in time, she buried her head deep into the bowl, releasing every piece, all the contents of her stomach. Over and over again, unable to stop the reflex, holding tight to the cold porcelain for fear she would fall in if she let go. Finally, relief. She felt her stomach relaxing, her throat closing, as her body realized it was over. There was nothing left.

The cold tile felt like ice against her hot cheek. She pressed her face hard against the smooth, cool surface, wanting nothing more than to melt away. She'd rather be a pool of water, evaporating into nothing, rather than this broken, lost girl. Anywhere was better than this ... Her eyes flashed open. She knew what she needed to do.

Pulling against the bathtub, she lifted her weak body up and started the water. Without removing her sheer white nightgown, the blood stain still visible between her legs, she allowed her body to fall into the water. Pressing her body against the bottom of the tub, the water now reaching her shoulders, she waited. Waited for the end.

She learned that day that her body wouldn't allow her to drown. After several seconds of burning lungs and her mind refusing to lift her head, her body decided to take over, forcing her up for air.

Her screams echoed through the empty house. She tried over and over, but every time, her body won the battle over her mind. She would have to find another way. Still wet, she roamed the house, frantically attempting to find anything to end this life.

There was no gun, which was surprising considering the type of man he seemed to be. She had thought for sure he would have a gun, at the very least to control her with it, but then she laughed at the idea that he would need anything other than his large, fat, disgusting body. He knew he had her overpowered the moment he saw her. She was sure that was another reason he picked her, coupled with the fact that she was a leper in this town who no one would believe, or miss for that matter. He was not a stupid man; she'd give him that.

Pulling the drawers out in the kitchen, she finally found one that would do. Holding the sharp silver blade over her wrist, she realized she wasn't shaking. For some reason, she thought she would be scared at the thought of cutting her wrist, yet she was calm. Peaceful. She pressed the cold, piercing blade against her skin; blue veins jumped and danced, begging to be sliced. Her body wanted this; it would not fight her as it had before.

The blue in her veins drained as a thin waterfall of blood flowed down her arm and dropped one by one on the floor. She could feel the relief washing over her as she realized she would soon be free of everything. Suddenly, she realized it was not relief, but nausea, once again. She raced to the sink, barely making it before yellow bile spewed out.

The blood rolled down the side of the sink, mixing and creating an intricate dance with the yellow bile still circling the drain. She watched as the two flowed next to one another, then slowly they mixed together, creating a new color that now seemed to settle in at the base of the sink, refusing to go down the drain. At that moment, she knew.

Her first thought was still to go through with killing herself. Being pregnant did not change anything. If anything, she convinced herself that killing herself now was more important than ever. She needed to do it for the baby; no child ever needed to be brought up in this life.

Pulling the blade back to her wrist, she hovered over the dried blood. *Do it, do it,* her mind screamed. Hopelessly, she wanted to glide the knife across her wrist, ending her life, but she couldn't.

The knife dropped to the floor. The sound of it crashing against the tile rang throughout the house. It was over. It was all over.

Chapter Thirty
Present Day

"Oh god, you are still here." Her body lingered in the doorway as if she were waiting for mine to fade away, a bad ghost in her kitchen. But I would not fade away, much to her dismay.

"Yes, Mama, I just went to the store for groceries." Having used a small portion of her most recent Medicare check, I had been able to get us some decent food for the next few weeks.

The sun was barely cresting the horizon as I pulled Ms. Kay's truck back into her driveway, letting it coast in on fumes so that she would hopefully never notice that I'd taken it. I didn't have the energy to ask her to borrow it again. So, at four o'clock in the morning *(not really sleeping anyway)*, I put the truck in neutral and pushed it just far enough so she would not hear the engine turning over in the darkness. It had been a risk, but one that paid off.

"Why are you here?" My mother probed repeatedly. I continued to ignore the question as I unloaded the groceries. "Is your life really so bad? Why don't you just run back to Michael?"

It was incredible the things she could recall, like the words to say that would cut the deepest. If she could remember his name, then she could remember why I was here. She was baiting me.

"You know why I am here, Mama."

"Oh, do tell me again. I love hearing about how well *you* have done with your life." She laughed under her sarcastic smile, as she pulled the last cigarette from her pack.

I waited for her to realize that the lighter was also in the pack and not on the counter, which I was judging is where she thought it was based on the fact that she was pushing things around. Finally, she decided to put the cigarette back into the pack, at which point she saw the lighter. Shooting an evil look down at the lighter, as if it had betrayed her deeply, she pulled it out and lit the cigarette right there in the kitchen.

The smell swirled around the small enclosed room. Just that smell brought back terrible memories, like bullets hitting me one by one as she blew the smoke into the thinning air. It was all I needed, coupled with that smug look on her face.

"Fuck you!" I screamed, throwing the metal can of soup directly at my mother. The can landed hard against the wall, the side busting and soup exploding all over the kitchen. My mother stood there, laughing, the red soup like blood dripping from her face and nightgown. It didn't seem to bother her though; she was ecstatic over my breakdown. *Misery loves company.*

The pressure started to build in my chest, the pain burning in my lungs, desperate to be released as my mother's laughter curled around my body like a snake, squeezing tighter with each passing second. There was a moment I could feel it happening but couldn't stop it. My anger boiled over, needing to be released. As I pulled each item from the paper bag, my mind screamed at me to stop, but each time, I flung the item against the wall. My anger exploded violently each time.

In those few seconds, I had managed to destroy all our groceries for the next week: smashed apples all over the floor, butter melting on the hot tile, cream corn slowly crawling down the walls, and soda still hissing as foam shot against the baseboards. When the blackness lifted, I could see what my rage had cost us. An overwhelming feeling of despair took over as my screams turned to cries.

"You stupid little bitch. Look what you've done."

Pain pulsated through my mind with each caustic word my mother spoke; each pulse caused a flicker of a memory. For weeks, I had held the memories at bay, drinking away the ability to accept my fate, but suddenly, they were blazing through every inch of my mind. Everything I had suppressed all these years, all the abuse, pain, and neglect was riding in on a flaming chariot. Suddenly, I felt as if there was no escape. I was surrounded and alone. Glaring up at my mother, I saw my pain personified.

Every bone in my body wanted to pull at her, force her to feel my pain, but just as I was about to step toward her cackling, contorted body, I saw the destruction of my rage all around me. If I started, I knew I wouldn't be able to stop. Even though there was a part of me that wanted to kill my mother, I knew that would never work in my favor. I had to get out.

Bare, pointed twigs reached out from their trees across the overgrown path through the woods, slapping me over and over again on my burning cheeks as I ran from my pain. It was as if the forest knew I needed to be punished for my evil thoughts. Just as my lungs started to burn, a fire threatening to overtake them completely, the trees faded away, and I could see my salvation.

I stood at the edge of the dock, my bare toes slightly curled over the wooden boards. The smooth, serene water looked as though I could step off and walk across the top. Lifting my right foot, I started to lean over the dock as if I was stepping out onto a platform. But my mind knew better. It knew I would fall right through the glass, deep into the depths of darkness. That was what I wanted most of all. I wanted to step off this dock and fall deep into the lake, allowing it to swallow me whole.

Ending my life seemed like the logical option. I slipped into the lake unnoticed, my thin body barely making a ripple as it engulfed me, pulling me into its warm, safe embrace. There was a peace that encircled my body as I allowed the lake to take my life. It was over ... Finally, I could be free from it all.

Air rushed into my burning lungs, forcing the water out as I reached the surface. My body had refused me, pushed me toward life. My fingers crawled at the blades of grass as I pulled my body up onto shore. Violently coughing every drop of water from my lungs, I rolled my broken body over onto the grass. Maybe I could just stay here, waste away into nothing, allow the quicksand to take me all at once. Anything was better than returning to that house.

"Norah, Norah, wake up," an angel called from the distance, beckoning me to death ... wait, no ... I knew that voice.

"Caroline?"

"Yes, for the love of God, I thought you were dead."

"No such luck."

"What the hell are you doing out here?"

As the world came back into focus, I realized I was still in the grass, my clothes still damp from the lake water, as the sun was starting to melt on the horizon.

"I must have fallen asleep." I attempted to lift myself, but my arms were stiff and my legs useless. Caroline reached out a steady hand and lifted me up just enough to look me eye to eye. *Shit.*

"You didn't just fall asleep out here. Please tell me you were not attempting to drown yourself." I had every intention of saying no, but my face betrayed me. "Good God, Norah."

"Just please, don't. You have no idea."

"I know what depression looks like. I know what hopelessness feels like. I know you might think I don't get this shit, but I do."

There was no possible way she could understand the depth of my anguish. "Come on." She pulled me up from the ground, giving me a supportive arm as I struggled to stand. "Let's get you back to the house."

My energy and resolve were gone, so I let Caroline lead me back to the one place I never wanted to go again. As the house came into view, I realized I would never be able to break free of this place. No matter what I tried to do, it would still be standing there, looming over me in the darkness. Just then I saw her, the shadow of my mother leaning against the porch door, the red glow of her cigarette. *Burn it.*

"Where the hell have you been?" There was still a hint of satisfaction to her voice, as if she knew she had broken me and relished the fact. Instinctively, like a caged animal, I reached out to her, a low growl releasing from my throat, but Caroline pulled me back, my claws just missing her neck.

"No, no, not the day to go to prison for killing your mother. You have to plan that shit out right," Caroline jeered. There was the dark side of me that actually found that idea more acceptable than taking my own life. Without my mother, I could burn the house down along with all the memories and pain, then maybe I could finally move on.

"Dear God," Caroline gasped as we walked into the kitchen. Had I not seen it before, or created it, it would have shocked me as well. "Jesus, Norah, what happened?"

"Attack of the produce?" I winced, attempting to ease her growing concerns. The more concerned Caroline became, the more difficult it would be to hide the truth.

"Well, shit, it's a wonder you survived. Go get yourself some dry clothes. I'll clean this mess up." I attempted to protest, but Caroline waved a stern finger in my direction, eyes narrowed in challenge. I did not have the energy to argue.

As I pulled the mud-stained clothes from my body, I could feel the veil of despair lifting, as if the lake water had extracted the pain, letting it seep into my clothes so that when I pulled them from my body, the pain would go as well. The fresh white t-shirt and jean shorts hung, loose but refreshing, on my skin. I felt different, if only for a moment.

"Are you eating?" Caroline had managed to clean up the entire kitchen in a matter of minutes. It would've taken me days, and of course, I would have needed multiple drink breaks. I was sure she didn't need those.

"Caroline, I am fine."

"That's a load of horse crap. I know it's not the best time to point this out, but a true friend should tell you. You are letting this," she motioned to the air around us, encircling the entire house, "kill you. Frankly, I don't want you to die. I think you still have a lot to give this world."

"Not really."

"Stop that. Stop doing that; you are only making it worse. Shit happens."

"I am shit. I didn't just step in it; I am the pile of shit."

"Well, that's a horrible analogy. You have never been a pile of shit, nor will you ever." She crossed the space between us, placing her smooth, delicate hands on either side of my face, forcing me to look directly into her eyes. This was serious. "You are a person of circumstance, horrible, awful, never-should-have-happened circumstance, but that is not who you are as a person. You are a good person, a person worth a life in this world. Please remember that every day. Do not let your circumstances dictate your life. Take control. I know you can win this battle."

Tears rolled over her fingers, a river being split into different directions by the land. As she removed her hands, she gently wiped the tears from my cheeks, returning them to a dry, barren desert. Words were lost in that moment as I realized I was not the only one on the battlefield.

Reluctantly, Caroline left me alone with my mother and myself in this house. She made me promise to not kill myself or my mother. I made the promise but was not sure I could keep it. I received explicit instructions to call her if I should ever feel the need to harm myself or my mother. She had saved me in the moment, placed a band aid on my pain, but band aids always seemed to fall off eventually. I just wasn't sure how long mine would last.

Aimlessly, I roamed the house, my mind conjuring up flames as the thought of burning the house settled in. My fingers slid softly over the wallpaper in the foyer as it made its way up the staircase and down the hallway to my bedroom. The dancing tulips brought back memories of sitting at the top of the stairs, listening to my mother being beaten or drinking herself into a stupor. There were pink flowers hunched over, wilting. To me, they never looked like

169

flowers but ballet dancers, moving in unison in an elaborate dance just for me. So many nights I watched that dance. I even started to give them names at one point.

My old friends.

"Help, help!" my mother screamed from the porch, the tiny wilted dancers fading back into sunken tulips. I stared out toward the kitchen, listening to her screams echoing through the house. *I should rush to her side, see what is wrong.* But instead, I just stood there, watching her sitting in the rocking chair, just screaming, reason unknown. Maybe the alcohol was slowing me down or numbing my ability to give a shit, but either way, I did not really care to rush to her aid.

Finally, her screaming, more annoying than anything else, started to get to me. As I walked out onto the porch, she stared up at me, her big brown eyes filled with fear as she continued to scream.

"What are you screaming at?" She didn't stop, just turned, staring out into the darkness, opening her mouth and screaming, over and over again, as if she were stuck on repeat.

"Stop!" Screaming at her did not make a difference; she was louder. Without thinking about it first, a pure reflex of frustration, I slapped her hard against the cheek. Instantly, a thin line of blood highlighted her cheek, revealing the consequences of my harmful actions. But she stopped. Then her eyes refocused with a possessed, evil look draping over them as she stared right at me.

"Mama, are you there?" I stepped back, giving her space, unsure how much memory of me had returned. She just kept staring at me as I slowly backed away. Any moment now she was going to literally kill me with her eyes. Best to just leave her alone at this point.

Back inside, I poured another drink, my hand still shaking from the slap. Turning my palm over, I could see the redness spreading like fire across my hand. Squeezing it tightly, I pushed the thought from my mind. My hand did not hurt but felt good. The slap had been a reflex, something I never intended to do, but deep down, I couldn't suppress the feeling of satisfaction. The last drips of the vodka falling into my glass ... this would definitely take the edge off my dreams tonight.

Chapter Thirty-One
Little Girl

The little girl held her knees tight to her chest as she rocked back and forth on her small twin bed. Her hands were cupped tight around her ears as she listened to her mother screaming over and over again. Glass shattered upon the wall, the falling pieces creating a wind chime sound as they hit the floor one by one. Then, there was an eerie silence, and the little girl knew her mother was gone, unconscious. He was too smart to kill her, for the little girl had learned that he knew just how much he could hit them without killing them. Her body shook as she heard his large, all-too-familiar footsteps starting down the hallway. He was coming. Now it was her turn. He was almost to her door when she heard it. The doorbell. Her saving grace, or so she thought.

She listened, envisioning the scene in her mind; the door creaked in pain as he pulled it open hard against its rusted hinges. She couldn't imagine who was on the other side, why they had come. No one ever came here. The voices, muffled and raspy, floated under the door. Eventually, her curiosity won. She glided down from the bed, barely cracking the door to slide through, as she made her way to the top of the staircase.

At the door, she could only see their shoes, black boots with thick, high laces. The blue trouser leg swept across the top of the boots, a yellow stripe down the outside.

"Uh, we received a noise complaint," the officer stuttered, his voice squeaky, that of a young boy. He seemed scared of the large drunk man. He was a police officer and had a gun. The little girl didn't understand.

"Really? Which one of these godforsaken neighbors called it in?" he demanded, pushing his way past the cops and yelling from the front porch into the darkness. "Mind your own damn business!"

"Now, you know we can't tell you who called," another officer stated. This one sounded older, his feet firm on the ground and his legs much larger than the other.

"We just need you to tell us everything is okay, sir." The little girl wanted to call out, *No!*, but she remained silent, trapped in fear.

"What goes on in my house is none of your business," the man slurred.

"Come on, Joe, just tone it down," the officer angled.

Suddenly, it was all clear to the little girl. That officer knew the man personally, possibly even as friends. They were not here to save her, much to her dismay. She placed a steadying hand against the wall; the small pink flowers seemed to reach out to her. Desperately she wanted them to pull her into their world so that she could dance with them.

The door slammed hard, pulling her from a trance. Quickly, she tiptoed back to her room, placed the chair up against her door, and prayed. *Please, please, please take me away from here. Please, please, please don't let him come in.*

God did not answer her prayers.

Chapter Thirty-Two
Present Day

Swinging open her bedroom door with much more force than I anticipated, I slammed it against the wall, quickly looking around the room. *Where is she?* The morning had come too quickly, and I was in no mood for this again.

My head was pounding as I moved unsteadily down the hallway, slipping on my socks into the kitchen. *Nothing.* Out onto the porch. *Nothing.* Just as I was about to look for signs that she'd gone to the bar again, I saw her, standing out in the field.

"Mama!" I yelled, but she did not turn around. "Mama!" I yelled again.

I ran over to her, her white nightgown covered in dirt and her feet black with mud. She was screaming uncontrollably. *Not this again.* I grabbed her shoulders and attempted to gain her attention, but she just kept screaming in my face, each wave crashing against my fractured mind.

Finally, I just couldn't take it anymore. I slapped her hard across the face, not knowing anything else to get her to stop. She fell hard to the ground. The cut reopened, the blood falling down her cheek. *Shit.*

I watched in silent horror as she curled up into a ball at my feet and continued to sob. *Great, now I have to deal with this.* Forcefully, I pulled against her free arm, but her body refused to move.

"Come on, Mama," I pleaded, trying again to lift her with no success.

"No," she suddenly screamed back at me, as she recoiled tighter into herself, her free hand burying deep into her chest. Her spine coiled as a snake under her thin nightgown as her head nestled into the damp, dewy grass.

"Mama, you can't stay out here. Come on." She refused my help, pushing my arms off her shoulders again and again. Finally, I gave up. It was too early for this shit, and I needed coffee.

From the porch, coffee in hand, I watched my mother. Her body appeared as a baby animal curled up in the grass. Slowly sipping my hot coffee, I wondered just what was wrong with her today. The random screaming was new, another sign that she was losing herself to the disease—*fingers crossed.*

Maybe Caroline was right, I could wait this out. Of course, I knew physically I would live longer than my mother—her health was touch and go—but mentally, I wasn't sure how much longer I could take all of this. There was a part of me that knew it was going to get worse, that I had only suffered a fraction of what was to come. That was what scared me, the unknown ... not knowing what would come next, not knowing if I could survive it ... The bandage was starting to feather.

I watched her all morning, moaning and thrashing in the grass. I wasn't sure what memories were haunting her, but she was definitely being haunted by something. Finally, about noon, it stopped. Her body lay motionless in the grass.

Kneeling down over her sleeping body, third cup of coffee in hand, I checked ... Yes, she was still alive. *Mixed feelings.* The smell of coffee wafted in the air, causing her eyes to flicker. As her eyes opened, I smiled down at her, every hope that she was going to wake up with no memory of me; this was always the best-case scenario. It would be nice, with all I was having to deal with, if she actually forgot who I was. Then, maybe, she wouldn't be so horrible.

"Where am I?" She attempted to pull her body off the ground, but she was too weak, moaning in pain, as if her arm was badly injured.

"Okay, let me help you." Surprisingly, she actually let me help her up. I guess she had no other choice, or she didn't recognize me just yet.

"Coffee," she demanded as we walked back into the kitchen. I complied, wanting this vague, unknown cloud that had fallen over my mother to never lift.

Cupping her hands around the warm mug, the cool air drifting through the screen onto the back porch, she drank, with a look of pure satisfaction on her face over the taste of that first sip. I never saw her take so much pleasure in a cup of coffee without rum.

"What is your name?" I probed, unable to help myself, the joy of my mother's memory being wiped clear of me was too inviting.

"I know my name. What a stupid question." I just stared at her, waiting. I could see she was trying but couldn't seem to put her finger on the answer. She didn't know her name. "It's just that ... Well, my name is ..." Anxiety was building; she was losing control.

"It's okay, I know your name. It's Lillie, Lillie Crawford," I assured her. She seemed to calm down at the knowledge of her own name, sitting back in the chair and taking another sip of coffee.

"Who are you?" Now, this question I was unsure of how to answer. If I told her I was her daughter, I knew she would explode. I should lie. No good would come of telling her the truth.

"I'm your daughter." It was reflexive, *damnit.*

"Oh, my dear, sweet Norah."

She reached out, her soft, wrinkled hand, brushing lightly against my cheek as she took in every part of my face, as if she had never seen me before now. Her eyes searched my own, looking for love, and for a brief moment, she almost found it, but then it faded into recognition.

"What are you doing here?" she snapped, the realization dawning on her that she did not love her daughter but hated her, more deeply than anything else apparently.

Her face contorted, twisted with hatred. Tears burned in my eyes. I almost had it. I almost had that feeling of being loved by my mother. I pulled the rum off the top of the fridge and filled both our cups.

Had I known the nightly eloping and screaming was going to be the next phase of my mother's illness, I would've invested the last of our money into a chain for her bedroom door. Night after night, my very little piece of REM sleep was being disturbed by my mother screaming bloodcurdling fear into the night.

The first couple of nights, I caught her still in bed, wrapped up in the sheets, sweat pouring from her body, her eyes tightly shut, as she howled out in pain. I figured her memories would just fade away, like puffs of dandelions in the wind, but I was starting to realize that her memories were going to put up a fight. They clawed at her nightly, causing her visible pain that made her appear possessed. Her body contorted, followed every time with a fearful shriek.

The third night, I tried slapping her again, but it only made it worse. Her body lurched this way and that, taking the hit as if her mind was expecting it. Finally, I decided it was best to just let her live it out in hopes that in the light of day the memory would be gone.

It wasn't until the sleepwalking started that I realized we had a real problem. My mind had become desensitized to the nightly screaming, so when she started to scream, it didn't even phase my own dreams. Suddenly, my eyes shot open, but my mind still hazy as to the reason. Then I heard it, the old, rusted creaking of the door swinging shut.

The early morning chill prickled at my bare skin as I ran out into the darkness after my mother's disappearing body. Her white nightgown glowed against the black backdrop, making it easy to follow her out into the fields behind our house. I picked up the pace as I realized she was headed straight for the woods. If she made it to the tree line, I would surely lose her for good.

"Mama!" I called after her, hoping the sound would cause her to pause, but instead she quickened her own pace. *Shit.*

Just before she disappeared, she stopped. *Thank god.* I was only a few seconds behind her, reaching her just as she started to scream ... again.

"Mama, Mama!" I attempted to wake her up by violently shaking her shoulders. I knew you weren't supposed to wake up a sleepwalker, but this was getting ridiculous.

"Stop, no ... please, just stop!" I released her, the fear in her opened eyes taking me by surprise, and she dropped to the ground. Her sobs echoed through the frosted night air.

I didn't know what to do. I tried to console her, but she pushed me away, begging me to leave her alone. I tried to lift her, carry her back to the house, but she was dead weight, pulling back against me and screaming. Sweat rolled down my temples as I tried over and over again to move my mother's limp body. I finally gave up.

"Fine, stay out here. I don't even know why I care." There was no obvious retort to my jab, another sign she was not right of mind at this moment.

It was too late to attempt to go back to bed, so I made some coffee. Within the next hour, the sky came to life with red and pink ribbons floating across the morning horizon. My mother had remained in the grass, thrashing and screaming in small spurts of pain, but for the most part, she slept out there peacefully. It seemed to be the only place she was able to get any sleep these days.

Then the rotten wooden boards flexed under the weight of the mailman, alerting me to his arrival. Creeping, a stealth animal on the prowl, I slunk behind the door, waiting for him to slip the small white envelope through the mail slot. Many white envelopes fell to the floor, but there was only one that I cared to open.

Unfortunately, I could not wait even a day to go get food. We had been out for two days, thanks to my little tantrum after the last trip. Every spare speck of food had been somehow cooked and eaten by mostly me in the last twenty-four hours. The vodka could only keep my hunger at bay for so long. Not surprisingly, my mother, having mostly survived on vodka her entire life, responded differently to the fasting. Every time I tried to feed her, she pushed me away, screaming violently in my face. So fuck it. *Starve to death* was my new saying these days.

As for myself, though, I needed food ... and alcohol.

Pulling on my common disguise of an old, faded Blue Jay's baseball cap over all my identifiable, frizzy hair, then tucking any stray pieces up into the sides as best I could, I then covered my face with large mirrored glasses and made sure to wear the largest clothes I had. I was going for a homeless look, which worked well. At least no one recognized me anymore. I was almost ready to venture out on my bi-weekly trip to the grocery store. The only thing left to do was grovel at Ms. Kay's feet for use of the truck. Of course, I thought about just taking it, wondering if she'd even call the cops, but during this late morning hour, it would be too much of a risk. And I needed something to eat tonight other than bread crumbs.

"Well, I suppose you can *borrow* it." Her eyes narrowed over the barrel of the shotgun, a piercing, all-knowing stare. I realized I had not gotten away with stealing her truck last time.

"Just one more thing ..." I glanced back over my shoulder at the house, the shadow of my mother neatly tucked away in her flower chair with a cigarette and drink in hand visible from her porch.

"Can I shoot her?" Ms. Kay growled, squeezing her wrinkled, yellow-nailed fingers around the shaft of the gun, an evil look clouding her witchy eyes.

"Sure, be my guest." There was no shock in Ms. Kay's eyes at my disdain for my mother, and in that moment, I saw she had the same. One day, if I didn't die first, I would ask her what happened between her and my mother. But not today. Today I needed to focus on getting food and liquor.

It was always the same cashier at the Piggly Wiggly. I'm sure she had grown to know me as the crazy, drunk lady who clearly didn't know how to cook; otherwise, I'd purchase more than essentials and junk food. Each time I checked out, she gazed down at me over her fat pig nose and said, "Liquor store hasn't opened yet." So often I wanted to punch her in the nose but refrained, knowing full well that it would bring Mark front and center, then subsequently Caroline, who seemed to have reduced her amount of checking in lately. I'd like to keep it that way.

"You are later than normal," she mused as she flippantly scanned each item, my blood pressure increasing with each cent. My mind was too cloudy these days to do the math, so I guessed. Knowing I had one hundred dollars for food, I only got the basics to survive. I crossed my fingers that it was all under a hundred.

"Yes, I know."

"Liquor store's open."

"Yes, I know." I wanted to rip the glasses off my eyes, reveal the true horror of my situation to this stranger, then grab her by the hair and ... *Oh shit!*

Thrusting through my dark fantasy, Caroline plowed through the doors. Quickly, I pulled my cap down further, pushing my glasses deeper into my face and praying she wouldn't see me. She seemed distracted enough, rushing down the first aisle and out of sight. Maybe I had been saved.

Suddenly, just as I started to pull the bills from my pocket, she was behind me, over-aggressively putting a pack of tampons down on the counter.

"Norah, Norah, is that you?" I had tried to turn away, put my back to her, but her thin fingers wrapped around my shoulder and pulled me back around.

"Oh, Caroline. Hi."

"Glad to see you are somewhat alive," she mused, taking in my homeless appearance. I noticed there was something different about her. It had been a week since she showed up at my house when I attempted to drown myself. As she shifted on her feet, I noticed she wasn't wearing her typical mom jeans, and she had makeup on, although it was slightly roughly applied.

"Yeah, are you going somewhere?"

"Oh, uh, no, not really." The shift in her tone betrayed her lie, as she quickly smoothed her disheveled hair. A deep feeling of insecurity settled in as it occurred to me for the first time—which was odd—that Caroline was keeping me at arm's length. The Christmas party had been filled with people that she had allowed me to meet, and it had been a disaster, in my opinion. It was clear most people had no desire to see me around this town again. Maybe she realized she didn't want me around either. Again, I was just a wounded bird for her to nurture and bring back to good health. Not an actual friend. The idea that I was right hurt.

"I gotta go." Quickly, I gathered my groceries and made my way for the exit. Having only the one thing to purchase, she was behind me the next minute as I threw the bags into the back of the pick-up truck.

"Norah, wait," she called, pausing when she finally reached me just before I pulled the door handle open. "Are you okay?"

"I'm fine, Caroline."

"Sorry I haven't checked in, I just ... well." Nervously, she bit her lower lip. There was something she was not telling me. I knew, though; she didn't need to say the words.

"Caroline, I am fine. Please, you don't have to take care of me."

"It's just I've been very busy lately with things."

"I know you have a great husband and wonderful children to occupy your world. You don't need me constantly mugging it up."

"No, no that is not it at all." Her reassurances fell flat, her eyes revealing her concern, but not empathy. Of course, maybe that was too much for me to expect from her, as it would be rare to know anyone who could truly empathize with what I was going through. "Norah, please, my life is messed up more than I care to admit. Nothing is ever perfect."

"That's not true."

"Yes, it is, and if your life wasn't so fucked up right now, maybe I could talk to you about it!" Clearly, I had pushed an imaginary button that hurt Caroline to her core. I just couldn't fathom how. But before I could even speak, she was gone, storming across the parking lot to her van. I cared slightly about it, but then again, I didn't actually believe her. Nothing was worse than what I was having to deal with. *Nothing.*

The moment I rounded the dirt path, the house coming into view, I knew something was wrong. The front door was wide open, a small empty glass perched on the broken fence frame and no mother in sight. Rolling the truck slowly into place, fearful she might jump out at any moment and claim I ran her over, I scanned the area. I had this feeling that she was going to attack me, which was an old, buried fear I always had as a child walking up to this house.

"Mama," I called out as I cautiously got out of the truck. *Come out, come out, wherever you are ...*

Groceries in hand, I labored through the narrow front door and into the kitchen, heaving the bags down on the counter. There was an uneasy silence to the house as I attempted to listen for any movement.

"Mama," I called out again, not wanting to be surprised. I hadn't been gone long, so I figured if she had started walking to the bar, I would've passed her on the way home. Or she would've been dead in the yard, killed by a gunshot wound.

She had to still be here, but where? "Mama!"

"Where the fuck have you been?" Just like an unwanted ghost, she appeared out of nowhere.

"Getting groceries."

"Did you get my vodka?"

"Of course." I pulled the handle from the brown paper bag. After my encounter with Caroline, I sprung for the handle instead of just the bottle.

Immediately, she snatched it from my hand and poured it over her melting ice cubes. I was pretty sure that was the glass from the front porch, but I was unsure how she got it. A vision of my mother crouched like a troll under the porch made me laugh.

"Why are you so goddamn happy?"

"I'm not happy, Mother. How could I be in this horrible place?"

"Then leave ..." She waffled her fingers into the air, motioning for me to walk away.

"How I wish I could."

"You can. I don't need you here. No one needs you ... You are a pathetic, worthless little ..."

"Stop!" My voice vibrated through the air, bouncing off the walls and hitting me across the chest. A shrill laugh filled the silence, my mother's yellowed teeth showing as she cried out in laughter.

"Still that same ol' weak little girl."

"I'm not that little girl anymore."

"Bullshit, why do you think you came back home?" She laughed again, taking a long sip of her drink. Her personal gratification over my suffering became the straw that broke me.

I went to grab a can from the bag, raising it up, my mind trying to catch up to my actions and remind me how horribly this ended last time, but just as I was about to throw it, my mother hissed, "Oh please, this again ... You could never hit me."

My arm slowly released, the can dropping back down onto the counter. "Like I said," she stumbled closer, an evil curtain falling over her eyes, "you are that weak little girl." The smell of smoke and liquor pulled at my mind, forcing the painful memory to the surface. I couldn't take it anymore; I couldn't let her hit me again.

"Stop it!" I screamed, slapping the glass out of her hand. It shattered against the floor, tiny pieces cascading all around our feet. She glared at me, waiting, baiting me to do it. She wanted me to hit her, and I wanted to hit her, more than I ever thought I would want to.

"Ha, you can't do it." She smirked, victory all over her face. "Make me another drink."

"Make it yourself." I leaned against the counter, attempting to gain composure, my hand shaking with my desire to hit her.

I never saw it coming, too distracted by my own menacing thoughts. Her hand hit hard against my cheek, her long nails scraping along my skin as she allowed the hit to linger. At that moment, I reacted. It was survival in my mind.

Pushing back hard against my mother's chest, she fell to the ground, the shards of glass skating over the tile floor as she flailed in pain, but I couldn't stop myself. Falling to my knees, I pinned each hand down, refusing to let her hit me again. Then my own fist made contact with her cheekbone. I could feel the pain vibrate through my own hand as her bones cracked beneath the pressure. With each hit, I could feel the pain, anger, hatred, transferring out of my body and into my mother. It felt ... *good.*

I could still feel the adrenaline coursing through my veins as I continued to hit my mother over and over again, just as she had done to me so many times. She deserved every hit. She screamed back at me, but I didn't stop. Every hit brought back memories of being on the other end, but this time I had the power. I had the control. For a moment, I was free from the pain.

Suddenly, I realized that the person now screaming was myself. My mother was limp. Leaning back on my feet, sweat pouring from my body, I knew I had gone too far. Her shoulders were already beginning to swell, and her right eye was bright red. I didn't see my mother though; I saw me. It was as if there were a mirror between us, only I was no longer the one lying helplessly on the floor.

Chapter Thirty-Three
Mother

"What the hell is that?" He pushed her away, her misshapen, top-heavy body falling awkwardly back on the bed. For months, she had attempted to hide the growing signs of her pregnancy. She had no idea how he would take the news.

"It's a ..." She couldn't say the words out loud; the fear she harbored over having this child was overwhelming. In no scenario did this work out well.

"You're fuckin' pregnant?"

"I think so."

"You think so?" He laughed, pulling his pants back up. "You really are stupid. You better count your blessings that I agreed to marry your ass. There ain't no one else that would be willing to put up with you. You know that, right?"

His words sliced at her skin, over and over again, reminding her she would never be able to leave. He made sure of that. The scars on her face, the pattern matching that of the boiling water as it streaked down her face, would always remind her she could never escape.

"Well, guess I have to find my pleasure elsewhere till you have that awful thing." Her eyes grew wide in shameful excitement over the idea that the abuse would stop, if only for a few months. If she had known, she would've told him the moment she knew for sure.

Being pregnant gave her false hope. For a time, the physical abuse stopped as she realized he might want this child. He didn't hurt her anymore, but as the months dragged on, she saw the true depth of his evil. There was no excuse she could give that he would take to allow her out of the house, no doctor's appointments, no grocery shopping ... *nothing.* She could hear the bolt latch from the outside of the door when he would leave, the bars on the windows obstructing her view of the world. She was more trapped than ever.

When the time came, the pain was so deep and frequent, she couldn't help but cry out. He refused to take her to the hospital. She begged over and over, reaching out to him for help, but he just watched as she suffered the fate of childbirth. When it was over, she was numb from the pain. The cries of the baby made a distant hum in her ears. She wanted to die. She wanted the pain to take her, so she closed her eyes.

It took a long time for the woman to heal, forcing him to continue to seek fulfillment of his needs elsewhere. But she didn't mind. It gave her time alone with the little girl. Her big doe eyes that would stare at her all day, the way she would snuggle onto her breast for milk. It was a comfort she had never felt before.

Growing up, her own mother didn't often show her affection for fear of what her father would think. It wasn't until later in life that she realized she was different from her siblings, her color slightly darker, eyes a deeper brown. She was no more her father's daughter than the dog was. Secretly, her mother would tell her of the love she had for her biological father and for her as a daughter, but she could never openly accept the girl for fear that her husband would take her away. That was how it all started, a deeply ingrained fear of the truth by others. She often wondered if that was the true reason she stayed.

The woman vowed it would be different for her daughter. She would love the little girl despite her father. But as the days turned into years, she grew to look more and more like her father. Every time she looked into the girl's face, it would change into his face. The little girl never had a chance of being loved, not after what her father did to her mother.

Chapter Thirty-Four
Present Day

Gradually, I lifted my mother from the ground, her weight suddenly less than before. Like a torn ragdoll, she flopped into my arms, only making a low moan, but not waking. I carried her, as a mother carries her baby, pushing open her bedroom door with my shoulder and ever so gently laying her down, her body sinking into the feathered mattress.

For over an hour, she slept while I lightly wiped the blood from her face, held ice on her bruises, and regretted every moment of hitting her. I knew what I had done was wrong, the shame settling in my stomach making me sick, but I also felt something else. There was a darkness that felt vindicated, a piece of me that did not feel sorry for her, because she had done the same thing to me, a child, for years. I lived in shame my entire childhood because of her abuse, and now I was the one in control. Shameful as it was, I did feel better.

The feeling I got from beating my mother unconscious loomed over my mind, deepening the depression I was already suffering. Each time I braved a glance at my mother, I could see the damage of my anger. While I excused my violence, having suffered hers for years, it did not stifle the degrading thoughts in my mind. I never thought of myself as a monster, someone who could hurt another with no remorse, but now that was changing.

In an effort to quell my thoughts of killing myself and my mother, burning the house with both of us inside, I drank. Pouring drink after drink till I could no longer think, my mind became numb and fuzzy. I had to escape, even if I wasn't really getting out of this place, at least I could forget ... sleep until it was all over.

However, at this particular moment on this particular day, I wanted to kill her more than ever.

"Miss Crawford, will you please ask your mother to calm down?" the young rookie officer pleaded yet again. In my drink-induced sleep, I had failed to hear my mother creeping from the house in the early evening. Apparently, we had run out of vodka. That was my fault.

"What would you have me do? I've told you she's ill. Maybe take off the cuffs?"

His eyes grew wide in fear. "No, I am definitely not doing that."

"Then I've got nothing for you."

My mother continued to scream through the door that she didn't know what was going on, which was a possibility, but for some reason, I felt like she knew exactly why she was in the back of the cop car. The phone had not stopped ringing, over and over again like a boulder bursting through my mind, until I finally answered it. It had been the police. My mother had been caught again.

"I'm going to take her down to the station, charge her," he affirmed, as if I were unaware of the process. I wanted to scream in his face, *I am a lawyer!* But it was counterproductive at the moment.

"I understand you have a duty, officer, but I am here now. I can take her home and assure you that this will not happen again." The last thing I wanted was to face Chief Morris and his smug face ... No, I was not going to the station. Not going to happen.

"Fancy seeing you back here again." Chief Morris grinned, looking down over his long, fat nose, which I wanted to punch. I could take a night in jail; *do it.*

"Ms. Lillie Crawford is being charged with disturbing the peace." The officer's voice shook as he spoke, clearly nervous, or maybe scared of the chief, or maybe even my mother, who was still putting up quite a fight in the cage, which we could all hear, considering the station was so small.

"That is quite enough, thank you, Officer Hamin." He waved the officer from the room, leaving us alone. The chief closed the door gently, moving slowly around to his desk, taking a long look in my direction. *Great.*

"I thought you were going to ensure nothing like this happened again, Miss Crawford." *Please, step a little closer so I can punch you.*

"The agreement was that I would stay to assist my mother and help prevent any further disruptions in your small town; however," I sneered, "my mother is still a woman of her own doing."

"That you agreed to manage, if I recall."

"I am doing my best here. You have no idea how difficult all this has been." I threw my hands up, overwhelmed and unable to communicate just how horrible it was taking care of that woman.

"Just arrest her. I don't care anymore. I'm never going to be able to get that horrible woman in a home anyway." I was stuck with my mother at this point, so a few nights in jail would be a nice reprieve.

"Miss Crawford," he said calmly, as if saying my name that way made him seem more authoritative, "all I want is for you to keep your mama on a short leash."

"Which I feel I've done, but honestly, I really just don't give a fuck anymore."

"I can tell."

"Oh—" Just as the words were about to escape my mouth, the door opened.

"Officer, thank you for coming." Mark's identifiable figure loomed in the doorway. "I believe Miss Crawford and her mother will need an escort back home."

"No, no—" I turned from the chief back to Mark and back again in protest. "I am perfectly capable of getting back home."

"Clearly you are not." He glared down at me. "I can smell the alcohol on your breath."

"That's old.'"

"Not enough." He waved a dismissing hand as Mark stepped aside. Rolling my eyes in defeat, I was out of energy and conviction to fight anymore.

Once again, I found myself waiting for my mother's release. The moment her face came into focus, I wanted to hit it. I wanted to knock that smug, disgusted look right off her face. She really had a way of sucking all the life out of a person, chewing it up and then just spitting it back out, as if it wasn't even good enough to eat.

"Norah, my car is this way." Mark motioned as I kept walking to Ms. Kay's truck, determined to not ride home with Mark.

"No thanks, I got this."

"Norah, I can't let you drive," he affirmed, calling out as I increased the distance between us with each step through the graveled parking lot.

"Arrest me!" I yelled back. "I could use the break."

I knew Mark wouldn't follow me, never arrest me, and I was well aware of the fact that I was abusing our distant friendship, but I didn't have anything left inside anymore. Nor did I want to ride all the way home with him knowing that Caroline didn't think their life was so perfect.

"There is no excuse for this," my mother sneered, sliding into the passenger side.

"What are you talking about? I just prevented you from getting actual charges. Chief Morris sounded serious this time. You can't be doing this shit anymore."

I was quite sure that Chief Morris would never charge my mother with anything; their history ran too deep. My mother had something on him, that I was sure of, even as a child. Whatever it was still scared him. But I wanted her to feel the gravity of her situation. Getting arrested had become this pointless timeout with no true consequences that deterred her behavior. Short of locking her in the house, I needed some way to stop her from leaving to go to the bar.

"What are you talking about? I had to come down here in the middle of the night because you were found stealing. Good-for-nothing piece of shit ..." Suddenly, I realized my mother was not living in the present but trapped by a fading memory of our past.

There were few things of consequence that happened in this small town, the yearly high school prom being one of the few. Unfortunately, I never made it to my senior prom, having been arrested for stealing. It took my mother twenty-four hours to realize I wasn't home, another hour before the police showed up at the door.

In my mind, I was not actually stealing, just borrowing, as I had every intention of returning the blue chiffon dress the next day. Caroline and I had gone dress shopping the week prior. Of course, she picked a tight-fitting, mermaid-frame baby-pink dress, while the only thing that didn't look completely wrong on me was the flowing, off-the-shoulder number at the only boutique in town. It didn't matter the cost, not really, as I couldn't afford anything. But as I glanced down at the tag, Caroline gushing over my glowing appearance, I knew I had to hate it. As I knew I would be faking an illness the night of prom. There was no world in which my mother allowed me to go.

Yet, for some reason, that evening she passed out early, completely drunk, and I knew she'd never notice my absence. Turns out even awake, she didn't notice. Caroline called, over and over again, insisting I meet Mark and her at Oscar's for dinner. She was desperate to not be alone with him on Prom night.

So, just as the sun melted behind the trees, I slipped from the house. I had assured Caroline weeks ago that I had a dress to wear, when, in fact, I didn't even own a dress. My only option seemed to be to borrow one. I never even thought she'd notice, as I'd return it by Monday when the store reopened.

But an hour later, I was being booked by Officer Morris.

My mother was currently reliving that particular moment. Her hands positioned as if she were driving, the same look on her face, the reference to me stealing. I was fifteen to her again, an insolent little girl that had interrupted her good buzz. It had been Monday morning at nine o'clock.

"I should've left you in there to teach you a lesson. You never seem to learn. Are you just stupid?" she screamed, never taking her eyes off the road. *Unnecessary.*

"You did leave me in jail, Mother. You left me in that jail for two days. You can't even remember it correctly, even when you think it's happening right now."

"Don't you dare open that mouth and talk to me like that. I will cut out your tongue and feed it to the dog."

We never had a dog, *ever.* She had never threatened or tried to cut out my tongue either, so this was new. I told myself to let it go. She was unwell, and her mind was playing an evil trick on her and me.

"I should've cut you out of me the moment I knew."

Wait ... what?

Slamming on the car breaks, my mother lurched forward, hitting her head hard against the dashboard. I never did put the seatbelt on her, a fact I neglected when I chose to slam the breaks out of anger in the middle of the road.

The weight of her words dropped onto my chest, the tightness intensifying by the second. My mother's hatred for me had never been a question, but to hear her confess that she should have had an abortion was another level to her hatred. I assumed I had done something, that initially she did love me but then changed. Whether it was from drinking or watching her suitors prefer me, there had been a time she loved me. But now I knew; she'd hated me all along. I loathed the guilt that spilled over me at the thought that I as well had wanted to *cut it out of me,* as she so horribly put it.

Without thinking, I left the car on the side of the road with my mother unconscious inside it. Walking nowhere, anywhere but here.

There was not much to this place, especially at night. Most of the road lights were out; the only glow in the darkness was the moon. It was full tonight, casting a yellow haze through the evening fog. Stars filled the sky, making it feel as if I were standing amongst them on that road. Someone told me once that stars were wishes made over the years. The ones that came true were the ones shining the brightest in the sky. I put a star in the sky once. I never saw it shine.

As I roamed the empty streets surrounded by empty fields on either side, I couldn't help but feel completely worthless. My own mother admittedly wanted to kill me before birth. She didn't grow to hate me. She hated me all along. What I thought was anger toward her life was true hatred toward me as a person, as a child ... as *her* child. I knew I had reasons behind wanting an abortion, feelings of inadequacy about being a mother, but they were never produced by ill feelings toward the child, which in my mind wasn't really a child at that time. I had pushed that idea from my mind and focused only on the fact that I was a horrible person. But, clearly, my mother felt differently. *What could cause her to hate me so much?*

Home. That was where my walk took me. The sun was rising in the distance. I had walked all night. It was almost hilarious ... *almost.* My feet had subconsciously led me back to the one place I never wanted to go again, as if reminding me I had no other choice. This was my home; this horrible, detestable excuse for a house was actually the place I called home. My life was further than rock bottom. It was buried so deep underground, I might as well be dead. My only hope was that the oxygen would run out soon.

I heard it before I saw it—a truck coming down the road, Ms. Kay's truck bouncing behind it. As the truth drew closer, I couldn't imagine who could have found it on the side of the road and would think to return it to me. Maybe my mother was directing the person, or maybe she was at the hospital, still unconscious ... wishful thinking.

No, as the truck drew closer, it was so much worse than all of those things. It was Brett. Slowly, he backed the truck into the dirt driveway, waving out the window to make sure I was aware that it was him. Oh, I was aware, acutely aware, and mortified. Once it was parked perfectly, he gently escorted my mother from the cab of his truck. She scowled at me, then retreated into the house. I was not going to be forgiven for that one, best to give her time to forget. *Maybe a few hours?*

"Everything okay, Norah?"

He was genuinely concerned, which I understood, considering how this looked. He found this car with my mother unconscious on the side of the road. He did the gentlemanly thing and returned these lost items to their owner: me. But only a fool would believe that everything was fine.

"We, uh, ran out of gas." My flat, disinterested tone gave me away. Brett's eyes glared down into my own as I shifted mine away. Last time he thought I needed actual mental help; Lord knows what he was thinking of me now. Nothing good, that was for sure.

"Your mother said you hit her."

"Well, isn't that just peachy," I jeered, glaring back at the house, the shadow of my mother in the kitchen. Most likely pouring a stiff drink. The last thing I needed was Brett now looking at me as an abusive alcoholic.

"It's nothing like that. I just slammed on the breaks, and she hit her head against the dash."

"She said it's not the first time."

"Brett, you have to understand my mother is ill. She doesn't really know what she's talking about."

The shame I had been burying with alcohol was now slapping me across the face, forcing me to wake up and see how truly horrible of a person I was for beating my mother. There was something about Brett, of all people, knowing that I had the ability to become this monster, that caused a deeper wave of shame to crash over my body, so forceful and vicious that I was surely going to drown.

"I get that. I know that." He nodded in agreement, but I could tell he still didn't understand; no one could ever understand. "I know things were hard growing up with that evil woman. I just hate to see you lose yourself to it."

"What am I supposed to do?" The words were released from my mouth, unfiltered by my clouded mind.

"Norah," he whispered, allowing me to fall into his arms. Instantly, I was crying, unable to stop the dam from breaking. For

191

a long time, he allowed me to snob helplessly into his chest, soaking his flannel shirt. There was something about the strength with which he held me that made me believe I could be broken, because he could keep all the pieces held together. As long as he never let go, I could stay this way.

All too soon, the moment ended, as I felt him pull back against my body, each shattered piece falling to the ground. It was foolish to think we could stay that way forever, or even that he could hold me together. There were too many pieces, lost and chipped; I could never be a whole person again. Not now.

"What can I do to help?"

"Nothing, really nothing, Brett." I sniffed, wiping tears and snot from my face.

"You said that last time."

"And I meant it. Just please leave us alone. There is nothing you can do."

A part of me was screaming for help, telling myself to accept his offer. However, if I accepted his help, I would have to reveal the truth ... that I was truly a monster. If he knew the truth, the real truth, not just the slight assumption he had now, he would never look at me the same way. No one would ever help someone like me, *a monster.*

He didn't move as I walked away, putting an unwanted distance between us with every step. I could feel his eyes watching me, hear the silent whisper to turn around and change my mind, but I didn't. I closed the door without ever looking back.

In the foyer, my own reflection glared back at me. Years had aged the mirror's appearance, the cracks making rivers through the calm lake of glass, the dirt an unyielding morning fog. Through it all, I could still see the person I had become. I hated this person, loathed every feature of her face. Without thinking, I smashed my fist into the glass.

Making my way out to the porch, I attempted to light a cigarette. I never smoked. I usually gagged at the smell, but for some reason it seemed the best thing to do in this moment. The alcohol wasn't doing the trick, the pain in my hand growing every second, so I had to try something else. The light flickered over the end of the cigarette, taking a moment to catch the nicotine. Smoke blanketed my face as the smell conjured up memories from my childhood. My mother always smoked after hitting me, like people smoke after sex. There was something about the smoke filling my lungs, the rush of nicotine to my brain, that made me see the point of it all.

Chapter Thirty-Five
Little Girl

The girl's screams echoed through the house. Her arm was pinned down, held firmly by his knee. Slowly, he released the smoke from behind his cracked lips, leaning down to make sure her face was engulfed in the cigarette haze. Coughing violently, her lungs burned.

"I thought you liked this," he taunted, tipping his head and narrowing his eyes.

Then, turning the cigarette over in his fingers, he pressed the burning tobacco on her pinned arm. Pushing the flame against her arm, she screamed, the pain erupting in loud, sporadic cries.

Please, God, save me! Make it stop, she thought.

He continued to press the tip of the cigarette into her flesh over and over again, deep red marks scarring her pale skin. At some point, the pain stopped, but it was only the shock setting in. He continued to push the lit cigarette against her shaking arm until it was extinguished.

"Don't let me ever catch you stealing from me again!" With that, he released her arm, grabbed his drink off the kitchen counter, and disappeared. She couldn't move, unable to wake her body from the shock. She lay there, silently crying.

Earlier that evening, as he snored in his armchair, the little girl slipped into the kitchen, gently pulling the stool up to the fridge, reaching her hand up, and feeling around until her fingers touched the cold plastic. She pulled down the small box, pausing briefly when she heard a loud snore, before silently replacing the stool and escaping out the back door.

She watched her mother do it numerous times a day. Every time he hit her, she would pull the box down, slip the long white stick from the container and light the cigarette. Her mother's face would start to change, the pain receding like a wave that crashed against the shore. The girl thought that if it could make her mother feel better, maybe it would work for her, too.

Pulling the lighter she stole earlier from her mother's pocket, she pulled a cigarette from the pack. The fire blazed between her small fingers as she attempted to light the white paper. It was a particularly windy day, making it difficult to get the thing to light. She needed a place to block the wind, but did she dare go closer to the house?

Finally, she decided to hide on the side of the house. No one would come looking for her there. Her mother napping, just as he was, both of them already in a drunken haze in the early evening. With the house sheltering her from the wind, the cigarette caught fire and came to life. Taking in a deep breath, the smoke filled her mouth and lungs. Instantly, her body rejected the nicotine, pushing it from her lungs in a violent cough.

The smoke traveled up through the cracked window and right under his nose. The girl was young, and she didn't realize the window above her head was open. She couldn't see how the smell of the cigarette woke him, like a bear catching a familiar scent.

The moment he appeared on the side of the house, seeing the girl smoking his cigarettes, she knew what would happen next. She was frozen in fear, unable to run, unable to fight back, and she just let him do it ... each and every time.

Chapter Twenty: Present Day

"Those things will kill you." Her voice was unmistakable. No one had a raspier, thicker accent.

"Yep, more than you know." I flicked the half-smoked cigarette out into the yard. "What do you want, Ms. Kay?"

"Just checking to see how your mama is doing these days?" She stood at the bottom of the porch step, waiting for an invitation that would never come, not while she had that shotgun in her hand.

"She's fine."

"Darling, your mother has never been fine." My mind prickled with suspicion as to the nature of their relationship. I figured now was a good time to ask.

"Ms. Kay, how long have you lived next door?"

"My entire life."

"You never moved away? Had a life?" This was all playing into my all-too-well-thought-out theory that she was a one-hundred-year-old witch.

"Of course, sure! I explored the world, as you young folks say, but there is no place like home." That was exactly what the witch told Dorothy to say. It all was too much. I couldn't help but laugh.

"Did you take that shotgun with you?" I jeered, still laughing, unable to control it. I wasn't sure if she was finding it all too amusing, but I really didn't care. The sinister laughter at her expense felt too good.

"Well, no, you can't take a shotgun on a plane. Have you ever been anywhere in your short, little life?"

"Actually, I used to go places all the time." Suddenly, my laughter turned into tears as every memory of vacations with Michael returned.

"Something bothering you, dear?"

"No," I assured her, fixing the hole in the dam. There was no point in thinking of things that would never be again. Those memories were from another life, clearly not even mine. More likely they were just a long dream, or maybe I had been in a coma with one foot in heaven and the other planted on the ground. A hazy mix of both worlds. Because there was no way that had actually been my life—ever. This right now was my true life; I never should've forgotten that.

"It must be hard taking care of your mama."

"Yes, it is."

I stared, eye to eye, with the woman who knew I was being abused all those years and never said a thing. Now, concerned as ever, she talked to me ... *Why the sudden heart to heart?*

"I better get back inside." Suddenly, I no longer cared for the story, as I realized she was the last person I wanted to talk to.

"Just let me know if you need anything."

The offer stopped me in my tracks. After all these years, now she was offering to help, making it clear that she was not incapable of helping. It was actually a choice she made all those years.

"You know what ..." *Stop. What's the point?* But I couldn't stop myself. "I did need something. I needed you to say something, anything to anyone." Wildly my hands flew across my face, the patch over the hole in my dam giving way again. There was an instant look of horror on Ms. Kay's face. "How could you never say anything?" I pleaded, desperately wanting to know why no one ever seemed to care enough to stop the abuse.

"I should have."

"What?"

"I should've said something. I am sorry for that. I can see that now."

"Only now?" I scoffed, not believing that she never thought to report my mother, as if the thought hadn't occurred to her all the times she heard me screaming.

"I just thought ..." Her eyes glassed over, a film of memory dancing over her foggy-gray irises. "Doesn't matter."

"It never seems to, does it?"

It mattered to me though, my entire childhood. There was never a moment I didn't feel alone in my situation with my mother. Even when I would crawl into Caroline's bed or hide away in the library with Brett, I still felt alone. We were just kids; there was nothing they could do no matter how much I tried to convince myself that they could. But Ms. Kay ... Chief Morris ...all my teachers who saw but never asked. They all could've done something. Yet they all chose to look away. They all chose to ignore what was right in front of their faces.

That night I couldn't sleep. Every time I closed my eyes, all I could see was Ms. Kay rushing over into my house, shotgun blazing and threatening to shoot my mother if she ever touched me again

... *foolish dreams.* No one ever came to save me. I had to save myself, pull myself out of the ashes of this house and make something of my life. Of course, at this moment, it was all for nothing. I was right back where I started, which is probably why I decided to give up. Why even bother trying to better my situation? Between the drinking and taking care of that ol' bitch, my life path was going to be pretty short now.

"Mama, Mama ... wake up." I shoved her shoulders, her heavy snoring a prominent sign that she was not dead as I had hoped. "Come on, get up. It's almost noon." If not for the smell, I would've left her to sleep, but the moment I walked into the room to gather the countless dirty pairs of underwear on the floor, I could smell it. The longer I waited, the worse it would be.

Dramatically, I pulled back the covers—*mistake.* I smelled it before I saw it, which was crazy when I thought back, because the shit was literally everywhere.

"What the hell?" I attempted to cover my nose with my elbow, unsure if I got any shit on my fingers from pulling back the covers. "You've got to be kidding me. Wake up!" I slapped her hard across the back, bringing her back to life.

"Jesus Christ! What the hell?" my mother shrieked, attempting to grab at the covers.

"You shit all over yourself." For a moment, I saw a flicker of embarrassment, but it would take more than that to embarrass my mother. After all, she frequently woke up in her own vomit, so shit was not too far off.

"Damnit, come on. In the bath."

Pulling her hard by the arm, I forcefully attempted to move her stiff body out of the bed and into the bathroom. Tearing at her white nightgown, she started to cry. Ripping her underwear off, the smell overwhelming and almost causing me to vomit, I threw them into the trash can. No reason to clean those.

"Get in," I demanded, pointing to the empty tub.

"Stop it, please."

"No, you need to get clean. You are filthy."

Reluctantly, she stepped into the tub. Pieces of shit ran down the drain, as the frigid water cascaded over her skeleton body. Once again, my worst moment had just been topped. Her screams, only paused by her sobs, pulsated through the small room and rang in my ears as I continued to allow the hard, cold water to pierce her body.

She continued to cry out as I forced her to sit down in the bathtub, water barely over her ankles, but I was too angry to care. There was no way I was cleaning up in there; she'd have to soak it off at this point. She shivered, the water still running cold, but I was short on compassion this morning. I tried to wash her, pulling back against her arms, dumping the water over her tangled hair, but she wouldn't stop screaming. Finally, I couldn't take it anymore.

"Do it yourself," I screamed, so close to her ear she flinched and covered it with her hand. I threw the soap at her, hitting her hard on the shoulder. Suddenly, I found new conviction in my thoughts to leave.

As I shoved each piece of clothing into my suitcase, my mind taunted me, saying *"Where will you go?"* Another piece of my mind still held on to the battle: *"Anywhere is better than here!"* Dealing with the fact that my mother couldn't take a proper shit but could still remember how to slap me was a never-ending battle. We'd be at it forever at this point, so it was time to go. *"Go where?"* my mind hissed. Suddenly, the rope that another piece of my mind had been holding so tightly lost its grip. I threw the clothes I had been packing against the wall, screaming in frustration. I was surrounded, with no way to get out. There was no way I was going to survive this. I collapsed in exhaustion on the bed. *Lights out.*

Suddenly, I woke up. I heard it before I realized what it was: a blood-curdling scream. Maybe it had been my own. I had fallen asleep, my clothes still all over the room, suitcase against the wall. The hangover was coming; I could feel the headache pushing forward, and my stomach started to turn. Checking my watch, I realized it was the middle of the night. Another scream cut through the silence. Suddenly, I remembered I had left my mother in the bathroom. Another scream ... *oh shit!*

Racing down the stairs, I flew through the bedroom door and into the bathroom. There she was, lying on the floor, shaking. At first, I thought she was having a seizure, but then I realized she was just cold—freezing, in fact. Quickly, I wrapped the towel around her wet, cold, naked body. Rubbing my hands up and down, I attempted to warm her body. I knew I should call an ambulance; she was clearly hyperthermic, but then I saw the bruises all over her body. *How could I explain them all?*

199

I ushered her into the bedroom, slipped a nightgown over her bruised shoulders, and slid her into bed. She was still shivering; at that moment, I did not see my mother but a little girl, cold and alone. Without thinking, I knew what I needed to do, so I got into the bed beside my mother, curled my fingers around her thin arms, and held her. After a few minutes, her shaking subsided, and she drifted into a deep sleep. I thought about moving, returning to my own bed, but I felt a comfort I had not felt in a long time lying there with my mother. So I stayed.

Chapter Thirty-Six
Little Girl

"You are filth." Her mother shoved her hard into the bathroom, only releasing the hold she had on her ponytail when the girl was fully in the room. She stood in the doorway blocking any attempt of escape. "Clean yourself off."

Tears streaked the girl's face, her eyes burning and her body shaking as she slowly pulled off her shirt, making every attempt to cover her naked chest.

"Not fast enough," she screamed. Buttons spun on the floor as her mother threw her white blouse out into the hallway. The girl flinched as her mother pulled at her shorts, lifting her feet before her mother could completely knock her over. With that, her mother stopped, stumbling back in disgust. Her underwear was stained red with blood and shame.

The girl didn't know what to do; she was only eleven years old, confined mostly to the house with no one to talk to. Her mother was the only person she could ask ... That was a mistake.

"That is just filthy. Get in that bathtub now, and clean yourself," she demanded.

The hot water pricked her skin as the blood bled into the water, turning it a murky brown. The trails of blood reminded the girl of the black snakes she used to see slithering through the garden beds along the house. Fear consumed her, as she had no idea what was happening; her mother never told her, just called her filth over and over again. The girl's body started to shake as she wrapped her arms around her chest, attempting to shield her body from her mother. Her mother was right. She was filth.

"All the way in." Her mother forced her down into the water, holding the top of her head until it hit the solid bottom of the tub. The water was too high; she was drowning.

She thrashed against her mother's firm grip. She thought for sure that her mother was going to kill her, drown her for bleeding. Then, suddenly, her mother stopped. Her mother was soaked, flower dress clinging to her thin frame. There was a look of shock on the mother's face, but the girl still couldn't figure it out. *What had she done? What was wrong?*

Ann Brooks

The girl could see it in her mother's eyes; something was off. It terrified the little girl, not knowing what her mother was so afraid of.

"Please, Mama, what is happening?"

"You are becoming a woman. There ain't no good in that."

The little girl thought her mother was fearful she would leave now that she was a woman, according to her words. But that was not why her mother was scared. It would be another month before he noticed, and she realized the true fear behind her mother's eyes.

Chapter Thirty-Seven
Present Day

The morning brought a haze of drunken misunderstanding as my arms curled around a cold figure. My own body blazed with heat, and in my dreams, I feared I was going to melt the cold figure in my arms. Suddenly, my eyes shot open, realizing that I was holding my mother. As I moved away from her, she was so hard, still, and cold that I thought for sure she had died in her sleep. For the first time, it gave me mixed emotions.

"Mama," I whispered into her ear, gently pushing a thin strand of misplaced hair behind her ear, trying to figure out if she was alive. As the thought of her death settled into my own lost mind, she suddenly twitched. Taken off guard, I stumbled back in the bed and fell completely.

"No!" she screamed from the sheets. "No, no, no!" Quickly, I climbed back up on the bed thinking she had been yelling at me to stop, only to realize her eyes were still closed. She was having another nightmare. Her body was shaking, and in my longing to feel close to someone again, I gently wrapped my arms around her shoulders, pulling tighter in an attempt to calm her nerves as she screamed.

"Get off me!" she suddenly bellowed, twisting beneath my arms.

"It's okay, it's okay," I tried to reassure her as she continued to scream. Then I felt a piercing shock of pain in my forearm, my mind taking a few moments to understand what was happening. *She bit me!*

"Jesus!" I yelled, releasing my hold and pushing her hard off the bed. "What the hell?"

"Don't you ever touch me again, you disgusting, little bitch." She clawed at the bed as she tried to raise her body from the floor, her words erupting from her mouth as she did so.

"Mama, I was just trying to help you." There was no point in an excuse, but my mind had become desperate for her to let me back in. Depression had fallen like a dark blanket around me, my mother's comfort last night giving a sliver of light through a hole.

But now she was violently stitching it back together, leaving me alone in the darkness.

"Get out of my room. Don't you dare touch me ever again. I want you out!" She was screaming, now throwing any item on the floor she could wrap her fingers around as I made my escape to the door. "I hate you! You worthless ..."

Her screams faded as I closed the door, leaving her to her own destruction. Even though I knew it was foolish to think that somehow things had changed overnight, I couldn't shake the feeling that, although she was here the entire time, I was truly alone in my depression. Only my inner monster kept me company.

"Open this door, Norah. I know you are home." Caroline banged against the door; any moment she was going to break it down. I stood on the other side of the door, refusing to open it. I knew the moment she looked into my eyes she would see me as a monster. In the last few days, I had allowed it to take over completely. He was mostly fueled by vodka.

"So help me, God, Norah, if you don't answer this damn door, I am going to break it down!"

I had avoided all calls after our confrontation in the parking lot, knowing that I wasn't a friend to her anymore. She was better off just forgetting about me.

"I know you are in there. Open the door!" She was pissed, her fist hitting hard against the wooden door that was barely holding together, much like myself. There was no use resisting. She was going to find out soon enough, better now than dealing with it later, so I pulled the door open to reveal the truth.

"What the hell?" She just stood there, the anger dissolving from her face as she realized. My oversized college sweatshirt was covered in coffee stains. I was getting clumsy in my drunkenness. I had on baggy, holed sweatpants. I hadn't brushed my hair in days, nor taken a shower. Even out of disguise, I now appeared homeless. "You were supposed to call me!"

"Why?" I figured after our last conversation she never wanted to talk to me again, and I had resolved that there was no helping me through this hell hole.

"Because ... Oh god, is that vodka on your breath? Jesus Christ, Norah. It's ten o'clock in the morning." Her face contorted in disgust.

"I know. I got a late start today."

"This is not the time for jokes. This is serious. Look at you!"

"No, thanks."

She scoffed as I continued to avoid the truth of what she was saying. I walked away, leaving the door open, and went to make a drink in the kitchen. She followed, covering her mouth as she made her way through the house. I guess it did smell.

"This is bad," she confessed, glancing around the kitchen, her eyes wider than normal.

Dirty soup bowls were piled up in the sink. That moment with my mother, feeling her against my body and for a second thinking that I was not alone or that I could possibly have her to help me through this, was completely shattered by her ill response to my presence. She had refused to come out of the room for days, the smell growing, but suddenly my "give a shit" was rendered numb by alcohol. Every time I tried to find a reason to get up and do something, I lost it like a shadow in the darkness.

"Just leave," I groaned, not having anything left inside me to deal with a Caroline intervention. *Just leave me here to die.*

"I just—" She stopped, unable to continue, the tears forming in the corners of her eyes. She was working hard to keep them at bay. The thought of Caroline crying over my crumbling life made me regret ever opening the door.

"It's okay. I'm fine, I promise. It's just been a rough couple of days. That's all." I shrugged, hoping she would accept my lame excuse for the state of things. Judging by her glare, it was not working.

"You're lost out here."

"Don't do that." I could feel it, deep inside, threatening to explode.

"Honey, you have got to pull yourself out of this."

"What's the point?" I pulled the flask from my sweater pocket and poured the vodka into my coffee. She pursed her lips in deep disapproval over my coping methods. I dragged my slippered feet into the living room, throwing my body down onto the couch in defeat.

"That is not going to solve this problem."

"Problem? What problem?"

"If you are not already there, you are becoming a drunk. I hate to say it to your face, honey, but there is the cold, hard truth for you."

"As if I didn't notice," I snapped back, fully annoyed by her judgment. "As if I don't notice that I'm completely falling apart. Trust me, I know. If anyone knows, it's me! But what's the point? I've got nothing ... nothing!" The raspy croak to my own voice was foreign to me, as if I was having an out-of-body experience, looking down on this broken, drunk person, not realizing that it was me.

"Stop that! You stop that right now." Caroline marched over to the couch and forced me up by the arm.

"You are not this person."

I scoffed. Clearly, I was no better than my circumstances.

"You are a good person."

Hardly, I literally beat my own mother.

"You are strong."

Highly unlikely, evident mostly by my current state.

"You need to snap out of this."

For a moment, I thought she was literally going to try and *slap* me out of it, but she released me, her face contorting from anger to fear.

"Are you even eating real food?" I didn't have to answer; just by looking at me, she could tell that my diet was mostly alcohol. She disappeared into the kitchen.

Caroline to the rescue, as always. Suddenly, I realized that Brett must have called her after the little incident with my mother being left for dead on the side of the road. Of course, that was weeks ago. So *why now?*

"Okay, so you have eggs. I'll make you an omelet." I was too hungry to argue. "What do you want in it?"

"Bacon and tomatoes."

She nodded, thankful she didn't have to fight me on the subject. I had been surviving on oatmeal, mostly, and soup for dinner. A warm meal with some protein would probably be appreciated by my body. Of course, I worried it would give it false hope. It would be back to oatmeal and soup when she left.

As she cooked, the smell filled the kitchen, bringing to the surface a memory that reminded me why I had stopped cooking breakfast, the real reason. Bacon and tomatoes were a bad choice. I could have at least picked two other ingredients. Maybe then I would not be crying right now.

"What's wrong? What happened?" Caroline immediately stopped cooking and rushed over to me.

"Michael used to cook me breakfast, an omelet with bacon and tomatoes."

Attempting to calm myself, I tried to find the humor in my choice. I actually found it funny that it hadn't even occurred to me that I was asking her to cook me the same thing that Michael did every morning. *Just when I thought I was making progress ...*

"Why are you laughing ... and crying?" Caroline started a nervous laugh, probably because she just wasn't sure what was going on.

"My life. I'm laughing at my life and the thought of Michael, as if I did have love and goodness in my life at one point." Caroline was no longer laughing. "Of course, I would screw that up. I never should've allowed myself to be that happy. I should've known I would have to pay."

Caroline wrapped her arms around me, pulling me tightly against her quickly rising chest. She squeezed, making sure that I knew she was here to hold me together. Crying on her shoulder, literally, I could feel myself slowly falling apart. She was not strong enough to hold all the tiny pieces together. No one was. I tried to manage this scattered life as if the pieces could actually be put back together, but no. That was foolish. The pieces didn't even match.

"You did deserve it. You still do." Caroline held my face in her hands, assuring me that I was worthy, but she didn't know how I had been treating my mother. If she did, she would not look at me that way.

"No, I really don't. All of this is a punishment, and this is what I deserve."

"Why would you say that? God is not punishing you."

"There is no God."

"It's a figure of speech. Take it for what it means to you. You are not being punished," she assured.

"If you knew, you would understand."

"Oh, trust me, honey, I understand. You think I don't see what is happening here?" *Was it that obvious?* "You are killing yourself, giving up. You are pushing away everyone who has ever cared about you. Mark even said you drove away from him drunk? Brett told me he found your mother on the side of the road. I mean, Jesus Christ, Norah. What the hell?" My face sunk into my hands, attempting to hide the shame of it all. "I know Michael came to see you, tried to help you. Why didn't you accept his help? Or Brett's help? It's like you want to die." Her eyes were glassy, flooded with tears, but she held it together.

"What would you have me do?"

"Stop drinking, for one. Take a shower. Stop beating your mother."

So she did know. *Thanks, Brett.*

"Just try to give a shit about something! Anything!" She threw her hands up, clearly exasperated with it all. I understood her feelings. I was tired of it all too, but luckily for her, she got to walk out of here. She got to go home to her real, loving family, while I was forever stuck in this hell.

"If I say I'll try, will you leave?" The words preceded thought, unaware of the damage they would cause. They were like a giant wrecking ball, crashing through our friendship.

"I can't keep dealing with this shit."

"Then don't. I didn't ask for your help." I took in a deep breath, trying to calm my anger before I took it too far. "Look, you came by to check on me. Thank you, but I assure you I am fine. Now, I really am busy." My eyes shifted to the door, a polite Southern way of saying, *Get the hell out of my house.*

"After all that we have been through, that is how you want to play this?" She stared hard with her strong hands on her hips, waiting for my response. I could not take it anymore. Looking away, I shrugged my shoulders.

"Fine." *Is that what that word sounded like?* The word was firm and spat out with aggression as she grabbed her purse off the counter and left.

Just as I was about to be free of her, most likely forever, she stopped, doorknob in hand. Looking back over her shoulder, the tears now streaming down her porcelain face, she said, "You know, for once, I didn't come here for you. I came here for me. I needed you, but clearly you are incapable of seeing that. I really never thought I'd see the day when you turned into your mother. After everything ..." She slammed the door.

Before her car could disappear behind a cloud of dust, I was pouring another drink. I attempted to flush away all memories of Caroline, the look on her face when she saw me for the first time, the pain in her eyes when I shoved her away, but most of all the shame that for the first time in my life she needed me and I couldn't be there for her.

It took about ten shots of vodka, at least half of the bottle, before I could feel myself losing control. I stumbled through the house, drink in hand, memories flooding my mind. *Why won't they go away?*

"Go away!" I screamed through the empty halls, slapping each depressing dancer on the wall, wishing they would all just disappear. I wanted everything in this house to disappear, the fire taking it all, even the ashes left behind.

Caroline's words brought to life the realization of the truth of my consequences. From the day I arrived, I felt an instant wave of change. A wave that had only grown stronger in the depths of the ocean, the wind fueling this power as it neared the shore. The moment it hit, it would surely kill me. I never knew by staying here that I was signing my own death warrant.

Chapter Thirty-Eight
Little Girl

The little girl was helpless, lying on the broken bed, unable to move. Her body had given up. Everything was numb. She feared that if she allowed her mind, or body, to wake up, then all the memories, the torture, the pain, would come flooding back, killing her at this very moment.

She could still smell him on her, the liquor and sweat. Immediately, she wanted to wash him away, but her body was too damaged. There would be large bruises on her legs and arms, already starting to show. She listened as the rain fell on the roof, focusing on each drop as it hit, counting them one by one, anything to keep her mind off of what had just happened.

After a long time, the rain stopped, warmth from the sun gliding through the window and washing over her cold body. She could hear the birds chirping in the tree outside her bedroom window. How she wished she was a bird, to soar over the world, looking down on everything. It would seem so small, she thought to herself. Just like she felt now—small.

She heard the front door creak, the light footsteps of her mother; she was home. If she found the little girl, if she knew, she would kill her. With no other thought than survival, she pulled her loose, faded denim shorts up over her thin waist and disappeared out the window, a familiar branch catching her, lowering her to the ground as she took off into the trees.

She ran fast and hard toward the lake, pushing through it all, the pain in her lungs and limbs taking away from the pain of the abuse. She ran until she could not run anymore.

Gasping for air, her hands fell to her knees as she attempted to catch her breath. She was almost there, the lake glistening in the distance. Through all that she was enduring in that house, she prayed every day, every second. She prayed that God would take her away from this horrible place, give her a mother who loved her, would hold her at night and maybe even read her a bedtime story, just like a real mother would do for her daughter. But it had been years ... years of abuse. In her mind, there was no God. She had clearly died already and was in hell.

Chapter Thirty-Nine
Present Day

Gasping for air, pulling against the water, I needed to breathe ... *I am drowning.* The water surrounded me. There was no escape, as if I were in a box filled with black water, instead of in the lake. Suddenly, there was a bright light ... *an angel? ... This is my death.*

I gasped for air, pulling myself out of the nightmare. Covered in sweat, breathing heavily, I honestly feared that I was drowning. *It was just a dream, just a dream.* Placing a stable hand over my chest, I tried to calm down. The dream felt so real, but it wasn't. My mind realized that now, but I needed my body to catch up. *Calm down, deep breaths.*

There was a part of me that couldn't help but think that the dream was symbolic; I did, in fact, feel as if I were drowning in this place, mostly in alcohol these days. Thinking of alcohol, my head was pounding. I needed coffee, Advil, and another stiff drink.

My memory of last night had hazed after that tenth drink, most of my recall clouded in darkness. *Maybe I just went to bed?* The thick, dry taste of alcohol soured my mouth. *I needed to brush my teeth.* Just as I was putting the brush in my mouth, I could feel the vomit rising in my stomach, forcing me to lurch over the sink. Pulling myself back up, feeling a sharp pain in my front temple, I unknowingly glanced in the one mirror I had not removed from this house. Falling backward, stumbling onto the toilet, I could not believe that the person in the mirror was me. Surely, that was not *my* face.

Before I braved another look, I gently ran my fingertips over my cheek. *Ouch!* There was definitely something wrong with my face. Slowly, I moved toward the mirror, an anxious beat to my heart at what I was about to see. The large purple-and-black bruise underneath my left eye gave my face a Frankenstein appearance. *What happened?*

With each blink, my face pulsated in pain, my lips barely able to part without a piercing pain vibrating throughout my face. My entire body was sore. I could feel the stiffness in my limbs, my body's rebellion against movement, but the pain was all centralized in my face. Gently, I attempted to wash my face, blood dried along my cheek and lips from whatever clearly hit me last night. For a moment, I figured it could be my mother, but then realized there was no way she had the strength to cause this level of damage. I must have fallen, hit something myself. The fact that I couldn't remember was really not good.

Pain seared through my arm as I pulled my blood-stained clothes from my sticky body. There was still a winter chill in the air, but somehow, I was covered in a thick layer of sweat. No doubt from my nightmares of drowning. After I pulled on some dry, semi-clean clothes, I made my way downstairs. First on the agenda was finding my mother; maybe she, even in her mental state, could tell me what had happened.

The door barely opened, but just enough so I could see her bed was empty, and I made a mental note to wash her clothes today. Without thinking much about it, I followed the silent hallway back down to the foot of the stairs to the swinging kitchen door. Looking up as I entered the kitchen, as my mind thought she'd be standing there, drink in hand, I didn't notice as my foot tripped over an object on the floor.

There she was, lying motionless. *Oh God, she's dead!* The scene unfolded behind my broken, hazed eyes, as I saw the blood covering her body, her arms oddly sprawled out to her sides, face drowning in a pool of blood. *Did I finally snap? Did I kill her?* I felt as if I would vomit again, a sickening feeling strangling me as thoughts of killing my mother flooded my mind. *What happened?*

"Oh, God, Mama, I am so sorry. Please wake up, please."

I wasn't sure if I should touch her, my shaky hands hovering over her body, unsure of what happened, what to do next.

"Please, wake up, please, Mama." Not like this. She could not go like this. She had to wake up. *Is she breathing or not?* She lay there, *lifeless*, my own body absorbing her lifeforce and exploding in frantic anxiety.

I fell back onto the wall, shock taking over and paralyzing my body as I started to cry. All I could assume was that in a drunken blackout I had killed my mother ... *I killed my mother.*

Suddenly, she gasped for air, life violently pushed back into her body. *Holy shit!*

"Mama, Mama, are you okay?" I tried to help her, but she moaned at my touch. "It's okay. I'm here." Her breathing was labored. Now was the time, no excuses. Pulling the phone down, my fingers barely able to push the numbers, I waited, anxiously, to hear another voice.

"911. What's your emergency?"

"Yes, my mother. I'm not sure what happened, but she needs help."

"Yes, ma'am, help is on the way. Please stay on the line to answer a few questions."

The woman's voice faded into the background, my mind unable to answer any of her questions as my anxiety rose, taking control. I paced the kitchen, my mother gasping for air on the ground. I knew there were going to be questions, ones I could not answer. Not only that, but I also had a massive black eye. It looks as if we got into a fight ... *what happened?*

Being drunk was not an excuse. I was well aware of that. I prosecuted a case once, where a woman, who was blackout drunk, stabbed her unfaithful boyfriend. Remembered nothing. She went to prison for twenty-five years ... *Oh, God, I can't go to prison.*

The doors slammed outside. They were here. I still had no explanation, no memory of what actually happened last night. *This is bad, very, very, bad.*

"Ma'am, where is your mother?"

"In the kitchen." Holding the door, two EMTs rushed by me with large medical bags in their hands, their fresh scent a stark contrast to the liquor still sweating out from my pores.

"Ma'am, can you hear me?" The EMT immediately started to assess the situation, checking her vitals, trying to get her to respond, but nothing. She was still gasping for air, not talking.

She is dying, help her!

"We are going to take her to the hospital." One EMT disappeared and returned quickly with the stretcher. Within minutes, my mother was hauled out of the house, unresponsive. *Oh God, what did I do?*

I followed the EMT, thinking I could ride with them, but the EMT stopped me. "Sorry, ma'am." He closed the doors. *But why? Why could I not go?* She was my mother; I should be able to ride with her. As the ambulance pulled away, I realized why I wasn't allowed to go. A police car, lights flashing, was right behind the ambulance.

Of all the cops in this town, Mark just had to catch this case. Of course, I was quite sure he intentionally showed up to this particular call. I could envision him sitting in his patrol car, cup of coffee in one hand, while fidgeting with his phone in the other, numbly passing the wasted hours while on call. Then, suddenly, a frantic call across the radio, a woman possibly dead. Then the address, and Mark knew.

"Just walk me through what happened."

"I told you. I don't know." My head was pounding, my leg shaking uncontrollably as I attempted to smoke the cigarette Mark had reluctantly lit for me as we watched the ambulance disappear in the distance. *Just a few questions,* he assured, then he would take me to the hospital. Yeah, I'd heard that before. This was a very clear, cut-and-dried domestic dispute case. This was an interrogation, whether Mark cared to admit it or not.

"Just tell me what you do remember." Mark reached a comforting hand across the space between us, but I backed away. I didn't deserve comfort.

"Yesterday, I did some cleaning." I was too embarrassed to reveal the conversation I had with Caroline.

"What was your mother doing during this time?"

"What does it matter?" The formal line of questioning seeded anger into my mind. Mark shot me a *just-tell-me* look.

"She was mostly sleeping in her room, pretty much all she does these days."

"And that is all you remember?"

"Yes, Mark. Come on, what the hell is this?" I could see he knew that Caroline had come over and was probing me to confirm the fact, but again I did not want to get into any details of what happened. Better to add that interaction to the *do-not-remember* column.

"I'm just trying to help you, Norah."

"I told you I don't remember. I was drunk. What do you want from me?"

"I want to believe that all this was an accident, and you didn't just try to kill your mother."

"What? Oh please. You know that I wouldn't do that."

"Actually, I'm not sure. Caroline told me—"

"Oh, fuck off." I threw the cigarette out into the dry grass, the last few living blades catching ablaze, then dying in the wind.

"How did you get the cut on your arm?" *Oh shit,* I hadn't noticed the dried blood on my forearm in all the commotion of the morning. Gently brushing at the dried blood, a new scar to keep my old ones company, I saw all the pain of the past now joined by my present pain. Quickly, I pulled my sleeve down over my arm to hide them.

"Clearly, I cut myself."

"Did your mother cut you?"

"This is ridiculous. I told you I don't remember!"

"Okay, have you been drinking already this morning?"

"It's coffee." That was a low blow. Of course, that was all I wanted in this moment.

"Really? Because I can smell it on your breath."

"Residual." My eyes narrowed. Suddenly, I got the feeling that he was not on my side, as if he were trying to get me to confess that I tried to kill my mother when he knew very well I could not remember. Or maybe he was pushing me because he thought I was lying. Either way, he was pissing me off.

"Okay, Norah, if you don't want to talk to me, then fine. You can talk to the investigating officer."

"Love to," I sneered, a thick distaste for Mark swirling in my mouth. Normally, I'd wash it away with some vodka, but I had to drive to the hospital now. Deal with my possibly dying mother, then with him.

Deep down, I knew Mark was trying to help, be a friend in a horrible situation. But a black film had fallen over my eyes, preventing me from seeing the truth. My depression, shoveled by my guilt, dug a deep black hole in my mind. Even if someone threw me a safety rope, I don't think I would've seen it. Not in that moment. In that moment, I was lost.

Chapter Forty
Little Girl

There was a dark silence in the house. Quickly, she shoved the clothes into her school backpack. It was time. He had been drinking all day, and he was drunk and passed out in the chair at this point in the evening. She knew this was her only moment to escape. She didn't know where she was going, just that she *was* going—that was all that mattered.

She was no longer a little girl anymore; he took that from her the moment she became a woman, as her mother called it. Night after night, while her mother drank herself into a coma, he would force himself on her small helpless body. All she thought about was getting away from him, no matter the cost.

She crept down the stairs, avoiding all the creaks as usual. The door was only a few steps from the bottom stair. She was going to make it. She was going to be free. She reached for the doorknob ...

"Where do you think you are going?" Her mother appeared in the kitchen doorway, just a few feet from her salvation. Fear consumed her. She was caught. "Your little ass is going to pay for this."

The ice clinked in her glass as she took a long sip, eyes filled with hatred. The girl knew she could outrun her mother. If she could make it to the woods, then she could hide. The chance of her mother finding her would be slim. Maybe she could still make it. She reached for the doorknob ...

Suddenly, a sharp pain burst from her arm. Looking down, she could see the large shards of glass sticking out and the blood covering her entire arm. Suddenly, a deep wave of fear crashed against her entire body, causing it to shake.

"You will never leave this place, you little bitch." Her lips curled into an evil smile, her yellowed eyes glowing in the faint moonlight and frizzy hair wildly dancing around her stoic face. Scoffing down at her arm, not a flicker of concern on her face, she turned back to the kitchen, leaving the little girl alone and bleeding. Resolved to her fate.

The blood dripped slowly onto the floor. She could not leave now, not with the glass cutting this deeply into her arm. The pain was nothing compared to the realization that she was never getting out. She thought this time would be different.

For years, the little girl had begged for help, prayed to the stars for a God that never came. Tonight, she didn't pray. She knew the only way out now.

Part Five: The Aftermath

Just as the roar of the wind beats against the walls, the water rises just above your face, and the realization sets in that you will die. Suddenly, it all stops. The noise fades, leaving nothing behind but a ghostly silence.

It takes a moment to recognize that the storm has passed, that it's safe to emerge from your shelter. There are no windows to peer through to see the end coming or know that the storm is truly over. It's more a feeling. The pressure that had been building, pressing in all around you, is gone. The walls do not flex against the wind, nor does the water rise any higher, but it starts to recede. It is over. The storm has passed.

As surely as the storm crashed against the shore to claim your life, it is gone. The swirl of the clouds loosens as the dark clouds slowly dissipate into the distance. The sun breaches over the horizon, and you realize you survived, but at what cost? Because now, you must live in the aftermath of the storm.

Chapter Forty-One
Present Day

"Your mother suffered a severe blow to the head. It appears as if she fell in the kitchen, hitting her head on the corner of the table. See this mark just here?"

The juvenile doctor wisped his finger over the deep cut just above her left temple. My mother lay sleeping—more like comatose, in my opinion—in the hospital bed, her thinned gray hair still flecked with blood, and the stitches across her forehead a blazing emblem impressed upon her by my monster.

The arduous ride with Ms. Kay, who refused to allow me to drive off in front of Mark smelling heavily of liquor, to the hospital was thankfully met by silence on her end. Yet, my mind would not be silenced as I attempted to unlock the darkness clouding my mind of the events of last night. If I could just remember ...

Maybe I would learn it was self-defense, that she attacked first; that wasn't out of the realm of possibility by any stretch of the imagination. Of course, I had thought about the fact that if I remembered beating my mother to her near death, then I could no longer deny the monster was in control. I had the feeling my mind was blocking it from my memory more than it being lost in a haze of drunkenness. Every minute I was awake, this dark monster took hold and refused to bring light to what had happened.

As I looked down at my mother, helpless and injured, I felt a deep need to take her hand, curl her bone-thin fingers into my own, and feign remorse. There was a part of me that was filled with guilt over what happened, no matter the circumstances, but at least I called for help. That was something she never did for me, no matter how badly she beat me. So there was a part of my sorrow that was faked, but I still couldn't shake the fact that there was a part that was not.

"This is what caused the loss of blood, causing her to lose consciousness," the doctor was saying as I pulled my mother's cold, clammy hand into my own hot, rough one. Immediately, anguish filled his youthfully chiseled face as he presumed my own grief. "Much longer, and we might be having a very different conversation." His deep-brown eyes shifted as he spoke, unwilling, or maybe unable, to face me directly as he told me to my face that I almost killed my mother.

"She seems fine now." *Fingers crossed so that I'm not arrested for attempted murder.* Despite her sleepiness, my mother did actually seem fine. She was breathing independently, a notable lack of wires and machines hooked up to her body as you would see with a dying patient. Everything *felt* fine.

"Well, we took some CT scans of her brain." Effortlessly, as if he planned it all along, he flipped the thin black X-ray from his folder and slid it up onto the board, a bronzed ring on this left finger catching the afternoon light. A light flickered on, bringing to life a picture of my mother's brain.

"So you can see here." He traced his smooth fingers over the dark canyons, deep rivers weaving through my mother's brain. "You see, a healthy brain appears more sponge-like. However, your mother's is more like a coral."

Glaring at the picture made it all real. Every memory lapse, every scream, every endless search for something unknown. It was all there, lost in the crevices of my mother's mind. *She wasn't faking it all this time.*

"Here, these dark holes." He pointed to the various points, insecurely shifting his eyes between myself and the picture to ensure my attention. "That is the disease eating away at your mother's brain."

"Yes, I know about her disease." *Regrettably, in all matters, I am very well aware of her disease.* "What does all this mean?"

"Well, see this small white spot here?" His finger circled a small, barely noticeable fuzz on the screen. "That is bleeding in her brain, caused by the fall."

My mind struggled to focus on the small, almost insignificant, speck on the corner of her brain. Something so small surely couldn't cause more damage than the disease literally eating away at her brain.

"There are two possible outcomes. This bleeding will stop on its own, causing only minimum frontal lobe functioning loss, or it could grow, eventually killing her. It is a very slow and very painful death." There was deep compassion on his face as his thick brows raised, widening his eyes, and his mouth pulled into a tight line as he undoubtedly delivered the heartbreaking news.

"What do you recommend we do?"

"Well, see the fact is ... I ..." He shifted nervously, giving me the feeling that this might be the first time he had to deliver such dire news. After all, he was barely a man, more a doctor-child. As with everyone we encountered in this process, I assumed he thought that I loved my mother, cared about her wellbeing, and wanted her around as long as possible. But all that was a lie, I wasn't even good at faking it, so it was hard for me to understand how others did not see my clear disdain for my mother. Yet, in this moment, the guilt was festering in the pit of my stomach, causing an actual concern for my mother's wellbeing in this particular incident.

"It's okay. Just tell me."

"It is difficult. With your mother's disease, the surgery to stop the bleeding may be futile, cause her more pain, and have a long recovery process that she may never truly be able to cope with, as she suffers from Alzheimer's. Even if we go through with a successful surgery, it will not guarantee the return of any lost functioning." He glanced over at my dying mother, and judging by the look in his eyes he was already signing her death warrant.

"I understand."

"It is your call as her daughter," he added, as if somehow that would make me feel better.

"Do you love your mother?" I asked the doctor as I stared down at my own, trying desperately to find even an ounce of love for this cold, hateful woman.

"I don't understand the question?"

"I'm trying to ascertain if you love your mother. If so, what would you do?" My guilt pulled at my mind to find the right decision on my mother's fate. With no love in my own heart, I reached out to the doctor for guidance.

"I do, in fact, love my mother. By that, I would take her home. Make her comfortable and spend the last moments of her life by her side."

"Thank you."

For a long moment, we both stared at each other, a growing sense of empathy between us both as each of our eyes glazed over with tears. Maybe he did understand more than I was giving him credit for. Somehow it felt as if he saw the truth of our relationship, or it could have just been the truth of our situation. He did not romanticize the fact she was dying, which, in turn, encouraged me to accept it in a peaceful manner. He excused the thought that what was happening to my mother was my fault and instead pronounced it as an accident. While on paper it was only a head wound, in my heart it seemed as if I was being absolved of her illness as well. Unknowingly, I had taken on the burden of guilt for her disease all this time.

"So we'll keep her another night for observation, but pending any dramatic changes, she should be able to go home soon." With that, he flipped her chart closed and slid it into the small envelope at the end of her bed. He paused ever so slightly at the door, as if there was more to say, but then decided against it and left.

There was a familiar coldness to the dark, silent hospital room. The night played tricks on my mind as I dreamed of the last time I found myself alone in a hospital room, dealing with the loss of the only child I'd ever be able to claim. Endlessly, I tossed over and over on the small, very uncomfortable chair bed next to my mother, who remained in her comatose state all night and into the early hours of the morning. My only reprieve was a nurse who came every few hours to check on her condition.

"I do think she should wake up soon," the nurse assured me when I stirred in the chair, the first rays of the rising sun peeking through the window. Finally, I could wake up, escape my dreams.

"Thanks." It was all I could muster considering I was still torn over what I truly wanted of my mother's conditions at this point. If she woke, remembered the events of that night, I could find myself going to jail. Worse, my monster would be confirmed. But if she didn't wake, then the shameful guilt would consume me, leaving nothing behind. I wasn't sure in this moment what would be worse.

"Caroline," I whispered into the phone, praying she didn't hang up at the sound of my voice. In the glowing morning light, I realized that I needed her most. I was never going to make it through this one without her strength and conviction. So even though I was a horrible person, and she might never speak to me again, I had to try.

"Norah? Is everything okay?" After everything I said, I thought for sure she would be harsh with me, but instantly I could hear the softness in her voice. It brought painful tears to my eyes, a knot so large in my throat I found it hard to speak.

"It's, it's my mother," I choked out.

"Where are you?"

"The hospital."

"I'll be right there. It's okay, I'm coming." My body crumbled, the phone dropping down by my side as I sobbed in relief. For the first time since my return home, I actually acknowledged that my mother needed me to be there for her now. Caroline also needed me as well. Seeing my mother laying there, knowing what I most likely did, I realized I could never pick up the bottle again. Not only to be better for my mother, but for Caroline as well. I just didn't know how to get there without her help.

There was a blank void to my thoughts as I waited for Caroline to arrive at the hospital. My eyes fixated on a small flower, wilted in the wallpaper on the walls. It was familiar to me to see the figures on the walls. Lost friends of a lonely childhood. But the moment Caroline entered the room, I pulled my mind to the present, reminding myself that I did have a true friend. A person who, no matter how horrible I had been, was going to be there when I needed her the most.

"Caroline, I am so sorry." I wanted to be strong, show her that I was ready to pull myself together and try to be there for her, but the moment she wrapped her arms around me, I couldn't stop crying.

"It's okay. It's okay." Gently, she stroked my hair, her soothing voice a wave of relief rushing over my bare body, refreshing every sense.

"No, it's not." I pulled away, forcing her to look at me for who I truly was. "I've been absolutely horrible."

"You are not horrible. You are a victim."

"That's no excuse."

"I know that."

There was a deep truth in her words, a feeling of shame that had yet to claim a name until this moment. I had been excusing my own monstrous behavior, blaming my mother's ill treatment of me as a child as the reasons for my neglect, pushing my friend away, assured I was justified in my actions. But I was not. I had allowed the monster to take over, encouraged it with hate, and fueled it with alcohol. I had been unaware that what I needed most was to acknowledge that I was victimized, and that it did not excuse my behavior, but instead, it should propel my recovery.

"I don't know what to do."

"Yes, you do." Caroline stepped back, taking both my hands, staring at the monster within me and not shying away. "Every second, you make a choice. Make one you know is right, stepping one foot at a time in the right direction. That is what you do."

"What if I can't? What if I don't know the right choice to make? Or I can't find it ... I can't find the next step."

"I know it feels overwhelming, because you are at the beginning. Your life has been torn apart, and you don't even know where to start the cleanup. But I am here. I will be here to guide you."

I could feel the enormous weight—the pressure that had been pushing down on me for months, causing my lungs to strain for air and my body to succumb to the pain—suddenly being lifted. There it was, what I so desperately needed all these months ... *love.*

Chapter Forty-Two
Mother

There is always a moment. A moment a person wants to give up. The tide has rushed upon them, pulling relentlessly over and over again against their efforts to survive. The ripe current is fueled by unknown forces within, unstoppable and unbeatable by a person who has grown weak from a continual battle to swim. As she started to let go, allowing the waters to take her down, she felt a peaceful calm, too alluring to let go of now.

The woman stood in the kitchen, the smell of cigarette smoke seeping into every crack in the house, yellowing the walls and clogging the air, a nasty film of disgust over her life in this place. She finally gave in and lit the cigarette right there in the kitchen while she was cooking dinner.

Blowing the smoke out smoothly from her lungs, she could feel a wave of relief. Her lungs did not fight the smoke; the opposite happened. They accepted the smoke with open, greedy arms. For years, she lived in the house as he blew smoke all over the walls and in her face. It was only natural for her to start as well. She came to feel the same way about drinking. Being numb, lost under the water, was better than fighting against his ruthless will.

For years she had tried to swim, find something to hold on to as he ravaged every piece of her body, stole every moment of time, and worse, poisoned her mind. Each time she showed any affection to the little girl, he would bellow about how much she resembled his own likeness. How her eyes glowed with a fire as his own, her skin a porcelain reflection of his dominating genes. It caused a bile to rise in her mouth, forcing her to push every feeling of the girl from her body, as she had no choice but to acknowledge that the girl was not hers to have, but his alone.

There was a moment—call it a hesitation—as she turned the knob on the door. Her mind knew that it was wrong, that under normal circumstances he would never have let her leave the house, let alone at this late hour. She was assured he would hunt her down, pull her by her hair, and chain her inside the house when he finally found her at the bar that evening. But as the evening carried on, her mind falling into a drunken blackness, she failed to notice his lack of appearance to drag her home.

At the time, she couldn't figure out what was different. Just a feeling she got when she walked into the house. It was too quiet, too still. Her mind searched for the missing piece—then she realized. He was not sleeping. She could not hear his snores echoing through the house, nor the creak in his chair as his body drifted back and forth under this breath. He was gone. A wave of relief washed over her body as she thought about him with another woman. Silently, she prayed he would leave her, find comfort in another and just disappear. Selfishly, she had taken his recent ambivalence toward her as a sign that her prayers had been answered, if only for a short while. Yet, it was not her prayers being answered ... it was a true monster lying in wait.

As she stumbled further into the house, bracing herself on the kitchen counter as she attempted to reach for her hidden pack of cigarettes, her mind swirled with alcohol. Pulling the singular stick from the pack, she allowed her mind to dance in the thought that he had finally left. Just as she flicked the light, the cigarette catching flame at the end, she heard it.

Above her head, she heard the base boards flex under a heavy weight. *He was here.* Fear shook her body as she realized her daughter's bedroom was just above her head. Frozen in a surmounting guilt, she listened as his body rhythmically flexed against the boards. Her unblinking eyes filled with shameful tears that then cut down her cold, hardened face.

She did not move when she saw the large shadow glide by the doorway and disappear down the hallway. Squinting through the night, she could see his all-too-familiar figure lumbering away, the click of his undone belt slapping against his upper thigh.

Her mouth ran dry as she accepted her daughter's fate. Yet, as she steeled her mind for what she knew to be true, she pushed the image from her mind, keeping a final thought that she was wrong. Not wanting it to be true, but knowing she needed to know for sure, she made her way up the stairs, strategically missing every creak of the boards. Gently, she pushed the door open to her daughter's bedroom. As she peered around the edge of the door, praying to find her sleeping, her worst nightmare was confirmed as her daughter scrambled to pull her torn clothes over her broken body.

Before she could say anything to her daughter, she disappeared out the window. The air caught in her lungs as she wanted to scream to her daughter, scream at him for doing this to her, scream at herself for letting it all happen. She had failed the girl on so many things in her short, tragic life; this was the final piece. Her feelings were a mixture of fear, hatred, and rage. She couldn't figure out who they were directed to. All she could think of in that moment was, *I thought I raised my daughter to know better ... to see the monster and hide.*

Chapter Forty-Three
Present Day

"Mama, are you hungry?" I probed, as my mother blankly stared out into the abyss of our backyard. It had been three days at the hospital, a regrettable release, and now four days into my mother still not speaking.

"Mama, you in there?" I waved my fingers in front of her face, something I would never have done before for fear she would bite them off, but this time—nothing. It had been nothing for almost a week now. The fact she woke up meant little as I realized her eyes had opened, but not her mind. That was still closed, turned off.

For a time, I figured it was better this way. This way allowed me to cope better. No longer did I feel the overwhelming anger threatening to pounce on her at any moment, nor the depression over my insidious behavior. As I no longer had to deal with a monster, my own monster had gone dormant for the time being. Caroline had shined a flicker of light in the darkness.

But then I realized that all of this was because of my inability to control myself. If I hadn't poured the last drink, if I had more control, I could have stopped myself. Even if I didn't push her, beat her, I, at the very least, wasn't there when she fell down. She was basically comatose because of my actions, and my elated feeling over it only deepened my guilt.

Gently, I brushed a stray piece of gray hair away from her stoic face. She was lost in there. I wondered if she would ever come out.

"I'll make you some soup, okay?" I waited for acknowledgment, anything to show that she understood. I knew she had to be starving, as she hadn't eaten any of her lunch, nor more than a few spoonfuls of oatmeal for breakfast.

Trying to get her to eat had been difficult. Mostly, I had to pull her mouth open, sliding the warm spoon over her tongue, then tilting her head back for each sip of soup. Though eating was not the only thing she was no longer able to do. It was as if the blow to the head had immediately moved her to the final stage of Alzheimer's. She had lost her speech, all functionality, and was now only a living statue that mandated my servitude at every waking moment. As she finished the soup, I could smell the soiled adult diaper that my mother was required to wear at all times. That was my recommendation, not the doctors.

"Okay, let's get you cleaned up," I announced, replacing the empty spoon into the bowl. She had accomplished eating half of the bowl, which had exhausted the last of my strength. I wasn't quite sure which part had been easier, the obstinate mother who bellowed and screamed but still could feed herself and kind of take care of things, or this shell of a person who was more of a lame pet than anything else.

Every second of the day, I kept waiting for her to curse at me, try to hit me, show any sign that my mother was still in there. There were even moments I found myself wanting to scream at her, slap her against the cheek just to see if that would bring her back to life. But, as I gazed into her glassy eyes, I saw nothing. A void of darkness.

Gently, I lifted her arm, a signal she had learned meant it was time to walk; *that* she could still do. But it was just a labored shuffling of her bare feet, the nails yellowed and curled into her toes, and peeling dead flecks of skin scuffed off as she walked. There was the crunch of the diaper as it shifted between her thighs, breaking through the ominous silence of the house as I ushered her toward the bedroom.

I changed her much like a mother would change a baby. Caroline had shown me how when we got home that first day. Pulling her legs apart, then slowly peeling back the tags on either side to reveal my mother's private area, which mostly showed up as a heavily covered, hairy, pixelated image. *Thank God.* Her lack of forethought to fight me made the process quick and easy in comparison to how things had been going whenever I tried to assist my mother with bathing or bowel movements.

I kept telling myself that this was for the better, the fall, hitting her head, being lost. At least she no longer screamed in pain through the night, her nightmares now lost to the blank space in her mind. My disposition toward her had turned more nurturing, less brutal than before, which was showing in her lack of bruises and slightly more colored skin tone. Of course, deep down, I was only making excuses for my hideous behavior. Trying to justify my shame, my guilt over what I knew I had done to my mother. It was one thing when it was the disease killing her; it was another thing when I took the last piece of her mind and stomped it into the ground.

The following evening, as I was pulling our cheese toast from the oven, I heard the porch door swing shut. *Damnit.* She was loose. It was not often she walked by herself, but it had happened once before, just around the house for a few moments. But the moment I heard the door close, I knew it was my mother. Quickly, burning my arm in the process, I threw our dinner to the side and rushed outside.

Stopping short at the bottom of the stairs from the porch, I marveled at the woman as she glided through the tall grass. Her yellow dress flowed in the spring breeze, the sun just catching her face, making it appear as if she were glowing. I watched her as she aimlessly walked, her fingertips lightly brushing against the blades of grass as her body effortlessly moved through the weeds.

As I reached her in the yard, it started to rain, drops cascading down from a seamlessly clear sky. Slowly, she raised her hands, the rain falling all over her body as she tilted her head back, opened her mouth, and allowed the rain to fall into the back of her throat, as a child does in the snow, catching each piece of childhood joy on their warm tongue.

"What is this called?" *She speaks?* Her words resonated through me as I realized that all was not lost. Though she never opened her eyes, still allowing the light rain to fall onto her glistening skin, it seemed as if she was alive again.

"It's called rain."

"It's wonderful." As if the fog had been lifted from her mind, she was suddenly clearly aware again. Just as my jubilance erupted at the thought of her return, another feeling settled into my mind. If she was returning, then all of it would return. The hatred, the screaming, the fear and anger. It would all flood back to her, and I wasn't sure if I would be strong enough to handle it again.

"Well, open your mouth," she probed. "Let it touch your tongue. It really is quite amazing."

"Mama, do you know who I am?" My hesitant words seemed to go unheard as she continued to relish the feeling of the rain washing her free from the fog.

"Oh, the feel of it on my skin ... It's so refreshing." There was nothing about this woman before me that reminded me of my mother. I could never even imagine her enjoying the rain as this person was before me. It was clear to me that this woman was not my mother. Even her tone of voice was different. *What was happening?*

Here she stood, all her pain, concerns, all her life, just washed away by the rain. She was experiencing it for the first time. At that moment, I envied her ability to relive a moment such as this, her mind oblivious to the truth. All I felt was the cold, damp truth of the rain, knowing it could not truly wash anything away, as I had tried.

"Just enjoy it," she encouraged me, grabbing me by the arm, evoking a searing pain where I had just been burned. She forced my arm out to my side, just like hers, to feel the full experience of the rain. At first, my arm spiked with pain as the direct hits from the water irritated my burns, but then the pain started to wash away with the water. And I guess my fears of my mother's full return started to lessen as well.

Leaning back, I allowed the light rain to drop over my face, into my mouth, and over my entire body. I wished this rain would wash away all my scars, memories ... everything. At that moment, I realized that my mother's disease was actually a blessing ... *an answer to our prayers.*

The cold winter days were fading into rainy spring nights and humid mornings. The smell of the coffee was just what I needed on this particular spring morning. I poured a heavy, dark cup and made my way to the porch. Just a nice, quiet morning. Suddenly, I heard her.

"Help!" she called from her room. Leaving the steaming coffee on the porch table, I rushed to my mother's bedroom.

"Are you okay?" I burst into her room, out of breath. She was lying in bed, moving quite awkwardly, as if she were a turtle caught on their back. "What are you trying to do?"

"Please, I just need to get up. I don't know where I am. Please help me." She reached out to me, and for the first time I did not hesitate to help her, as this woman was not actually my mother but only my mother's body. I pulled her up from the bed. Relief washed over her face.

"Who are you?" She stared into my eyes, desperately wanting to find the answer. I avoided it. I didn't want to risk the return of my real mother.

"No one, just here to help." She nodded, accepting the lie. I ushered her toward the kitchen, sitting her down at the table. I made her a cup of coffee. "Here." Sliding the coffee cup over to her waiting hands, I demonstrated with my own how to hold it and blow against the steam. She mimicked my actions, as she always did. There was a consistent wait time on things for my mother now as she looked to me to show her everything.

"Eggs?" She just stared at me, unsure of how I wanted her to answer. I had forgotten myself, as I knew better than to ask. These days I just told her what we were doing, or eating, or drinking.

The bottle of vodka had yet to be moved since we returned home from the hospital. Without my mother's glaring disgust for my existence, I found it easier to deal with the situation. And somehow my mother, despite her years of being an alcoholic, suddenly forgot that part as well. The lack of withdrawal symptoms was fascinating. Of course, I came to the conclusion that all the alcohol ran out of her body along with her blood and mind that night.

These days I honestly wasn't sure if it was the lack of memories that turned her into this person or if it was the blood slowly fading out over her frontal lobe, erasing her personality, leaving behind a fresh slate. Either way, I found myself shamefully grateful for this personality change.

Placing a plate down in front of both of us, fork to the side, I hesitated to see if she would recall what to do. She stared at the fork, then up at me, waiting. Slightly disappointed, I picked the fork up on my own plate, signaling to her to watch, put eggs onto the fork, and ate them. She nodded and attempted the same, except most of her eggs fell on the floor.

"Oh, come on, you are making a mess," I snapped out of frustration, instantly feeling regretful. This person was not mentally my mother, but she still physically looked like her, which made it hard to see the distinction when I got angry. Often, I would forget that she was not doing these things to torture me but that she could not remember or do them herself. Then there were the memories that still haunted my dreams, dredging up deep-seeded hatred. With no alcohol to block these thoughts, the pain was raw on the surface, putting my mind on edge.

"I'm so sorry, please don't hurt me."

She cowered beneath me, hands blocking her head as if I were about to hit her across the face. *How did she forget everything, but not that?* I wondered if she still had some memory of that night; otherwise, I questioned what would make her act that way. A person learns that others will hurt them. It is not something ingrained in our genes. Either she remembered that night, or another time where someone hurt her.

"No, I'm not going to hurt you, just ..." I sighed, raising up my hands in surrender, then realizing she probably didn't understand the gesture. "Just go out on the porch, and I will clean it up."

While my mother's speech had returned, she still seemed to sleep most of the day. In order to keep my hands busy and my mind occupied, I started gardening—something I had discovered I rather enjoyed doing in order to pass the time. It started with a weed here, a flower there, before I was knees deep in the dirt, covered in mud and sweat. Flakes of dirt dusted my sweaty skin, my shirt covered with smears of dirt, and my nails lined with mud. There was something about going back inside to take a bath that turned me off. I wanted to clean myself freely, not worry about the dirt I would track into the clean house or the thin film that would taint the bathtub's white porcelain. I wanted the freedom of a swim.

The house had been silent for hours, my mother no doubt still deep in a dreamless nap, which she did the most these days. So I made my way through the forest, my feet automatically following the well-known path, moving side to side, as it curved through the trees. Everything was a vibrant green after another rainstorm, one that had soothed me to sleep last night. Birds chirping, squirrels wrestling the leaves, frogs croaking—there was life in this forest, one I had failed to see until this moment. Maybe that was why I enjoyed it so much as a child. It was a place full of life instead of death and fear.

As I emerged from the forest, I stopped short, seeing that someone was already here. A woman, judged only by her thin frame and long dress, was standing just far enough in the distance that I couldn't make out who it could be. I'd never seen another soul at this lake, ever. It was a hidden alcove off the lake, long since cut off by receding waters that no one else knew about. Intrigued, I hesitantly made my way toward the person on the edge of the dock. As I drew nearer, I watched her beautiful yellow dress blowing in the spring breeze, a vibrant dance around her thin body. As the dress swirled around her, the light radiating off her damp skin, I received flickers of the person hiding behind this brilliant display.

What was she doing here?

As I approached my mother, a low hum, peaceful and soft, sent chills through my body. She was singing. I had never, in my entire life, heard my mother sing. She never even listened to music or tapped to a beat. *Suddenly she could sing?*

"Mama, are you okay?" Her trance broke at my touch as her eyes sprung open, and she stopped singing. For a moment, I waited for the cruel look to return to her face; this was the moment. I never should've said *Mama.*

"Of course. Isn't it just wonderful out here?" She took in a deep breath and smiled as she gazed out over the lake, a peacefulness in her eyes that seemed to calm the waters themselves. I breathed a sigh of relief as I realized it was just a false alarm. She was still gone.

"Yes, it really is. How did you find this place?"

This hidden haven amongst the forest was *my* place. Yet here she was admiring it. My mind knew that there would be no way for another person to happen upon this place; she had to know it. She had been here before, most likely numerous times in order to have found it in her current condition.

"I know this place well."

Suddenly, thunder boomed across the sky. In the distance, I could see the deep gray clouds growing, threatening to burst open at any moment. *Great, more rain.* Every afternoon, like clockwork, those clouds would form, bringing spring weather on its wings.

"We should go."

"Yes, let's go home." My mother hated that house. She never wanted to be there, nor did I. She never called it home, always *house, hellhole,* those sorts of things. But now she spoke of it as if she longed for its comfort and warmth. It had neither of those.

I followed her as she seamlessly made her way back down the path through the trees. It was a route carved over many years, mostly overgrown, but I did not need a clear path to know the way. The fact that she could follow it as well, making her way directly back to the house, was astonishing.

It had been a few days after we moved in, the summer air thick against my skin, my mother drunk and screaming as I disappeared into the woods. My intention was to hide, give my mother time to pass out, but then I saw it. A path where the grass wasn't as tall, where the branches didn't reach out as far. I followed it, not knowing who the creator was but thankful when I found the lake. *Had she been the one to make it?* It was an odd feeling to think we traveled the same path, as if suddenly our fates were more intertwined than I realized.

Chapter Forty-Four
Little Girl

"There is only one way out," her mother slurred, clearly drunk. She had the girl by her arm, pulling her hard toward her as she scrambled in fear. Her mother was begging her to see the truth, but she didn't understand. Her mother wasn't making sense. She knew her mother was infuriated that night; she could see the flames of hatred through the darkness. But it wasn't her fault. How could she stop him?

"How could you let this happen? How could you not see?" Her mother screamed the words over and over again, the gun shaking violently by her hip.

"I didn't ..." she stuttered in fear, tears flooding her mouth each time it opened. "I couldn't ... please, don't, Mama, don't!" she cried out, thinking her mother would surely push the cold barrel of the gun to her head and shoot. It had not been her fault; she had tried to fight, but he was too strong. If it was anyone's fault, it was her mother's. She left her alone with him.

The girl had thought about death many times, even more often since he started to visit her room late at night. There was no world now in which she could wash him away. He would forever be a part of her, a fact she loathed so intensely that she wanted to die. But, as her mother waved the gun into the air, the threat of death at her doorstep, she panicked. A piece of her mind was still holding on to life ... to hope.

"How could you let him do this?" Her mother's words were poison as they seeped from her mouth, snot dripping down her tear-covered face, the alcohol a suffocating gas. The words confused the girl. She never *let* him do anything—*he* did. She didn't understand how her own mother could hate her so much for something he was doing. If anything, she should hate him, beat him, leave him ... but instead, she was a coward.

Releasing her daughter's arm, stepping back, she raised the gun to her own temple. Only then did the girl realize her mother's true intentions.

"This is our only escape."

The shot vibrated through the silence, shaking the girl to her core. Her breath caught in her lungs, her heart paused in her chest, as she watched her mother fall to the ground. It all happened so fast, yet in her mind she was frozen in the moment, a picture she never wanted trapped in her mind forever.

Her mother killed herself.

There was an unbearable silence in the house as the girl waited for him to return home. Her mother's blood snaked through the grout of the kitchen floor tiles, flowing to every corner, as each piece of her mother escaped. It was hours that she stayed by her mother's dead body, trapped.

His return was early in the evening, the last rays of sunlight disappearing just moments before she heard the boards creak on the porch. It was in those seconds before he would enter the house and see what she did that the girl's mind broke free. Leaping to her feet, she ran. His screams followed her into the forest, but she didn't stop. She didn't stop until she was surrounded by silence and darkness.

They stood there, shoulder to shoulder at the funeral, a grieving family. He even held her hand, which made her cringe. She desperately wanted to run away, but that little girl inside her was trapped in fear. Each person shook his hand, sadness in their eyes. No one saw; no one realized. They bought into the picture he painted with her mother's blood.

If there was ever a moment to show this town the truth behind the veil, now was her chance. She no longer had her mother, and there no reason to stay, so it was perfect. But she too was a coward, unable to even pull her hand from his own. The feel of his skin upon her own made the bile rise in her stomach. There had to be another way, at least for her. Her mother's escape was not the only way.

That night, the girl stood at the door, bag in hand, as he snored loudly on the couch. No mother to stop her this time, no mother to stay for this time either. Tears silently fell down her hot red cheeks, a shaking hand reaching for the door. Glancing down, she could still see the bloodstains on the floor and the deep scar on her forearm. She took a deep breath. She had to do this. She had to escape. Her mother's way could not—would not—be the only way out of this place.

If not for herself this time, for the growing child inside her.

Chapter Forty-Five
Present Day

"How is she doing?" Caroline leaned over the coffee cup, removing the lid, then gently blowing the steam from her face. She had arrived early that morning with coffee. She had called a few times over the last couple of weeks, but this was her first visit. As I stared at her over my own coffee cup, I couldn't seem to figure out what was different about her this morning.

"Well, different for one."

"You told me she was better on the phone?" Confused, she glanced through the screen door at my statuesque mother slightly rocking back and forth in the chair.

"Depends on how you define better."

"She still a mean ol' bitch?" Caroline jeered.

"Ha! No, actually, I really can't even consider her my mother."

"Well, I never thought I'd see the day your mama wasn't drinking, that's for sure."

"She never even asks for a drink. She just sleeps, or roams the yard, or just sits there. That's it." My eyes pricked at the thought of all my mother had lost in a single blow to the temple. I wasn't sure if I considered it a blessing that I took all that hatred and pain from her or an injustice that my mother had lost her soul.

"Has the bleeding gotten worse?"

"I don't think so. She did start talking again. But even that is weird, because she never says anything my actual mother would say."

"Well, that's a good thing right?" We both laughed at the concept, a slight pinch of pain fluttered through my heart.

"When do you go back to that handsome doctor?"

"You mean the child that is somehow a doctor? Not sure. I keep thinking, what's really the point of going to see all these doctors? They never do anything for her. Nothing will actually change or get better, so why go?"

"Peace of mind, maybe," Caroline struggled, only slightly agreeing with my logic.

"Don't think I'll ever have that at this point," I muttered, the monster inside only kept at bay by my mother's docile nature and my guilt over her losing her mind. But it was still there, gnawing away at my thoughts, filling my life with darkness, the haze of depression still circling my mind.

"It's not easy to come by these days." There was a distant, sorrowful look in Caroline's eyes, one I had only seen once before, in the parking lot that day she screamed at me that her life was not perfect. In my drunken fog I had failed to see that my friend was clearly going through something. Now, it was glaring headlights coming at me from the opposite direction. I wanted to be there for her; I needed to be after all she'd done for me.

"What's going on, Caroline?"

"It's fine, Norah, I know you have so much to deal with. I'm just so happy you are doing better." She ran her fingers nervously through the tips of her hair, as she always did when something was bothering her. I briefly relished the fact that I could still read my friend's tells.

"You're right, I am doing better. Better enough to be here for you, so tell me." While I still wasn't completely sure I could hold Caroline's hand in the way she'd held mine our entire lives, I had to at least try. I owed her that much at this point.

"It's just that ... well ... I ..." She tapped her fingers anxiously against the laminate counter, biting her lower lip and holding back the words. Instantly, I knew.

"Oh, Caroline, I am so sorry." I wanted to reach for her, but she held up a firm hand to keep me at a distance, visibly forcing the tears back in her attempt to be strong.

"It's not what you think." The pain of what she needed to tell me was noticeable, but I had missed the shame in her eyes. "I cheated." The words were released like a fish from a hook, the tail slapping me across the face.

There were so many reasons Caroline did not want to tell me what happened, for her own shame and my own grief. She knew each word would be harder for me to hear, knowing the pain I'd suffered from Michael's affair. But her strength bled into my own, forcing me to reach across the counter and clutch her hands into my own.

"What happened?"

"You don't have to do this." I felt her try to pull away, but I held tightly to her hands, refusing to let her go. Conceding, her eyes blinking back the pain, she resolved to tell me.

"It's hard to say the exact moment it happened. More a gradual change overtime. First there was fighting, then silence, a sign we had both just given up." She pulled her hands together. I allowed her to release our hold to each other as she wrung her fingers together. Slowly, she started to turn the wedding band over on her finger, then pulled it off completely.

"It was like one day I woke up, and suddenly I was cheating on Mark." Leaving the ring on the counter, her hands disappeared into her lap, as if she physically refused to be married anymore as she talked about her affair.

"You know there was just nothing between us anymore, then there was this other person putting in all this effort. Suddenly, I was happy again at the thought of talking to him, seeing him, being with him. It just all got out of control so quickly. Before I realized what I had done, what I lost ... it was already gone." The first tear finally escaped. I watched as it made a new trail down her face, as her affair had forged a new path for her life.

"Who is it?" I asked as gently as possible, not wanting to overstep the line of how much she was willing to tell me.

"Oh gosh, you don't know him."

"Everyone knows everyone in this town."

"Not you anymore; you've been gone for over twenty years. New people have come to this town." She shifted on the barstool, looking down at her feet, giving away her secret.

"Oh, shit, Caroline, are you serious? The bartender?"

"Well, I mean how else do you think I knew you were there?" she confessed, slapping her hand hard against the counter, then pulling it up over her face to hide her shame, as she realized everything was now out in the open.

"Have you told Mark?"

She shook her head, pulling her hair tight against her temples as another wave of tears escaped. "I can't tell him. He'll leave me. I'll lose everything."

She was right. She would lose everything. I was all too familiar with losing everything over something like this. Except, I had been on the other side; I was Mark. Even after all this time, the experience and feelings were still so raw that I couldn't stop but feel the pain Mark would surely endure when he found out. That feeling of betrayal by the one person you trusted most would consume him, devour every piece of his life, then spit it back out in a crumbled, disgusting mess. And there would be nothing he could do to stop it; he would just have to watch it all blow away in the dust. Suddenly, I felt horrible for how I had been treating him these last months.

"I've ended things. After our conversation, seeing how crushed you were by what Michael did, I realized I couldn't do that to Mark. I still love him."

"Uh, I ..." I couldn't see how that was possible. To love someone yet deceive them so deeply. Then, as if a dam released the waters all at once, the memory of all those broken moments with Michael rushed over me. The times I pushed him away, refused his touch, denied him healing. All the conversations I dismissed, my selfishness taking up every part of our relationship. I can remember that moment I understood where he was coming from, why he did it.

"Sometimes," I managed to choke out between my broken attempts to quell my tears, "people become broken. They become lost. Whether it's like my mother, who lost her memories, herself, or how you lost your marriage. Either way, we have to believe that we can be rebuilt. We have to." The words were stopped by the lump settling, unmoving in my throat. My eyes needed to blink, but, knowing that it would release the tears I was so desperately trying to hold back from Caroline, I fought the urge.

"I really want to believe that, Norah, for all our sakes."

Chapter Forty-Six
Little Girl

There had been another bullet. The girl could've taken the gun and killed herself, which was what her mother wanted. Her mother wanted them both to die that day, convinced that was the only way to escape their torture. But the girl saw a different path, another way to break free. Formulating her plan over weeks, slowly stealing money from his wallet as he slept, keeping him endlessly plied with booze so that he was too drunk to force himself anywhere, let alone on her body, and keeping the growing child inside her belly a guarded secret, she waited night after night until the right moment, but it never did come.

Each night he seemed to jump and shake at any noise, bellowing out for her to come to him. While he was too drunk to do anything, he wanted her. He'd clutch her hand tightly, his body and her fear a rock keeping her tethered to the bottom of the ocean. But if she waited any longer, she might run out of time. The window to get to a doctor to have the baby cut from her body was closing. She had to take any chance she had, no matter how deep her fear; it was time. With only a week left, she pulled the door silently closed behind her, steadfast in her convictions despite the small bump that had started to form.

It was a long, arduous bus ride to Montgomery, the closest place to find a doctor who would do such a thing. Each shift in the road she swore she felt the baby alive in her stomach. The entire time, she kept reminding herself that the thing inside her was *him*, and nothing good would come of having another person like him in this world. It had to go. There was no way she could keep it. But in the dark corners of her mind, on the loneliest night, she thought she could love the child.

Chapter Forty-Seven
Present Day

I watched as my mother danced as a child through the tall grass. Her pink butterfly dress flowing in the breeze made it appear as though tiny butterflies flew all around her. She never went back through the trees, nor down to the lake, but just stayed around the garden. I had come to realize that she preferred being outside, a break from the constant sitting and staring at the wall.

Pulling a chair out into the yard, I slipped down into it, resolved to wait her out. After all, there was no reason to pull her away from her joy. If only I could find that joy as well. I envied my mother's ability to forget. I wanted to forget everything ... the abuse ... Michael ... the baby. I wanted it all to go away. Caroline's confession only made things worse. There was something broken inside them both. I knew that if she told Mark, asked for forgiveness, he would give it, as I would to Michael. Love seemed to have a way of doing that for normal people like them. For me, it wasn't going to be so easy.

"Everything okay?" Ms. Kay called to me from her back porch, shotgun in hand.

"Yes, it's fine," I said, waving my hand at her to go away.

"Your mama ain't right. You know that?" she called to me from behind her screen door, her raspy, annoying voice radiating through the silence.

"I've been aware of that my whole life, Ms. Kay."

Suddenly, she was standing right next to me, my body flinching at the thought of her stalking through the tall grass, a lion unseen by its prey. I made a quick inventory of her possessions, thankful to realize she'd left the shotgun on the porch. The relief that she wasn't out here to kill me relieved most of the anxiety of having her standing next to me with no witnesses except my deranged mother. She could bury me in those woods, and no one would ever find my body.

"What's wrong with her?" *She's finally at peace.*

"She fell, hit her head. Now she just seems ... well, lost."

"That is for the best. Your mama's got some dark demons." Ms. Kay shrugged, attempting to turn around to leave us alone, but my mind just had to know.

"What do you mean?"

"Like I told you before, I've lived in that house over there for a long time," she began. "I knew your mama when we were both kids." There was no part of my mind that could picture Ms. Kay as a child. Nor had I even given thought to my mother as a child. I always just knew them both as the people they were today, as that was the only time I had ever played a part in their lives. The thought that they had a scene before I knew them was intriguing.

"Never thought of my mother as a kid. What was she like?"

"Sad." That was not at all a word I would use to describe a child, giving way to more questions than answers.

"What is that supposed to mean?"

"Well, she grew up in that house with your grandparents, and well ... it just..." Her face seemed puzzled, lips drawn in, eyes squinted, as she struggled to find the words to explain the enigma that was my mother.

"So you knew my grandparents?" People whom I had never met before, nor was I ever allowed to speak about. I assumed my mother never really knew them herself, not in a true sense anyway. There was something she visibly hated about them, but I never learned why.

"Yeah, I knew your mean ol' granddaddy and that awful woman." Deep lines of disgust crossed her face. "I know your mama beat you and was a drunk." The blunt statement slapped me hard across my chest, causing my heart to skip a full solid beat. "But that woman out there went through worse at the hands of your granddaddy. She would never want you to know, but there wasn't a day that went by that your mama didn't have bruises on her body, and not a night I didn't hear her screaming in that room."

"Wait, so you are saying my grandfather abused my mother?" Suddenly, I was in a slow-motion movie, hearing the words but not able to process them, nor understand the gravity of them.

"He did more than that." Her eyes were filled with a deep, knowing fear that sent a chilling shiver through my body in the warm afternoon sun.

"What does that mean?"

"Just know that your mama, well, that woman ... she never had a chance." Ms. Kay was firm in my mother's excuse for abusing me, but as I had learned in these last months, being a victim was not an excuse.

"So all this time she was abusing me, she had been through the same thing?"

"Don't think of it like that ... It's not like that. Your mama tried to break free of your grandparents, but they broke her. Your mama is broken, a lost soul really."

Her words settled onto my chest, an overbearing weight that I could never lift. Gradually, as the fog dissipated, revealing the truth of my mother's life, it all started to come into focus. Her hatred for this place was not centered on my presence here but the memories of her abuse. As were my own. Like our path through the woods, I started to see that I had followed her ghost as it led me in the same direction.

"Why did no one do anything about it?"

"We tried," she affirmed, shaking away the glassiness in her own eyes. "Called the cops, but they didn't do nothing. Nor did social services." Suddenly, I realized what my mother had over Chief Morris all these years. *Guilt.* He was probably a young officer at the time, clearly being a good twenty years older than my mother. *Was this why Ms. Kay never said anything?*

"Come to find out, your granddaddy knew some powerful people. Ran some gamblin' clubs for the local cops. There were calls made, whispers passed around town, but at the end of the day, your mama was collateral damage in their eyes."

"How could everyone just look away?" I didn't understand the circumstances; I didn't see the truth of time back then, only that there was a moment in history when it all could've been stopped. The violence, the abuse ... all stopped.

"I was just a scared kid back then," she affirmed. "I tried to be friends with your mama, thought maybe that would help, but it only made things worse."

"How did it make it worse?"

"It just did, okay? No point in talking about those things now." Ms. Kay nailed a thick nail into that coffin, refusing to tell me the story. "It wasn't until your mama got pregnant that she finally found the courage to leave."

Ann Brooks

Ms. Kay turned away from me, swiftly pulling the escaped tear from her red cheeks. My mind hesitated, denying the truth of her words. It was stuck on repeat, just saying her words over and over again but never moving past them. Never allowing my thoughts to formulate the conclusion.

"How did she get pregnant?" I choked out, my mind screaming at me to close the book, failing to read the ending because it would change too much. But I couldn't. Dark thoughts filled my mind as Ms. Kay just nodded at me, confirming the worst ...

"Your mama did the best she could, but coming back here was too much for her to handle. Now, I am not excusing what your mama did to you, but I thought you oughta know."

She gently placed a hand on my shoulder. I desperately wanted her to leave me alone ... hug me ... slap me ...

My mind was lost in the wave, unsure of what I needed. Silent tears escaped as I realized what I truly was ... *I was my grandfather's daughter.*

Chapter Forty-Eight
Little Girl

"Push, push," the nurse urged, holding tight to the girl's ankles as she attempted to push with all her might. "You're almost there. I can see the head."

Sweat poured from her forehead, her teeth pained as she clenched down again, forcing the pain from her stomach and into her legs. Fire exploded through her body, so overwhelming that she thought she would surely die from it all. "Stay with me now ... Push!"

Again, she tried, but she was growing so weak. Darkness started to circle around the corners of her eyes. She could feel her body giving up, relinquishing herself to the pain. She reached out, but there was no one there to grab hold of, only the disheveled, elderly nurse, who reeked of smoke, yelling at her to push from between her knees.

The burning pain grew deeper and deeper, her legs threatening to fall to the ground in defeat, every nerve turning off as her body went into shock. The walls started to shake, moving like waves, as her eyes started to roll into the back of her head. She couldn't do it. It was too hard. She was dying.

"You did it!" the nurse cried, pulling the baby into her arms. "It's a girl."

The baby's screams erupted throughout the room, bringing her back to life. It was over. She had done what she needed to do. The baby was born, healthy, into this world. There was nothing else for her to do but die.

Gently, the nurse wrapped the baby and held her up for the girl to see. Tears fell silently down her temples. *I have a little girl,* she thought. There was a part of her that didn't even want to look at the infant. For months, as she grew in her stomach, so did her disgust for the baby. There had been no salvation for her here, only a crowded shelter full of desperately pregnant women such as herself. She had planned to leave it at the hospital, leave the moment she could walk. She told herself it would be better that way, but then the nurse stood there, holding the little thing in her arms.

She found herself unable to resist as the nurse leaned over and placed the newborn on her bare chest. Naturally, the little girl curled into her mother's breast and she could feel her heart beating with her own. They were one. Looking down into the little girl's brown eyes, she realized those were her eyes, not his. All her hatred suddenly washed away. This was her daughter, not his. She looked so innocent, helpless.

Suddenly, her fear of being a mother faded, and for the first time in her life, she thought that she could be a good mother. She could raise this little girl safely. She would find a way to give this little girl a better life, something she never had. She could look past how she was made and see only this precious little girl. At that moment, it was all possible.

"What's her name?" the nurse asked.

She stared up into the nurse's eyes, tears falling down her face as she smiled. "Norah. Her name is Norah."

Chapter Forty-Nine
Present Day

Collapsing onto the ground, the grass almost higher than my head, I cried, unable to control the tornado of thoughts causing catastrophic damage to my mind. There had never been a doubt that my mother loathed my existence, that she fought her own demons on a daily basis, but never had I considered that I was her true demon. My life alone was a constant reminder to her that she was raped by her own father. I knew the screaming was my own, but it felt so far in the distance.

The rays of sunlight drew back into the storm as it rolled across the horizon. I couldn't move, the storm drenching my clothes and stiffening my bones. All this time, the truth was right there; if only she had told me who I was to her, then maybe I would've understood. Endless questions swirled in my mind as I became trapped in a never-ending circle of shame. There was a part of me that thought I would never move from that spot again.

I just kept going over every detail of my life, filling in all the holes where I never could get answers before, no matter how many times I asked my mother. I knew deep down my mother always hated me. Now I understood why. *How could she ever love me?* All the times she could not look at me ... beat me ... called me hateful things ... It was her way of coping with who I really was ... not her *daughter* but a reminder of her abuse.

Finally, the broken picture was coming into view. My mother, who suffered abuse and rape by her own parents, had succumbed to the same demons, drowning in alcohol and using violence to release her own pain. We were the same. I drank away my pain and beat out my anger as well. Was this just the people we were to be because of what he did? Was the only way to get past this to become like my mother: *mindless? Lost?*

Sitting in the literal dark, my own darkness came into view. I could always feel it, lurking just beneath the surface, a monster fueled by something I never could understand. I thought it was my mother. Knowing that she could house that level of anger and hate, I just assumed I would be able to do the same. In every step of my life, I attempted to manage my anger, pushed my hatred down, and avoided the darkness. Yet, I had to admit that it was always stronger in this place, just like it was for her all these years. Finally, our monster had a name ... a face. Now, I could clearly see the source of my anger, fear, darkness. *It was him.*

The pressure closed in around me, threatening to take every piece of me and tear it apart. I felt trapped in a massive, unrelenting wave. At times, I could barely breathe, gasping for air through my cries, reaching out, trying to grab on to anything that was solid, but there was only the water crashing down on me over and over again. I just needed someone, anything ... just something to help pull me out of the wave before I was lost forever.

Then, there she was. Standing over me, reaching out her hand to help me up. The innocent look in her eyes as she offered her hand, a gaze of unfamiliarity in her eyes, as she no longer knew who I was. I realized it was possible for her to save me. *Could God have finally answered my prayers?*

My arm was weak as I lifted my hand and allowed my mother to help me up. I could feel her straining to lift me, her own body fragile, beaten down by life at every moment. Suddenly, I was overwhelmed with empathy for my mother. All I ever wanted was for someone to save me, help me out of this pain. Take me away from this horrible place, but no one ever came. Just like no one ever saved my mother. No matter how much I hated her, how much I wanted to leave her, at that moment, I found that what I wanted most was to be her savior, just as she was offering to be mine now.

There was something about knowing my mother had suffered worse, endured years of abuse and torture, letting it destroy every part of her life, that changed me that night. I realized that while my mother had allowed it to take every piece of her apart, I didn't have to. Seeing her now, the person she could've been, I realized that I did not want to be my mother. I did not want to succumb to the hatred anymore. I wanted to forget. I wanted to move on. There had to be a way to survive all of this, pick up the pieces, and start again. I just never thought I would find it in my own mother.

Chapter Fifty
Little Girl

Lillie stood in the doorway, no longer a little girl. The foyer was still stained with her own blood, a harsh reminder of the abuse she had been trying so desperately to forget. As she stared down at the little girl next to her, her mind flashed back to her father, in that room ...

She turned away, barely able to look at her daughter. Tears filled her eyes, burning to escape. She tried so hard to love her, but every time she looked at her ...

This place was the same, even the smell of liquor, smoke, and sweat still swirled around her, as if it had seeped into the walls. Would she never be free of him? Even in death, he continued to haunt her.

"Mama, will this be our new home?" She could see hope in her daughter's eyes. A deep part of her wanted to slap it out of her, just to make sure she knew that there was no hope in this horrible place.

"Home is a strong word for this place."

"Can I pick a room?" The little girl's excitement was nauseating. How badly she wanted her to see this place for what it really was ... *Hell on Earth*. She should burn it to the ground, walk away from all the painful memories. That dark part of her thought about doing it while her daughter was in the house, then maybe she could be free of it all.

That night she drank, shamed by her horrible thoughts. It was not the first time she'd thought about killing her own daughter. She knew what those thoughts made her—a monster. The only thing that made her forget was "one more drink." That's what she always told herself: Just one more drink, then it will be gone.

It was never truly gone, though. It was always inside her, no matter how much she drank. She climbed the stairs, each heavy step bringing the memory of her father coming up these same stairs flashing across her mind, as if she were being stabbed in the gut over and over again. By the time she made it to her old room, she was bleeding to death inside, unable to support herself. Then she saw it.

The little girl was lying in the bed, so peaceful, just sleeping. But she didn't see her daughter; she saw herself, helpless and weak. Screaming, she started to hit the girl violently. It was not her daughter anymore. She was beating herself. She was so angry she had allowed him to do that to her for all those years.

"Fight back!" she screamed at the little girl.

The little girl begged, screamed for her to stop, but she couldn't. The little girl needed to understand. She needed to fight, to run away.

"Go!" she kept screaming down at herself, over and over again, with each hit. Finally, she collapsed, exhausted. *Why would she not run? Why would she not go?*

There was never going to be a good life in this place for her, not in this house where her own mother shot herself. This would never be home. But she had nowhere else to go. Her daughter needed a place, even if it was evil. A part of her thought that maybe she could change things, maybe this house could become a home.

For years, she clung to the idea that the house would change, which it did, but not in the way she had thought. The house changed her, made her hate herself and her daughter more than ever. Every moment in this house brought back a painful memory. In the end, she couldn't stop herself. It was the only thing she knew how to do ...

Chapter Fifty-One
Present Day

"This is the third night in a row."

Caroline held up two bags of to-go food with her fingers, dangling treats to gain entrance into hell.

"Please, Norah. I can't go home. I can barely look at Mark."

I pulled the door back, waving her into the kitchen.

It was the same each night, Caroline arriving at my doorstep with bags of food, resolved to avoid Mark. While she had ended the affair, finally said it out loud to another person, making it more than a dream, she was still struggling to figure out what she was going to do next. Their relationship was still broken, and no matter how hard she was trying to talk to him, connect with him, she said he was just pushing her away. So she chose avoidance. Join the club.

Caroline's frequent visits were a welcomed distraction from my recently gained knowledge. For a moment, I thought about revealing my truth to Caroline, but then I held back. I knew this time I needed to be there for her no matter what. My issues would have to come later ... or not at all.

"I just don't know what to do," she confessed, properly setting the counter for our dinner, her mind needing to occupy itself with mundane, repetitive actions. I understood the feeling all too well. I watched as she flustered about the kitchen, pulling out knives, forks, and napkins, setting each piece across from each other. No place for my mother. She would not eat this food anyway. These days I was good to get her to eat some oatmeal for breakfast and soup for dinner.

"I try to talk to him, touch him, but he is pulling away from me." Her eyes searched my own, desperate for guidance. She looked to me as a person on the other side, *Mark's side*, who could help her fix their broken marriage. She kept running scenarios by me, asking if I would've taken Michael back if he said this or did that. Unfortunately, for her, I would take him back every time, but it had not been my choice, which was what she was struggling to understand.

"It's not my place to tell you what to do."

"Please, tell me!" she begged, our dinner fully displayed and ready to eat. The smell of fried chicken floated around the small kitchen, the memory of eating dinner at Caroline's house, when her mother would bring home this exact meal after her shift at Oscar's, rushed back into my mind. Caroline had earned her fierce convictions from her mother, a woman never willing to give up. She tried, and frankly that was all Caroline needed from her mother. That was all I ever needed, thinking that my mother refused to try all those years, but now I knew how incapable she was of doing so.

"I think you should tell Mark."

"No, no, no, what good will come of that?"

"Look, you are both hurting. It's not just the fact that you had an affair, it's that things were broken long before that time. You used the affair thinking it would fix something or, I don't know, allow you to have something better. But then you realized you wanted Mark. You wanted to make it work. You need to give him the same opportunity."

"How is telling him about the affair going to do that?"

There was no part of me that wanted to talk about what happened between Michael and me, but I could see that Caroline needed to understand, and I couldn't think of any other way to explain it to her. So, steeling my veins, preparing to reopen the wounds, I pulled back the bandages that were covering up my scars from Michael.

"After we lost the baby, I couldn't even look at Michael. I pushed him away, refusing to talk to him. I wouldn't let him touch me. In the darkest hour, I wanted him to leave. I had given up. But the moment he told me about the affair, suddenly I realized that I did still want to fight. That I did still want him in that way."

"Did you tell him that?" There was empathy in her question, that maybe, as she was, I had been too scared to say the words. And for a time, I had been scared, but there was a deeper fracture in our relationship. One I was never willing to fix.

"It didn't matter really. I couldn't give him a child. He wanted that more. But it's different for you and Mark. If you tell him, then you will see if he really has the conviction to make things work or if maybe he doesn't." I winced, knowing the truth would sting.

"And if he doesn't?"

"Then you move on. One step at a time, just like you told me. But at least then you will know."

"Don't forget to call me every day," Caroline insisted as she gathered her bags, making her way to the front porch.

"I will. But you need to focus on Mark. I'm fine."

"Like hell you are." She waved her long arm around my shoulders. "But maybe one day, I can see that for you now."

Watching Caroline make her way to the car, shoulders hunched over, I felt as if I could see the heavy weight pushing down upon them. A weight that I had so arduously carried throughout my life. I had not revealed my mother's secret to her for a few reasons. I didn't want her to look at me differently, nor burden her with my ongoing, never-ending saga of issues. But most of all, it didn't feel right to tell my mother's secret to anyone, because that was what it was to her. She had given up an entire life to conceal the truth, never once telling me what happened to her, just allowing me to think she was just naturally an awful person.

Attentively, I pulled the dress down over my mother's frail frame, bones drastically noticeable, eating having become an elusive action for her these days. I pulled the brush through her thinning gray hair, attempting to tame the last of her curls. Just like my own, there was no managing these wild things. Eventually, I gave up; it's not like anyone was going to see.

My mother had become a shell of a person now, the few moments of understanding gone. In the last few weeks, she had lost her speech again, reverting back to a comatose state. There used to be a light in her eyes, if only for a moment, but now that was lost. I had thought she was becoming a new person, one unencumbered by her abuse, but then that person faded as well, leaving nothing behind at all. Surprisingly, I found myself wanting my mother to return, acknowledging that I wanted to find a relationship with her, feel something other than what I had felt my whole life.

After revealing my pain to Caroline, the wound now festering underneath loosely applied bandages, I was starting to realize how desperate I had become to confess my sins to my mother. Even though my true mother wasn't inside that mind anymore, somehow I thought she would still be able to hear me. It was the only way I could think of to move on ... *to heal.*

"Mama, I know how hard it was for you," I confessed to her through the darkness. She was lying in the bed, tucked in for the night as I gently stroked her hair back from her face. She liked the feeling, her eyes closing and fading off. "I want you to understand

255

that I know that now. I know what you went through." Her eyes flickered open as she curled her boney fingers around my own, holding my hand tightly.

"Can I tell you something?" I waited, but there was no reply, just a vague expression in her glassy eyes. I was never going to be able to tell my mindful mother of our unspoken connection; this woman would never understand, but maybe there was a part of her trapped inside that could still hear it.

"I never wanted to be a mother, for obvious reasons. But the moment I saw those two blue lines, I'm not really sure what happened. It's just that for so long I told myself I didn't want this *thing.*" I couldn't bring myself to say the word yet. "That when suddenly I did want *it* ... well, none of that turned out to matter much, I guess. In the end, I wasn't able to keep the ... the ... *baby.*" The moment I said the word, the first tear escaped from my burning eyes. I braced myself to continue, pulling tightly at my mother's fingers wringed within my own.

"I told myself I didn't want ... *her.*" The floodgates opened, making it impossible to continue to speak for the next five minutes. When I looked up, I found my own mother, tears falling down her own cheeks, carving a path where they would eventually dry away into the pillow.

"Mama, are you there?" I pleaded, desperate for any sign she was listening, any sign she understood. *Nothing.* There was no emotion other than the silent tears.

"It was a girl. For a moment, I told myself that I was going to be a great mom, that Michael would be a great father, keeping me stable so that I could be everything you never were to me. It's silly, but there was a part of me that thought I could erase everything you did by being this great mother to this little girl. Somehow, I don't know why, it's stupid really, but somehow, I thought that would make it all go away."

"I told myself that I didn't want the baby, that I would never make a good mother, but now I realize that was a defense mechanism. Somehow, I think I knew I would mess it up, so I just told myself that I didn't want to be a mother. I was just scared, but deep down ..." The words caught in my throat. "Deep down, I did want that child, so much that the thought of losing another was unbearable."

"In the end, I got sick. There was nothing I could do to stop it, to make it better. I was helpless. That is the true, real, selfish reason I couldn't go through it again. Not because I didn't want a child, not because I couldn't deal with losing the child again, but because I couldn't deal with not having control over my life."

"Ironically, though, by attempting to keep control over my life, it swirled further out of my control. Michael couldn't accept not having a child. There was so much of me that wanted to be angry with him, but I couldn't, because I felt it too. *I wanted a child.*"

Suddenly, I could feel the slight squeeze of my mother's hand in my own, as if she could feel the pain in my words. Looking into my eyes, she smiled. "Mama, you see, I understand why you couldn't give me up. I know why you kept me. I understand that now. I would've done anything to keep my child, to have that precious little girl in my arms. After everything that happened to you, everything I was to you, I know you should've let me go, but I understand why you didn't ... *couldn't.*"

Leaning down, seeing her eyelids starting to fade, sleep taking over her mind, I whispered into her ear, "I forgive you, Mama."

The next morning, as normal as every other morning, I walked into my mother's bedroom at nine to wake her up.

"Mama, Mama, wake up." But this time, she wasn't responding, her body cold and still. Quickly, I checked her chest. It was moving ever so slightly, her heart slowly beating underneath her thinning rib cage. "Okay, it's okay, Mama," I assured her, as if somehow that made a difference. Really, I was the only one in a panic.

Pulling the phone off the table, I dialed 911. "Help is coming, Mama, just hold on."

I'm not sure why I encouraged her to hold on. It was not like she was still there. It was instinctive to want to help her keep on living. Isn't that how it always is? Death is so final. We fight against it, but really, in her case, *what was I fighting against?* She was already lost.

"Looking here," the too-young doctor was back, flipping a CT scan up onto that same board, "the bleeding stayed in the frontal lobe, but here ..." I could see it. He didn't need to point it out or tell me what it meant. I already knew.

"I know, doctor. She's gone." There had been a feeling last night as I gently kissed her on the cheek that I couldn't quite explain, but now I knew. It was the very last piece of her floating away, only the stem of the dandelion left in its place.

"How's she doing?" Caroline emerged through the door with a large bouquet of flowers and a much-appreciated and needed soda.

"She's dying." Caroline gasped at the blunt response, quickly looking to the doctor for confirmation that I was being dramatic. But he gave her none, just politely excused himself from the room.

"Jesus, Norah, I don't know what to say."

"Nothing. You just say nothing. Just give me that soda." Quickly, she placed the flowers down on the table and handed me the bottle. Pulling a chair next to me, she reached out and took my hand.

"I'm here," she assured.

Of course, Caroline would do just the right thing. It was all I needed at that moment to know that I was not alone in this. No matter how this woman had treated me, she was my mother. Of course, she wasn't really the mother I remember but the mother I had those last few weeks, the one free of anger and pain. She was the mother who reached across a canyon of emotions to hold my hand and help me up. That was the mother I was with now. That was the one dying in this hospital bed.

"Caroline?"

"Yes, what do you need?"

"I need you to know something."

"Right now?" She was clearly confused that I would pick this particular moment to take the focus off my mother's situation, but this was important. Just as I needed to tell my mother, I needed to tell Caroline this.

"My mother, it's just that ..." It was harder than I thought to form the words, the volcano of emotions threatening to erupt at any moment. I thought I would be able to tell her, to say the words out loud, but they just wouldn't come.

"It's okay," she assured. "You don't have to say it. I know your mother was a mean ol' bitch, but I know this is hard. Losing a parent is always hard, no matter the situation."

I smiled. That was not what I wanted to tell Caroline.

"Thank you."

Even though I didn't say the words out loud, did not tell her who I truly was, she understood that this was hard for me, which was all I really wanted her to realize. I wanted her to see that I did find a place where I could now mourn the impending loss of my mother. I wanted her to know this, because when the time came, I was going to need her the most.

It's hard to describe the feeling of watching someone die. A part of me felt like she had left that morning when I found her lying on the kitchen floor. Now I was waiting for her body to let go, cut the final strings of life holding her to this world. I believed that her soul was already gone, left with all her memories and pain. *Maybe there is a God?* Maybe there was a place where she could be at peace. At that moment, I prayed that she got to leave her sorrow behind. In death, she would be free of all of it. If God did nothing else for her in this life, he could at least do that.

"We need your signature." The nurse held out the pen. Six months ago, this would've been so easy. I would've signed and walked away without even a single thought, but now ... now my hand was shaking. Sign this piece of paper, just a simple signature, and my mother's life was over. The machines that kept her alive would be turned off. Even though I knew she was not in there or trapped, begging to be released, it didn't make it any easier.

The nurse gave me an understanding look as she left the room. Suddenly, the room was silent, the noise of the machines gone. It was just us now. I took her frail hand into my own. Her body having melted away, face sunken, she didn't even look like a person anymore. I leaned over, kissing her lightly on her forehead, and whispered in her ear, "It's okay. You are free now."

"How are you doing, honey?"

Caroline placed a gentle arm around my shoulders. She was being a good friend, but that question made me cringe. Every person asked that question as if by some miracle I would suddenly say, *"I'm fine, all is good, don't worry about me."* Maybe that was what they were all hoping for, then they would be off the hook. *"She's fine, no need to fuss over her anymore."* I could lie to all the others, but not to Caroline ... She would see right through me.

"I don't know how to answer that question, honestly. I don't know what I am feeling." Tears burned and threatened to escape, but I pushed them away. *No crying.*

"It's okay. You don't have to know."

It was reassuring to hear. The moment she gave me permission, I started to sob, all the pain and sadness pouring out of me for the first time. For the last twenty-four hours, I told myself to be strong. That was what people expected, but now that Caroline had given me permission to let go, I did.

The day before, I was asked a million questions, over and over again. People wanted to know, *"What were her final wishes?"* Well, she didn't have any real *final wishes,* because she had lost her mind, so now it was up to me to determine everything. My greatest need was just to be allowed to break down, if only for a moment. I just needed some time.

There, in my mother's kitchen, Caroline gave me that time. She held me as I cried over my mother's death, something neither of us thought I would ever do in this lifetime. I hated my mother all my life, only to discover in her last moments of life that I could in fact forgive her for it all. All of that poured out of me onto Caroline's shoulder.

"What can I do?" she asked once I was able to calm myself down.

"This, this right here is what you can do." Her comforting arms wrapped around my own, our bodies pulled close to each other, as I melted into her strength, allowing it to refuel my own depleted tank. "Thank you so much. You will never know how much I appreciate you."

"Aw, honey, trust me. I know." With that, she made me laugh for the first time in a long time, which brought back every memory of our friendship, built over time in a way that no one could truly comprehend. There was an effortless comfort to her friendship, that ability between us both to know each other better than ourselves. Somehow through all the fog, we could still see each other in the distance, a guiding light to safety.

"Truthfully, I don't want a funeral. No one will come, and if they do, it would be a lie. Is that okay?" I put a lot of thought into this over the last few days. *What would I do with my mother's body? Would I have a funeral?*

"Yes, of course. What do you want to do?"

"Just something simple."

"You just let me know when, where, what—and I will do it."

"Thank you. There was a point not too long ago when all of this would've killed me, but having you, that changed everything for me."

There were so many emotions between us over a lifetime of friendship, but love was the one that had prevailed. It always did.

That evening, the house was eerily quiet. It wasn't like there had been much talking, but at least she had still been present. Now the house was dark, empty; it felt different. I could not bring myself to sit on the porch. It just didn't feel right going out there without her to sit beside me. After everything, each emotion since my mother's death took me by surprise, especially this one. I never thought I would miss her, especially after all the times I wanted nothing more than to just be free of her.

As I curled into my bed that night, I couldn't help but feel her absence. She was never in this room with me, but somehow, it now felt as though she were missing. I thought I would never fall asleep, tossing and turning, never finding the right place.

A glowing light in the distance floated through the darkness of my dreams. As the light grew closer, I could see her face surrounded by a beautiful light. "Mama?" My voice echoed out into the distant darkness.

Suddenly, a vibrant moving picture was painted around us, the brushstrokes gliding all around, brilliant blues and greens bringing the lake to life. The colors waved in her movements as she skated across the glassy lake.

"Mama, what is this?" She smiled, her face blurred in the paint, but for some reason, she had a beauty to her that I had never seen before.

"This lake was always so beautiful. I would come here trying to escape it all." Her voice echoed around me, taking up all the space. Each stroke of the brush was connected, moving to the sound of my mother's voice, just as we were connected by this place. "There was always something about this lake."

"I felt it too. I just never understood it until this moment." Her hand reached for me, but she was still too far away out in the lake, my feet firmly planted on the dock. "I'm so sorry, Mama," I called, as I reached out for her as well, desperate to be connected.

"No, no, no, dear girl. You have nothing to be sorry for. You freed me." Her forgiveness did not absolve my shame. "We cannot change these evils in our life, but now I see that we can overcome them. Have strength."

"I don't think I have any left."

"Oh, sweet girl, you have no idea. It is not strength you need to have." Suddenly, she was right in front of me, her face clearly formed. She placed a reassuring hand on my cheek, but I couldn't feel it. I desperately wished I could feel it. "I will be with you. I will carry you. Just let go."

The lake began to melt away; my mother's face started to shift and move. *No, I need more time ... Not now!*

"I need you to know something." As she spoke the words, her face changed, the paint flowing in all directions as the artist attempted to keep up with the movements of her mouth. "I do love you, and I am so proud of you." Large smears of paint flowed down her face; she was crying.

"I know, Mama, I know," I assured. A true peace swirled in her deep brown eyes, illuminating them and making them glisten like the setting sun on the lake.

"There was never a moment, dear girl, that I didn't wish I could be more for you. I am so sorry I could not be there for you."

"It's okay. I know the truth now, Mama." There was a cascading pain down her melting face. "I forgive you," I added quickly, desperately wanting to erase her pain.

I held her hand to my cheek, the paint dripping down through my fingers as I pressed it harder into my skin, wanting to feel her touch, but it was only a cold brush of wind.

"I need you to do one thing for me. Find peace in this life. Find a way to let go. I never could, but I hope that you can."

"I promise, Mama."

"I will always be watching. Know that I love you."

"Wait ... did you find peace?" She just smiled as if that in itself was the answer. She started to fade away, floating over the melting lake, leaving me alone all over again. I called out to her, but she kept getting farther away.

"I'm so sorry."

Suddenly, I was back in my bed. The bright moon illuminated the room in an ominous yellow, cutting through the dark. The warm night air pressed against my bare skin, sweat beading from every pore. I didn't remember leaving the window open. Sitting up, I placed my own hand against my cheek, closed my eyes, and saw my mother again, gently touching my cheek and telling me that she would always be with me. *Was it only a dream?* Yes, it was just a dream, but it didn't feel like that to me; it was much more.

Knowing my mother was finally granted her peace, whether it was just a dream or something more, I chose to believe in something more. God was never my favorite. In fact, most of the time I cursed him and disowned him, but now, I was beginning to see things differently. There was this part of me that knew my mother was forgiven, washed clean of her sins and those done to her. Finally, she was allowed to be in a peaceful place. If that wasn't the work of God, I wasn't sure what was.

On April 23, the summer heat kept at bay, if only for a few more days, I laid my mother to rest. Holding the urn in my hands, Caroline's hand on my shoulder, I stared out over the lake. Even though she never told me, this felt like the right place to leave my mother's ashes. Carefully, I removed the top of the urn, the wind surrounding me as I prepared to release my mother. *She is here.* Reaching my hand into the urn, I pulled out a handful of ashes.

"Be free." The words were only a whisper lost in the wind, the ashes cascading over the lake ... *our lake.* As each ash flew from my hand, the dark flakes peppering the crystal blue of the lake, I could feel every ounce of pain, fear, anger, and resentment releasing with it. We were both letting go, each ash a piece of both of us.

My life had been swallowed by the storm, tossing and spinning me around so harshly to a point where I could never see getting out. I still could not fathom how I made it through the storm, but here I was, tears falling down my face as I released my mother into the lake, feeling her absence in every piece of me at this place.

I released another handful of my mother's ashes, the sun breaking through the clouds. The air was growing calm, the wind settling down. I could not help but think that it was just like the turbulence of my life suddenly smoothing out. The pressure was lifting from my chest, the air filling my lungs fully for the first time as I realized I was changing. *Was this my mother?* For the first time, there was hope in my heart, a shining light in the distance piercing through the never-ending darkness. The storm had passed.

"She is at peace now," Caroline whispered.

"Yes, I believe she is."

I could not bring myself to leave the lake, not until the sun had long since melted over the horizon, filling the sky with brilliant pink and orange clouds. I lay in the tall grass, counting each star, every wish I ever made here as a child. Only in my mother's death could she grant my wishes. As if my mind were cleared of all other things,

I could see how all the stars of my past connected, leading me to this place. It might not have always been pleasant, definitely not perfect, but it was my path, just as the one my mother had walked.

"Thank you for staying with me, Caroline." I reached over and squeezed her hand. "And I am proud of you." I didn't see, but I could feel that she was crying.

She hadn't wanted to talk about it, but I knew she'd told Mark about the affair. Something I knew had to take courage, which I had never considered when Michael told me the truth that day in the kitchen. I had focused so much on my side of the story that I'd failed to see his, until Caroline. I saw her labor over her choices, find the bravery to accept the consequences of her actions at whatever the cost, and risk everything she held closest to her heart. The affair did not mean she loved Mark less or valued their life less, as I had assumed with Michael. It just meant she was lost; they had become lost to each other. Looking up, I felt as if their stars were still connected, as they always had been.

"I should get home."

"Me too."

As we walked the path back through the trees, then to the field beyond my home, the patterns of the stars seemed to follow us, each one leading to the next, the bigger picture unseen, until all the stars were connected as one. That was what I saw that night in the sky. Long after Caroline left my side to return home to her own family, long after the sun said goodnight, I finally saw it. I saw my path, my purpose.

Chapter Fifty-Two
Present Day

The road hit hard against my feet, one after the other, the air tight in my lungs and my muscles burning, begging me to stop. *Keep going.* I ran against the wind, pushing me back with every step I took, but I did not stop. I kept running, faster and faster until I felt as if my lungs would collapse.

"Good job, that was three miles today." Caroline stood, water in hand, wiping the sweat from her brow as my feet stumbled to a stop at the foot of the dirt driveway up to the house. Throwing my hands down on my knees, my lungs screaming for air, I took in as much as possible with each deep breath.

"I feel like I'm dying," I gasped, trying to drink the water, but my lungs refused to stop breathing. Clearly, the three miles were not as challenging for her athletic build.

"You'll get used to it," she assured.

"Not something I'm looking forward to."

Exercise was Caroline's release, something she'd done since we were kids. I, on the other hand, never exercised. But Caroline had convinced me that it would help ease my grief and clear my mind. There was something to it that I did find soothing, as my thoughts were purely focused on the road, on the push I had to find within myself to keep going. Each time I finished, the accomplishment I felt started to bleed over into other parts of my life.

"Don't lie; you like it," she quipped, slightly jabbing me in the shoulder.

"Sure, keep telling yourself that." She laughed but knew that I needed this time with her just as much as she needed it. It was our therapy in different ways. Caroline needed a distraction, if only for an hour, from everything with Mark. I never knew when she was going to talk about it, so I was always at the ready. Sometimes she would bring him up immediately, our entire run consumed with conversation, while other times she never talked, silence following us. Those were the days she'd run ahead, powering through the last mile, pushing all her pain and frustrations into the run. I learned to let her go; there was no way I could keep up.

"How are things going?" Pulling my foot up into my hand, I pulled back hard on my leg to stretch out the sore, tight muscles.

"I just thought ..." She sighed, biting her lower lip, debating whether or not to tell me. There were so many times she held back, afraid of how I would look at her if she told the truth. But I had realized so much through Caroline. "I just thought that if I ..."

"It will take time, Caroline."

"I knew that. I mean, I know that. I know what I did was horrible. I'm lucky he's even willing to still talk to me, let alone be with me again."

"Is he talking yet?"

"He did the other night. Said he was having a hard time getting over everything."

"I'm sorry, Caroline. Just give him time." Placing a friendly, supportive hand on her shaking knee, I added, "I'll always be here for you, through every step. You're not alone in this."

Through the darkness, Caroline had been a singular guiding light, but there was a time I didn't have her to look to. I had been alone, drowning in the dark waters, the waves crashing down on me with no end in sight. The moment I had her to reach for, a stable hand to pull me from the depths of my depression, I had a fighting chance. I had no intentions of letting Caroline go through this alone. I didn't think of myself as anyone's guiding light, but for Caroline, I would sure as hell try to be.

"I can't imagine a life without ... What if he ..." Her voice caught in her throat, and she couldn't continue, but I knew what she was going to say.

"You'll get through it. I did." She looked at me with a mixture of pity and pride emanating from her eyes, then she reached out to take my hand.

"You did," she repeated, squeezing hard.

Part Six: Calm after the Storm

It takes time to clean up after a storm. In the aftermath, it seems overwhelming. Like nothing will ever go back to normal, nothing will ever be fixed. But then, piece by piece, day by day, things start to move forward until one day it's over. All the signs of the storm are cleaned away. While the debris is picked up, your home repaired, and your fears calmed, there are still signs of the passing storm that will never leave. The tree line is different, having lost so many during the storm. The sky is a deeper, cloudless view, as the imbalance of the atmosphere has been corrected. There is a calm that settles in as you realize you survived, emerged from the storm, and recovered. Something not everyone can say.

Chapter Fifty-Three
Three Months Later

The moment my mother died, her hand holding on to my own, her last breath escaping her lungs, I knew that it was no longer a lie. It was now our truth. In her last moments, there was true love between us. A love that transcended all other things.

Three months had passed since my mother's funeral. Still healing, my heart slowly mended over time, just as Caroline had told me it would. The edges were still sharp and raw, but it was a process. One moment I was fine, not even thinking about it, but then I could smell the freshness of the morning dew or the thick, sharp aroma of coffee, and a memory would bring me to tears on the kitchen floor.

Thankfully, summer breathed new life into this place, the hot weather and soothing lake bringing in vacationers to provide a much-needed distraction to the town. People were everywhere. Seasonal shops opened, beckoning people to the streets, crowding the once-barren downtown with deep, frivolous pockets, which was just what this town needed to survive. It felt and looked like a completely different town with its open flower markets and outdoor seating along the sidewalks. Even my mother's house—*my house*—felt different.

As I walked through the house, there was a new light to this place. I had taken my time getting to know it again, no longer shrouded by darkness but pulling in the light that was always there, just blocked for so many years. I took down all the shades, cleaned the dingy windows, and moved all the furniture to the opposite walls so that nothing blocked the light. The amount of sun she'd blocked all those years was oppressive. With each item I touched, there was a memory. It had been therapeutic to go through each item, seeing the memory without the darkness. Understanding the nature of my mother's pain gave me a different perspective on each moment. Boxing up most of her belongings, and some of the old ones from my room, I realized that, as I could give away these things, I could also give away my tainted memories of this place. There were only a few items I decided to keep; the rest, I donated.

Redecorating the house, even if I did just move things around, finally made it feel like *my home*. While my mother's flower chair, with full cigarette burns and drink stains, remained, I never found the courage to sit in it. It was more of a stable reminder for me to stay strong in my convictions. As easy as it would be to take a seat, take her place, I never would. The chair was everything my mother hated about herself, and now I saw it as a blazing emblem of my own strength.

Shutting the door on my childhood bedroom was a symbolic moment. Having cleaned out all my childhood belongings, pulling the door closed one last time was the closure I so desperately needed in my previous life. As I walked back down the staircase, holding the laundry basket of clothes, to my mother's room, I could feel the weight of my former life in this house fading away. The door would always remain shut to that part of my life in this place. I was determined to have a new beginning in this home. If my mother could find her salvation, then so could I.

Ironically, after so much time spent avoiding it, my favorite place had become the sunporch. Once the shades had been pulled back, I saw the beauty in all its pieces. From the porch, I could see out over the expanse of the fields. Nightly, the fireflies would dance on the top of the grass, a private show just for me. It was here that I felt at peace, as if my mother were still here sitting right next to me. I found myself talking to her, as a mother and daughter would. There were times I could almost hear her talk back. In my own way, it was how I was dealing with the loss of her. It was my way of feeling like I had a relationship with her, one that I never had in life.

I had even replaced the mirror in the foyer with a fresh, clean piece of glass, a stark metaphor for my own life these days. There was no longer a foggy film or shattered pieces over my life anymore, just a clear, whole mirror revealing my true nature. My hollow cheeks were now plumped with fat, my sunken eyes full of life again, as it felt like my body itself had woken up. Finally, it had been able to truly heal. The small scar above my eyebrow was simply a testament to time passing. Each line on my face not only showed my age but each lesson learned. The scar from that night healed, just as I had. I never did learn of what happened that night I lost my mother, only knew that deep down I was responsible one way or the other. I was not sure how long she would have lived or how she would have lived if that night had never happened, but that was the thing about letting go. It only worked if you let go of everything ... even things within yourself.

This house held so much pain, but now I feared it was the only place I would be able to find *her* anymore. Surprisingly, that meant the most to me these days. I had lit the match numerous times, thinking I could burn it down, but it never happened. I couldn't do it. It was because of her ... this deep-down need to still feel connected, something I never thought I would ever feel for my mother. So, as it turned out, I didn't burn the house down; keeping the memory of my mother alive here meant more to me now.

A horn blared, cutting through my thoughts. It was time. I did one last makeup and hair check, noting that my hair was less frizzy and more naturally curly in the humidity of the summer, and my skin held a more olive glow from the sun. There was barely a time I could remember now that I didn't look this way, the rare memories of what I had become fading quickly now.

The black van waited for me at the end of the drive. Pulling back the sliding door, my silent, solitary life was suddenly filled with laughter. Caroline waved me into the seat, pushing a button to close the door, which almost caught my foot. The two younger girls were shoved into the back of the cab, while her eldest, whom I'd never met before, was in the captain's seat right next to me, sharing a large, toothy smile that reminded me of Mark. Charlotte, home from college, held a striking resemblance to her mother, pronounced mostly by her bright blue eyes, despite having her father's signature smile. I could not imagine what it was like for Caroline to learn she was pregnant twenty-one years ago, how much she gave up to have their daughter, but now we were here. A life almost missed, which brought tears to my eyes.

Had my little girl survived, what life would I have had then? My mother's life would've meant nothing. She surely would have died alone and drunk, either by accident or neglect. My own life could have continued with Michael ... but what mother would I have been then? Knowing the truth, knowing my mother, that had changed me, and for the first time in my entire life, I actually thought that I could be a mother. The kind of mother I always wanted, needed, dreamed of. I never could have done that without coming back home.

"Buckle up," Caroline rushed. "We want to get good seats, and we are so late."

"Okay, I'm ready."

It was hard to know if I was actually ready for what I was about to immerse myself in today. For the past three months, and really longer if I considered that last month with my mother, I had isolated myself. I had found a much-needed comfort in being alone, allowing myself ample time to grieve and process all my emotions. But now, as we rode to Alexander City for one of the biggest summer events, I was about to find myself completely surrounded.

Initially, I had no plans to go, my solitude the shelter for my pain. But then there was a moment—I couldn't explain it, nor did I try to Caroline—when something in my mind told me to go. My logical thoughts claimed it was just a whim, but my heart told me it was my mother speaking to me, urging me to go. The next day, I called Caroline and accepted the invitation to join her and Mark, along with the girls, at the 4th of July celebration at the Amphitheater in Alexander City. An event that would surely be attended by every resident and vacationer on Lake Martin.

"We're here," Caroline announced.

The kids pressed their hands against the windshield to get a view of all the cars and people as Mark weaved the car through the endless rows of parking. Finally, he located a spot only just big enough to open the trunk; thank goodness the van side doors slid open. Otherwise, I never would've been able to wedge my fuller figure out. Mark unloaded all the chairs, a large bag with blankets, a picnic basket which held dinner and wine, and, lastly, the wagon to carry it all in, as we stood around the back watching all the people arrive.

The open field was already mostly covered with blankets, chairs, and running children as the sun was just starting to touch the tips of the trees in the distance. It was still hours before the show, but Caroline had assured me that this was part of the event as well. We followed behind Mark as he snaked the wooden wagon through the various camps to the center of the amphitheater. Watching the others as Mark took the time to set all our things out, I took in the small moments everyone was finding. The happiness they all seemed to be exuding. The connections they all seemed to have with others.

Suddenly, I had a deep feeling of loss as I looked at all the families. For a moment, my mind hallucinated as I saw Michael with his family in the crowd, but just as quickly as I blinked, it was gone. I never heard from him again, not even when my mother died, but now I knew I didn't want to ever hear from him again. That was my previous life, clouded in darkness and secrets. The moment my mother died, she gave me the gift of being reborn. Looking back at Caroline and Mark, the path that they had been on just a few short months ago changed in a single moment for the better, I knew I would find a greater love in my life.

Only when you can admit your faults, accept every raw, scared piece of yourself, can you truly allow someone else to love you fully. In the end, through my dreams, I saw that love from my mother. For now, that was all I needed. For Caroline and Mark, it took her confession to break down every piece of themselves. Together in the last three months, they had slowly, tenderly, rebuilt themselves. Once Caroline was able to forgive herself, understand the reasons for her actions, and resolve to never allow herself to get to that point again, only then had Mark been able to forgive her. Their stars still connected, but their path shifted as they regenerated a deeper love for each other. Watching them now, a piece of me longed for my star to connect to another's, but each night that I looked up into the sky, I wasn't able to see it. My path was a singular star weaving through the sky. But that's the thing about the stars in the night sky: Every season they seem to change.

Caroline placed a comforting arm around my shoulders and handed me a plastic cup of wine. While I had not taken up drinking again, I still did enjoy the occasional glass of wine; moderation was key. Mark was putting out the chairs, and the kids were gone, off to meet up with their friends. Caroline gave me a slight smile, seeing the pain on my face as I observed the other families.

"Cheers," she said, raising her glass to mine. I lightly tapped my cup against hers with a forced smile. "It's been a hell of a year," she offered as a toast.

"Yes, it really has," I agreed, letting out a deep sigh, attempting to push the feelings of loss away, choosing to focus on all that I had gained. "Thank you for everything."

"It was nothing." She waved it off. "You did the same for me."

We smiled at each other, knowing that I could never match all she had done for me over our lives. Never again would I discount the friendship I had with Caroline or how much it truly meant to me.

"Well, ladies, your chairs await," Mark announced, motioning for us to sit. There was a large red-and-white checkered blanket spread across the grass and three folding camp chairs sitting next to each other. I wanted to sit down, take my place amongst their family, but I knew it didn't feel right in this moment. As much as they had welcomed me in, there were still pieces that hadn't been put back into place. They needed this time to each other, to find a moment to add a few more pieces.

"Actually, I think I'll walk around, if that is okay?"

"Sure, of course." Caroline appeared slightly concerned but still let me go, taking her rightful seat next to Mark. Turning back around as I made my way down to the lake, I saw Mark slide his arm around her shoulders, validation of my actions.

Standing alone by the lake, listening to the cheerful noises in the distance, I forced myself to let go. Releasing my arms on either side of my body, feeling the warm winds drifting over me from the lake, I took in a deep breath. Feeling the full thickness of the summer air, the taste of salt and cedar, I allowed it to consume me whole. A feeling of comfort washed over my body as I knew my mother was with me in this moment. I could hear her voice whispering in my ear, *Let go.*

"Norah?" The sound jolted me from my thoughts. Quickly I pulled my hands to myself, embarrassed to have been caught in a vulnerable moment. "Is that you?" It had been too long since I'd heard his voice, but my mind had not forgotten his tone, nor my body the feeling he gave me.

"Brett." My words were a whisper as if he were only in my imagination. I needed to reach out, touch him to ensure he was really standing before me. It had been so long, his memory foreign to my mind as he stood before me, that charming look on his face.

The last time I spoke to Brett I was pushing him away; my pain had felt so deep I never thought I'd be in the place I was now. Standing before him, the feelings still palpable between us, I desperately wanted to tell him the truth. Confess all my reservations, faults, fears ... but then I was sure he would walk away. I still felt the same insecurity as I had with Michael. *I wasn't good enough.*

"How ya' been?"

273

"Fine."

"I've heard that one before," he scoffed, his half-cocked smile filled with pity. "I heard about your mother. I'm sorry I didn't come by," he confessed, his tone resonating with seriousness.

"It's okay. I never expected you to, or anyone really."

"I still should have come by. I am truly sorry." He stepped closer, my own skin feeling the heat of his, sending a wave of warmth over my body. The space between us was so minimal yet filled with so many emotions. I wanted to tell him, but I hesitated.

"I ... well ... I wanted to know ..." His voice trailed off as he scanned the crowd nervously. I knew what he wanted to know, or at least I hoped I did. Even after all the horrible sides he saw of me in the last year and the shame that flustered in my stomach, I could still feel that magnetic pull between us. An old, unresolved feeling still floating in the air. "I wanted to know if you are doing better?"

"I am, actually." There was a sense of pride, something I had rarely felt in my life, at being able to say the words, especially to Brett. Of course, I wasn't sure if that would be enough. I knew I needed to explain more to him why I pushed him away, refused to let him into my life. But just as my mind started to form the words, that old fear crept into my thoughts.

"So ..." Suddenly there was a small person grabbing at his leg. Looking down at the boy, his crystal-blue eyes, deep-red hair, and half-cocked smile, I knew it had to be his son. "Oh, hey, Collin. Everything okay?"

"Yes, Daddy, I just wanted to ask if we can sit with Jackson? Please, Daddy, please?" His little hands folded together as he begged, his eyes growing wide and his bottom lip popping out. The look on his face was familiar—*childhood Brett.*

"Sure thing. First, I want you to meet my friend, Norah." Shyly, he hid behind his father's leg, slightly waving, giving me a skeptical look. "Go along, I'll be right behind you." With that, the boy bounced back up the hill toward the crowd.

"You have a son?" My mind was still trying to carve out what it all meant while also filling in the gaps of all our conversations. I was baffled that it had never come up, nor ever been mentioned. I did consider that he intentionally didn't bring up the fact he had a child; maybe that was too close to the vest. Something he didn't want me to know, because he was keeping me at arm's length. Of course, I would've kept me at arm's length in the state I was in.

"Yes, he's eight now."

"His mother?" Pain immediately flooded his face, giving me my answer.

"She left. Shortly after we lost my father. Went out one day and just never came back home. We found out a few years later that she had overdosed."

A burst of emotions exploded between us as so many things came into clear view. Suddenly, I understood that what I thought had been Brett's judgement, had been concern that I too, would die. Which, honestly, wasn't out of the realm of possibilities during that time. In a split second, I realized I had misunderstood it all and maybe there was a possibility of us together. But quickly, the rush of the wave receded, dragging my emotions back with it. There was a deep pain, my own waving back to his. I feared that no matter how much he felt it too, that his own fear would hold him back. I had been an addict. I had been lost. There was a part of me that knew he might never be able to get past the fear I would leave as well.

"Brett, I am so sorry."

"Does that change things?"

"What things?"

"Norah." He reached for my hand, our fingers slightly touching, unsure if they could hold on to each other but desperately wanting to. "I've owed you an explanation for a long time now. You have been through so much, and I hate thinking that I added to that. I should've been honest with you from the beginning."

"No, I didn't give you much of a chance. I pushed you away. You were right to think I needed help. I did, but I just couldn't bring myself to accept it."

"You misunderstood me that day." His fingers instantly wrapped around my own as he pulled my hand to his heart. The rhythmic beat and heat radiating from his chest was a spark as he tried to relight a dying flame. "I overstepped; I know that now. I never should have presumed to understand your relationship with your mother."

"No, no. You were right."

"Norah, I wanted to help you. That day, I saw how much it was changing you and I just ... I missed being there for Colin's mother and I didn't want to miss being there for you. I've always just wanted to be there for you."

There were so many times I wanted to let someone be there for me, but even at my loneliest, darkest place, I never felt as if I deserved the help, so my mind refused to accept it. Now I could see that I had to want to be pulled from the water; I had allowed it to take me down to the darkest depths, never looking for the steady hand to pull me up. Once I realized I didn't want to let it consume me, all I had to do was to accept the extended hand.

As the tide slowly shifted, I could feel my heart shifting in this moment as I realized there had always been a deeper level to our connection. From the moment I returned, seeing him in that coffee shop, I'd felt a magnetic pull toward Brett, an imaginary connection of our stars. Standing before him now, seeing every piece of his life come into focus—the son, the loss of his wife—I started to understand.

"I just thought ..." I paused, unable to say the words, knowing now that no matter how much we wanted to ignite the flame, he couldn't risk losing me as he had his wife. It was his regret that pulled us together, realizing now what Caroline meant that night after the Christmas party. He had been through enough. I would not add to that.

Taking a deep breath, I pulled all my strength. I needed to say it. "I don't think I can be the person that you deserve. I'm a million messy pieces, and I can't ask you to put me back together again, not after everything you have been through."

"Just stop. You. Are. Perfect." Each word was spoken with volition and intent, his firm, strong hands encasing my face, forcing me to look at him. "From the moment we met, all those years ago, I knew you were different. I knew you were the person, the woman, that would complete me fully someday. I'm not scared. I want you, Norah, every messy piece of you."

His words, his powerful, life-changing words, vibrated through every cell in my body. I couldn't believe what I was hearing, that he had felt so strongly for me all this time. The flame ignited. Suddenly, my constellation was complete. Each star, each step in my life, was connected, the big picture visible. The moment he said the words, my fears were gone, the insecurities of never being enough for him were all washed away. I had let go of it all, just as my mother had taught me.

"I've felt it too, all this time. There was so much going on in my life that shadowed it, but it was always there."

"So after all this time?" I could see the want in his eyes, as he realized that I felt the same for him as he did for me. He wanted the real, unabridged version of *just me*. I couldn't wait to say the word, bursting to tell him. The moment I said it, I knew the last level of my walls would be demolished. This was it.

"Yes."

Ann Brooks grew up in a small town off the Gulf Coast of Florida, where she cultivated a passion for the water. She grew up immersed in the arts, learning to sing and perform at a young age with a local children's choir. Even as a child, she held a unique ability to develop detailed and elaborate stories.

Through her personal hardships as a teenager, she developed a deep inner need to help others through their own emotional battles. Graduating from the University of Florida with a degree in Psychology, she set out on her mission to help children struggling with mental illnesses. Taking her first job with a local nonprofit behavioral health organization, she discovered the horrifying, heartbreaking, and long-term effects of the cycle of violence. Through these life-changing encounters, the story *A Lost Woman* was born.

These days, she lives with her husband and two children in her hometown, just two houses down from her mother. By day she works with children in an elementary school while spending summers either on the beach or at their family retreat nestled along the inner jetties of Lake Martin in AL, where her two young sons love to fish and swim. Nurturing her love for writing by night, she labors to create a balanced life of work, family, and reaching for her dream of being an author. This is her first novel.